The Devil whispers his sweet commands . . .

A cold, damp wind bit into me. Seth was behind me as I walked ahead, around the outside of the house.

The tower's very stones drew me and seemed to hold me. The sound of the sea in the near distance was hypnotic.

I stopped and confronted Seth. "You aren't going to tear this down," I stated.

The wind blew his hair back from his face and carved his cheekbones higher. He frowned, at me or at the battering wind.

Everything I said, everything I did, was coming to me automatically now, as if some spirit guided me. I could only hope the spirit was benevolent.

I held out my hand. "You can give me the keys now, Seth. You won't need them anymore. . . ."

THE STONE HOUSE

DIANNE DAY

POCKET BOOKS

New York   London   Toronto   Sydney   Tokyo

Map taken from *Islands, Capes and Sounds* by Thomas
Schoenbaum, published by John F. Blair, Publisher.

This book is a work of fiction. Names, characters, places and
incidents are either the product of the author's imagination or
are used fictitiously. Any resemblance to actual events or locales
or persons, living or dead, is entirely coincidental.

An *Original* Publication of POCKET BOOKS

POCKET BOOKS, a division of Simon & Schuster Inc.
1230 Avenue of the Americas, New York NY 10020

ISBN: 0-671-63991-9

First Pocket Books printing March 1989

10 9 8 7 6 5 4 3 2 1

POCKET and colophon are trademarks of
Simon & Schuster Inc.

Printed in the U.S.A.

ACKNOWLEDGMENTS

I wish to thank the following people, who were helpful to me in gathering material for *The Stone House:* Betty Shannon of Beaufort, N.C.; Gavin and Yvonne Frost of New Bern, N.C.; and Dr. John Butts, Chief Medical Examiner of the State of North Carolina.

FOR ANN, WHO GOES WITH ME

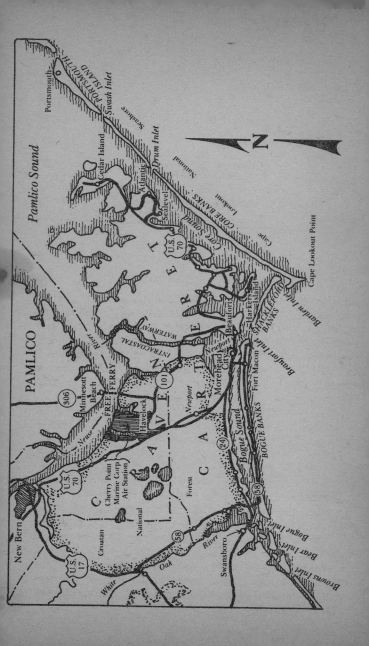

1

I was living on the edge. I didn't realize, at first, that I'd been pushed so far; I wasn't like Alice, who fell down the rabbit hole and saw Mad Hatters and giant caterpillars smoking pot and all those other things she saw. I just knew that all of a sudden, things were different. Light had a terrible clarity, music was excruciatingly beautiful, my skin was alive to the textures of everything I touched, everything that touched me. All very interesting, and also *strange*.

There were times, such as now, when the strangeness took over. When that part of the mind that screens the many messages received by the senses ceases to function and there is suddenly too much of everything. Uncensored, reality seems unreal. Panic looms. One becomes aware, for instance, that driving sixty miles an hour may be legal, but it may not be safe. Wind whips past windows; bright colors of autumn-leafed trees rush by in a blur. You are alone in a machine, a ton-heavy mass of metal, hurtling down the side of a mountain. The interstate is a mere ribbon of road, a thread of civilization through a wild world. I felt afraid.

I stopped my car in the breakdown lane of the West Virginia Turnpike. This episode would pass, they always did, and I would continue on my way from central Ohio to the North Carolina coast none the worse for it. There were some times when I thought, tentatively, that all of this was actually good for me. Certainly it was good that I no longer had to practice law, in spite of what my friend the psychologist had said. I smiled, remembering, and with the smile felt normal again. I slipped the car back into gear and back onto the highway.

My friend the psychologist had said, "Don't do it, Laura! It's a mistake to give up your whole career when you're only thirty-three years old. It's another loss, on top of the three significant losses you've already had. You'll push yourself too far!" But she was wrong. Leaving a job and a profession I'd never liked, never really wanted, wasn't a loss. It was a gain, it was freedom.

My friend had been right about other things, though; she'd helped me to see that under the circumstances my strange feelings were normal. In her professional jargon, "appropriate." All the old patterns of my life had been disrupted, that was why I felt so strange.

As I wound my way out of the Alleghenies and across a corner of Virginia, I reaffirmed my decision to leave my old life behind. I thought I probably felt much the same as the boy who had lived for so many years in the clear plastic bubble must have felt when they took his bubble away—the world was all familiar and yet not familiar at the same time. Everything was there looking the way it had always looked, and yet it was all new, to be explored. Living on the outer limits of my experience, still in the familiar, yet ever pushing just a bit beyond. On the edge. The boy, I was sure, hadn't wanted to go back in his bubble. I didn't want to go back in mine, either, nor could I if I'd wanted to. My bubble was destroyed.

Even in a place as innocuously American as Mount Airy, North Carolina, doubts return with the dark. In a motel room's bed I read far into the night, a paperback book my talisman against shadows. At last I fell into a fragile sleep. The next morning I left Mount Airy to complete my trip with a new awareness: it was true that I was completely free, as never before; it was also true that I felt vulnerable, as

2

never before. A paradox. I supposed one must accept such paradox, when living on the edge.

"I don't know quite how to tell you this, Miss Brannan," said the girl behind the desk. It was a pretty little desk, either antique or a reproduction. The girl was pretty, too, and the lines of worry on her young face looked out of place.

I suggested, in my sensible Midwestern way, "Just tell me."

"We—we expected you, of course, and your room is all ready, it's the very best room, on the harbor front, but . . . but your sister isn't here!" She looked stricken.

"Oh. Well, that's no big deal. I'll take my things in and shower and change, and by the time I've done all that, she'll probably be back. If you'll just give me the room key . . ." I held out my hand.

"No! I mean, sure, here's the key. But no, I'm not so sure she'll be back. You see, we don't know where she is. No one has seen her all day, and when the maid went to do her apartment, she told me the bed hadn't been slept in. But her car is here. Jonathan is out right now asking around town if anyone has seen Kathryn last night or today."

"Jonathan?"

"Jonathan Harcourt. He's the night manager, he lives here, too. Oh, I'm sorry. I forgot you don't know everyone. You see, we feel we know you already. Kathryn talked so much about you coming, and how you're half-owner now and all. My name is Polly, Polly Wilson. I'm the assistant manager. I usually go home at six o'clock and Kathryn takes the desk until Jonathan comes on at eight, but tonight I guess I'll stay. It's all so confusing, I don't know what to think!"

Polly was right, it was confusing. I was sluggish from two days of driving, but even so, I felt the first stirrings of alarm. My sister had begged me to come, insisted that she needed *me,* not just the money. I hadn't been about to make such a move until the legalities of our partnership were finalized, and Kathryn had complained bitterly about the delay. Would she go away so suddenly, on the very day when I was

3

finally due to arrive? Not likely. Alarming Polly any more than she was already wouldn't help, though. I tried to say something soothing.

"I'm confused, too, but I'm sure—"

The door behind me opened abruptly, cutting off my words. A wave of energy preceded the man through the door, and his angry voice reached my ears just before a strong hand gripped my shoulder and turned me around.

"Kathryn! Where the hell were you? I waited . . ." He stared down at me, and the anger in his face gave way, but his fingers still dug into my shoulder. "You're not Kathryn."

"No, I'm not." I heard a note of annoyance in my voice. I had never liked to be mistaken for my sister. "I'm Laura Brannan, Kathryn's sister."

"I see." His eyes raked over my face, my body. "I didn't know she had a twin sister."

I felt abraded by those blatantly curious eyes, as if he had scraped the surface of my skin with sandpaper. "We aren't twins," I said automatically. It was what I'd told people when we were growing up, and they had compared me to her. I shrugged my shoulder, a hint that he remove his hand. He did, but still he studied my face.

"No, you're not. Your eyes are different. Not just your glasses, your eyes are . . . smoky. They have a lot of green in them."

That's one for your side, I thought. Kathryn's eyes were a clear, medium gray. I studied him, too. He was handsome, in a severe way. Long, thin nose in a longish face, deep-set brown eyes under heavy dark brows, hair that had once been as black as mine but was now all silver-gray, and longer than men wore their hair in Columbus, Ohio. He had high cheekbones with slight hollows beneath, a lower lip a little fuller than the upper, and there was a depression, like a thumbprint, in his chin. He was much taller than I, as most men are. His body seemed lean in the dark business suit he wore.

"There's something else," he went on. "Your expression, I think. You seem, how shall I put it? Much softer than your sister."

4

I knew what he meant, but I didn't like it. I never liked statements of that sort from a man. It wasn't that I was no longer Laura the Lawyer, or that I felt vulnerable a lot of the time now and it must show. I just snapped at him. "If you're going to stand there undressing me with your eyes and making hasty judgments, the least you can do is tell me your name!"

"Sorry." His grin was engaging. The man could obviously be charming. "Seth Douglass." He grabbed my hand in a firm handshake.

"I gather from what you said when you barged in here that you were supposed to meet Kathryn somewhere this afternoon?"

"Yes. I'm sorry I yelled at you like that, but you do look so much like her, and I was stood up. She was supposed to meet me at the Stone House two hours ago."

"The Stone House?" asked Polly. Poor, confused young Polly—I'd forgotten her.

Seth Douglass nodded. I had no idea what or where this Stone House was, and I didn't think it could be relevant. My first mistake, but I was brand-new in town—how could I have known?

"We have a problem here," I said. "I've just arrived, and Polly tells me no one has seen Kathryn since yesterday evening. Apparently she didn't let anyone know she'd be out today, she didn't take her car, and Polly is concerned."

"If she didn't take her car, perhaps she went somewhere by boat," said Seth.

Polly brightened. "Of course! We should have thought of that! As soon as Jonathan comes back I'll tell him. There are several boats we hire when guests want to go out. There's Cox's and Benthall's, and—"

I interrupted her. "I really must get to my room. I'll check in with you later, Polly. Nice meeting you, Mr. Douglass."

He stood between me and the door. Three long strides, and he opened it for me. "Seth, please call me Seth. Let me help you with your bags."

"No, thanks." I brushed past him. "You must have things to do."

5

"I did, but I waited so long for your sister, it's too late now. The business day is about over."

Suit yourself, I thought, stalking the short distance to my car. I simply couldn't handle him or any more of this until I'd showered and changed clothes. My mind felt as grubby and wilted as my denim dress. Besides, if I didn't get Boris into the room before he woke up, there'd be hell to pay.

With his long legs Seth got there ahead of me, bent down, and looked into the car windows. "You don't exactly travel light, do you?"

I pulled the keys out of my pocket and unlocked the passenger side. "I've come to stay. My sister and I have gone into partnership."

Hand on the rear door handle, Seth paused. "I see. I didn't know." His expression was rapidly calculating.

I knew that look. In my former profession I'd encountered it often enough. He was sizing me up, which meant he expected to have to deal with me in some way, whether as ally or opponent. I'd found it best in such situations to meet the assessment head on, and as quickly as possible. Damn, I thought, I don't need this right now. But with an inner sigh of resignation I pulled together my tattered strength.

"Look, Mr. Douglass—"

"Seth."

"Seth. I'm not quite as"—rapidly I searched for a word that wouldn't be too negative—"shall we say, disorganized as my sister when it comes to dealing with things. I can see my partnership with her makes a difference to you. Let's get it out in the open. Why?"

I caught a flicker of respect in the brown eyes. "Business. She recently acquired some property I'm interested in."

"Impossible. You have to be mistaken. The only property my sister owns is this inn, and since I signed the partnership agreement ten days ago, half of the Trelawney Inn now belongs to me. She cannot have owned other property, or it would have come into the agreement; nor can she have acquired any property recently without my signature. I am, or I was, a lawyer, and I assure you I have a thorough

6

understanding of these things. And of Kathryn's financial situation."

"You seem very sure of that." Seth drew his heavy, dark eyebrows together. "This is new information to me. Well, I'm sure you don't want to stand here any longer. Let's get these things to your room. Which room, by the way?"

"Number three. I have no idea where it is. Harbor front, Polly said."

"I know the way, I'll show you."

He was busy with the large pieces of luggage while I slipped the strap of my carryall over one shoulder and slid the cat carrier from the front seat with both hands. Boris was a heavy cat. I felt him stir and heard a low, tranquilized growl as I lifted the carrier in my arms. Boris definitely did not like to travel, and I definitely would not have come to North Carolina without him. Boris was my "family," and I knew him a heck of a lot better than I knew my sister!

"This way. Is that a cat or a small dog?"

"Cat. A very large cat named Boris. Himalayan."

Seth grinned. "I like cats. And big dogs. Don't like small dogs much, though."

The Trelawney Inn had originally been two houses, one behind the other, both built in the early nineteenth century and both long and narrow. In a flash of inspiration, which he'd apparently later regretted, Kathryn's eccentric husband Carroll Trelawney had purchased both houses and, with the blessing of the Beaufort Historical Association, restored them and built a connecting link. The link was architecturally indistinguishable from the outside, or from the inside. I thought, as I followed Seth Douglass down a very long central hallway, that the original houses must have been very alike to begin with or they could not have matched up so well.

"Here we are. Door's open—after you."

I went into the large, rectangular room, and my eyes were immediately drawn to the row of small-paned windows that looked out across Front Street to the harbor. Nine panes over six, historically authentic, I remembered. "Oh, this is spectacular! What a fantastic view! All that water, the boats . . ." With Boris in his carrier still in my arms I went and stood before the windows, enchanted.

"It's beautiful, isn't it? I've fallen in love with Beaufort myself. I intend to make it my home, as soon as I can. And you? Did you come here to stay, sight unseen? A well-organized, logical legal person like you?"

I glanced up at Seth and saw amusement soften the severity of his face, tug at the corners of his mobile mouth. He seemed so tall standing close by my shoulder. I felt a lurch from Boris and ignored it. "I've seen pictures, of course, and done a little reading, enough to know that Beaufort, North Carolina, is a beautiful little seaport with a long, interesting history. And I know there's an economic upswing in the town—it's a good time for an investment."

"And yet, those aren't the only reasons you came. There's more, I can see it in your eyes."

My confidence wavered, even as I felt a current of warmth flow from Seth Douglass to surround me. "My sister needs me," I said.

"Umhm. The question is, what do you need, Laura Brannan?"

"Mowr!" Boris demanded. I was spared.

"Here, let me take the cat carrier. Where do you want to put it down?"

"I'll do it," I said, seizing my chance to escape. There was entirely too much going on all at once here. "Perhaps you wouldn't mind bringing in the rest of my things?"

"Glad to."

When he had gone I set the carrier on the floor and opened the top, then removed a groggy, grouchy cat. I stroked him for a moment, appreciating the softness of his long, thick hair. Boris would have been a big cat even if he were short-haired like his Siamese cousins, whose color and markings he shared; with his own long Himalayan coat he was huge. I placed him in the middle of the king-sized bed.

"Welcome to your new home, big guy," I said.

"Mowr," replied Boris. He blinked his blue eyes once, yawned, and began to lick himself. When he had finished his grooming, I knew he would be fully awake. I yawned, too, and stretched, working out some of my own kinks.

Seth was back, arms full. "Where do you want this stuff?"

"Anywhere. Just put it down on the floor, and I'll sort it out later. Thanks for your help, Seth."

He deposited his armload in front of a fireplace on the opposite side of the room from the windows and ignored the note of dismissal in my voice. Long and lanky, he ambled to the big bed at the end of the room and scratched Boris between the ears. "Good-looking cat. Huge, isn't he?"

I began to wonder how to get rid of this man. "Yes, he's big all right."

"How long have you had him?"

"Five years. I'm very fond of him. He's been with me through—" Just in time I caught myself. "Through a lot of things. Boris is my family."

"Except for Kathryn." Seth stuck his hands in the pockets of his trousers and came to stand in front of me. His voice was quiet. "I know from her that both your parents died a few months ago. Double suicide. I'm sorry."

I said nothing, rather than one of the many things I could have said about my parents' death. Two of my three significant losses. Seth went on.

"Look, it must be pretty difficult for you to have driven all the way from . . . where?"

"Columbus, Ohio."

"From Columbus and find that your sister isn't here to greet you, get you oriented and settled in. How about if I come back in a couple of hours? If she hasn't turned up, I'll buy you a drink and dinner."

"Thanks, but I think not. I can do my own settling in, and I'll have something to eat here. The inn's food will be fine for me tonight. You've been kind to help. Now, if you'll excuse me . . ."

"They only do light meals here. Are you sure that's what you want?"

"You don't give up easily, do you?" I flared. With sudden, devastating clarity I knew that my anger was defensive. All the soft places in me wanted to open up to this strong man. I wanted to be with him, to lean on him, to let him take care of me . . . if only for one night. But those yearning soft places were sore, still damaged, maybe forever. I lifted my chin and kept the anger in front of me like a shield.

"No," he said, "I don't give up easily." Hands still in his pockets, he ambled to the door, where he turned. He nailed me with a piercing gaze, his long face dramatic with its arched black brows and waves of silver hair. "Not when I see something I want, I don't." And then he was gone.

I had my supper with Jonathan Harcourt, who looked nothing like his impressive-sounding name. He was comfortably slouchy with the beginnings of a paunch, and his sandy-blond hair was improbably thick and bushy in a corona around the bald top of his head. He had kind eyes, pale blue, and tortoiseshell-rimmed glasses that kept sliding down the bridge of his nose. His soft voice matched the kind eyes—there was a sort of abstracted benevolence about him. He could have been anywhere in middle age. I wasn't surprised to learn that until the past couple of years he had taught English at a junior college, a job he had given up to write full time, though he'd not yet published anything. He'd come to Beaufort because it was quiet and he loved the sea, and when he'd begun to run out of money, Carroll Trelawney had offered him room and board and a small salary in exchange for tending the inn's desk and telephones at night. An ideal arrangement for a night-owl writer, said Jonathan.

Now he gazed past me out of the windows in the tiny third-floor dining room. I'd been surprised to find the kitchen and dining room at the top of the house until I saw the view, and then I realized the wisdom of the location. From this high up one could see the contours of the whole harbor, across Carrot Island and Horse Island, to where Beaufort Inlet opened between the Shackleford Banks and Bogue Banks, to the sea beyond. Coming as I did from the land-locked Midwest, the ocean was a wonder to me, a mystery.

The sun had set in a rosy, golden glow, and now both sky and water turned an ever-deeper blue. Navy blue. For the first time in my life I understood where that color got its name. And I thought I understood for the first time, too, how my sister, Kathryn, who had always been materialistic, acquisitive, and unromantic, had lost her head and chosen for her second husband a seagoing nomad of only modest fortune. Not to mention that Carroll Trelawney was more than twice her age. She had been caught, as so many others had, as I myself was being caught, by the lure of the sea.

"Perhaps we should call the police," said Jonathan.

"Oh, surely not! Not yet," I said, more positive than I had a right to be. The search of boats for hire, like the inquiries up and down the street, had yielded nothing. Kathryn had simply disappeared. But in the world I'd come from the police meant crime, violence, and drugs, sometimes death. This was my new world, Beaufort had begun to work its charms and spells on me, and I wanted none of the old, ugly things here. Not in this place. No, we must not call the police.

Jonathan Harcourt regarded me thoughtfully across the table. "Do *you* have some idea where she might be? This is a small town, I've asked everyone I can think of, but I didn't ask you. Did she mention anything she had to do, maybe to get ready for your arrival?"

"No, she didn't. I called her from my motel last night at about this time, to tell her how far I'd gotten and what time I thought I'd get here today. She answered the phone herself, said she was relieved to know I'd finally be here. That's all."

"Hmmm. More coffee?"

"Yes, please."

Jonathan took our cups to a small sideboard set out with carafes of wine, plates of cheese and crackers, a basket of fruit, and two insulated pots of coffee. A few guests had been in the room earlier for wine and cheese, but only Jonathan and I had remained for supper. The bacon, cheese, and mushroom quiche had obviously been heated in a microwave but it was good nonetheless, and the salad greens were

11

fresh. Though the Trelawney Inn provided fuller fare than a bed-and-breakfast, no real cooking was done on the premises, and most of the guests ate lunch and dinner out.

Jonathan returned with the coffee and a bunch of green grapes which he put unceremoniously in the center of our table. He lounged in his chair and munched grapes, but I could almost hear him thinking. At length he said, "I'm sure she would be relieved to have you here. That's why I can't figure it. Why would she pull a disappearing act when she was about to be let off the hook?"

My mouth went dry. In spite of my best efforts to play ostrich, the situation was getting to me. I took a quick sip of coffee. "I'm not sure what you mean," I said.

"How well do you really know Kathryn? You haven't seen her in years, except for the time she went back to Ohio for your parents' funeral, right?"

"That's true." He might appear to be in a well-meaning fog, but there was nothing wrong with Jonathan's powers of observation and deduction. I didn't really know, had never really known Kathryn, not even when we were children with barely a year's difference in age between us. In honesty, I'd never liked my sister very much. Perhaps because I was the elder I'd always felt guilty about that, and somehow vaguely responsible for her. A responsibility I'd never defined, and never fulfilled. I'd been the smart one, the sensible one, and when our brother was killed in Vietnam, I became the oldest child. All the parents' hopes and expectations had then been pinned on me. I was the one who had to give up my dreams of becoming a ballet dancer, dreams that when I was sixteen were not unrealistic. I was the one who stayed at home and went to Ohio State and became the lawyer my brother Brian was supposed to have been. Kathryn got to do as she pleased, she had the boys and the dates and Wellesley, where she'd flunked out in her sophomore year. No, I didn't know her then or now, I only knew that I still felt the guilt and the responsibility and that was part of why I'd come here to Beaufort.

"She'd be relieved," said Jonathan, "because she's got no head for business, for one thing. This place has been tottering on the edge of going under ever since Carroll took off eighteen months ago."

"I know that, she told me herself. What I don't understand is why he left. Kathryn didn't seem to understand, either. It seems to me that she didn't so much mind being without Carroll as she just felt inadequate managing the inn on her own. Do you know what happened?"

"Carroll Trelawney will never stay married very long to anybody but that boat of his. Once the inn was restored he'd tired of playing the charming, eccentric host; it lost its fascination for him. Seemed like your sister had ceased to fascinate him long before that."

"I see."

"Nooo . . . I'm afraid you don't, not really." Jonathan pushed his glasses back up his nose with a forefinger and straightened up in his chair. Elbows on the table, he leaned toward me with more intensity than I'd yet seen in him. "I'm going to tell you some things you may not like, but I think you need to know. First, I'm sure you're already aware that if you didn't wear glasses, you'd be a dead ringer for your sister. What you don't realize is that because you look so much like her, folks around here are going to expect you to *be* like her—I know I did, unconsciously, as soon as I saw you. I didn't really want to have dinner with you tonight because of that. But, well, I'm a writer and I'm curious about everything. I notice little things most people don't, like the way you hold your head a little to the side and listen, really listen, when someone talks to you. Like the way you walk with your toes a tad turned out and with a sort of lilt to it, almost like a dancer. And there's a tiny quiver to your chin sometimes, as if you'd been recently hurt or wounded or something. It's . . . endearing. All those things are not like Kathryn Trelawney. After talking to you for a while over supper, I see you aren't at all like your sister. Other people, however, won't know it, and because of the resemblance you'll be in for a hard time until they do get to know you."

"They, ah, don't like my sister?"

"She's hard to like. Everybody was nuts about Carroll, you couldn't help but like the guy. And she was his wife, so she was included along with him. But without Carroll, Kathryn has alienated a lot of people."

"Why? How? What is it that she does?"

Jonathan shrugged. "If she comes back, you'll see soon enough. If she doesn't, well, I don't know. Maybe it won't matter. There's one other thing you ought to know, whether she comes back or not. Carroll told me before he left that he was going to put a fair amount of money in a bank account for Kathryn, for her personal use and to help her operate the inn during the slack times until some of the debt is paid off."

"But he didn't, he couldn't have! I've seen Kathryn's financial statements, I had her whole situation investigated before I agreed to the partnership, and there's nothing like that."

Jonathan sighed. "How well I know! I've been doing the bookwork at night, because Kathryn couldn't or wouldn't keep it up. The question is, what happened to that money? I knew Carroll pretty well. He was eccentric, but he was fair, and generous to a fault. He was also honest. He left the money all right. That money disappeared, I never saw hide nor hair of it for the inn's operation. And now Kathryn's disappeared, too. Strange, don't you think?"

"She'll be back," I said rather desperately, "she'll be back tomorrow, I'm sure she will."

Jonathan bowed his benevolent bald head, in deference to my stubbornness. "Maybe."

2

I couldn't sleep. Every time I dropped off it was only to be awakened by sounds new to me—the creaks of the old house, the faint rattle of wind against the windowpanes, a metallic clinking that had unnerved me with its persistence until I realized it must come from the wind in the rigging of one or more boats docked in the water right across the street. Boris slept on my feet, as usual. Time and again through the night I resisted the impulse to pick up the bedside phone and ask Jonathan at the desk if Kathryn had returned. As usually happens in such situations I fell into a deep sleep around five A.M., and was less than grateful when my live-in feline alarm clock awakened me.

"Mowr? Mowr, rowr!" Boris insisted.

"Yeah, okay, give me a minute!" At home—no, I corrected myself, that wasn't home anymore—in Columbus I could have let him outside and gone back to sleep. But here I had set up his litter box in a corner so he wouldn't need to go out. He must be hungry.

"Mowr?" Watching me.

I sighed, stretched, and swung my feet over the side of the bed. The room was chilly, though yesterday had been Indian summer warm. "Coming, master!" I wiped heavy sleep from my eyes and put on the glasses without which I was blind as a bat, and tried not to step on my great cat as he rubbed against my ankles.

My room had an adjoining private bath and dressing room with closet space along one side, and on the other side under a narrow counter with a small, oval sink was a mini-refrigerator. I appeased Boris's immediate hunger with some of the milk I'd brought down from the kitchen, then pulled on a robe and splashed my face with cold water. I felt groggy and out-of-sync. I gave Boris the last of the cat food I'd brought with us, and made a mental note to buy more. That done, I wandered to the windows and pulled back the curtains.

The sky was an incredible clear blue; the water, equally blue, danced with points of light. Some boats had people busy on their decks, some rocked patiently with their naked masts pointed to the sky, waiting for their owners. Suddenly I wanted nothing more than to be in that third-floor dining room with its sweeping view. With only a trace of guilt I decided to forego the dancer's exercises I usually did first thing every morning.

I dressed quickly in a khaki skirt, loose-fitting navy cotton sweater, and canvas espadrilles. My short black hair was curly and needed little attention. A quick touch of lip gloss, and I was ready.

"Not this time, big guy," I said to Boris as he followed me to the door. "If you don't stay in the room for at least twenty-four hours, you'll get lost the first time I let you out." I opened the door just enough to slip through, then closed it behind me.

I went up the stairs at my end of the long building and was surprised to find Jonathan Harcourt sitting at the same table we'd occupied the night before. Otherwise, the dining room was empty.

"May I join you? I thought you'd still be at the desk. Where are the other guests?"

Slouched in his chair, Jonathan looked professorial in a gray cardigan that had seen better days. "Not at this hour. It's almost nine o'clock, and it's a weekday. What few guests we had last night are out on their boats by now. Aren't you eating? If you want eggs I'll have Evelyn, the housekeeper and cook, make them for you. She's in the kitchen."

"No eggs, thanks. Right now, this is enough." I sipped at the orange juice I'd brought from the sideboard, then stared greedily out the window. It was this view I was hungry for, not food.

The blue water shimmered in the harbor. Farther out, in the open sea, the blue was darker and crested with white. The sunlight seemed to be made of crystal, it was so clear, so bright. A midsize sailboat with its sails still furled backed from its dock under power. Much farther away a fishing boat, big and bulky, heavy with nets, approached the inlet, which looked surprisingly narrow from here. In the middle ground a sleek white motor launch proceeded slowly out of the sheltered side of the harbor, around the island I'd learned was called Carrot Island. I watched it as I asked, "Do you know how Carrot Island got its name? Surely they don't grow carrots there!"

Jonathan chuckled. "No, they don't grow carrots. It's an estuarine sanctuary now, nothing there but sand and scrub, and good shelling on the other side. It seems to have been called Carrot Island ever since they were making maps, as far back as the 1750s, for sure. Now, Horse Island next to it, that's a different story. Look, you can see three of the wild horses from here."

"Yes, I see them! Are they really descended from horses left there by the Conquistadors?"

"That's what some people say. I doubt anyone knows for sure. I'll tell you one funny thing, though. Recently those horses were moved from Shackleford Banks—down there"—I nodded that I understood—"and now sometimes they'll swim over to Carrot, but they never swim back to Shackleford. Nobody knows why, it's a mystery. Since you're so glued to that window, Laura, let me get you some food. I'm sure the muffins on the sideboard are lukewarm by now. I'll go to the kitchen and be right back."

"Yes, thanks . . ." Those islands were so close! It was a pity they could only be reached by boat; canoe-paddling skills wouldn't help much here. Perhaps someone would take me there; someone would have a boat I could rent or borrow, maybe even teach me how to use it.

"Here you are. Hot muffins, bacon, sausage. I didn't know which you wanted so I brought both. And coffee."

I pulled myself away from the enchanting view, and smiled my thanks. "Won't you sit down again, have another cup of coffee, and keep me company while I eat?"

"No, thanks. I've got to go. It's my bedtime, you know. You have plans for the morning?"

"I don't know, I haven't thought . . . I don't suppose there's been any news about my sister?" I had to ask, though I felt I knew the answer.

"No." Jonathan pushed up his glasses and rubbed the bridge of his nose in a gesture I realized was typical. "Laura, if I may ask your help. With Kathryn absent, Polly's about stressed out. She doesn't work well without direction. I can't be on the desk all night and make decisions for her in the daytime, too. Maybe you could, ah, just talk to her, calm her down?"

"Sure. I can certainly try. Is there anything else, anything specific you want me to do?"

Jonathan smiled, shaking his head and shedding warmth the way a shaggy sheepdog sheds its coat. *"You're* asking *me? I* can't get over how different you are from Kathryn Trelawney! No, dear lady, you're the owner. Not me. *I* work for *you.* Get it?"

"I guess so, but I don't really think that way, who works for whom. I'd rather just say we'll work together." Suddenly I realized how much I had to learn, what a mess I'd have on my hands if my sister didn't come back.

"You're the boss. If you say 'together,' then together it is. I'll be up again by three. If there's still no word from Kathryn, I think we'd better go to the police."

I knew he was right. I said, "All right."

When I talked to Polly I found that the source of her stress was an overactive imagination. Overnight, she had jumped to the conclusion that my sister was never coming back because "something terrible" had happened to her. I discouraged speculation about what this terrible something might be. Instead, I asked what her usual routine was and noted that as she explained things, she calmed down. Then I got her to tell me about herself, and soon she was chattering happily. I learned that she was even younger than I'd thought, had been in her job only four months, and had no previous experience of any kind. No wonder she needed direction! I told her to do just as she usually did in the mornings, and to make a note of anything she was unsure of and we'd deal with it together later in the day.

Polly nodded, then asked a sensible question. "What do I say if anyone calls for Mrs. Trelawney?"

"Just, ah, just say she's not in and ask for a name and a number where they can be reached. Okay?"

She looked dubious, but she nodded without further question.

"Now, I'm going to take myself on a tour of the inn. If you'll just tell me which rooms are occupied so that I don't disturb anyone?"

Business was not exactly booming. Aside from my room and those permanently taken by Jonathan and my sister, only two of the other fourteen rooms were occupied. Perhaps that was usual for mid-October, but I began to have the uneasy feeling that more was amiss here than my absent sister.

The guest rooms were charming, each somewhat unique in furnishings and decor. Most had fireplaces that seemed in working order, as you would expect in such an old house. Houses. About half of the rooms had private baths which must have been carved from the rooms next door, except in the connecting link which fit in so seamlessly that it was impossible to tell where it began and ended. On each floor there were a cluster of rooms which shared a large bathroom, more luxurious to make up for the sharing. The restoration had been faithfully yet cleverly done, introducing modern comforts in an unobtrusive way. Though I didn't linger in my inspection, I was increasingly impressed. The Trelawney Inn seemed to me a fine property. Pride of ownership, an entirely new feeling, stirred in me. Surely we could make the inn a great success, even without the force of Carroll Trelawney's personality behind it!

When I reached the third floor, I avoided the dining room and kitchen. I didn't feel up to meeting the housekeeper-cook. What had Jonathan said her name was? Evelyn. I felt instinctively that a meeting with Evelyn would produce a new set of problems, and I had enough problems already. I suspected that my sister was a poor manager, that was why Jonathan felt overburdened, why the assistant manager was so new and young and inexperienced, and perhaps that was also why there were so few guests in October when the Carolinas were warm and pleasant enough to pass for summer elsewhere. As I returned to my own room I had a horrible thought: what if Kathryn had known she was a poor manager and had simply copped out, what if my sister had deliberately skipped out on me?

Boris came running and I picked him up. He responded with the muffled rumble of his purr. I held him against me on one arm, like a baby, and he put his front paws and head over my shoulder.

"Well, what do you think, big guy? Would she do that to us?" She might, I had to admit it. What she had told me was that she couldn't cope with the financial end of the operation. She hadn't implied that it might be more extensive than that. But what other explanation could there be for her absence? With every hour that passed, her return seemed less likely.

For a few moments I felt completely at a loss, abandoned, alone. Was I crazy to come here? Certainly there had been times in recent months when I'd been afraid I was losing touch with reality.

"Oh, Boris," I murmured into his soft fur, "the truth is I don't really know what I'm doing!"

Silently I began to cry. Not the first time I'd cried for myself, and it probably wouldn't be the last. Without realizing it, I'd counted on my sister for . . . for *something*. I wasn't sure what. Support? Affection? She had never given me either one. No, not for those things. What, then?

At our parents' funeral I'd seen that she needed me. Kathryn was one of those women who cannot function without a man in her life, and Carroll Trelawney had deserted her. She needed me. That was what I had counted on, her need for me. And of course I could pull myself together for someone who needed me, I was good at that, I'd always been good at that!

The tears silently rolling down my face turned bitter. I'd gone about this partnership and this move in such a logical, businesslike way, being as careful as my legal skills had taught me to be. But all the while what I was unconsciously doing was repeating an old, old pattern. Kathryn needed someone, and I was family. She needed me, she was my sister, she was someone to love. And if I gave her what she needed, then she would love me in return. It was a pattern so ancient in me that I had repeated it without knowing that I did. The trouble was it didn't work, it never got me what I really wanted—love—not from my mother and father, not from the man who'd been briefly my husband, and now not from Kathryn. She was gone, she couldn't even stay to play the game for a little while.

Well, enough was enough. I sniffed, wiped my face with my hand, and got cat hair in my nose. I put Boris down on the floor. "I promise you, my friend cat, I'll never make that mistake again!"

"Mowr?"

"I said *never*. That's right, never."

For the first time I saw the dolphins. They swam in a wide circle perhaps fifty feet from where I stood on the grassy shore at the westernmost end of Front Street. I counted ten of them, not leaping and playing as I'd seen them do on television, but slowly, gracefully moving their gleaming dark gray bodies in circular procession. There was a rhythm to their movement, and a deep, essential quiet, as of some ancient, stately ritual. I was entranced, my problems, large and small, forgotten. Revolving, revolving, the dolphins swimming in their magic circle wove a spell of peace wider than the water, warmer than the midday sun above. The dolphins drew me. I found my feet halted at the water's edge; I found far, far within me an archaic yearning I could not name. The dolphins called to me, and wordlessly I answered. And they came.

Two dolphins curved away from the circle, carving an arc through the water, and then side by side they lifted their heads and leapt in a joyous arch. Across the water I heard them whistle and click. The others broke their circle, leaping, whistling, clicking. The two swam to me. I knelt on the cool, soft grass, hardly daring to breathe. Closer and closer came the pair, shiny-wet and beautiful. Five or six feet away they stopped. They hovered, poised nearly upright, round heads well out of the water, wearing a seeming-smile. They looked at me with their dark, liquid eyes. Eyes, the windows of the soul.

"What are you?" I whispered. "What do you want from me?"

They opened their smiling mouths, so close to me that I could see their tiny perfect teeth. Then they turned to each other, giving me their profiles. How intelligent they seemed, how alien, yet how wonderful! In unison the dolphins looked at me once more, dipped their heads, then tucked themselves into a deep dive and swam away underwater.

"Wow!" I said aloud. I straightened up and shaded my eyes with one hand. The dolphins were gone now . . . if they had ever been there at all. For a few moments the smell of salt on the air was too pungent, the sharp, clean breeze seemed to pierce my skin and pass through every pore to lodge chill along my bones. Heightened senses. Living on the edge. I blinked against the too-blue sky, too-blue sea. It will pass, I told myself . . . and it did pass.

My encounter with the dolphins had not been imagined, it was real. Strange and wonderful, and true. I thought about it, puzzled over it. The experience settled into me with all the weight of an important event. We have all felt that way a few times in our lives—we meet someone, or do something, or find ourselves in a particular place, and deep inside a bell rings. Signals: This is important! Remember! Why I should feel that way about a couple of dolphins, I didn't know, but the feeling was undeniable.

I ran my fingers through my hair, an old habit, an attempt to restore order to its unruly thickness. My hair had always had a mind of its own, and no amount of brushing or hairspray could change it for long from what it most resembled—a black, curly mop. Of course, Kathryn had had more patience with hers. She'd been more willing than I to spend time and money on herself that way. I was thinking about Kathryn again as I returned to the sidewalk and walked back along Front Street. Kathryn, with her 20/20 vision and clear gray eyes, had perfect eyes, not nearsighted and clouded with green, as mine were. Kathryn's shoulder-length, professionally styled, salon-straightened hair was impeccable. In high school and college I'd no longer thought we looked so much alike, but that she was prettier than I. I'd been surprised at our parents' funeral to see that she no longer had her hair styled and straightened. Carroll and his boat and the wind, she'd explained, had broken her of the beauty-salon habit. She'd reverted to nature, and her hair was as much a curly mop as my own.

I crossed to the boardwalk and idled along, looking at the boats although I knew I should return to the inn for lunch. I stopped dead in my tracks, frankly staring.

Like the dancer I'd so much wanted to be, I had an objective appreciation of a beautifully developed body, male or female. This one was male. Gorgeously, gloriously male. He wore grubby-gray deck shoes and tight, faded, frayed cutoff jeans, and nothing else. He was doing something with a rope that hung down along the mast of his boat, so that he strained upward, hands above his head, his back to me. His shoulders and arms were magnificent, his muscles rippled smoothly under the tanned silk of his skin. His hair blazed copper-red in the sunlight, a healthy mane of waves, neither long nor short.

"Damn!" the gorgeous creature swore under his breath. He dropped his arms, moved a quarter-turn around the mast, then reached up and tried again. I saw him now in profile—hairless chest, flat abdomen, bulge of his sex in jeans that rode his hipbones well below his navel, his thighs long, calves strong. He had a beard which like his hair was red, full, and neither long nor short.

He tugged on the rope with a grunt of satisfaction, moved another quarter-turn around the mast, and tugged. Then he looked at me.

I knew I'd been staring. Quickly I turned my gaze to his boat. I took in the polished teak deck. The unpolished brass needed his attention soon. The name in black and gold letters on the stern: *Hellfire.* But first I'd seen the very odd look on his face, a mixture of surprise and revulsion. No doubt he disliked being scrutinized by strange women.

"Your boat is beautiful," I said.

He crossed the deck and glared down at me. "Who the hell are you?"

I forced my eyes to look up into his, which were green and angry. "I'm Laura Brannan, and I didn't mean to offend you. All this"—I gestured with a sweep of my hand—"is new to me. I was just admiring your, ah . . . *Hellfire."* I stepped back a pace. It was hard on the neck, this looking up. Plus which, with his size and his blazing wealth of hair and beard, it was rather disconcerting, like talking to an angry god.

He sank into a crouch, which brought him closer to my level, and proceeded to undress me with his eyes. "Laura Brannan. Welcome to Beaufort, Laura. You must be new in town if all this"—he copied my hand gesture—"is new to you."

"Yes, I'm new. Do you live here?"

"In a manner of speaking. I live on the *Hellfire,* and right now Beaufort is my home port. I'll be here through the winter, at least."

"An unusual name for a boat, isn't it? Why do you call it the *Hellfire?* And speaking of names, I presume you have one?"

He grinned, a flash of white teeth. I noticed how well-shaped his mouth was, framed by the glorious beard; noticed, too, tiny wrinkles in his tanned face, especially around his eyes. The wrinkles told me he was not as young as I'd at first thought, which made his body all the more remarkable.

"I call her the *Hellfire* because she flies before the wind like a bat out of hell. My name's Nick. Nicholas Westover."

"How do you do, Nick Westover."

"It's a little late to be so formal, don't you think?" Once again his eyes invaded my body. He leaned down, extending his arm and hand to me, saying, "Nevertheless, how do you do, Laura Brannan?"

I gave him my hand for the handshake he offered. It turned into something more, a physical joining more intimate than any handshake had a right to be. I pulled back, but he didn't release me, he only drew me closer.

His voice dropped a notch, matching the intimacy in our touch. "Would you like to come aboard? Let me show you my . . . *Hellfire.*"

I couldn't find my voice. Nick was dangerous, as dangerous as he was gorgeous. I knew this, just as I knew that never before in my life had I felt such a strong physical attraction to a man on first meeting. Never, ever had I invited a sexual overture, as I had invited this one. His green eyes, wickedly glittering, told me he knew exactly what I felt.

"No," I said at last, "I can't. Not today. Perhaps some other time. I have to get back to the inn."

"You're staying at the Trelawney Inn?" He still held my hand captive, without effort, though his body was extended from the deck of his boat in what must have been an uncomfortable position.

"More than that. I'm one of the owners. Kathryn Trelawney is my sister."

Now he dropped my hand. A curtain fell behind those green eyes. He sat back on his haunches. A hard edge came into his voice. "I might have known."

Jonathan had warned me, and this was my first taste of it. "You think I look like her."

"When I first saw you, yes. But when I came closer, heard your voice, no. Otherwise I wouldn't have . . ." He didn't finish, he didn't need to. We both knew what he meant. He went on. "You may as well know, your sister wasn't my favorite person."

I caught his use of the past tense. *"Wasn't?"*

"Wasn't. I don't have anything to do with her anymore. Besides, I heard she's missing."

"Yes, she is. Do you know anything about that?" The lawyer in me still didn't like his choice of the word *wasn't*. And the woman in me didn't like the implication that he had once had things to do with Kathryn.

"Only what I heard when I got in last night, just after sundown. That Jonathan Harcourt was down here, asking if anybody knew where she was, if anyone had taken her out yesterday." He stared straight at me, eyes guarded, expression impossible to read because of the beard that masked the rest of his face. "Good riddance, I say. I'm sure you'll do better without the bitch."

Facial clues were unnecessary, after all. I blinked and backed away from the cruelty of his tone. And yet, when he spoke again I waited to hear what he would say.

"Don't go, Laura. You're not like your sister."

"That's true, I'm not. But I do have to go."

"Tomorrow, then. Come back tomorrow."

"Perhaps I will. If not tomorrow, another time. You know where to find me." I walked backward, a step at a time. Repelled yet attracted, I found it hard to leave him.

"If you don't come tomorrow, you can be sure that I will . . . find you."

I turned then, not trusting myself another minute in Nick Westover's presence. What kind of man was he, and how could I feel this immediate, irrational urge toward him, especially when he so obviously hated my sister?

I quickened my pace until I was almost running. And ran straight into the arms of Seth Douglas.

3

He needn't have put his arms out, of course, much less around me. I'd looked over my shoulder without slowing my steps, wanting to fix in my mind exactly where the *Hellfire* was docked, and I merely bumped into Seth Douglass.

"Whoa, slow down!" He caught and held me for a moment, then with my shoulders in his hands moved back at arm's length.

"I'm sorry, Seth, I guess I wasn't looking where I was going." I felt flushed, slightly breathless. I ran my hand through my hair and forced my breath to come evenly.

"What's so interesting back there?"

"Boat called the *Hellfire,* and the man on the boat, I suppose he owns it. His name is Nick Westover. Do you know him?" I couldn't help but notice the difference between the man I'd just left and Seth, with his long, aristocratic nose, thick black brows and silver hair. They were as different as fire and ice.

Caution in the dark brown eyes. "I know him slightly. Why? You look as if he may have said something that upset you. And you *were* practically running, one is tempted to say running away."

"He hates my sister, Kathryn. That's all." A part-truth is better than none, I thought.

"Well, I wouldn't let that worry me too much if I were you. That man's regard is of no great value to anyone." One eyebrow arched in disdain. "I was looking for you, and since I've found you, we may as well have lunch together. Unless you've eaten?"

"No. Lunch will be fine. Where?"

"Away from here, if you don't mind. I have something to tell you that requires some discretion and privacy. I left my car at your inn."

I checked my watch. It was a quarter after one. "All right, but I should be back around three. And I should stop and tell Polly."

Seth shepherded me across the street, his hand light yet firm between my shoulder blades. "No need for that. She knows I hoped you'd have lunch with me. She told me where to look for you."

His take-charge attitude irritated me as much now as it had yesterday, but because I was so curious to know what he had to tell me, I went along with it. I noticed that he was unconsciously polite, a rarity in my experience. He didn't walk too fast for me, he did walk on the outside—a useless, antiquated custom but nice somehow. He opened the car door, held it, checked to see that I was safely in, then closed it. Nice, I had to admit.

"Your car looks like you," I said when he got in beside me.

"How's that?"

"Conservative, very correct. Charcoal-gray pinstripe suit, black BMW with four doors. It fits."

"Ah, but have you noticed my tie?"

I hadn't. I leaned over to look as he backed and maneuvered the car down the driveway. His tie was paisley silk, turquoise and gray with flecks of gold, on a black background. Elegant, but unexpectedly exotic. "The mystery of the Orient," I quipped. "You have a secret longing to be a Persian prince."

He took his eyes from the road for a second and smiled at me. "I have secret longings all right, but so far that isn't one of them. All I meant was, I'm not as conservative as I may appear to be."

"You appear to be a banker or a stockbroker or something like that. What *do* you do for a living?"

"I build houses. And hotels, and condos. And in the past, a couple of shopping malls. I'm a developer." He glanced at me, as if he expected some reaction to this announcement. "That automatically makes me a bad guy to a lot of people around here, especially in Beaufort. Which is why I wanted to get you out of there and on my home turf before we talk."

"Are you sure you aren't just being paranoid?"

"Not paranoid. Realistic. Beaufort is a very small town. You'll soon find out that everybody knows everybody else and most people are friendly, so naturally they talk. Anything said in public might be overheard, and you can be sure it would be repeated. I'm being careful, that's all."

I was beginning to think Seth Douglass was careful about a great many things. Was this prudence, or did he have something to hide? In any case, he sounded less than enthusiastic about Beaufort, a town I'd already begun to love, and I charged to the defense. "You don't like Beaufort? How can you not like it? Beaufort has charm, and character, which is even more important. It's one of the most unusual, most beautiful little places I've ever seen!"

"I agree, completely. Don't get me wrong. I like Beaufort so much that it's changed my life. I intend to stick around this area for a long, long time, which is why I want to be accepted."

"You mean you're not . . . accepted?"

"No. Not yet. It seems I have yet to prove myself."

"I don't understand."

"I can understand their point of view—'they' being the natives and those who have lived here for some years. And you'll understand, too, in time. You can't learn everything in one day, Laura, and right now you have other priorities."

I sighed. "Yes, you're right. What you wanted to discuss with me, does it have to do with Kathryn?"

"Yes, it does."

I waited for him to say more, and when he didn't, I

prompted, "We couldn't have more privacy anywhere than we do here in your car."

"I don't discuss business when I'm driving."

The tight reserve that seemed to be so much a part of this man was back again. I looked out of the car window. We'd gone over a bridge, through some sort of beach town with a roadside collection of tacky stores, past some imposing condos or apartments, and were now on a straight, flat road with bushes and houses along the sides. Not much to see.

"How much longer?" I asked.

"Ten minutes. We're going to Emerald Isle."

"Oh." I'd studied my maps, and I knew that Emerald Isle was at the south end of Bogue Banks. I was surprised that the ocean wasn't visible from the road. After a couple of minutes of silence I tried another question. "What do you have against Nick Westover?"

"I don't have anything against the man. I believe what I said was that his opinion of your sister, or of anything else, should carry no weight."

My patience was dwindling. "For heaven's sake, I'm not going to sue you if you venture an unguarded opinion! Talk to me! Have a conversation, one friend to another—loosen up and say what you think. Or do you fall apart if you're not Mr. Rigid twenty-four hours a day?"

Seth stiffened. His voice cut the air like cold steel. "Mr. Rigid?" He released a long, heavy sigh that sounded nearly human. "Oh, damnation! You're sharp, Laura, I give you credit for that. You must have been a good lawyer. Maybe some day you'll tell me why you gave it up."

He looked at me, and I looked back. Not now, I thought, I don't let you get me talking so you can get yourself off the hook. He seemed to get the message because he continued. "It's been said before. I'm rigid, too severe, too controlling. My ex-wife said all those things, and more. But you've picked them up on very short acquaintance."

"It wasn't hard to do."

"Well, I'm trying. At least give me credit for that. One friend to another, you said, and I'd like for us to be friends. So, about Westover. He's a rogue, an outsider, a lawless man. He stays on that boat of his, answers to no one. If you ask him what he does for a living, he'll tell you he's a bum. If you press him further, he'll say he's a *rich* bum. That much is true. Early this year he wanted to buy a property on Ocracoke that I own with three other people, so we investigated him. He has money, a lot of it. He's the son of wealthy parents, a reclusive old-line Virginia family. Never worked a day in his life because he never had to and apparently didn't want to. Whatever else he does, he covers his tracks. The man is thirty-eight years old, and there's no record of him doing anything concrete since he graduated from prep school."

"Did you sell him the property?"

"No. I didn't trust him, and the Ocracokers didn't trust him, either. I value their opinion, and I honored it."

"Why? What did you think he was going to do with your land, use it for a white slavery business or something dastardly like that?" I was teasing, but I was impressed by this further evidence of Seth's cautiousness.

"What an imagination you have, Laura! Actually, you're not far off the mark. He said he wanted it because he wanted to build himself a house on, quote, 'land sacred to Blackbeard the Pirate.' And Blackbeard did have fourteen wives."

"Blackbeard the Pirate? That's crazy. He must have been kidding."

"He wasn't kidding, and it's not crazy, either. Blackbeard spent a lot of time on Ocracoke. He careened his ships there, and Ocracoke Inlet was one of his favorite hiding places."

"I thought Blackbeard was a myth, a storybook figure, like Captain Hook in *Peter Pan.*"

Seth shook his head. "No, not so. Pirates aren't fairy tales, and Blackbeard was all too real. There are places he's supposed to have lived in all over this part of the coast, including one in Beaufort. I'll show it to you sometime."

"Okay. So Nick Westover knew what he was talking about with the Blackbeard thing, and he had the money, but you still didn't sell him the property because you didn't trust him. Why didn't you trust him?"

Seth shifted uncomfortably in his seat, withdrew one

31

hand from the steering wheel, and rubbed the back of his neck. "It's difficult to explain. I told my three associates it was because of my respect for the local people, who were quite definite about not wanting him there. But the locals weren't any more specific with me than I was with my colleagues. I've been . . . uncomfortable about it ever since, because I don't usually make decisions that way."

I'll just bet you don't, I thought. To his credit he went on, though he struggled with the words.

"There was something in the way he talked that I just didn't like. Sure, he sounded a bit sarcastic when he said 'land sacred to Blackbeard,' but there was a look in his eyes that said he meant it, *sacred*. That gives me the willies, it's almost . . . almost obscene. Blackbeard—Edward Teach was his real name—was a bad man, a very cruel man. To use a word like *sacred* in connection with him seems a lot like, well, I hesitate to say it, but it seems a lot like worshipping the devil!"

"Oh, come on . . ."

"I'm serious. You wanted what I really think, and I'm telling you. Or trying to. I admit it doesn't make much sense, especially when you consider that ostensibly what's keeping Westover in these parts is the Dolphin Guard. A volunteer dolphin guardian with a soft spot for a bloody pirate? It's a contradiction in possibilities! Therefore, I didn't trust him, and I don't want to have anything to do with him. Nor should you."

I wasn't ready to have Seth Douglass or anybody else make my choice of friends for me. Far from putting me off, the things I'd just learned about Nick made him all the more fascinating. A lawless man who was interested in dolphins was an irresistible attraction for an ex-lawyer who'd had an encounter with the dolphins that very morning!

I said, "The business about the pirate is probably only some kind of misplaced romanticism. Harmless."

"You're a romantic yourself, if you think so." He was severe again.

"Maybe I am," I said evenly. I'd never been one in the

past, but people do change. I knew I was changing. Living on the edge does that to a person. "Tell me about the Dolphin Guard."

"Some other time. We're here now." He pulled into a space alongside other cars parked around a wide cul-de-sac. The end of the road, apparently. I'd been so absorbed in the conversation that I hadn't noticed our turning off from the main thoroughfare.

"Here? Where? I don't—"

"Shhh. Listen. And look carefully."

I listened, and heard the sound of breaking surf. Wonderful, unfamiliar to my formerly landlocked Midwestern ears. Then I looked carefully, as he'd said. Below us, beyond the hood of the car, something man-made blended unobtrusively into the landscape.

"Come," said Seth softly. I left the car and stood beside him. "It's called the Dunes. I think this is the finest thing I've ever built. Do you like it?"

"Oh, yes, I do. It's incredible!" What I'd seen from the car was the roofline of the Dunes. It was sand-colored and sand-textured and curved to the contour of the natural sand dunes.

"The steps are over here. We go down. You see, I've built into the dunes, for protection both of my structure and of the dunes themselves."

Halfway down the steps I said, "Wait, please." There was too much to see, I couldn't take it all in at once. The vastness of the rolling sea, the beauty of the smooth sandy beach, so white and clean. The cry of seagulls. No sounds of man, only the sounds of nature, and the taste and smell of the sea in my nostrils and on my lips. And finally, the building of which Seth was so proud. It was rambling, one story, walls of wood weathering to a silvery gray under their unusual roof, many windows facing the ocean. "I love it. But it's huge!" Then I remembered the other cars. "Who lives here? What kind of place is this?"

Seth laughed. He took my hand and led me down the remaining steps. "It's a residential hotel, with an excellent restaurant. I don't own it, of course, I only built it. But it has been my home for the past two years. There's a lot I'd like to tell you about this place, why and how I had the architect design it the way it is, but I'll have to save it for another day. We're tight on time if I'm to have you back at the Trelawney Inn anywhere near three o'clock, and there's a more pressing matter to discuss."

We sat at a table with only a wall of glass between us and the beach and the ocean, calm and murmuring at low tide. A bamboo screen on one side and a ficus benjamina on the other gave us privacy from the others who were lunching as late as we.

"I hate to ask you to look at me rather than the ocean, Laura, but I do have something important to tell you. I'm afraid it may come as a shock, going by what you told me yesterday. Kathryn Trelawney does own the property known as the Stone House, and the five acres of land that go with it."

"But, how—" I was speechless. It simply couldn't be possible!

"I was wrong about one thing. She didn't acquire it recently, as I'd thought. She bought it sixteen months ago, just two months after her husband's departure. She paid $175,000 cash. She owns it free and clear."

Stunned, I said, "Except for the inn, which is in debt, Kathryn has no assets. Of course, there is our inheritance. She got less than she should have, that was one reason I . . ." I stopped, halted in my protests by the seriousness in Seth's dark eyes. He wouldn't be telling me this if he weren't certain.

"She apparently chose not to disclose her ownership of this property. I'm sorry. I don't know why, but she has been keeping it secret. I was surprised myself when she contacted me about a possible sale. No one in Beaufort knew she owned it, and she has been secretive about our negotiations."

"Somebody knew. The people who sold it to her."

"The estate of the former owner. It was all handled by

lawyers in New Jersey. I spent the morning at the Carteret County Courthouse researching this. Here, I've brought you copies of the paperwork."

I looked. Our lunch came. I read every word, and it was as he said. I picked at my food and tried to think. "If she was keeping it a secret, why did she come to you?"

"I've let it be known that I'm interested in a sizable waterfront property on the sound side of the Core Banks, and there aren't that many. Word of mouth is always the way to find the best places, that's what I was counting on, and Kathryn heard. As I said, she was secretive about it. Wouldn't talk anywhere but at the Stone House itself, and it's an isolated place. We met there twice, alone. She insisted on that, and she insisted that I tell no one. I *am* interested, but her terms are tough. She wants $200,000 cash, no bank financing, no mortgage deal of any kind. Nor will she consider selling less than the whole five acres. Even I have trouble coming up with that amount of cash. At the meeting we had scheduled yesterday I intended to ask her for more time."

I could find no way around the truth. "My sister lied to me." But why? Why would she do that? "Is there anything . . . peculiar about this Stone House?"

"I wondered about that, too. It does have a long and interesting history. It's so old that no one really knows when it was built. The central core of the house is a tower, built entirely of ballast stones. It may have been, probably was, used as a watchtower in Colonial times."

"You mean, like a lighthouse?"

"Not exactly. Stone House is on the land side of Core Sound. A lighthouse would have been built on Core Banks, on the barrier island where it would be visible from the open sea. There *is* a lighthouse there, at the southern tip, Cape Lookout. No, if it was used for a watchtower—and I think it must have been, in those days people around here weren't building themselves Norman-type stone towers for no useful purpose—it would have been used to keep track of what boats were in Core Sound. My guess is that it was built by a merchant who wanted to keep an eye out for those pirates I was telling you about. It could even have been built earlier, by the Spanish, and abandoned by them."

"No one has ever done whatever you need to do to date it?"

"Not that I've heard of. Of course, it has been added on to at various times, always in stone. I haven't looked into the matter thoroughly because I'm not all that interested in the house itself. Architecturally it's a hodgepodge, a curiosity. If I do acquire the property from your sister, and from you now that you're involved, I'll probably tear down all but the old tower. I certainly wouldn't want to live in it."

"That seems like a shame, somehow. But I still don't have a clue . . ." I didn't finish the thought, either in my mind or aloud. Instead, a new one jumped in. "Oh, I just remembered something Jonathan Harcourt said. He said Carroll Trelawney told him he intended to leave money here for Kathryn, to help her until the inn was making a profit. But Jonathan never saw evidence she had such money, and it puzzled him. That's where she got the cash to buy Stone House! It must be, it fits with the time of Carroll's leaving." I felt a minor triumph at putting these pieces together, but the feeling soon vanished. "It doesn't tell us, though, why she would keep the Stone House a secret, especially from me. Or why now she's decided to sell. Did she tell you why she wanted to sell it?"

Seth shook his head. "No. But I've bought a lot of property in my time, and from the way she was acting I'd say she needed the money."

Now it was my turn to shake my head. "Not unless she contacted you before I agreed to the partnership, and from what you've told me, she didn't. I've given half of everything to Kathryn, and by our agreement she did the same with me. We're well enough off. It's not money, it has to be something else." I was troubled, deeply, and confused. I ran my hand through my hair and stared unseeing through the glass.

"Well," said Seth quietly, "it won't remain a mystery much longer. When your sister returns from her unexpected trip, wherever she's gone, she'll have to tell you. You'll want to confront her with this. When and how you do it is up to you, that's why I brought you here, so that nothing will get out until you decide to make it known. Just remember, I still want to buy the property as soon as I can get the cash together."

In my confusion, I couldn't believe I'd heard him right. My thoughts were all for my sister, the apparent peculiarities of her behavior, and what all this meant to me, and here was Seth focused on a mere thing, a material piece of land with a house! "That's what you're *really* interested in. Your business. Acquiring that piece of property, and nothing else. Well, isn't it?"

A muscle in his cheek twitched. His eyes flashed once and were still. "No. Of course it isn't." In the silence that fell between us, our eyes locked; then slowly, deliberately, his probed deeper into mine.

I felt invaded, and I struck back. "Stone House is no longer for sale! You can forget your precious property acquisition!"

"I imagine Kathryn Trelawney will have something to say about that." I heard once again the cold steel in his voice.

"Whatever she has to say, she can say to me." I threw my napkin on the table. "Now, I believe we've finished this lunch."

Seth's car on the drive back was filled with uncomfortable silence. I knew I'd overreacted, but I couldn't bring myself to admit it to him. I longed for someone to confide in, someone who might help me find my way out of all this confusion and doubt. But Seth Douglass was not the right person for the job; we always ended up snapping at each other. Kathryn could, of course, be waiting at the inn, and that would solve all my problems. Correction: *some* of my problems. No matter what happened, no matter how I looked at it, I had some heavy stuff to deal with. As we turned in behind the Trelawney Inn, I loosed an involuntary sigh.

"Are you all right, Laura?"

The warmth in his voice surprised me. "Yes, I'm all

right," I said briefly, gathering myself to leave when he stopped the car. "Thank you for the lunch, and the information."

Seth caught my left hand and held me back. "I apologize for seeming callous back there. Let me help you, Laura. You're more worried about your sister than I realized, aren't you?"

"I can handle it," I said, but I was yielding. The gentle pressure in his touch seemed to promise the support I wanted, needed.

"I'll come in with you," he offered.

My eyes stung with beginning tears. I blinked hard and pulled my hand away. "I can handle it," I repeated. I was good at handling things, I'd always been the one who handled—everything.

But I hadn't always known Seth. As soon as my hand left his he was out of the car, and his long legs brought him to my side before I'd shut my door behind me.

"Okay." He smiled down at me, a genuinely kind smile that softened his face and turned his eyes to deep brown velvet with caring. "You handle it. I'll just be here in case I'm needed. I'm coming with you." And he did.

Both Jonathan and Polly were behind the desk. One look at them told me that Kathryn was still absent. The men shook hands. Polly chirped something about messages. I felt curiously still, dead inside, as Jonathan ushered me and Seth to the inner office and shut the door.

"I'm ready to call the police," I said. My voice in my own ears sounded faraway, as if I were now inside the boy's plastic bubble. I couldn't believe any of this was really happening.

4

We didn't have to go to the police station; the officer did us the courtesy of coming to the inn. But that was the extent of his courtesy. He seemed determined to give me a hard time. I confess I've never liked to deal with the police, though like most lawyers I've had to, often. I tried to put my discomfort down to old police-paranoia, but as the officer persisted in asking me questions I could not possibly answer because I hadn't been present when my sister disappeared, my control snapped. My new vulnerability rose up and swallowed me whole. I, who had never shed a tear in the most difficult of my lawyer days, began to cry. I had to take off my glasses, wipe my cheeks with cold fingers. Dismayed, I heard my own voice come out brokenly: "I don't know! Can't you understand? I wasn't here, I've never been here before in my life!"

The tears were humiliating, but they got me off the hook. The policeman turned to Jonathan Harcourt. Jonathan rapped out his answers as if he were uncomfortable and wanted to get the questioning over with as quickly as possible. Seth's turn was still to come. Though he was out of my line of vision, I was acutely aware of his presence as he stood behind me, his hand on the back of my chair.

"Did Kathryn Trelawney have any enemies?" The classic question; it had been bound to come.

I shook my head.

"None that I know of," said Jonathan.

"Mr. Douglass?" asked the policeman.

"I don't know." Seth hesitated, cleared his throat. "I didn't know her very well," he said finally.

"Then why are you here?" the officer probed. "You have something to contribute?"

I twisted around in my chair, to look at Seth. I expected him to tell of the appointment he'd had with Kathryn at the Stone House, of her failure to appear. But he did not.

He raised one heavy eyebrow and responded without the feeling his words implied, "I'm here to lend support to Laura Brannan. This is all very upsetting to her, as you can see."

I stared at Seth, trying to see through his impeccably suited facade. Why was he deliberately withholding information? Perhaps he thought his missed appointment with Kathryn was irrelevant. The policeman watched us both, I knew, so I turned back around, feeling like a conspirator in Seth's omission. I wouldn't call him on it, but I wondered. Why?

When we were alone again in the office, Jonathan growled indecipherably and pushed his glasses up to the bridge of his nose with a forefinger. Then he slouched down in his chair behind the desk. Kathryn's desk, I thought.

"I'm glad that's over," I said.

"He was pretty rough on you," said Jonathan. "I'm sorry."

"Yes, he was," I admitted, "and for what reason? Surely he can't think me responsible for Kathryn's disappearance!"

Seth came from behind me to sit in the chair vacated by the policeman. "No," he said, "I'm sure he doesn't. More likely he was testing you because you're a stranger to him. Do you know the man, Harcourt?"

"I've seen him around." Jonathan paused, thinking. "The name's familiar, though. Sanders. Sergeant Sanders, wasn't it?"

"Uh-huh," I said, and Seth, too, nodded.

"There are a lot of Sanders. It's an old name—there have been Sanders here back to Colonial times, before the Revolution. I traced the old names a while back, just out of curiosity to see how many have stayed on, and as I remember there are still a number of Sanders living on Harkers Island."

"Interesting," said Seth. "They must be a tenacious bunch to survive for hundreds of years on a spot like Harkers Island. Are you a local history buff, Harcourt?"

"Not really." Jonathan smiled at Seth—it was the first time he'd looked benevolent all afternoon. "I'm a writer. I just like to dig up local color, and I like to talk to people. Why'd you ask if I knew Sergeant Sanders?"

"I'd rather know why a family would have to be tenacious to survive on Harkers Island," I put in.

Seth looked at me. "I thought from the Sergeant's, ah, shall we say, challenging manner that he wasn't too sympathetic to our concerns about Kathryn's absence, and I wondered if that was just his habitual way of speaking. As for your question about Harkers, the best answer would be to take you there one day. How about it?"

"I don't know," I hedged. "I'm feeling a little . . . disoriented. Disloyal, too, perhaps. I shouldn't let myself get sidetracked on local history at a time like this." The residue of my crying pricked in the back of my throat and in my nose, and I sniffed. "I guess I'm upset. I'm paranoid about the police. I've had some rough dealings with them as a lawyer back in Columbus, but I know they always do their job."

An uncomfortable silence fell among us. The men seemed no more satisfied or encouraged than I. Jonathan drummed his fingers twice on the desktop. Then he said, "I'm sure they'll do all the usual things—whatever those are—to look for Kathryn. We already know there were no accidents around here the night she disappeared, there are no boats missing, nobody took her anywhere by boat, and she hasn't shown up in the emergency room of any hospital from here to Jacksonville. I don't know what else they can do. But"—

Jonathan pushed himself away from the desk and stood up—"I'm going to relieve Polly so she can go home and have dinner with her mother. The girl's getting frazzled."

"I'll take a turn on the desk," I volunteered, "It's time I learned. If you go on duty now, you'll have a horribly long night."

Hands shoved in the pockets of his sweater, Jonathan looked kindly down on me. "Thanks but no, thanks, Laura. We'll get you started tomorrow. You must be a little frazzled yourself."

"I-I guess you're right." I sighed.

Jonathan left the office and closed the door behind him. I sat undecided. A part of me wanted to be alone and quiet, with time to sort out all the input of the past twenty-four hours; but another part of me was curious, wanting to know Seth's real motives. I doubted he'd stayed for the police interview just to be helpful to me. And why hadn't he told Sergeant Sanders of his appointment with Kathryn? What was he thinking about now, what was going on behind those deepset dark eyes?

The curious part of me won out. I tried to sound more conversational than confrontive. "I couldn't help but notice that you didn't tell the Sergeant about waiting for Kathryn at the Stone House. You must have a reason."

A half-smile touched Seth's lips. "Of course. And you'd like to know?"

I nodded. I watched him carefully, out of training and habit, looking for the body language, the facial expressions, the hard-to-define nuances of communication that separate the telling of truth from the telling of lies.

Seth shifted in his chair and crossed one lanky leg over the other. "Let's just say I'm cautious by nature. And I honor my commitments. Your sister asked me to keep our negotiations regarding the Stone House confidential, and she could still show up anytime. She wouldn't thank me for telling the police or anyone else that we were supposed to meet there."

His facade was impossible for me to penetrate. He seemed relaxed enough, and I'd already recognized his cautiousness.

42

Perhaps he was telling the truth, but something nagged at me. Suddenly I had it.

"You forgot about Polly," I said. He looked surprised. I went on, "Yesterday when you burst in here and thought I was Kathryn, you said she was to meet you at the Stone House. In front of Polly."

Seth scowled, pulling his heavy eyebrows together. "So I did. Well, that's another side of me, Laura. I have a temper, I admit. Kathryn Trelawney could be a difficult woman, she'd already been difficult with me, and then to be kept waiting . . . ! If I didn't want that property as much as I do, I wouldn't have chosen to do business with her in the first place. So my temper was at the flaring point, and when that happens, I—well, I'm not so careful."

"I doubt it matters. Polly forgot about it right away. Are you aware that you're talking about my sister in the past tense? She *could* be difficult, you said."

Now Seth was definitely uncomfortable. "What are you driving at?"

"Nothing. Just making observations. On the one hand you say she could show up at any time, and on the other hand you speak in the past tense, as if you don't expect to see her again."

"I wouldn't attach too much importance to that if I were you." He regarded me darkly. "We all have that same conflict, don't we? There was every reason for Kathryn to meet me the day before yesterday. I know she is, or was, anxious to sell. And there would seem to have been every reason for her to be here for your arrival. It's only logical to assume she'll turn up soon, isn't it? And yet, in your gut—or to put it more delicately, in your heart of hearts—do *you* expect to see her again, Laura?"

"Yes," I said stubbornly, "of course I do. Kathryn wouldn't go to all the length she went to in order to get me to come here and then run out on our partnership. We were never close, but we're *sisters!*"

Seth looked at me in his intense way, as if he could see written behind my eyes the things I didn't say: that in my "heart of hearts," as he'd put it, I had a bad feeling about Kathryn. Not that she'd run out on me, it was darker than that. More sinister. Gathering in the shadows of my mind was a horrifying certainty that someone, somehow, had prevented and perhaps was still preventing my sister's return.

"Um-hm," said Seth. Then he stood and reached out a hand to me. "That's enough speculation. You've done what you had to do, you reported the disappearance to the police. I think we could both use a drink, and then you should think about dinner. As well as I remember, you ate very little of your lunch."

I gave him my hand and let him pull me to my feet. I felt a return of the gentleness that was so surprising in one with his handsome severity. I wanted to go with him, to drink, to forget—but I couldn't. Because Seth's gentleness might be deceptive. Because I'd had another thought and shoved it down, lest he see it in my eyes: Seth Douglass could be the someone who detained my sister. I really knew very little about this man.

"I appreciate your thoughtfulness, and your support, but I'd like a raincheck on the drink. I'm tired, and I want to rest in my room for a while." I gave his hand a squeeze. "I'm sure we'll be in touch."

I did want to rest, but my cat Boris had other ideas. I came in the door of my room, and there was Boris sitting right in the middle of the rug. He blinked his blue eyes once, then raised his nose slightly, wearing his expectant expression. I knew what he expected, but if I ignored him, maybe he'd give up for an hour or so. I acted preoccupied and took the long route around the room to the bathroom, following the far edges of the rug.

"Mowr," said Boris. I pretended not to hear.

I took my time. Washed my face with cold water, brushed out my tousled hair, and then shook it back in place again, cleaned my glasses. Then I looked at myself in the big mirror over the sink in the dressing room. The day had taken its toll—this day and many others before it. My face looked white and small, lost under all the hair. My clear-rimmed glasses, carefully chosen for their proportions—I thought they brought out a suggestion of high cheekbones—emphasized eyes that at the moment looked bewildered. Knowing I was going to lose out in my subterfuge with Boris, that he wouldn't forget, I put some blusher on those pale cheekbones.

When I came back into the room, Boris was sitting in front of the door that by now he'd figured out led to the outside. He stared at me, meowlessly.

"Yeah, you've made your point," I said to him. "I'll take you outside. You do have to start learning your way around sometime."

The door that had been the house's front door was near my room. It had been fixed in the restoration so that it could no longer be opened from the outside, because the Inn's main entrance was at the rear of the two linked houses, closest to the parking area. But from the windows of my room I'd seen chairs on the open porch across the front of the house, and that was where I wanted to go with my cat. I tried the former front door and found that I could go out that way, even if I could not get back in.

"Come, Boris," I said, opening the door. He preceded me with cautious dignity, pausing on the threshold to sniff and survey the territory. "You're a good boy," I encouraged. "You've got too much sense to dash out in a new place without knowing where you're going, don't you?"

Boris looked up at me. "Mowr," he agreed, lifting his plume of tail in the air. He came through the doorway and I closed the door behind him.

Maybe Boris has more sense than I do, I thought. I chose a rocking chair and sank into it. Perhaps I could rest here as well as I would have on the bed in my room.

"Don't you dare run off!" I warned the cat in my sternest tone of voice. He turned his head and blinked, then continued to explore the porch. I closed my eyes resolutely against the boats and the blue water of the harbor across Front Street. It was still warm this late in the day. I rocked, oblivious to occasional passing cars; I heard the creak of the rockers on the porch's old floorboards, felt the caress of warm, light breezes on my skin.

One by one, images rose behind my closed eyelids: a nightmarish flashback of too-vivid autumn colors speeding by me on the West Virginia turnpike; my sister's face the last time I'd seen her, as we said goodbye in the airport after Mother and Father's funeral; dolphins swimming in a magic circle; a nearly naked, copper-haired man named Nick Westover, his eyes a green blaze over letters that spelled out *Hellfire* . . .

I awakened with a start that would have brought me out of the rocking chair, except for the weight of Boris, settled in my lap, anchoring me to my seat.

"You scared me half to death," I scolded him, but gently. It's hard to scold a purring cat. How long had I slept? I glanced at my left wrist and saw only whiter skin against a fading tan where my watch should have been. I'd forgotten to put it back on after washing my face. Amazing. Usually my watch was indispensable, as much a part of me as my glasses, and as far as I knew I'd never forgotten it before. Though I didn't realize it now, the forgetting of the watch was symbolic—already I sensed on an unconscious level that nature rules time as well as everything else here by the sea.

Without the watch I relied on the sun. Its glowing red half-disc was sinking behind Carrot Island, shedding a ruby path across the water. Long, low, horizontal strands of cloud were purple on top, gold underneath. One, two, three, four, five boats, two with sail and three without, came in an unevenly spaced procession to their moorings. I appreciated the beauty of the moment. Such a sunset was glorious, nature's benediction, a blessing at day's end. And yet, I could not feel blessed. Even as I stroked Boris's soft fur and my lap vibrated with his purring contentment, I could not be at peace.

Dreams. I had dreamed. All those images in my head, and one remained: a long, elegant face with the hint of a cleft in the chin, a mouth by turns either sensual or severe—Seth Douglass. In his own way a handsome man. A disturbing man. I had dreamed about him, I was sure of it; and while I couldn't remember the dream, it had disturbed me.

"It's probably not important," I said aloud to Boris, "I'm easily disturbed these days. Come on, kitty, let's go for a twilight stroll along the boardwalk."

I felt in the pocket of my skirt. Yes, my room key was there, and so was the folded twenty-dollar bill I always carried in a pocket or if I had no pockets, in my bra—a useful habit I'd developed after once having my purse stolen. Right now it meant I could stop in a grocery store on our way back without having to walk all the way around the inn and through it to my room, just to get my purse. I shifted Boris to the crook of my right arm and set off.

On this walk I looked not at the ever-present boats and water, but at the people. A preponderance of men over women, they were at least my age, most older, all with faces full of character. Some smiled easily at me, as if they were amused by the sight of a small woman with a large cat carried like a baby in her arms. I wondered which of these people were transient, visitors only, and which lived here and were my neighbors. This small seaport seemed a remarkably classless place, where men and women, old and young, were unified by the sameness of their casual dress. Seth in his business suit would have looked out of place. I frowned at the thought. I wanted to forget about him.

The tables and chairs of a sidewalk, or more appropriately boardwalk, restaurant attracted me, and I sat down with Boris on my lap. A waiter appeared, dressed in jeans, T-shirt, and apron. He was the youngest person I'd yet seen in Beaufort, aside from Polly. I ordered a glass of white wine, and when he offered a menu I took it without thinking. Then I realized that I was hungry. When he brought the wine I ordered shrimp salad, trusting that as long as he was in my lap, Boris would be no trouble.

Where do dolphins go at night? I wondered. Do they ever sleep? This restaurant was near the western end of the boardwalk, and at a distance of about half a city block I could see the grassy place at the end of Front Street where I'd stood when the dolphins came to me. The sun had set now, but the westward sky shone with a rosy-golden glow which reflected on the water where the dolphins had played. The memory was strong, and stirred in me something mystical, archaic, older than knowing. I longed to see them again. Unreasonable and childish though it was, I felt that the dolphins were wiser than I. If I could find them again, if they could only speak to me, they would have all the answers.

I shared my shrimp salad with Boris, finger-feeding him on my lap under the cover of the table. The food was very good; my thoughts were not. Something about Seth bothered me, and wouldn't let go. I wanted to trust him. He seemed, well, to be honest with myself, he seemed attracted to me. That in itself was enough to make me wary. Since the breakup of my marriage it had been hard for me to trust a man, especially an attractive man who was attracted to me. Seth's failure to tell the police about his scheduled meeting with Kathryn gnawed at me. Was he honest? If he could lie by omission to the police about that, might he not also lie to me about his reasons? Seth wanted the Stone House property badly, that was clear. What if he'd lied? What if Kathryn had come to meet him and had told him she no longer wanted to sell, that he couldn't have it? He would have been angry, very angry. Just how strong was the temper he admitted having? Might he have been angry enough to—to what? Well, to do something to teach her a lesson; surely he wouldn't hurt her. Surely no one would hurt my sister.

Boris, still on my lap, stiffened and growled, a low, warning rumble. At the same moment I realized that someone stood near, and I jerked my head up, startled from my unpleasant thoughts.

"Hello, Laura Brannan." It was Nick, Nick Westover, looking quite civilized in a black turtleneck jersey and pale blue stonewashed jeans. "May I join you?"

Boris growled again and thrust his head up mightily, nearly upsetting the small round table. Glasses and silverware rattled dangerously as he put his ears back and glared at the stranger. "Don't mind him," I apologized, grabbing my wineglass with one hand and the scruff of Boris's neck with the other. "Hush, Boris!"

"It doesn't seem to like me."

"He, not it. Boris is a male cat." Boris relaxed somewhat in my grip, but he would not put his head down. I knew his eyes were fixed on Nick.

"Do you always take your cat out to dinner with you? No, don't answer that, let me guess. You're really a witch and he's your familiar, a demon in cat form, and you never go anywhere without him." Nick's green eyes gleamed, mocking.

I laughed. "I hadn't planned on eating dinner. I had my cat on the porch with me at the inn, getting him used to his new home, and then I decided to go for a walk at sunset, and I just brought him along. Then I found this place and we just stayed . . ." I let my voice trail off as the waiter came to the table, and Nick ordered a beer and another glass of wine for me.

The waiter stayed a moment to light the candle within a glass globe on the table. The candlelight touched Nick's wealth of hair and beard to flame, and I thought that it would take more than civilized clothing to tame this man. Shadows played across his face, adding a hint of his true age to his tanned youthful face. He caught my scrutiny, and smiled, a knowing smile. This man could charm me, and he knew it. I smiled in return.

"Well," he said, "cat and all, I'm glad you stopped here. I hadn't expected to see you again so soon. Have you been enjoying your first day in town?"

"Yes and no. I like Beaufort very much, but my sister hasn't come back yet and I'm worried about her. We reported her disappearance to the police this afternoon."

"Oh? And what did they say?" He smiled again, but this smile was different, sardonic, darkly amused. The darkness of that sardonic smile didn't fit my concept of Nick—with his bright hair, he should be of the sun, of the light. Seth was the dark one, dark-brown of eye and black of brow, and hair that had once been black, though now it was silver as moonlight.

I roused myself to answer Nick's question. "They didn't say anything, or rather he didn't. Jonathan Harcourt and I talked to a Sergeant Sanders, and all he did was ask a lot of questions." I noticed that instinctively I had failed to mention Seth to Nick.

The waiter returned with our beer and wine. I stroked Boris rhythmically, willing the cat to relax his guard. "It's okay, big guy," I whispered, but still he was tense. With his ears so flat against his head, he probably hadn't heard me. I hoped Boris would calm down, because I wanted to stay here with Nick.

He was saying, "They won't find her. All they're good for is writing traffic tickets."

Well, I thought, Seth did say that Nick was a lawless man. The contempt in his voice shouldn't surprise me.

"You take my advice," Nick continued, "and forget about your sister. Unless she comes back on her own, and I'll bet you a million bucks she won't, you'll never see Kathryn Trelawney again."

"I hope you're wrong," I said, but I sounded uncertain. I was so afraid he was right.

Nick leaned across the table. His eyes were fascinating, gleaming like green jewels in the near-dark. "Besides, she couldn't hold a candle to you, anybody can see that. I'm sorry I insulted you by thinking you were Kathryn when I first saw you this morning."

The words he said were words I had often wanted, in my youth, to hear: I prefer you to your sister. And yet I felt no pleasure. My response came out of all the old places in myself. "People have always done that, mistaken me for her, I don't take it as an insult. Everyone thought we were twins, until they got to know us, and then they'd see that Kathryn was prettier than I. So, you see, you're wrong. It's the other way around—I'm the one who can't hold a candle to her."

Nick reached for my hand. Boris hissed and spat. I grabbed the back of his neck again and let Nick's fingers close over mine on the table. His touch was charged; it went through me like lightning.

His voice was low and rough. "Listen to me and believe

me, Laura. Maybe she was your sister, but Kathryn Trelawney was no better than a whore!"

I gasped, snatched my hand away. But his eyes still held me. I remembered this morning he'd called her a bitch. Under that green gaze I felt small, nearly helpless. Strength I thought I didn't have welled up and I said steadily, "I suppose you know of her whorishness from first-hand experience."

Nick threw his head back and laughed, teeth flashing white within the red beard. Boris struggled; it took both hands to hold him now. From the corner of my eye I saw people at other tables looking at us. Nick Westover's laugh was far from discreet, and I was embarrassed. How much had those other people overheard?

"I-I have to go," I stammered. I stood up and scanned for the waiter. He, too, had been looking at us and he came immediately. I thrust the twenty-dollar bill from my pocket at the waiter, saying, "Please take your tip out of this, too."

Boris quieted in my arms, perhaps sensing I meant to leave. He put his paws on my shoulder and his head on his paws.

Nick had sobered. "You won't stay?"

I shook my head.

"Then, I'll walk you home." He tossed a dollar for his beer on the table and got up. "We still haven't finished our conversation."

"Well . . . oh, all right." I stood awkwardly, anxious for the waiter to return so that I could escape the sidelong glances that still came our way.

The lighting along the boardwalk was not as bright as on the city streets I was accustomed to. There were no other walkers in sight, and few cars passed. The waters of the harbor were black, without even the moon's reflection.

"Is it cloudy?" I asked. "There doesn't seem to be a moon."

"Yep, it's clouding over. Rain tomorrow. The wind will come up in the night, you'll see."

I heard our footsteps on the boards. They had a hollow ring.

51

Nick stopped. "You want to know if I, oh, shall we say fooled around with your sister?"

"Not really." The truth was that I both wanted and didn't want to know.

Nick stood an arm's length off, looking down at me. He didn't speak right away, but waited, as if considering what to say. And when he did speak, his voice was oddly hoarse. "Okay. I did. But she came on to me, she came after me first. And then she, she . . . well, that's not important. She was what I said she was, and you might as well know it. I never met her until after her husband had left, but there's plenty of people will tell you she was unfaithful to him. You'd never do that, Laura. You'd keep your promises."

I swallowed hard. He sounded so strange, and he waited for me to say something. So I said, "I do keep promises."

Again, that strange hoarseness, as if from some excess of feeling. "I know you would. You're . . . good, even I can see that. I wish . . ." But he didn't say what he wished. He fell silent, and simply looked at me.

Revolted as I'd been by what he said about my sister, the revolt was all in my mind. My body felt again in the night as it had in sunlight, the power of this man's sexuality. He drew me like a small, pale moth to the flame that was himself. My voice came out in a whisper. "How can you say those things about me? You don't even know me!"

Nick took a step toward me. His fingertips, hard and callused from working his boat, brushed my cheek, then locked in the thickness of hair at the back of my head. Boris growled, but I held him fast. Nick had me enchanted; it was all I could do to breathe evenly.

"I don't have to know you," he said. "I feel the difference in you, the difference from your sister. I saw it in your eyes this morning. I see it now. I feel it now." He moved closer. His hand tightened in my hair, pulling my head back, my chin up.

Boris gave a great, unearthly cry, more like banshee than cat. At the same time his claws came out, pricking into my shoulder, and he twisted sharply in my arms. My cat hurled himself at Nick's face so mightily and so suddenly that I let go.

Large he may be, but Boris is all cat—with agile, deadly grace he turned in the air, extended a paw with claws unsheathed and scratched Nick's face; then landed gracefully on all four feet. In the instant I took to look at the long scratch along Nick's cheekbone, already welling with dark blood, Boris had dashed across the street and disappeared.

"I'm sorry! I can't imagine, he never did anything like this before," I babbled, "but you must understand, I can't lose him! Boris is all I have, he's my family, I have to go after him!" I ran. Lacking feline agility myself, I stumbled on the curb but quickly recovered. If Nick called after me I didn't hear him, for I was calling Boris.

My cat sat on the steps of the inn's porch. Boris has a gift for being able to place himself in the exact center of any given space, and that was where he was now, exactly on the middle of the top step, in a direct line with the middle of the front door. He sat tall, his face with its dark masklike markings enigmatic, truly a magnificent, priestly creature. It was not hard to imagine Boris in an earlier cat-incarnation sitting just so, a sacred cat in the center of the pillared porch of some Egyptian temple.

So many feelings flooded me all at once that I was dizzy with them: relief, anger, exhaustion, love. "You're pretty smart to know where you live, big guy," I said as I approached him slowly, my hand out palm up, waiting for him to nuzzle me. I certainly didn't want Boris to run again, for I was too tired to follow. He pushed his cool nose into my hand, and I picked him up. I couldn't scold him. Certainly I was alarmed by what he'd done, but the thought uppermost in my mind was, Thank God I haven't lost him, too!

5

October blurred into November. I studied the workings of the inn as avidly as I had ever researched any case, and I learned quickly. I was surprised to find that all the records had been kept by hand. It took hours to dig out cost comparisons and occupancy rates. I could not find some things that common sense told me should be there, such as a mailing list with names and addresses of former guests. In spite of the fact that I knew almost nothing about computers, I thought we needed one; I also thought we needed some strong public relations. I learned innkeeper jargon: high season, low season, off-season. Though I couldn't find the documentation, I believed Jonathan when he said that two years ago the inn had been breaking even in the low and off seasons, and turning a profit in summer, the high season. Now we were in the red, losing money rapidly. I didn't need either a computer or a hotel-management consultant to tell me that what we needed most was more guests.

I hired an accounting firm to take over the financial records and get them on computer as an interim solution. I felt I had to study the computer situation myself before making a decision on what to buy for the inn, and at the moment I hadn't the time. I set Polly to making up a mailing list of former guests by hand, Jonathan to writing a new brochure which removed Carroll Trelawney and introduced me as the new co-owner of the Trelawney Inn; I even endured having my picture taken for the brochure. There I was on the page, side-by-side with an older photo of Kathryn, whose absence, of course, we didn't mention. And I assigned the public relations task to myself.

It was difficult, at first, going into so many new places and situations as a stranger with no one to introduce me. Seth offered, and so did Jonathan, but I turned both down. I didn't want to be linked in people's minds with Seth, and Jonathan had already carried more than his share—especially since his salary was, I thought, scandalously low. I intended to give him a raise at the first of the year, no matter what.

When I introduced myself to the owners of the several bed-and-breakfast houses, I was surprised to find that they, like me, had all come from somewhere else. Beaufort natives I met at a meeting of the Historical Association, and all kinds of folks fascinated with the sea at the Hampton Mariners' Museum. I went to the town hall and the county courthouse and talked to anyone I could find; did the same in the shops and restaurants. I visited the chamber of commerce headquarters in Morehead City and reaffirmed the inn's commitment, and came away with another mailing list. Everywhere I went I was received at first with caution, but I asked questions and listened and encouraged people to talk to me, and they warmed. As days went by and I continued my rigorous, self-set P.R. program, I noticed less skepticism and more of a welcome. One male shopowner put it into words: "I've been looking forward to meeting you, Laura Brannan. I've heard good things about you." So, my campaign was working, at least on the local level. I found it rather remarkable and admirably tactful that not one person asked for news of my missing sister.

Our brochure looked good in spite of the fact that we'd practically bribed the printer to turn it out in record time.

For several nights I sat up into the small hours with Jonathan, addressing the brochures to our two mailing lists, the one made up by Polly and the one I'd gotten from the chamber. I hoped they would get out in time to attract a full house over the long weekend at Thanksgiving.

I kept myself so busy that I almost forgot I was living on the edge. I pushed myself *too* hard, kept up a near-frantic pace. I told myself this was necessary, there was so much to learn, so much to be done. Polly couldn't keep up, and I continually worried that she'd make mistakes on the reservations. I hadn't the heart to fire her, and so I did much of her work as well as my own, double-checking her work after she left for the day, confirming by telephone the reservations she'd made. Yet no matter how I filled my days with activity, always there loomed just beyond the corners of my vision a dark shadow cast by the mystery of Kathryn's absence.

Realities I refused to acknowledge by day became spectres and dreams at night to haunt me. I could not become accustomed to the creakings and groanings of the old house, or to the clankings of the rigging of the boats in the harbor, or to the whispers of the wind around the windows. I slept poorly and woke often. Night after night I dreamed of death in many forms: I saw my parents together in mutual suicide, struggling to breathe, bodies twitching in futile, unconscious agony; saw my sister lost, wandering in some dark, nameless space. I saw disasters—urban buildings in flames, shipwrecks with drowning people screaming, plane crashes that flung pieces of wreckage and pieces of human beings over the landscape. I dreamed that I was threatened by someone or something that wanted to take my life, and these dreams were the most frightening of all. Sometimes the threatener was a man dressed all in black, face covered by a ski mask with empty eye-sockets like a death's head; sometimes a formless monster sat on my chest and sucked the breath from my nostrils, and I, suffocating, couldn't throw it off because its body was made of smoke. Sometimes I fled, on foot or in my car, faster and faster until I fell or crashed with the world and wheels of stars spinning around me. The dreams were so frequent and so frightening that I dreaded sleep as much as I longed for it. Slowly but surely, I was becoming afraid of night and of the dark.

Jonathan commented on the change in my appearance. It was mid-November and five weeks since my arrival. He looked at me over the tortoiseshell tops of his glasses, which were, as usual, halfway down his nose. "As they say in English novels, you're looking a mite peaked, Laura."

"Hm? Oh, hi, Jonathan. I didn't hear you come in." I glanced at the digital clock on the office desk. It said 3:30 P.M. "Did you just get up? I hope you slept well."

"I did. And I can't help but wonder when was the last time *you* slept well. Those blue shadows under your eyes didn't get there from just a few late nights addressing brochures."

"Speaking of brochures, they're paying off already! We got three reservations in response to them today. Go out and ask Polly—she'll show you. Two are for Thanksgiving and one for all of next week!"

"I don't want to talk to Polly. Right now I want to talk to you, Laura, whether it's my business or not." Jonathan pulled a chair up to the desk and sat down.

I noticed he looked less rumpled than usual, in a tweed jacket and a white dress shirt whose open collar seemed actually starched. I ran my hand through my hair, pushing it back out of my eyes. "Okay, you have my undivided attention."

"You've been working too hard. You never stop. I doubt you ever go out anywhere unless it's to talk to people about the inn. Now, do you?"

"Well, no." I thought of Seth, who had often called, sometimes come by; I'd refused him so repeatedly I was sure I must have offended him by now. Fleetingly I thought of Nick, whom I hadn't seen or heard from at all.

"That's what I thought. And you're probably not eating enough to keep a kitten alive. You're a small woman, and if you ask me, you're getting smaller by the minute. To be honest, I'm worried about you."

Jonathan was always so mild, so easygoing. I'd quickly grown comfortable around him, but now he was making me most uncomfortable. "I eat enough," I protested, "it's just, ah, just that I'm not dancing anymore. There's no place to do it around here, so I'm losing muscle tone. I'm perfectly healthy, and you don't need to worry about me."

"All right, then, humor me because I'm probably old enough to be your father. I want you to stop working so hard and get out more, and have a decent meal once in a while, something more than what we can zap in the microwave upstairs." His voice softened, there was appeal in his pale blue eyes. "You don't have to save the Trelawney Inn single-handedly in your first six weeks, you know. You need a break, and tonight I'd be honored if you'd have dinner with me. I've made reservations at the Beaufort House for an early supper. Six o'clock."

I was touched. I smiled at him. "Jonathan, that's a lovely idea, but you know we can't. Polly leaves at six, and I have to take the desk until eight."

"Not tonight, you don't. I've already talked to Polly, first thing this morning. She's willing to stay on if I ask, and she hasn't done that in a long time. It won't hurt her."

I glanced at the open office door, and got up and closed it. Then I leaned against the desk and said in my most quiet voice, "I've been meaning to talk to you about Polly."

Jonathan grinned, and a twinkle came into his eyes. "I've been wondering how long it would take you to get around to that. I'm glad to see you aren't going to keep doing half of her work as well as yours forever. But as far as tonight goes, a few extra hours from Polly won't make a difference. Might even up the score a little bit, so what do you say?"

I pushed my hair back again, aware that it was too long and needed cutting—it always fell onto my forehead at the best of times, and now it was frequently in my eyes. "I . . . I don't know. Do you think Kathryn will be very upset if I let Polly go?"

There was a small silence. Then Jonathan said, slowly and deliberately, "I think Kathryn will never know. I don't know where she is, and I hope she's not in some kind of trouble, but I do not believe we will see or hear from her. If she were going to return or to contact us, she'd have done it by now."

I couldn't look at him. I walked around his chair and stood at the window, pretending to look out. I crossed my arms tightly, hugging them to my chest. Now that Jonathan had spoken aloud the thought I daily drove from my consciousness, I felt a reluctant relief. It is, of course, always better to face the truth; it was just that I'd had so many difficult truths to face within so short a time.

"I know you're right," I said, my back still to him. "I suppose I haven't wanted to face it because somehow Kathryn's disappearance is worse than the other things. It's the not knowing . . ."

"Other things?"

I turned around, embarrassed. I'd been thinking out loud. But this was Jonathan, kind, comfortable Jonathan, and I trusted him. I could tell him. Perhaps it would be good to stop holding so much in. "Yes. I don't like to talk about any of them, but in part you already know. You know that my mother and father died together—I'm not sure you know *how* they died."

Jonathan simply shook his head.

I continued. "They had a suicide pact. Father had cancer; Mother didn't want to live without him. I didn't even know Father was sick!" I skipped over a lot of things—the separate letters they'd left me, the irrational sense of betrayal I'd felt. "So I lost both of them at the same time. That was six months ago; well, seven months now. It was the beginning of May. Earlier, just after the first of the year, my husband left me. It was hard; we'd only been married for three years, and I expected it to last, made myself blind to the signs that should have told me it wouldn't. So you see, this has been a bad year for me. To have Kathryn disappear on top of losing husband, mother, and father has been hard to accept. Since we don't *know* what happened to her—"I faltered, swallowed hard, and pulled myself up to all of my five-feet-two—"it's been easier for me to hope that she hasn't left me, too."

"I understand. I don't want to take away your hope."

"It's all right, really. Five weeks is a long time. The police haven't found anything, we haven't heard anything. I'll be better off to stop avoiding the truth. I promise you from this moment on I'll be realistic. And I'd love to have dinner with you." I tried a smile, and it felt okay. Better.

"Good! I'll tell Polly. Now, shall we meet upstairs for wine and cheese with the guests first, or would you prefer to go for a walk?"

"It's nice out—I think I'd rather walk. Give me about half an hour?"

Jonathan nodded and looked pleased. I pressed his hand in gratitude as I went out of the office.

"I haven't done this before," I acknowledged. We were strolling along Ann Street, looking at the houses and the graceful, spreading shapes of the tall, leafless trees. "Every time I've left the inn, it was with a goal, a destination in mind, and I was in a hurry to get there. Well, except for the first day, the day I told you about when I saw the dolphins."

"Uh-huh, that's what I thought," said Jonathan. "You've done more with the inn in a month than I think you realize. Now maybe you'll take the time to get out more, get to really know the town."

"I've met a lot of people already."

"Yes, and the people are important, but I meant something more. The history and feel of the place. For example, here at Pollock Street is the boundary between Old Town and New Town. Chronologically it doesn't mean much, because there are as many pre-Revolutionary houses over in New Town, including the Hammock House, which is the oldest of all. But historically, on the original plot of land when the streets were laid out and named in 1713 by a man named Turner, the easternmost boundary of Beaufort was here."

Jonathan turned around and gestured back in the direction from which we'd come. "Ann Street was named for Queen Ann, who was the Queen of England at that time. The story is that she was pleased to have a street in the New World named for her, and she sent the elm trees, these very same elm trees, in thanks."

I looked at the quiet narrow street with its old trees that I now knew were elms, and the lovely little houses, most of them painted white, two-storied, with deep, overhanging porches. Only at first glance did the houses look alike. Though all were similar in size, each had its own individual details to set it apart. Almost every other house we'd passed had a shield-shaped historical marker placed near the front door.

"I had no idea everything was quite so old," I said. "You know, Jonathan, Beaufort doesn't look like I'd have expected a Southern coastal town to look. When I was a child we went to Cape Cod and to Martha's Vineyard and Nantucket one summer, and Beaufort looks like that. Like a New England fishing village."

Jonathan nodded his bald head with its wild halo of hair. "True. I've often thought so myself. Let's turn here and go back to Front Street."

"Sure." I walked beside him feeling alert, fascinated, open to the spirit of the place as I'd been on my arrival. I hadn't realized how much in the intervening weeks I'd looked at my surroundings only through the tunnel vision of my need to shut out everything but work. All so that I could avoid thinking of my lost sister. I breathed deeply the cool, fresh air, evening-damp, and felt alive again.

My learned companion continued to educate me. "Front Street wasn't a street for a long time, it was just a path along Taylor's Creek, which is what the part of the harbor that runs between the islands out there and the mainland has always been called—after another first citizen of Beaufort. Those houses over there to the East had a beach in front. Around the turn of the century there was a boardwalk running that way, about three-quarters of a mile long, and the water flowed beneath it. The town was a popular resort then, but only in the summer. It's becoming popular again, now on a year-round basis."

"I know. I did learn that before I came, and I was convinced that a partnership in the inn would be a sound investment. I still think so." We were approaching the restaurant now and crossed the street to walk on the present boardwalk.

"I never get tired of this place, in any weather, any time of year," said Jonathan. He leaned with his elbows on the railing and looked out across the harbor.

I stood with him, content in an easy, shared silence. The sun had gone down as we walked, and night descended with a suddenness that caught me by surprise. Twilight didn't linger long this time of year. As the light died the wind came up, sharper, colder.

Jonathan saw me shiver, and as if in response he began to talk again. "I never get tired of it, but it isn't always a peaceful place to be. This is going to be a bad winter, or so everybody says. Even in a mild winter the North Carolina coast up here along the Outer Banks can be hostile. Nature makes all the rules. Life has always been hard here, there's never been the prosperity of Virginia or South Carolina. That's why Beaufort looks more like New Bedford than Charleston."

"But I'm confused. Beaufort isn't on the Outer Banks."

"Might as well be. You do need to get out more, Laura. Learn your way around your new home. Shackleford and Bogue, they're the tail end of the Outer Banks. We're part of the Outer Banks, all right. Tourism has changed some things, brought a new prosperity, but it may be a false prosperity. With this bad winter coming you'll see what I mean soon enough. Now, that's enough history lesson for one day. Let's go eat!"

I soon made a habit of walking for at least an hour every afternoon before I took over the desk from six to eight. Sometimes I explored alone, and sometimes Jonathan came along, full of more local lore. The exercise alone was good for me, and so was the interest I now took in the area's history. I bought books and collected the pamphlets of the Historical Association. Whenever my steps took me to the western end of the land, I looked for the dolphins, but they were never there. I wondered if I would ever see them again.

I wondered, too, what had become of the *Hellfire* and Nick Westover. On none of my walks did I see either the boat or the man. It was certainly my fault, I reflected, that

Nick hadn't come or called. My cat had given his face a nasty scratch, and I should have sought him out the very next day to apologize. But I hadn't. Boris's uncharacteristic behavior that night had mystified me, and frightened me a little, and so I'd done nothing.

Seth Douglass, however, did not stay away. I looked up from the reception desk one evening to see him coming through the door.

"Good evening, Laura," he said. "I'm interrupting your work intentionally. Forgive me?"

I smiled, finding I was glad to see him. "I think I can manage that. Did you want to make a reservation for someone, Seth?"

"No. Mind if I sit down?" He pulled a chair near the desk and didn't wait for my consent. "I came to see you. I figure if you have to cover the desk, you can't run away or hang up on me. You're a captive audience, and I'm going to keep you company for a while. You can't be too busy on a Monday night."

"We're not, but that's changing. Slowly. We'll be almost full at the end of the week, for the Thanksgiving holiday."

"You've been working hard. Word is out, in the community. You've been to see a lot of people and you've made an impact."

"I'm glad to hear that," I said. Seth was relaxed in his chair, long legs crossed at the knee. I liked his casual dress better than the severe business suits he usually wore. His jacket was fawn-colored suede, well-worn but still handsome. He wore it over a cream turtleneck sweater and trousers with tiny gray and beige checks. I hadn't seen him in some time and I was struck all over again by the dramatic contrast between his silver hair and black brows.

"Maybe you've been working *too* hard?" A crease appeared between those eyebrows, and concern in the dark brown eyes.

"I admit it, I have been. But I've let up a bit. I'm getting out for a couple of hours every afternoon now, fresh air and exercise." I ran my hand through my too-long hair, thinking again of the problem I'd been pondering before Seth appeared. I decided to tell him about it. "I'm enjoying getting out, but I may not be able to do it much longer. You see, I have to let Polly go. I intend to tell her a week from today, as soon as we're through Thanksgiving. She just isn't able to do the work, and I have no idea how long it will take to find a replacement. I've never hired or fired anyone before, and I'm dreading it. Until I get a new assistant manager, I'll have to be here all the time."

"I see. Well, maybe I can help. I have a lot of experience with those things. If you'll tell me what you need, what qualifications you're looking for, I'll see what I can do. If that's okay with you, that is."

I didn't miss the deference in his offer to help; my previous few times with Seth he had been all too ready to tell me what to do about any and everything. Could it be that the man had changed? I told him the kind of person I hoped to find, stressing that this person could be either male or female. Then we went on to talk of other things.

I warmed to Seth. The suspicions I'd had of him seemed far in the past, an overreaction. I saw things I hadn't seen in him before: a rich baritone depth in his voice, how beautiful his hands were with their long, slender fingers. Very expressive hands, with both grace and strength. And his eyes—no hardness in them now; they were as dark, deep, and liquid as a forest pool. And yet from time to time he looked at me as he was doing at this moment, and those eyes softened in a gaze of quiet appeal that sent tiny pricks of pleasure playing across my skin.

There was a lull in the conversation while Seth continued to look at me in this way. When he spoke, his voice had softened to match his eyes. "These past several weeks, when you wouldn't see me or even talk to me on the telephone for more than a minute, have been some of the longest in my life." He leaned forward over the desk which separated us. "Perhaps it was for the best. I certainly had a lot of time to think. I *had* to think—I couldn't get you out of my mind. I'd like to start over with you, Laura. You've seen my bad side first, the too-tight control, the coldness, the anger. Give me a chance to show you that I do have other qualities."

"I can already see that you do." The desk was small, an antique, not much of a barrier. Seth's face was only inches from mine. He smiled, the faint suggestion of a cleft in his chin deepened, and my heart jumped.

"Then you will give me that chance?" He placed his hand before me on the desk, palm up and open. The gesture said, as if he'd spoken it, Come to me.

I looked at his hand, the long, slender fingers naked and wanting. My senses became acute; the moment separated itself out of time. The desk lamp shed golden rays over us, a hushed stillness was in the air, and I felt Seth's hand yearning for mine. I placed my hand in his, felt his strength close over me.

"Yes, I will," I said, with a hitch in my voice.

"Thank you." He said it softly, little more than a whisper.

That was all, the joined hands, the few words, and yet the moment seemed to stretch, to carry us into a new dimension. I trembled with the power of it, and then it was over.

"Have you eaten?" Seth's mundane question brought me all the way back to earth.

"No." Still he held my hand. "Evelyn puts something aside for me in the kitchen and I go up for it after Jonathan takes the desk at eight."

Now he did let me go, and looked at his watch. "Time passes quickly in your company! It's almost that now. How about, tonight, you let me take you up the street to Clawson's for supper?"

I hesitated. Clawson's had already become a favorite place for the few times I did eat out, but what had happened between us seemed special. I feared anything further might ruin it. I smiled. "It's a nice idea, but not tonight. I'd rather do it another time."

"Soon, then?"

"Soon."

We probably won't have many more days like this," said Seth. "I'm glad you could take time off and spend it with me."

"I'm glad you asked." I smiled across the car at him. December had followed close upon a very successful—from the Inn's point of view and therefore mine—Thanksgiving weekend. Though the season was subtly changing from fall to winter, this day was bright and clear, cool but not cold, the sky an incredible blue. We were headed north on Route 70, following the shoreline, and had just crossed a body of water called North River. It was not really a river, but rather a deep, narrow bay.

"Would you like to see the Stone House? It's quite near here."

"What?" The question jolted me.

"I said, would you like—"

I interrupted, not wanting to hear the words again. "Actually, I heard you. The question just took me by surprise. No, I'd rather not see it. I haven't begun to deal with—with anything associated with Kathryn yet."

A crease of concern, perhaps even disapproval, appeared between Seth's eyebrows, but he said casually enough,

"Okay, then we'll swing down and start with Harkers Island."

"Good." I studied the map in my hands intently, determined to drive out the ghosts conjured up by Seth's mention of the Stone House. "You know, this part of the North Carolina coast is just amazing. All the way from here to the Virginia border there's much more water than land. Why, there isn't much place we can go by car without going way back to the west!"

Seth chuckled. "Yep, that's right. We'll go to Cedar Island, and I'll show you where the ferry crosses to Ocracoke."

"Oh, can we go there, to Ocracoke?"

"Not today, not unless you want to stay overnight, that is. The crossing takes over two hours, and the morning ferry is long since gone. If you go at midday you'd get to stay no time at all before you'd have to turn around and come back. I don't think you'd want to do a day trip even in summer, when there are more ferries. There's too much to see."

"All right. I see now that the ferry routes are marked on the map." I fell silent, studying the map, remembering Jonathan's lessons and the things I'd read. The expanse of water was formidable, even on paper; the narrow islands that made up the Outer Banks lay exposed like fragile bones.

"I wish I could sail," I murmured. I felt Seth glance at me and looked up at him.

"You're so little, I'd be afraid you'd blow overboard!" he said with a grin.

"I may be little, but I'm stronger than I look. Heavier, too, unfortunately! You don't sail, either. What's your excuse?"

"I just never learned. I was always too busy building things. For many years my work and my play were one and the same. You can make a lot of money that way, but you don't become a very well-rounded person. That's changing, *I'm* changing, since I came here. If you really want to learn to sail, Laura, perhaps we could learn together. In the spring."

"Perhaps," I agreed. It was an interesting thought, and I let it occupy me for a while.

As we drove around the periphery of Harkers Island, I

began to understand what Jonathan had said about the tenacity of the people who had come here and stayed. Seth stopped the car in front of a sizable wooden building, a kind of warehouse for boats. Next to it was a short wooden pier.

"Let's walk out here for a minute," he said.

I climbed out of the car and immediately felt the bite of the wind. The sky looked like October, but in this exposed place the wind carried the coming of winter. I was wearing a favorite wrap, a fringed blue poncho of soft Peruvian wool which fell below my knees. The wind got into my hair, and I was glad I'd finally had it cut, or I'd have looked like a black sheepdog. I followed Seth out onto the pier.

I thought he looked marvelous, in jeans and boots and a white turtleneck jersey under a thick cableknit sweater of a silvery-green that picked up the silver of his hair. As I came up beside him he put his left arm around my shoulders and pointed with his right.

"Core Banks," he said. "If you look hard to the south, that's Cape Lookout, and there's a lighthouse there. No one lives on Core Banks anymore, it's all sand dunes. Sand constantly shaped by the wind and the water."

"The lighthouse keeper must get very lonely."

"Not anymore. The lighthouses are all automated, didn't you know?"

I shook my head, feeling ignorant. This was a totally new world to me, a world I wanted to learn much more about.

"When the earliest settlers came, there were Indians on Core Banks, a tribe called the Cores, or the Corees. There were also Indians here on Harkers Island, and they had made a causeway out of millions of empty oyster shells. It must have taken generations to build up that causeway. Then the good old white man came and soon discovered that crushed oyster shells can be used to pave roads and walkways, and they hauled it all away. In a few years white men destroyed the Indians' handiwork of lifetimes. From the air, in a small plane, I've seen the outline of the ancient causeway under water."

"You sound a little bitter about that," I observed.

Seth's grip on my shoulder tightened. "I am. And I feel

more than a little guilt by association." He looked down at me, his face serious. "The Indians knew how to live with nature. They were primitive, but they were wise in ways I'm just now trying to learn. I come from a breed of white-man developers. We're a very destructive tribe. We have no wisdom, only greed. We want to conquer the forces of nature and bend them to our will, but it can't be done. In the end we've destroyed the beauty of the beaches because we sought to possess that beauty and keep it for ourselves. We've cluttered the coast with our buildings and protected the buildings with seawalls until the beaches are no more. We've poured our refuse into the rivers and oceans until the fish and shellfish die. Hardy, honest fishermen who for hundreds of years have survived all the harshest blows nature can deal out can no longer earn a decent living. They starve, until their pride is broken and their homes are lost."

This Seth was a different man. His eyes flashed, his body was hard, his voice rich and ringing with passion. He went on.

"Only here in North Carolina"—he moved his right arm in a sweeping arc, while with his left he still held me fast—"on these barrier islands, we still have a chance. We may learn here to live without destroying. The very wildness of the Outer Banks, the treacherousness of the waters, has protected these beaches from people like me. Like I used to be. Until recent years, only very strong, brave, stubborn men and women could survive here. This is their place first, and no one must take it from them. I swear I'll die without building so much as one more simple cottage before I'll let this coastline be destroyed, by me or anyone else!"

I was impressed. "You really mean that!"

"You're damned right, I do. I'm dead serious." Now he smiled, and his grip on my shoulder eased. "But I didn't mean to get quite so carried away. Maybe it's just as well that I did. Responsible coastal management is my obsession. I know I've gone overboard, but making the right things happen requires serious commitment. If you're going to be around me for any length of time you may as well know how I feel. I'm thinking seriously of running for the state legislature, campaigning on this issue. What do you think of that?"

"I think it's wonderful to make such a deep commitment!"

"Thank you for feeling that way. Somehow, I thought you would." Seth ducked his head and kissed me swiftly at the temple. "You cold?"

"No. The wind is a little stiff, but it feels good." My face felt cleansed by the wind, and flushed from the brief touch of his lips to my skin. I had not felt so healthy, so full of life, for many months.

"Let's go back to the car. We have lots more to see yet. By the way, I like that blue thing you're wearing. What do you call it, a cape, a cloak? I'm afraid when it comes to women's clothes, I don't know very much, only what I like when I see it."

"It's a poncho, from Peru—I got it from a mail-order place. As long as we're talking about clothes, I like to see you dressed the way you are today. Somehow you're much more, er, down-to-earth in casual clothes than you are in the whole getup, three-piece suit, et cetera."

"In that case," Seth said as he opened the car door and handed me in, "I may never wear a suit and tie again!" He went around and got in behind the wheel. As he started the car he looked at me intently. "I hope you'll never go back to Ohio, Laura. You do like living here, don't you?"

I considered my answer before I gave it, considered the implications behind his question. I returned the steadiness of his gaze, taking in the elegance of his face with its fine long nose and sensitive mouth, strong chin; the long-fingered hands on the wheel, the lanky body that belonged more on a cowboy than a businessman. Elegant strength, that was Seth. I liked him more than I'd thought I could. I was attracted to him, and I was also wary, too recently wounded to know what I wanted from him or any man.

"I won't go back to Ohio," I said at last. "There's nothing for me there any longer. I'll be honest with you, Seth, even if what I say is not what you want to hear. My life right now is all mixed up. Everything here is different from anything I've known before, it's beautiful, intriguing, sometimes scary. I think I like it, but until my life straightens out, I can't say if I will stay here for good."

After a moment of silence Seth said, "I hope you don't think I'm pushing you."

He sounded touchingly boyish, and I smiled at him. "Well, you are a little, aren't you?"

His answering smile came easily. "I guess I am." He turned his attention to backing up the car and getting us back on the road. We drove along two lanes of asphalt pavement that was patchworked in places. The BMW rode easily over rough spots. Seth was a good driver, careful though he kept up a good speed. I particularly appreciated this because Roger Brannan had been a speeder and a risk-taker behind the wheel; he had conditioned me so that I was seldom comfortable in a car unless I drove myself.

That intrusive thought of my ex-husband unsettled me. I tried to concentrate on the view out of the windows. I noted trees and foliage, some of which I could name and some I could not; the sandy texture of the soil, the heterogeneous nature of the houses we passed. They seemed to have in common only an air of struggling to hold together under their dilapidated roofs. I remarked on the atmosphere of near-poverty to Seth, who said there were other, more substantial places, but they were nearer the sound, back through the trees, and could not be seen from the road.

Try as I might, I couldn't keep my mind on sightseeing. It was as if Seth's obvious interest in me had opened up a hole in the dam that had for so long held back my deepest, most desperate emotions. I felt suddenly like a pressure cooker— if I didn't let some of this out I might explode. As hard as it was for me to talk about my feelings, a fault my psychologist friend had often warned me about, I had to risk it. I had to.

Hesitantly, I began. "I'm sorry. I don't seem to be able to keep my mind on the scenery. I . . . I have a lot going on inside of me, Seth."

One black eyebrow arched up. "Anything you want to talk about?"

I wanted to talk, I needed the release, but the words

wouldn't come. I put my hand up to my forehead and pressed hard, closing my eyes, silently screaming with frustration and need.

Seth spoke gently. "Laura, the weeks I was away from you after we first met, I couldn't get you out of my mind. I told you that. I have a new priority in my life now, and that priority is *you*. I want very much to know you as well as you will allow me to know you. There is nothing you could say to me that I wouldn't want to hear."

The tone of his voice and the words he said unleashed my tongue, and my own words poured out, at first slowly, then in a torrent. "I was married, and the marriage was a miserable failure. His name is Roger Brannan. You see, I still have his name. Kathryn and I, our maiden name is Lawson. Roger is a doctor. We met when he was doing his internship and married when he began his residency, about four years ago. I was crazy about him."

I laughed at my own choice of words, and the laugh came out a harsh, broken sound. "Crazy is an accurate description. Where Roger was concerned, I had no sense at all. Remarkable, I've always been such a sensible person! Whatever Roger did or didn't do, I put it down to the stresses of residency. I told myself that when he had finished all his training and was in practice, things would change. And they did change, but not the way I wanted. Less than six months after he was out on his own, Roger divorced me. Just like that! He wanted a divorce so badly, he went out of the country to get it immediately. There wasn't even another woman, he just wanted to get away from me! Of course, I then divorced him here myself—I was a lawyer, right? It was no problem to prove desertion, and a foreign divorce isn't a hundred percent legal in this country. That doesn't bother a lot of people, but it did bother me with my tidy legal mind. So I'm not once, but twice divorced!"

"Don't, Laura. Don't be so hard on yourself. How long ago did this happen?"

"Not long. He left in January of this year. By March both divorces were final."

"And the wounds are still fresh."

"You might say that!" I said sarcastically. The air in the enclosed car was heavy with my bitterness—I could almost taste it.

"When was it that your parents committed suicide?"

"How did you know that was the way they died?" My voice sounded aggressive, challenging. I was nearly out of control and I knew it, but all the long dammed-up feelings had gathered into a ball and were rushing downhill. I was powerless to stop them.

"Kathryn told someone, I don't know who, and it got around by the grapevine. When did they die?"

"In May." I bit down on my lower lip to keep it from trembling. Anger was giving away to sadness. I didn't know which was worse.

"My God." Seth was silent, digesting this information. "You must have needed your parents after your divorce. Even I, uptight male that I am or was, turned to my mother. You must have felt that they deserted you, that they didn't care for you."

"No! That's not how I felt! I felt that I'd *failed!* Failed Roger as a wife, and failed them as a daughter. You see, my mother and father had—well, I guess you'd say they'd depended on me for a lot ever since my brother died in Vietnam. I stayed in Columbus for them, became a lawyer because that was what my father wanted, what my brother would have done. They seemed to need me for so many things. But after Roger left I was so wrapped up in self-pity I didn't even notice that my father wasn't well. He was *dying* of cancer, and I didn't even know! Afterward, they left letters, letters that hurt to read . . ."

I couldn't go on. I turned my face toward the window as the tears came. What had I done, why had I said so much? I felt ashamed, embarrassed, sick with the excess of my feelings. Through the blur of my tears I saw outside the car window a bleak landscape, miles and miles of flat marsh grasses and no other living thing. My heart, my life, felt no less bleak. Surely I had disgusted Seth, as I disgusted myself. Surely now I had driven him, too, away.

But he spoke again. "Is that why you gave up being a lawyer, because you'd only done it for them?"

I nodded, my head still turned away. I thought that I could never face him again. Seth said nothing further, and I closed my eyes and rested my forehead against the cool glass of the window. The coolness was some comfort to my burning face, and I was grateful for that.

I felt the car stop, heard Seth click off the motor, and I opened my eyes. We were in a large parking area. There were no other cars in my field of vision. I heard another click, softer, the sound of a seat belt being released. Still I didn't, couldn't, move or speak.

Slowly Seth moved across the seat and gently he spoke to me. "I don't want to hurt you, to cause you pain, but I know there is more. You don't have to say anything, just nod your head if I'm right. You decided to come to Beaufort because your sister Kathryn asked you to come. Probably, by the time you'd worked out the details and were on your way here, the wounds had begun to heal over a little. And then you arrived—and no Kathryn. She had left you, too, or so it must have seemed. All the old wounds opened up again, and a new one as well."

I nodded my head.

Seth released my seat belt and pushed it away. He took both my shoulders in his hands and turned me to face him. "Thank you for telling me, Laura. I won't pressure you, after all you've been through. But I will make you a promise. I promise I will never leave you, unless you ask me to go."

I didn't know what I was going to say until the words came out of my mouth. I spat them, I flung them into Seth's face, so close to mine. "Don't say that, don't ever say such a thing! You only say it because you think that's what I want to hear, and *I don't believe you!*"

Like a wild thing, my horrible words ringing in my ears, I threw open the car door and ran. I had no idea where I was, or where I was going. I saw only the surface under foot. It changed from asphalt to grass, to an edging of wood like a railroad tie. I ran like the wind, and when I reached the wooden edge I flew, right over into a drop of about three feet. My body, working better than my mind, took care of me and I landed safely on both feet, in sand. I was on a beach. The band of sand, about five feet wide, stretched as far as I could see and again I ran. The soft surface tugged at my feet, but I pushed on until I was exhausted. Then I collapsed in a mindless heap. Never before had I broken down like this, never.

Long arms came around me, enfolded me. Pressed my head against a firm chest, the wool of a sweater bumpy-soft beneath my cheek. Seth said my name over and over, "Laura, Laura," nothing else, just my name. I crawled closer into the comfort of his embrace, only half-knowing what I was doing. He took me on his lap like a child and rocked me.

Gradually I realized that I was safe. And warm, and comforted. I felt emptied out, but clean. A good feeling. I looked up at Seth from within the circle of his arms. His face seemed softened around the edges.

"I lost my glasses," I said.

"I know, and I'm afraid I stepped on them, running after you on the sand. I didn't want to stop—they're halfway back up the beach."

"I didn't know where I was going."

"Yes. I was afraid you'd turn and run into the ocean, and I'd lose you. You ran so fast—how did you ever learn to run so fast?"

"I used to be a dancer."

"That explains it."

Seth's lips brushed mine, moved to my ear, and back again. Softly, sweetly, he took my mouth and opened it like the bud of a flower. Only once. Then he stood up easily with me in his arms. It was a pleasant sensation, being carried. In all my adult life no one had ever done that before.

"I can walk," I said.

"No."

I closed my eyes and let him carry me. Lulled by the motion, I felt curiously happy. At peace.

The motion stopped. "Your glasses," said Seth. "Either we leave them, or I have to put you down so that I can get them."

I started to say, leave them; then thought better of it. "Glasses are expensive. I'd better have them."

"You promise if I put you down, you won't run away again?"

"I promise. Whatever it was that happened to me, it's all over now." Seth released me, and I slid down the length of his body until my feet touched the sand. I looked up at him, just now fully realizing all I'd said and done. "I'm sorry, Seth. I just, I don't know what I did. Went to pieces. Nothing like that has ever happened to me before."

"It's all right. I think I understand. The important thing is that you seem all right now." He bent down and fished my glasses out of the sand. "These, however, aren't in such good shape."

I took the glasses from him. One bow was broken off entirely, and the bridge was cracked, but the plastic lenses were intact. I couldn't tell if they were scratched or not. I shoved them into the pocket of my jeans, beneath the poncho. "I can't see a thing without glasses, but I do have another pair at home and perhaps I can get new frames for these. For now, please be sure I don't bump into anything."

"It will be my pleasure." Seth pulled me close against his side and tucked his arm around me. "In case you're interested, this is Cedar Island, and Ocracoke is about two and a half hours out that way."

I looked out to sea, and to my nearsighted and astigmatic eyes it was all one big blue blur; where the sea met the sky I couldn't tell. "Nice," I said.

Seth laughed, warm, intimate. "Come on, I'll lead you back to the car."

"This is a causeway," Seth explained as we drove back the way we'd come. "Cedar Island really is an island—there's no solid surface under all that grass you see out there. One day we'll come back and I *will* take you to Ocracoke. I'm sure you'll like it; you've never seen anything like Ocracoke, it's unique."

"I've never seen anything like this, either. It's so bleak. So lonely."

"Yes, but it's also unspoiled. There are other areas much lonelier than this. Particularly at the northern end, the Currituck Banks. I'd like you to see Currituck, too, someday."

I was amazed that we were having this normal conversation, after what I'd said and done. "Seth, aren't you angry with me, or disillusioned, or——or something?"

He looked at me for an instant, with unmistakable tenderness in his face. "No, Laura. I'm certainly not any of those things."

"But what I said to you before I ran from the car, that was terrible! I——" I stopped short. I couldn't say I hadn't meant it. He might be kind, and I might try to, but I couldn't believe what he'd said about never leaving me.

"It's all right. I know it must have been hard for you to tell me of your marriage and how you felt about your mother and father's death. I understand now, more than I can say, why it is that from the first day I met you you've seemed so vulnerable."

"Vulnerable," I echoed. I knew the word fit, but it was not a word I liked.

"You have a lot of fighting spirit, I see that, too. But the truth is that you've been badly hurt. I had no idea how badly, until today. So you went to pieces. Under the circumstances, it makes sense to go to pieces."

"Maybe not to me. I still can't believe I did it."

"Well, it was probably time for you to let go. I realize that I shouldn't have said what I did about never leaving you. I might have known that you aren't ready to hear something like that. However, now that I did say it, I won't take it back. Please understand, Laura. I'm a decisive man and I've been divorced a number of years. I know how I feel about you. For whatever it's worth, I meant every word. All I want you to remember is that I intend to be around and a part of your life until when or if you tell me to back off or to leave. Okay?"

"I . . . yes. I guess so. Okay." I sat in silence trying to figure out how *I* felt. I felt . . . warm. Warmed by Seth's words and the memory of his touch. I felt a pervasive sense of peace that was pleasant, and I was sure it was the aftermath of emotional catharsis. Most likely the peacefulness would wear off all too soon.

We had lunch at a place called Sealevel; then went back through Beaufort and Morehead City and across a bridge to Bogue Banks. Seth talked of history and the development of each place we drove through. Gradually, as I'd suspected, I began to feel like my old self again—which was to say, the peacefulness disappeared and I began to feel disturbed. When we reached Emerald Isle, I asked if we could stop somewhere and talk.

"Sure," Seth nodded. "Would you object to my place?"

"No objection. In fact, I'd like to see the Dunes again."

Seth had three large rooms; all faced the sea and had a lot of glass. One might have been on any beautiful beach anywhere. There was an entirely different feel here than in the places we'd been earlier. I didn't remark on this, for to do so would surely have sent him off into more rapturous explanations, and I had another, major, thing to talk about. I asked for mineral water rather than an alcoholic drink and settled into a corner of his couch.

"I want to talk about my sister, Kathryn," I began.

Seth frowned, but he said, "All right."

I took a deep breath, for courage. "Those weeks when I was working so hard, I shoved her out of my mind. Wouldn't let myself think about her, beyond taking care of technicalities like activating my power of attorney so that I could run the inn without her. Then Jonathan forced me to recognize that if we were going to hear from her we'd most likely have done so. That was a couple of weeks ago, and since then, thoughts have been coming thick and fast. I haven't pushed them away."

"Such as . . . ?"

"The police haven't done enough, and I'm not happy with what little they've done. Since she wasn't in an accident and there's no evidence of what they call foul play, the police seem content to assume she left of her own accord. I don't believe it."

"Oh? What do you believe?"

I pushed my hair back from my face and swallowed hard. I'd never said this aloud, and it was difficult. "I believe someone or something has prevented her return. I want to hire a private detective, and I want you to help me find one."

Seth looked very serious. His dark eyes probed into mine. "You really mean that, don't you?"

"Yes. Yes, I do." Now that I'd said it and the hard part was over, I rushed on eagerly. "Don't you see, Seth, it just doesn't make sense to think she left wilfully. Her clothes, her car, her bank account, all her possessions are still there. She wouldn't have left *everything* behind!"

He did not respond, but got up from the couch and walked around the room, hands thrust in his pockets. At length he turned to me. "She might have had her own private reasons for needing to get away suddenly. Reasons we know nothing about."

"Then that's all the more reason for us to dig deeper than the police have done. Isn't it?"

Seth's long face took on a brooding aspect. With his silver crest of hair, the heavy brows, and long nose, he might have been a hawk looking down on me. "No, Laura, I don't think so. From the way Kathryn acted with me over the sale of the Stone House, including the fact that she apparently went to some lengths to keep her ownership of the property a secret, I'd say she had something to hide. My guess is that she was involved in something she didn't want you or anybody else to know about, probably something unpleasant, possibly even illegal. If you do hire a private detective and go into this further, you might be opening a Pandora's box."

"Oh, surely not! Can't you understand? I have to know what really happened to her! I can't just continue to sit and do nothing."

"Think, Laura." He came to me, sat next to me, took both my hands in his. "If you found that Kathryn was involved in some illegal activity, say theft or smuggling or something like that, how would you handle that information? It's far better not to know. If you hire a detective, you're likely only to cause yourself more grief. Accept the fact that she's gone, and learn to live with it. That's your best decision."

None of the things he said had ever occurred to me. "I was thinking perhaps she was kidnapped," I said stubbornly.

"Without a ransom note? For what purpose would anyone kidnap Kathryn Trelawney? Your sister wasn't exactly the innocent-victim type."

I snatched my hands away from him and felt my chin quiver with disappointment. "You won't help me, then?"

"I'll help you in anything but this." He put a finger under my chin and tipped my face up to him. The texture of his baritone was persuasive. "Anything else, I'll gladly do for you. But I strongly recommend you drop the idea of the private detective. You will only hurt yourself more, and I don't want that."

Tears rose in my eyes. I was tired; my eyes were tired from being without my glasses. Seth saw the tears. He kissed my eyelids, first one and then the other, and I surrendered. I let his reasoning prevail over my doubts. My arms found their way around his neck and my lips sought the kiss which, when it came, was gentle.

When later, driving back to Beaufort, Seth said he had found someone to take Polly's place at the inn, I accepted that, too. Gratefully.

7

Zelda Crabtree was Seth's answer to my assistant manager problem. She had been his assistant on a shopping center project, and she had all the skills I thought the inn, and I, needed. In the interview she said that she was unhappy with her current position and asked that I not call them for a reference. I saw nothing wrong with this, and offered her the job on Seth's recommendation alone. She accepted immediately and said that she could start when Polly left on December fifteenth. Knowing that I had a replacement for Polly was a great relief.

In general, things at work were going better. Jonathan, relieved of keeping the books, returned to his own writing during his long night hours at the desk. Evelyn, the cook-housekeeper, went about her duties with the calmness I'd come to expect of her. She was a tall, thin, black woman who never said much but supervised her two part-time maids well and ordered her supplies prudently; she was, in fact, a treasure. Boris had made the entire inn his domain—he had become a sort of mascot, and guests and staff alike made a big fuss over him. Which, of course, he enjoyed enormously. We had the number of bookings I'd calculated was average for the time of year. All in all, I couldn't complain.

I should have been settling in, happy with the routine, like everyone else. But I couldn't quite do it. The catharsis I'd experienced with Seth helped, but not enough; nor could I completely follow his advice and learn to live with Kathryn's disappearance. An undercurrent of uneasiness was always with me. I still slept poorly and had nightmares often. I fought my growing fear of night's darkness, but still I was afraid.

Christmas loomed on the horizon, not as the joyous family celebration it had always been for me, but as an ordeal to be lived through. The one thing I'd learned, the one improvement in my life was that I no longer tried to bury my problems inside myself. When disturbing thoughts came, I thought them through. When I woke from a terrifying dream I forced myself to relive it, and searched for its meaning. When the weather turned cold and depressing, I went out into it, learning the different moods of sea, sky, wind, and rain as if I learned the moods of a new lover.

So it was that one particularly restless night I decided to confront my fear of the dark. I'd been to bed and couldn't get to sleep. I turned on the lamp and put on my glasses, but the thought of reading didn't appeal to me. My restlessness was physical, roaming through my muscles, compelling me to move. If I'd been in my former house, I would have gone down into my basement practice room, put a tape into the deck, and danced; but I couldn't do that here. The next best thing would be to go outside and walk, or even run. But it was dark outside.

I snapped off the bedside lamp and waited for my eyes to grow accustomed to the darkness. At first I stared into total blackness. It was like being suddenly blinded, and involuntarily my breath quickened, my pulse accelerated. Then objects began to take shape in the room—distorted, they grew from the dark itself. I focused on them, unblinking, until they lost their strangeness and became chairs, pictures within their frames, a floor lamp, the dressing room door. There. My pulse returned to normal and so did my breathing. I got out of bed slowly, not to dislodge a heavily sleeping Boris. The floor was cold on my bare feet, but I ignored that.

I walked to the window, held back the curtain, and looked out.

Streetlights, spaced far apart, were eerily luminous in haloes of mist. There was no one on the street, no one on the boardwalk. It was near midnight. I felt drawn to be out there. My feet wanted to carry me straight through the window and out into the night, nightgown and all. I stood there, feeling already the cold mist on my face and the wind in my hair. I told myself there was nothing to fear. Beaufort was as safe at night as it was by day; there were no muggers or rapists roaming the streets. I was only afraid of the dark, and it was no more dark out there than it was in this room. My fear was irrational, and to conquer the fear I must go into and through it. I must not doubt that I would come out safely on the other side.

I slipped my nightgown off over my head and hastily pulled a soft old sweatsuit over my bare skin. I put black Reeboks on my bare feet, and my favorite blue poncho over everything. Quietly and swiftly I left my room, went through the front door and out into the night.

I'd been wrong—the dark out here was different. It was not confined to a small space. This dark was vast and threatened to cover me up, blot me out until I disappeared. The streetlights were pale and sickly, no defense. My heart pounded but my feet went forward on a will of their own. Droplets of the cold mist collected on my face and in my hair; I shuddered with a sudden illusion that the drops were acid, eating through my skin down to the hard bones of skull. A gust of wind caught my poncho and flared it out behind me, as under a streetlight I saw my own shadow. My Dark Side, my own death—I was an acid-eaten revenant, clad in a black, flapping cloak. I gasped at the illusion and walked faster, my soft-soled shoes whispering upon the boardwalk. I must go through this fear, I must not let it conquer me, I said over and over.

Out of breath, hyperventilating, I stopped. I blinked and my vision cleared; shivered, cold and hot at the same time. I ran my hand nervously through my hair, blinked again and stepped closer to the railing. Inches away from me a boat bobbed ghostly white in the water. On the stern, wavering in the heavy mist, were black letters: *H e l l f i r e*. I had come out into the night, into the dark, into the fear, to stand before the *Hellfire*. I had almost forgotten about this boat and her owner. The boat seemed surreal in the night mist, shrouded like an apparition.

I ran from her. I left the boardwalk, left the waterside, ran across the street to the sidewalk. Sped past the blank dark windows of closed-up shops, past the handsome rustic facade of the Mariners' Museum, past centuries-old houses set back from the street. And as I passed I remembered a story told to me by Jonathan, of the ghost of a sea captain whose steps could be heard upon the walk up to one of these houses. My heart lurched in my chest. I was in the fear again, fighting it, losing the battle, for I thought I heard footsteps behind me.

The street ended in a cul-de-sac, beyond that only a few feet of grass, and then the waters of the harbor. That was where I'd seen the dolphins on a bright morning which now seemed long ago, but the thought did not comfort me. Now I could think only of the footsteps, ghostly footsteps that followed me, and I was trapped. I dared not look back over my shoulder, and soon there would be nowhere else to run.

There was a bench on the far curve of the cul-de-sac, a plain, ordinary, park-type bench I'd sat on many times. I ran up to it and stopped short, gripping the rough boards of its backrest in both hands. My own back I kept to the street. Still I heard the steps, they came on steadily, a dull, hollow *thump . . . thump . . . thump . . . thump*. The wooden board in my hands was solid, substantial, a link with reality. I told myself the fear was only part of living on the edge, it wouldn't last. It would go away. The Something which made the footsteps was not real, either; if I turned and faced it, it, too, would go away. I turned around.

The mist was thicker here, the streetlamps leaked a wan light. Wind blew, the mist swirled, footsteps sounded. I faced the Something, and it did not go away. It came on, a dark figure trailing swirls of luminous vapor. Closer. Dressed like a sailor—I saw the glint of brass buttons on a double-breasted coat. A smudge of white where the face should have been. It raised its arms; it called on the wind: "Laura!"

I felt the seat of the bench at the back of my knees, and I sat down, hard. My senses were confusing me, playing tricks on me. I thought I knew that voice. I waited, terrified and curious.

"Laura, is that you?"

"Y-yes," my voice came out first in a squeak. I swallowed and tried again. "Yes, it's me."

Now he came more rapidly, and the white smudge became part of a face under a navy watchcap, and the rest of the face was hidden in a beard, its fiery color subdued by the lack of light.

"Why were you running?" asked Nick Westover. He sat down next to me. "Until you stopped and turned around, I didn't recognize you."

My breath was still a little ragged. "For exercise. I couldn't sleep and so I decided to go out for a run. How, how did you happen to follow me?"

"I looked out of my cabin window and saw someone standing by the *Hellfire*. I couldn't tell who it was; in that long, flapping thing you have on you could be anybody. So I got my knife and followed." He turned his hand over, showing me the knife. It was short and thick and cruel, and gleamed with its own steely light.

I shuddered. "Ugh!" I said. "You frightened me, following me like that. Please put that thing away!"

"Why?" he grinned, teeth very white in the darkness. "Does it make you nervous?"

"Nick, don't tease me!" Suddenly I remembered the last time, how Boris had scratched him. "I hope you're not mad at me. I never did apologize for my cat scratching you. I'm sorry."

"I could get even with you right now, you know." His voice was light, still teasing, but he held the knife up, its wicked point millimeters from my cheek.

I didn't move a muscle. "Go ahead," I said, "I owe you one."

Nick hooked his other arm around my neck and pressed the tip of the knife against my cheek. And then his lips took the place of the knife. His voice was low, an intimate rumble. "I wouldn't cut that beautiful skin."

"Thank goodness!" I felt incredible, awash in relief that my fears had been for nothing, dangerously thrilled by the warm touch of his lips where the cold knife had been, shocked by the unfamiliar, sensuous feel of his beard on my skin.

"I do think I'll shanghai you back to the boat." He tightened his grip around my neck, then relaxed it. "I bet you could use a drink to warm you up, and I have some excellent brandy."

"I shouldn't, it's late. I shouldn't have gone out at all."

Nick stood and pulled me to my feet. "Ah, but you did. Here you are and here I am, and who's to stop you? Come on, I'm sure you must be cold."

There was no one to stop me, and I *was* cold, and I wasn't thinking straight. I went with him.

The boat's cabin was not as small as I'd thought it would be, but there was nowhere to sit except on one of the two bunks. I looked around and remembered what Seth had said, that Nick was "a rich bum." Subtle evidence of wealth was everywhere—in the boat's beautiful wood, in the heavy, creamy cashmere of the sweater revealed when Nick took off his dark-navy coat, in the small but heavy-cut crystal glass that held the best brandy I'd ever tasted. I felt like a bum myself in my old sweatsuit, not a rich one, either.

Nick lounged on the other bunk, leaning back on one elbow. He sipped his brandy and openly stared at me. I was suddenly aware that my face was totally bare of makeup, and under the sweatsuit my body was equally bare. I felt my cheeks flush.

"I haven't seen you around in a while," I said to cover my embarrassment.

"I've been around. Here and there."

"Guarding dolphins?"

"What?" He tilted his head, went from languid to alert in an instant.

"I heard that you work on something called the Dolphin Guard. I'm interested. In fact, I've wondered where the dolphins are. Back in October I saw a whole group of them in the harbor. They were swimming near that bench where we sat. I haven't seen them since, though I've looked for them almost every day. Do they go somewhere in the winter, migrate?"

"No, they don't migrate. You sure you want to talk about dolphins?"

"Yes. Very sure."

"Okay. Dolphins are sort of territorial, and one thing the Dolphin Guard is trying to find out is where certain of their territorial boundaries lie. The D.G. doesn't really know yet. Those dolphins you saw, they're still around. You get to know the individual ones by their size and their markings, and I know the ones you mean. They come into the harbor sometimes, but not often. You're more likely to see them out on the other side of the banks. They don't come through the inlet much, only if they follow a particular boat in. They do that sometimes."

I was thrilled to be talking about dolphins with someone who really knew the creatures, who might understand my fascination. Eagerly I told Nick about my encounter, spilling over with enthusiasm, ending with, "They seemed to be communicating with me somehow, as if they were intelligent!"

"Huh," Nick growled. He heaved himself upright on the bunk and reached for the brandy bottle on the floor. "Yeah, I heard they're intelligent. Got a brain bigger than a man's, they say. I don't know, I just go out and watch them when this woman who got me involved tells me to. I'm not really all that interested in the dolphins—thought I was interested in the woman, but she turned out to be not worth the effort. I keep on with the D.G. because it's something to do. They've only got volunteers. I guess they need me."

He really doesn't care, I thought, too disappointed to say anything.

Nick tossed back half a glass of brandy and his face flushed momentarily. As he reddened, I could see a long, thin white scar along his cheekbone. Boris must have scratched deep to leave a scar like that. And I saw his eyes take on a peculiar look. Haunted. When he spoke again his voice was brittle. "Did you ever notice their eyes? Sometimes when I'm watching the dolphins, I feel more like *they're* watching *me.* I tell you something—it gives me the creeps!"

Now I was more than disappointed, I was confused, and apprehensive. Why would a person who so obviously didn't like dolphins—or worse, had some decidedly peculiar feelings about dolphins—continue to be one of the Dolphin Guard? Especially since he wasn't getting paid. I really didn't understand what was going on here. I decided the best thing to do was change the subject.

I forced a laugh, which unfortunately came out sounding like a silly giggle. "I guess it's just as well I went for a walk tonight, even if you did almost cut me with your knife. I was afraid I wouldn't see you again."

That got his attention, and produced a knowing smile. "You wanted to see me again?"

"Yes. I've felt bad that I didn't apologize for what Boris did to you."

Nick came across the space between the bunks, crouched low, his head and shoulders filling my vision. He stopped with his face close to mine. "Left a scar, see?"

"I see. I'm sorry."

"Why don't you kiss it and make it all better?" His eyes glinted.

I was getting to know that look, that tone of voice. Nick was teasing again. In spite of my instinctive sense that Nick's teasing could get rough, I leaned forward a little and touched my lips to the thin white scar. "There," I said.

Of course he didn't stop at that. He came over me and I felt his splendid body pressing me down; felt the heavy, silky beard on my neck and against my cheeks. For some inexplicable reason Seth's face flashed through my mind, and with it the memory of his kindness, his slender fingers stroking gently, his lips coaxing, persuading a response. Not devouring, as this great red-haired hunk was devouring, at present, my ear. And so I struggled.

Nick raised his head and laughed. He pinned my arms with his hands as easily as if I were a butterfly on velvet. I pleaded with my eyes and with my voice. "Please, Nick, not this way!"

To my surprise and relief, he released me. He rolled onto his side, and I curled up into a sitting position, pulled my knees up and hugged them against my breasts.

"Don't worry, little Laura," he said. "I won't force you. Some other women I might, but not you. I was planning to see you again, cat or no damn cat. I just had some things I had to take care of first. To get ready for winter and all that."

I nodded. I felt as if I were all eyes, watching his every move. But underneath the sweatsuit my naked body burned, answering Nick's sexual call even if my mind did not. He was erect as he lay sprawled next to me; only a blind woman could have failed to see.

"Come on," Nick cajoled, "finish your brandy and I'll walk you home. I'll bring my knife in case anybody else mistakes you for a prowler."

So I finished the brandy, asked him to leave the knife, and made it home safely. Nick tactfully faded into the night before I tapped on the inn's main entrance door for a surprised Jonathan to let me in. "I couldn't sleep, so I went for a walk," I explained. It was the truth, after all.

At two o'clock I was in bed, again. I had completely forgotten about my fear of the dark. I lay there thinking of Nick with ambivalent feelings. I would be seeing him again—I'd agreed to go sailing with him on the next sunny day. He'd offered an irresistible enticement: he said we would look for the dolphins.

For the next several days the weather continued to be dank and overcast, and I was busy at the inn. Polly departed and Zelda Crabtree came. Training Zelda was easy; getting along with her was something else. I sat at the reception desk one evening, puzzling over this, when the door opened and a tree walked in. Or seemed to. Behind the tree was Jonathan, obscured by the branches of an evergreen taller and broader than he.

I laughed. "Oh, Jonathan, you look like Father Christmas himself! Where did you ever find such a gorgeous tree?"

"I got connections," he said with a wink. "It's a white pine. Like it?"

"Yes, I do. But I feel a little guilty. I should have thought of it myself. Of course the inn needs a Christmas tree!"

"You've had other things to think about. In the past we've had a tree upstairs in the dining room. So I'll take this on up there, unless you'd rather put it somewhere else."

"No, the dining room is the best place, I'm sure. What about lights, ornaments, and all that?"

"I'll ask Evelyn when she gets here in the morning—I'm sure she knows where those things are stored. Perhaps you'd join me, Laura, in decorating the tree after breakfast tomorrow?"

I felt a cloud pass over me and knew my face reflected the sadness I felt. "I don't know, Jonathan. I think I'd rather ignore Christmas this year."

"That's what I thought you'd say." Jonathan propped the big tree against the wall and took off his battered tweed hat. His pale, crinkly hair sprang out all around the shiny crown of his head. "But you can't ignore Christmas. It's like death and taxes—inevitable. You have to deal with the memories, and make new ones."

I saw a wistful look in his pale blue eyes and realized how selfishly I was focused on myself. "Do you have family? Would you like to go away over Christmas?"

He shook his head. "No family. I'm used to being alone. I'm a confirmed bachelor and before that I was an only child. My parents died years ago. The inn's like a home to me now, and you and the staff and the guests are all the family I need."

I studied his face, which so often looked full of good-natured mischief, like an elderly Cupid. Tonight he seemed more like a Cupid who had wounded himself with his own arrow. I guessed there had been someone very special to him, and that the loss of that someone was the reason for his confirmed bachelorhood. I guessed further that asking him about it would not be a kindness. So I said, "I'd be honored to decorate the tree with you."

We did it in the morning after breakfast, as Jonathan had suggested. I brought Boris with me, Boris being my family. We placed the tree in the center of the row of third-floor windows, so that the colored lights could be seen from the street and the harbor. The fresh scent of pine took Boris back to kittenhood: he frisked and pounced and batted at the lower branches with his paws while Jonathan and I strung the lights and hung the ornaments.

"Boris may knock off a few ornaments," I said, "but he hasn't tried to climb a Christmas tree since his first Christmas. I think he remembers how the tree crashed with him in it. It scared him half to death!"

Jonathan chuckled. "Boris is half human. I never knew a cat could have a personality like he has. No wonder you're so fond of him."

"Yes, I am. I don't know what I'd do without him."

We chatted easily as we worked, and when we finished we sat over second cups of coffee admiring the tree. It was beautiful, and I was glad Jonathan had talked me into it. My mood of satisfaction broke when I thought of going back downstairs to the office, where I'd have to see Zelda.

"Jonathan, what do you think of Zelda Crabtree?"

He looked at me over the tops of his glasses, which as usual had slid down his nose. "She's mature, and to my mind that's in her favor. Kathryn never should have hired Polly, she had too much youth and too little experience. Zelda seems capable, and you said she had good references."

"She had *one* good reference, from Seth Douglass. She used to work for him."

"What's on your mind, Laura? Maybe I should ask what *you* think of Zelda."

"I don't know. I'm not sure. She does the work very, very well, especially considering she's only been here a few days. She's efficient and responsible, and I could probably delegate all but the most important decisions to her. But I feel so uncomfortable around her." I ducked my head as I said this, feeling that even this admission was a failure on my part.

"Uncomfortable? In what way?" Jonathan pushed his glasses back up his nose. He looked concerned.

I shrugged. "Maybe I'm just paranoid. She seems to be always watching me. I think she doesn't like me."

Jonathan put his big hand over mine, like a friendly paw. "That's ridiculous. Nobody could dislike you, Laura."

I shook my head and forced a smile. "You wouldn't say that if you'd known me in my lawyer days, which wasn't so long ago. There were plenty of people who hated my guts!"

He beamed, clearly unconvinced. "Too hard to believe."

I appreciated his warmth, his uncomplicated friendliness. "You're a good friend, Jonathan."

"I hope so. Anything else on your mind this morning?"

I looked at the Christmas tree, its bright baubles and golden garlands catching the morning light and giving it back, colored and magnified, to the world. There *was* something else. I had another friend, and I'd thought of him during the memory-invoking ritual of decking the tree. "Seth Douglass," I confessed. "He has no family here, either. Perhaps he's going away for Christmas, I haven't asked. But if he doesn't I'd like to add him to our celebration. You and me and Boris, and Seth. I thought I'd find out from Evelyn how we can get a turkey cooked. The rest I could prepare ahead of time for the freezer. We can have a semi-festive dinner here on Christmas Day. Would that be all right with you?"

"If that's what you want," Jonathan said. He studied my face seriously. "Seth does seem very, ah, attentive to you."

"That's true." I smiled. Since the day we'd gone to Cedar Island, Seth had either called or come by nearly every day. I didn't know Jonathan had noticed.

The serious expression remained on his face. He said, "If you have any doubts about Zelda, perhaps you should speak to Seth about her. Didn't she have any other references besides him?"

"No." Suddenly I had an old feeling which I recognized,

though I hadn't felt it in a long time. It was the small panic of self-doubt, a possible mistake made, something important perhaps overlooked. "She said she was unhappy with the place she was working when I interviewed her, and she preferred that I not talk to them. So I didn't. Seth has had so much experience of people working for him, and I've none, so I took his word about her. I presume Seth is trustworthy."

Even as the words left my lips I realized I hadn't always felt that way about him. There had been a time not so long ago when I'd suspected he was keeping something from me; I'd gone so far as to suspect him of having something to do with Kathryn's disappearance.

"He has a good enough reputation around here," said Jonathan, "and from what I hear, he's earned it. Still, you might discuss your concerns about Zelda with Seth, since he recommended her to you. Now, it's way past my bedtime. I'm glad we did the tree together. I think we'll have a halfway decent Christmas if we give it a chance. See you later, Laura."

He walked part of the way to the door, then turned around and came back. I looked up, wondering what he had forgotten. To my astonishment, Jonathan bent and swiftly kissed my cheek.

"Thank you for coming here," he said. "You make a great difference in the quality of life around this place."

"You're welcome," I murmured. As swiftly as he'd bestowed his kiss, he was gone again. I sat wondering if anything in the world could be truly uncomplicated, including the friendship of Jonathan Harcourt.

My mood turned pensive; it matched the pale gray of the sky. We had been days without the sun. Beaufort's December cold was not so cold as I was accustomed to, but it was more chilling. Bleak. A damp chill that came from the water and on the wind, into and through you. Pervasive and penetrating. Winter was in the ascendant, winter ruled everything, including my heart.

8

Overnight the sky changed, and the sea sparkled silver-blue under a welcome sun. In a heavy, hooded OSU sweatshirt, corduroys, and rubber-soled sneakers, I presented myself before the *Hellfire*.

"Ahoy, there," I called to Nick, who knelt on deck, busy at some task.

He straightened up, and a grin appeared within his beard. "So, you remembered. Well, come on. Come aboard. You know the way."

I leapt over the gap between deck and dock. Being on board was different, more thrilling than a quick walk across the deck and down into the cabin in the middle of the night. Heady with anticipation, I stretched my arms to the sky and breathed deeply of the salt-tinged air. I no longer felt ambivalent; all my cautions about Nick blew away on the clean, cold wind that polished my cheeks and ruffled my hair. This would be the first sail of my entire life, and I intended to enjoy every minute of it.

Nick explained that he was changing the mainsail, putting on a heavier canvas which would lie flat to the strong winter wind. I confessed complete ignorance and offered to help if he would tell me exactly what to do. He declined, along with a lengthy technical explanation of the many features that made it possible for him to sail the *Hellfire* alone. Out of all the unfamiliar terminology I understood only the most basic things, such as that the type of boat was called a masthead cutter, and the *Hellfire* had been specially modified to enable Nick to sail her alone: for example, there was the modification of a wheel on deck rather than a tiller, and near the wheel were clustered controls for doing almost everything automatically. In addition, the boat could be sailed under power or with the sails alone.

"I'm impressed," I said; then I left the mysteries and mechanics of getting the boat out of the harbor to Nick. I gave myself over to pure enjoyment. We rounded Carrot Island and proceeded through Beaufort Inlet under power. Everything took on a different perspective from the water. The effect was disorienting. It was as if the world had suddenly gone out of proportion, and I was out of control.

Nick was the one in control. He was in his element. A magnificent physical specimen on land, at sea he was even more so. His head was bare, his abundant hair held back by a red and black bandanna folded and tied around his forehead. He wore a heavy wool ragg sweater, also black striped horizontally with red, and black trousers tightly fitted to his thighs and buttocks. Instead of deck shoes, he wore beautiful boots that must have cost him a fortune— soft black leather, flat heels, they fit so well I guessed they must have been custom-made. I envied him those boots, or a female version thereof.

I moved forward and stood in the bow. I looked out and down, below the bowsprit, fascinated by how cleanly the boat cut through the water. No wonder she was called a cutter! Then I looked ahead to the horizon, and felt a moment of disorientation so complete, it amounted to terror. The long blue line where sea meets sky seemed infinite, landmark of an alien planet. Though the sun shone above friendly-warm, the potentially destructive force of the great ocean slammed into me, a shocking surprise. From the safety of land I had always seen the ocean as a benevolent mother, seat of all creative power. Now I saw the mother's other side.

Shivering in the cold wind, I looked again down into the water, possessed by dark thoughts. Thoughts of drowning. Words came into my mind, learned long ago and all but forgotten: "Full fathom five thy father lies, of his bones are coral made, those are pearls that were his eyes . . ." Shakespeare, *The Tempest,* my junior year of college. There was more, I couldn't remember exactly—something about a "sea change."

I ran my hand through my hair, part nervous habit and part a futile attempt to keep it out of my eyes. These thoughts and feelings were so different from what I'd anticipated! Where was the pleasure of the senses, the spiritual exhilaration? Why was it that these days I must always first experience the dark side of all I touched? And how long would it be, how many times must this happen before I would be too exhausted, too defeated to keep struggling for the light?

I felt the *Hellfire* change course, though visually there was no difference in the never-ending vista of sea and sky. But when I looked to my right, I saw land not far away. If we'd turned right, starboard, then we were heading south, and that land must be Bogue Banks. Atlantic Beach, Pine Knoll Shores, Salter Path, Emerald Isle—I knew the names now. Even from this distance I could see shoreline dotted and clustered with houses and condos. Bogue Banks was on the verge of overdevelopment, Seth said.

Suddenly I sensed another change, an absence of something that had been there before. Alarmed, I whipped around, seeking Nick. Then I understood: he had cut the power, it was the sound of the motor that I missed. Now he raised the sails. My breath caught in my throat—here was the beauty, the thrill I wanted! The great white sails slowly climbed to the top of the mast, shuddered, and caught the wind. My heart pounded but with excitement, not fear. I was awestruck. The *Hellfire* flew before the wind and my spirits soared with her.

I made my way back to Nick on uncertain sea legs. "The *Hellfire* is magnificent," I said.

He only grinned in answer and wrapped an arm around my waist, pulling me against his side. I felt the power of the man seep into me, from flank to flank, a raw animal force, primitive, elemental. He handled his white-winged craft with fierce pleasure, riding the sea as if the very waters belonged to him. For uncounted minutes I shared his power and exulted, intoxicated by risk. I felt that Nick Westover was a man who could and would do anything. Anything!

Such power, too, has its dark side. Unaccustomed to intoxication of any kind, I became overwhelmed. No matter how physically perfect, a man who could so easily handle a large boat with one hand and a small woman, me, with the other was a man to beware of. I moved, to move away; he tightened his hold. He looked down on me, and I met his eyes and was burned by their green fire. I gave him a tremulous smile.

"I need to go below," I said, an excuse I presumed he would honor. He let me go.

Somewhere along the way we found the dolphins, or perhaps the dolphins found us. They were far off when I first spotted them, only a group of elongated dark gray shapes, arching in and out through the waves.

"Dolphins!" I yelled to Nick over the wind. He left the wheel and came to stand beside me. "Can you do that," I asked, "leave the boat to sail herself?"

"Yeah. Not for too long today in this wind, but for a while. I'm going below to get the binoculars."

While he was gone, my hope grew to a certainty: the dolphins were coming to us. There were a couple of fishing boats in sight, and another sailboat not far behind, but the dolphins had singled out the *Hellfire*.

Nick returned and silently held the binoculars to his eyes. After a few minutes he said, "I recognize them. They're the ones you want to see, all right."

I felt a rush of gratitude. Though he was one of the Dolphin Guard, I knew Nick didn't share my love for these creatures. He had done this for me. "Thank you," I said, "you don't know how much this means to me."

Unsmiling, Nick handed me the binoculars. "Well, I wanted to get you on my boat," he said, rather ungraciously.

I decided to ignore the comment, and occupied myself with adjusting the glasses to my vision. "Look how fast they're coming! I'm sure they're coming this way."

"I don't doubt it for a minute," grumbled Nick. He stalked away, muttering under his breath, "Damn dolphins!"

While he was gone I debated whether or not to ask him why he didn't like the dolphins, and by the time he returned with two cans of beer, I'd decided against it. I could keep my fascination with the beautiful creatures to myself; how Nick felt need not be any concern of mine. He had brought me out onto the ocean, and I'd found my dolphins again, and that was enough.

Nick went back to the wheel, and I watched my refound friends. The glasses brought me so close, I felt as if I were a part of their togetherness. They pursued us purposefully, yet their pleasure in one another's company was palpable. They swam in twos and threes, their bodies touching. Gradually I recognized that they were not all the same size, and I presumed the smaller ones were the children. Nor were they all precisely the same color; some were darker than others, and one had light spots on his or her side. I tried to count them but lost count because of the way they wove in and out of the waves.

I thought it odd, though perhaps it was normal, that when the dolphins got within about a hundred yards of the *Hellfire* they began to keep pace with the boat and would come no closer. I'd heard that dolphins liked to play in the wake and ride the bow waves, but these did not. Instead, they arranged themselves on either side of us, like a ceremonial escort. Like the Secret Service following the President, like armed guards following their captured prey. I shook my head to clear it, wondering why dark thoughts had seized me once again.

The dolphins stayed with us until Nick took the *Hellfire* into the harbor at Swansboro. They didn't follow, and I was disappointed. I'd called out with my mind, hoping that the two who had come to me at Beaufort would come again, but they did not. I couldn't help but feel that there was something slightly wrong, a little bit off, about the way they'd flanked the boat. I tried to explain away their behavior by rationalizing that the water was winter-cold, and thus the dolphins didn't leap and play, but the rationalization wasn't satisfactory. This dolphin encounter had been, in the end, unsettling.

"Lunchtime," Nick announced. The *Hellfire* rode at anchor in Swansboro Harbor. "We'll eat below; wind's too stiff out here."

"I suppose you're right," I agreed, following him through the hatch and down the few steps.

"Another beer?"

"Yes, thank you." I felt pleasantly light-headed from the one beer I'd had, and I wasn't averse to prolonging the feeling. "Why don't you let me fix lunch, since you've been doing all the work so far."

"If you want to," he agreed. "There's plenty of stuff in the refrigerator; you can choose whatever you like."

The galley was compact, but it did have everything. It was more like a real kitchen than what we had at the inn. Nick was obviously accustomed to eating well, and expensively. I fried bacon, toasted bread, and made hot crabmeat-salad sandwiches with the bacon crumbled on top. I found I was enjoying myself. I hadn't realized how much I had missed cooking, missed the feeling of being domestic, doing things for a man.

"I like this," said Nick. "You in the galley, cooking for me."

"I like to cook. Now, where do we eat? We can't very well eat on the beds, er, bunks."

"Abracadabra," said Nick, with a flourish pulling out a shelf hidden in the galley's countertop. "Like magic, we have a table." He opened a built-in closet. "And chairs." They were the folding kind, and he set them up.

"Very good. You're a genius!" I plunked the plates down, then forks and napkins. "Now, eat."

After an interval, Nick said, "I am, you know."

"You are what?"

"A genius. Of sorts." He grinned wickedly, a grown man playing mischievous little boy. Any minute now I expected him to wink at me.

Well, all right, I'd play. "Really. How interesting. What sort of genius are you?"

There was the wink. "A very unusual sort. You'll find out, little by little."

"Oh, come on. Don't be so mysterious. I can see you're a wonderful sailor. What other things do you do, genius level or not?"

We sat next to each other at the countertop-table, close due to the confined space. Nick narrowed his eyes, making frown lines on his still-tan forehead, and his nostrils flared with some emotion I couldn't guess.

"For now," he said, "the other things I do are my secret. One of these days I expect I'll tell you." He gazed at me with an intensity that made me uncomfortable.

In an attempt at lightness I joked, "Let me guess. You're a smuggler. You smuggle drugs. No, something more exotic. You've found a sunken treasure, and you're bringing it in a piece at a time because you don't want the government to know."

Nick was not amused. Instead, his frown deepened. How quickly he could change! One minute playful, dead serious the next. "If you really knew what goes on in these waters, Laura, you wouldn't joke about such things. But anyway, it's not money I'm after, I already have plenty of that. No, it's something much more important than money. Much more . . . exciting."

I shrugged. This game was no fun anymore, and I got up to clear the table. "Well, I can't imagine what could be so much more important than money, but I'll take your word for it. Now, I'm going to clean up the dishes."

"I'll sit here and watch you. I like to watch you."

I could feel his eyes on my back. Whereas before I'd felt

pleasure in cooking for him, now I was uneasy. I decided I'd better keep him talking. I asked, "Where do we go from here?"

"That depends on the weather."

"What about the weather? It's a beautiful day. A little windy, maybe, but—"

Nick interrupted. "That's it, the wind. She's blowing from the Northeast, and this time of year storms come from that direction."

"Is that why we didn't go the other way, north, along the Outer Banks?" I asked over my shoulder.

"Partly. And partly I just wanted to come down this way. There's probably nothing to worry about today, but we're in for a bad winter. The Coast Guard is getting ready, and that's a sure sign. I can feel it myself. We're going to have some unusually high tides—they get a little higher every day now. Unusual astronomical conditions."

"Oh?" I turned around to look at Nick. He had my full attention.

"Yeah. In a few days the earth, moon, and sun will be in a direct line, and the tides will be crazy. If we get a storm on top of that—well, you can guess. Destruction like nobody's seen for a long time! *You* needn't worry, and I've got a safe harbor at Beaufort."

"Well, maybe there won't be a storm until the tides go back to normal, the sun and moon go back to wherever they usually are."

"Yeah, maybe. Let's go back on deck. We might have time to sail down as far as Topsail this afternoon. They lost a lot of beach there in the last storm."

Viewing destroyed beaches wasn't exactly my idea of a good time, but we set off again and with a strong wind behind us, we did get to Topsail Beach. I looked obediently through the binoculars, but because I was unfamiliar with the way it had looked before, I could tell only by the condition of the beach houses what had happened here. Again I thought of Seth and his concern for the coastline— the more I saw, the more I appreciated his mission.

We picked up the dolphins again on our way back, and

they flanked the *Hellfire* as before. Nick fought to keep us headed into the wind, and I left him alone for the long trip back to Beaufort. I sat near the stern, thoughtfully watching the spreading wake of the boat. I wondered if it could possibly be that the dolphins sensed Nick's dislike of them, and that was why they kept their distance.

They left as suddenly and mysteriously as they'd joined us. As if on some inaudible, invisible signal the dolphins turned away and swam out into the open sea. I closed my eyes and followed them with my mind, saw them swimming smoothly in their mystical blue-green kingdom; sleek, rounded bodies swooping and touching, sensually, sensitively. Saw their smiling mouths, their fabulous dark eyes . . . and then a darkness came over my inner vision. It took on the feel of my bad dreams. A sea change . . . the sea changes . . . and behind my closed eyes I felt and heard a rushing that pulled me down, down, where I looked not into the eyes of the dolphins but into the black empty sockets of a human skull.

My eyes flew open. The *Hellfire*, beating into the wind, pitched endlessly. I was going to be sick. I leaned over the rail, holding tight with both hands. But I didn't vomit. The sickness was in my mind, in my soul, not in my body. The voice of memory returned, but this time it said, "Full fathom five thy sister lies . . ."

"Do you think he's jealous?" I scratched Boris behind the ear. He opened one round blue eye—his eyes are round, like the Persian side of his ancestry, which is also the source of all that long hair. I scratched him again. "Well, big guy, what do you think, is he jealous?"

"Mrmmph-um-urrurrurr," said Boris, closing his eye again and launching into a purr that shook the bed. He kneaded a place alongside my thigh with his paws, then turned around on it three times and settled there.

"Not going to help me, huh?" I punched my pillows in human imitation of Boris, and settled back against them to think this through on my own. Seth jealous, because of the day I'd spent sailing with Nick? It had been on the tip of my tongue to say coquettishly, Why Seth, I do believe you're jealous! Except that coquettishness wasn't in my behavioral repertoire, and to have two men interested in me at the same time hadn't happened before, either.

"Oh, well," I murmured, "a little jealousy never hurt anybody. I guess."

I'd been careful to explain to Nick that I had to be back at the inn in time to change clothes and be on the desk at six, and he did get us docked at five. We watched the setting sun on our way into the harbor. But then Nick hadn't wanted to let me go. It had been such a confusing day, beautiful and disturbing at the same time—not unlike Nick Westover himself. I'd gone tongue-tied trying to be gracious, to say thank you for the sail and at the same time to say no, thank you, I don't want to stay for a drink. In the end I just gave up and went below and accepted the drink. Only I never drank it. The cabin seemed so still, so silent, so warm after the sound and feel of the wind and waves. Nick threw back his drink in one swallow while I raised my glass to my lips. The barest taste of Scotch, stinging-smooth, had touched my tongue when my glass disappeared and Nick's lips were over mine, his tongue thrusting in, tasting of the same Scotch, stinging-smooth.

Now, safely in bed with the cat, I asked myself honestly how I had felt about that kiss. Why should it be so hard to know? How could I feel so attracted to Nick and yet repelled by him, too? Because the attraction was so entirely physical. Because there was something about it, about him, that felt primitive, dangerous.

I argued with myself, being my own devil's advocate. Mightn't I need to go with that part of myself that responded to Nick? Hadn't I been too civilized for too long, repressed my primitive desires long enough? I was, after all, teaching myself to confront my fears, to risk. Maybe Nick was simply a part of this whole pattern, a learning experience. His sexuality was certainly compelling. And it certainly did frighten me.

Yes, it frightened me. That was why I'd resisted his kiss, hadn't given in to the hot desire that flamed through me when his tongue touched mine. He was so much bigger than I that I felt surrounded by him; with one arm he pinned my body to his and with the other he held my head, forcing it back and up. To move was impossible; my only defense was to give him no response at all. By an effort of will I made my body go limp. My mouth, forced open by that demanding tongue, refused to answer his demands at all, though he didn't realize this for what seemed like a very long time. My neck ached and my willpower had worn thin when at last he raised his head.

"I'll be late," I'd whispered, "I have to go"; and he'd said roughly, "The day will come when you won't want to leave!"

But for this particular day I had left, and as I'd dressed in a rush and combed an impossible nest of tangles out of my hair, my mirror had shown me a face with cheeks colored high by windburn, and a mouth reddened and slightly swollen by that long, bruising kiss. This was the face that, a few minutes later, brought first an appreciative smile (You look so healthy! Have you been out in the sun?), and then, on closer inspection, a guarded look of appraisal (Where have you been today?) from Seth. When I'd told him that I'd spent the day on the *Hellfire* with Nick Westover, his stern reaction was a classic. His nose seemed to lengthen, his jaw and faintly cleft chin clenched; his shapely lips pressed into a hard line while the heavy eyebrows arched upward to convey both surprise and disapproval. "Oh, really?" was all he'd said. Which was when I'd wanted to play coquette, and didn't. Instead I'd suggested that he bring two glasses of wine from the dining room and tell me about his day. Our casual sharing of wine and talk while I sat at the reception desk was becoming a usual thing—but tonight Seth hadn't stayed as long or said as much as usual.

Well, there was nothing I could do about it, whether Seth was jealous or not. I snuggled down in bed, which disturbed Boris. He lifted his head long enough to give me a dirty look, then put it down again and curled the tip of his tail over his nose. He went back to purring, no doubt returning to some exotic cat-dream. I put my glasses on the bedside table and turned off the lamp, confident that tonight I would sleep well.

I fought my way out of heavy, dreamless sleep, for a moment so disoriented that I reached across the bed for my husband. I sat up abruptly, feeling the pang of loss that still came to me on waking up alone. I shook my head and ran my fingers through my hair; reached out for the lamp and then thought better of it. Something had awakened me, something had pierced through layers of sleep and brought me to consciousness. A sound? An unusual sound. I sat stock-still, listening. Pale moonlight sifted through the curtains at the windows, and I strained my eyes to see, as if the eyes could aid the ears. My efforts were rewarded. I heard footsteps, and I saw a shadow. My heart jumped up into my throat and stayed there. Someone was on the porch, looking through my window and into my bedroom.

I had pulled the curtains together as I always did before going to bed. They were white, rather sheer, and blurred the shadow's outline so that I could not tell if the watcher was man or woman. The room was large and my bed was at the far end, against the east wall—I doubted if I could be seen. Heart pounding, I felt on the bedside table for my glasses and put them on.

The shadow moved, again I heard footsteps, muffled yet distinct. The watcher wore soft-soled shoes. The shadow appeared in the second window, nearer my bed. Instinctively I drew up my knees, shrinking myself into the smallest possible ball. I held my breath. A peeping Tom? If I went to the window, would he expose himself? And where was Boris? He wasn't on the bed with me.

Boris had become an instant watch-cat. I saw him now, a small, bulky shape with night-glaring eyes, standing in front of the fireplace opposite the windows. As the shadow wavered at the second window, Boris began a low, guttural growl; then he screamed a cry that sounded half-human and in a running leap hurled himself at the shadow. He caught his claws in the curtains and yowled again over the sound of ripping, tearing cloth. The shadow disappeared, the footsteps ran, and I jumped out of bed. Without thought I sped to the door, turned the key and threw back the dead bolt, and did the same with the automatic lock of the front door. I left both doors wide open and raced across the porch. The cold turned my thin nightgown to crinkling ice and burned the bare soles of my feet, bringing me to my senses. I stopped on the top step, panting. Whoever the watcher had been, he or she was a fast runner. There was no one in sight, no point in running after someone who had already disappeared.

I went back to the door, remembering now the faint sound that had brought me from sleep: a kind of scratching or scrabbling at the windows, or perhaps at the door. I went back into my room, put on a robe and slippers, and got a flashlight. Returning to the porch, I shone the light around the windows, one at a time. There were no marks of any kind on the sills or the windowframes. Then I inspected the door more closely. Still there was nothing to be seen. Frustrating! I closed the door and watched it lock automatically. It looked solid and safe enough. Back in my room I flicked on the overhead light and locked myself in. Boris sat calmly in the middle of the Oriental rug licking his paws and restoring order to his fur. The curtain he'd attacked would never be the same again, but Boris was unperturbed. I laughed shakily and dropped cross-legged onto the floor with him.

"Mowr," pronounced Boris. He marched over and began to lick my ankle bone with his delicate, sandpapery tongue. I scooped him into my lap and hugged him.

"You were very brave, and I was very silly to run outside like that." I stroked him until I felt relatively calm. "You probably think we should tell Jonathan, but if I do that, he'll call the police. And really, Boris, I can't handle the police again. It was just a prowler, and anyway he found out he can't get in."

Boris looked up at me and for a moment laid his ears back. "Rorr," he said.

"Oh, you don't agree with me? Well, I'll tell you what. First thing after Christmas we'll get the inn a burglar alarm system. Is that better?"

"Mowr," said Boris. I took it that he approved.

9

At the last minute I decided to give a small party on Christmas Eve. There were no guests at the inn that night, though six were scheduled to arrive late on Christmas Day, and four of these six were staying through New Year's. The truth was, I was trying to keep myself busy; I didn't want time for thoughts or memories. I took over the small kitchen with its refrigerator-freezer and microwave oven and was as creative as its limitations allowed. As I worked, I realized how far circumstances had brought me from the intentions I'd had on coming to Beaufort. I'd intended to rent or buy a house as soon as possible, and to send for my furniture and all the things I'd left stored in Ohio. I certainly did miss having a real kitchen and my own equipment!

By 5:00 P.M. I had produced a good assortment of hot and cold hors d'oeuvres and chilled several bottles of domestic champagne, and dressed myself in the new red sweater I'd bought especially for the party. It was a clear, bright shade of red, with a softly draped cowl neck; I wore it with a long skirt of winter-white wool I'd had in my wardrobe for years. I also wore my "Christmas shoes," high-heeled green satin sandals that had seemed frivolous when I'd purchased them long ago, but in spite or perhaps because of their unusual color they went with almost anything. Putting on these shoes pleased me—shoes are my passion, and the strappy green sandals were fun, flattering, too. I don't look so bad, I thought, though I did wish I could wear contact lenses. The red of the sweater brought color to my pale skin and contrasted well with my black hair. I decided the party was going to be good for me, above and beyond the fact that the preparations had achieved their purpose, made the day pass quickly.

Jonathan, Boris, and I received our few guests in the dining room just after sundown. The Christmas tree glowed forth its many jeweled colors and reflected them in the windows, like stained glass. I'd placed candles in hurricane lamps all around the room and turned on no electric lights. The very air was soft and golden.

"I don't know how you got all this together in such a short time," said Jonathan. "Everything looks great, including you."

"Thank you," I replied. "I see you and I had the same idea about appropriate dress for this occasion."

"What?" He looked a little flustered. Jonathan, too, wore a red sweater, the V-necked kind, over an open-collared white dress shirt. On him the expanse of red took on the look of a Santa Claus suit, in spite of his gray trousers. "Oh, you mean the sweater. I, uh, I always wear this at Christmas. You should have put a red collar or a bow or something red on Boris, too."

"You've got to be kidding! He'd tolerate a bow for about five seconds, and collars of any kind just get lost under all his hair. A couple of years ago I got him a fancy collar with a big jingle bell and he hated it—he glared at me until I took it off, and he went around with his nose in the air for weeks after."

Jonathan laughed and reached down to stroke my cat, who sat on the floor between us.

Seth was the first guest to arrive, bringing spectacularly huge poinsettias. I thanked him, and he kissed me on the cheek. Next after Seth came Polly with her mother. Polly bore me no ill will, and chatted about the new job she'd be starting in January. Next to arrive were Eloise and Darlene, the part-time maids, with their husbands, and after them a couple Jonathan had invited. They were special friends of his and owned a bookstore-gift shop in Swansboro. Evelyn, the housekeeper, looking very attractive in a royal blue dress and gold necklace and earrings, brought her whole family: a solemn, black-suited husband and two handsome teenage sons. Trevor Blackburn, Kathryn's lawyer and now mine, came—to my surprise. I'd invited him because he was a recent widower, and I thought he might be lonely. I hadn't really thought he'd come.

A last, late arrival was Zelda Crabtree. To my shame I had to force my smile, the handshake, the words of greeting. Tall and gaunt, Zelda had overdressed in emerald-green brocade that was all wrong for her—the color turned her complexion sallow, and the low-cut bodice required more breast than she had available. She scanned the room and headed straight for Seth, teetering a bit on the way. Her heels weren't that high, and I wondered if she'd started celebrating before the party. Of course she'd go to Seth, she had known him longer than the others in the room. I watched her greet him. He turned to her with recognition in his eyes; polite as always he bent and touched his cheek to hers. He didn't have to bend very far. I couldn't help but notice that they looked well together, or would have if she had been as tastefully dressed as he. Like him, she was taller than average, and they both had the same long, spare-boned looks. But in Seth the lankiness was attractive, whereas in Zelda it came across as awkwardness.

Such critical thoughts were unlike me, and I resolved to stop them. I turned to Jonathan. "That's everyone I invited. Let's get some champagne and mingle."

The party flowed along smoothly, happy faces and cheerful voices mellowed by the candlelight, sparkled with champagne. I felt pleasantly muzzy, full of goodwill for these people who'd responded to my invitation on short notice and seemed to be having a good time. Even Zelda seemed to enjoy herself—every time I looked her way she was never far from Seth. As always when I was the hostess, I made an effort to spend time with everyone more or less equally. I moved at intervals from one cluster of people to another, keeping an eye on the food and drink in the process. The food ran out about when I'd thought it would, at the same time that conversation slowed down. I knew before long the guests would begin to drift away, which was as it should be. I moved unobtrusively nearer to the door and was soon saying good-bye-thank-you-for-coming. Jonathan left with his friends and explained that he would be back late, he was going to the midnight service at church.

Seth came up to me, Zelda trailing behind. He said, "I'm going to take Zelda home. She had car trouble and came in a cab. I'll be back to help you clean up."

"Oh, don't bother," my protest came automatically. "It's not as bad as it looks; I can do it in no time at all."

"Nonsense." He took both my hands in his and dropped his voice an octave. "I'll be back. I have no intention of leaving you alone on Christmas Eve."

"But—" I was about to say I'd see him tomorrow anyway, when he stopped my words by kissing me. Just a swift kiss, no one would have had time to notice it wasn't lightly given. Brief as it was, the kiss was moist and tender and wanted to deepen into something more. He whispered as his lips left mine, "Later."

I nodded and turned my attention to Zelda. I hadn't realized she was standing so close. "Thank you for coming, Zelda," I said.

She grabbed my hand in her bony fingers. "So nice of you to have this little party. You don't know how grateful I am to be working at the inn, Laura. Isn't it nice of Seth to take me home?" As she asked the question she leaned over me almost as Seth had done, and for a moment I had the awful thought that Zelda was going to kiss me, too.

I stiffened and wished she were not head and shoulders taller than I. "Yes, it is nice of him. I'm sorry about your car, and glad to have you with us at the inn. Merry Christmas." I felt about as sincere as a robot programmed for party-hostessing.

Over my shoulder I watched the two lanky people go, Seth

and Zelda; saw him slip his arm casually about her shoulders, perhaps to steady her; saw their two heads almost matched in height, his silver and hers light brown shot through with similar silver. I wondered why I hadn't realized before that they were about the same age—she seemed so much older to me, but she wasn't. I knew her age, forty-three, from her résumé. Seth, I knew, was over forty, how much over I'd never cared. Briefly I thought they might be sister and brother, but no. No sister ever looked at her brother the way Zelda had looked at Seth off and on through the evening. Could they be former lovers? Current lovers? What a preposterous idea! And yet the familiarity between them as they walked away was undeniable.

Evelyn and her family were last to leave. They were, all of them, lovely people. Watching the father and the sons in the way they related to her, I could see that Evelyn was the glue that held this family together, and I envied her a little.

Finally I stood alone in the decorously littered dining room. Boris had long since wandered off. I sighed and stretched, suddenly tired. I'd stopped drinking over an hour ago, and a final glass of champagne before tackling the mess seemed like a good idea. I poured it at the sideboard, let the bubbles tickle my nose, took a sip, and kicked off my green sandals; sat and put my feet up in a neighboring chair. Yawning, I stretched again: legs, ankles, toes.

I fell asleep sitting in the chair, fell into an abyss of dreams. All the thoughts I'd held at bay, through the day and through the party itself, turned into dream-images. I was Alice-in-Christmas-Wonderland. I fell down, down, through a dark, echoing vertical tunnel that went on forever; heard my voice calling, hollow and magnified, Kathryn-*ryn-ryn*, where are you-*are you-are you?* I tumbled and called, tumbled and called. At last I stopped falling, hovered upright in a black space, unable to tell up from down. Then a hole opened in the blackness, seemingly at its outer limits, like a door. In the door I saw a small figure in a white dress, her back to me, running away. Her curly mop of hair was unmistakable: Kathryn. Or was it myself?

I ran after her, never fast enough, always tripping, losing

my shoes, stumbling, tearing my stockings. I ran through a fantastically horrible wood, and there was my ex-husband Roger the doctor hanging upside-down from a tree limb. He looked impossibly neat, white coat clinging in defiance of gravity—he smiled and showed his white, perfect teeth. Then the smile grew to a leer, the teeth grew to fangs, and Roger became a snake. A huge snake. Swinging back and forth on its limb, the snake barred my way, singing, "Jingle bells, jingle bells, jingle all the way . . ."

I somehow made it past the snake and resumed my calling: Kathryn, where are you? I saw her, far away; she waved, and I ran after, not knowing if I followed my sister or myself. I ran faster now, my feet left the ground and I ran through the air, but not easily. The air was sticky, viscous, it pulled at me until my clothes hung in shreds. Suddenly the air let me go, deposited me in a breath-killing thump on the banks of a dark body of water. Face-up in the water floated my dead brother in his army uniform. Standing on a nearby rock and oblivious to all but themselves were my mother and father. Their hair was blue, and so were their lips; they were joined at the hip like Siamese twins and twisted their torsos so their hands could meet. They hopped in unison from one foot to the other and clapped their hands together, playing patty-cake. But the song they sang wasn't "Patty-cake, patty-cake, bakers man"; it was "We wish you a Merry Christmas, we wish you a Merry Christmas . . ."

From across the dark water a voice cried, "Sister!"; then the voice screamed, and in a flash of black and white, the small, curly-haired woman hit the water and was swallowed up.

"She's in the water, she's in the water, she'll drown!" I cried, struggling to go after the girl who was either Kathryn or myself. But I couldn't, I couldn't get loose, someone was holding my shoulders, someone was shaking me.

"Laura, wake up! It's a dream. Wake up, Laura!"

I opened my eyes. "Seth." I took off my glasses and, forgetting about the mascara I so seldom wore, rubbed my eyes.

"You fell asleep in the chair," he said. He brushed the hair

113

back from my forehead, and with his thumb smoothed the smudges I'd made under my eyes. He knelt on one knee next to my chair, and I was very glad to see him.

I grinned, feeling both happy and stupid. "It was just a bad dream. I have them all the time. It's nothing important."

"Not important? To me, it is. You deserve better than bad dreams." He pulled my head to his shoulder and hugged me, hard. "Oh, Laura, what am I going to do with you? I find you sobbing in your sleep, and you tell me it's not important!"

"I told you, you didn't have to come back," I said into his shoulder.

"I hope you're glad that I did," Seth murmured, stroking my hair.

I pulled away—this kindness on top of the horrible dream was turning me to mush inside, and I didn't want that. "Yes, I'm glad you did," I said. I stood up, needing to move, do something. I shook out the folds of my skirt and retrieved my green sandals, standing on first one foot and then the other while I put them on.

"Pretty shoes," said Seth, "pretty feet."

"Thank you, about both the shoes and the feet. I have a shoe obsession, I admit, but having pretty feet isn't a plus. I'd rather have been a ballet dancer, in which case by my age my feet wouldn't have been very pretty anymore."

"Um-hum," said Seth, coming to me, "and if you were a dancer you'd be all skin and bones." His glance roved over me, lingered on breasts a little too full for the rest of my body.

I made a playful face and spun away from him, sending my long skirt flying. "Compliments will not get you out of helping with the cleanup, sir! The kitchen is through those doors, and there's a great big trash can just waiting to be filled. You do that, and I'll gather up the glasses."

Seth grumbled, but not seriously. With both of us working we were quickly done, and I thanked him, adding, "If you're hungry I can fix you something. There are lots of things in the freezer."

He shook his head and said what his eyes had been telling

me as we'd worked side by side: "No food. What I want is you."

I looked up at him. From the day we'd gone to Cedar Island, Seth's behavior toward me had been tender but reserved, almost fatherly. Our few kisses had been restrained; our daily conversations had been pleasant, but merely friendly. Now as he backed me firmly against the kitchen counter, he was no father, and he was more than friend.

"I wish you could see your face," he said softly. "You're lovely. Your eyes are enormous, beautiful."

So were his. Seth's eyes blazed, a fire burned in their dark depths. My heart pounded, and I gripped the edge of the counter on both sides of me as hard as I could. His long legs and firm abdomen pressed against me, and his lips, hot, closed on the sensitive hollow behind my ear.

I shivered, holding the counter tight. I felt something from him, with him, that I'd never felt before. Never like this. He called forth from me a yearning that matched the yearning I felt in him—more than desire, deep and painfully sweet. His mouth moved along my throat, stitching the line of my beating pulse with tiny flicks of his tongue. He covered my hands where they rested on the counter with his and leaned into me, giving me his weight. I felt my body yielding, my lips opening, letting out a sound that was half gasp, half moan.

Seth paused to search my face and in that pause I could not breathe, so much did I want his kiss. Slowly, with deliberate skill, his lips closed over mine. I felt our hearts beat together. How incredible, how paradoxical—I felt that Seth and I were both old and new together; every exploration of lips and teeth and tongue was excitingly strange, and yet familiar. The kiss went on, neither of us willing to break it. I lost myself in Seth and knew that he was lost in me.

"You have no idea how often I've wanted to kiss you like that," he said finally. He smiled, I smiled. His hands moved to my waist, and I traced his fine long nose with a fingertip, touched the faint depression in his chin. I was dazed, speechless.

I gave myself a mental shake. It was time to get moving again. Taking one of Seth's hands in mine, I stepped away from the counter and pulled him after me, through the kitchen door. "You kiss great, Mr. Douglass, but the question is, can you build a fire?"

Seth made a wry, one-sided grin. "The truth is I'm probably a better fire-builder than kisser. Where do you want this fire?"

I stopped in the middle of the dining room and dropped his hand. I hadn't thought of that. Of course, it would have to be in my room. The dining room was the inn's only common area, and it was much too large for intimate fireside conversation. "My room," I said. "Do you mind?"

"What do you think?" He chuckled.

"I think you'll have to behave yourself, or I'll sic Boris on you."

"I think I can manage Boris. It's you I'm not so sure about!"

"Oh, really? Wait a minute." We were at the door of the dining room when I stopped. "Let's bring a bottle of champagne. Would you get one from the refrigerator in the kitchen?"

"Gladly. Glasses, too?"

I nodded as Seth with his long legs covered the distance much faster than I could have. Waiting, I admired the Christmas tree while at the same time I felt a stab of sadness. "I think I'll leave the tree lights on tonight, so that the people on their boats in the harbor can see it," I said when Seth returned. "Just for tonight, because it's Christmas Eve."

The doubtful crease appeared between his brows. "I don't like to disagree with you, Laura, but it isn't safe. I'd rather you turned them off."

"I suppose you're right." I sighed, bending down and pulling the plug from the wall socket. Then I flicked off the overhead lights we'd used while cleaning up. "But you know, Seth, sometimes I wish you weren't so cautious."

"That's a strange thing to say."

"No, it isn't." We reached the stairs and started down, me

first since the old stairway was wide enough for only one person. "You really are cautious about a lot of things, you know."

"Well, maybe it's a good idea for *one* of us to be cautious."

Seth's words sank into me, gradually making their impact. On the second-floor landing I snapped around. "Just what do you mean by that, *one* of us?"

"I mean, specifically, that I told you not to trust Nick Westover, and yet you went and spent a whole day on his boat with him. Alone, I presume." His expression was grim, but his voice was irritatingly calm.

Oh, how I wished I were tall enough to look Seth Douglass straight in the eye! "I heard your advice, and I chose not to take it. I can make my own decisions about people! I can take care of myself!"

Almost inaudibly Seth said, "Maybe right now you could use a little help."

In contrast to his calmness I was furious. "I'm doing just fine, thank you very much! Like I said, I can take care of myself!"

"And if I said that I want very much to take care of you . . . ?"

"I would say *no thank you!*" I turned my back on him and went down the remaining flight of stairs as fast as I safely could in my high-heeled sandals—the last thing I needed now was to trip on the stairs and prove myself wrong!

Neither of us spoke again until we reached my room. I preceded Seth through the door. Just over the threshold, he placed a restraining hand on my shoulder. I stopped, but didn't turn around. I knew my cheeks were flaming, that I was more upset than I should be.

"Laura, I'm sorry. I said earlier that I didn't want to disagree with you, but I did it, didn't I? Turn around, look at me." I turned. "I really am sorry," he said again.

"You're sorry we were fighting, but you meant every word you said. Isn't that so?"

To my consternation Seth laughed. "Yes, counselor, that's so. My God, you're feisty! I give up. Truce, okay?"

As angry as I'd been, it was a pleasure to see and hear

Seth's rare laugh. He was usually so serious, and in fact we'd seldom had anything to laugh about. So I smiled for him, willing to let go. "All right, truce. If that was our first fight, I don't think either one of us won."

"Maybe that's as it should be." Now he was serious again.

"Maybe." We stood for a long moment in the doorway, simply looking at each other. What Seth might be thinking, I had no idea; but in my mind I heard again his words, "as it should be." The words recalled the wonderfully strange feeling of belonging together that had come to me in the intimacy of his kiss. Suddenly I wanted him to kiss me again. I reached for him, stretching upward to place my hand on the back of his neck, and he bent to me. Encumbered as he was with champagne bottle in one hand and glasses in the other, he could hardly take the initiative, so I did.

I kissed Seth, gently, curiously. I sensed him holding back, responding but deliberately letting me lead—not an accustomed role for me. I wanted the kiss to deepen, and yet I could not do it. In my marriage, the only relationship I'd known for many years, I'd learned not to be the initiator. And so I withdrew from the kiss. Wordlessly, I took the bottle and glasses, and without looking back, I made a retreat into my dressing room and closed the door.

As I packed ice cubes around the base of the champagne, which I'd put into one of the inn's plastic iceuckets, I asked myself what I really wanted from Seth. This was not a new question, and I got the same old answer: I didn't know. Exasperated, I shook my head and, as I did so, caught a glimpse of myself in the mirror. My cheeks still held a heightened color, and my eyes, which usually looked cloudy, like green mist, were sparkling. Except for the always-unruly hair, this was not the same tired face I'd been seeing in the mirror every day for weeks. In a flash of honesty I admitted to my new-shining face that I would never know what I really wanted from Seth until I opened myself to the closer relationship he offered. What I saw in my own face were the bright colors of promise.

I returned to the room with champagne, glasses, and a

bowl of cashew nuts on a tray. Seth had proved that he was indeed a good maker of fires, and Boris was curled in the center of the hearth.

"No, don't get up," I said to Seth as he started to unfold his long legs. "I'll join you."

We sat on the floor in front of the fire, on the old Oriental rug worn to a soft silkiness. I took off my sandals, Seth took off his jacket and loosened his tie. He popped open the champagne, and with our first sips we wished each other a Merry Christmas. The traditional words hung in the air between us, lingered, and stretched into silence on a fading echo. Minutes passed. I hugged my knees to my chest and stared into the fire, not wanting to think, waiting for a glance, a word, a touch that did not come.

Finally I stole a sidelong glance at Seth. His face in profile was a portrait of still sadness. "Memories?" I asked softly.

He inclined his head, the corner of his mouth turned down bitterly. "I was thinking about my daughter."

I kept the surprise out of my voice. "I didn't know you had children. It must be awful for you not to be with them on Christmas."

"Not children, a child. One daughter, six years old." His voice was cold and flat. He drained his glass and refilled it, all the while not looking my way.

"What's her name? Do you miss her?"

"Her name is Margaret, and no, I don't miss her. Not really. It's a mistake to bring a child into a bad marriage, which is what happened. She was still a baby when I left, and she has a stepfather now. She calls him Daddy. She calls me Seth—I'm only a nice man who brings her a present on her birthday and sends gifts to put under the tree at Christmas."

"I'm sorry." An inadequate response, but the only one I could think of.

Seth shrugged. "I'm sorry, too, but not for Margaret. She has her own family now, complete with a little half-brother. I'm just sorry I've never been a real father." Now he turned his head to look at me. "Sometimes I doubt that I ever will be."

The firelight played upon his face, molding his aristocratic features in a shadowed burnt umber, somber as a Rembrandt. Locked in melancholy.

I gazed at Seth, aware that somehow in the space of a few minutes he had surrounded himself in a moat of isolation. "You are the most complicated man I've ever known," I said. "Every time I think I've made some progress in knowing you, you show me yet another side of who you are. Less than an hour ago you were close to me, as close as anyone has ever been. You were warm, I might even say passionate. But now you've isolated yourself in a kind of self-centered regret, and there's such a huge gulf between us, I don't know that I can cross it even if I want to!"

He arched one black brow and his mouth, which by turns could be expressive or sensual, curved into a bitter smile. "Self-centered regret, eh? That's good. Very accurate, no doubt. You've never spared me from the truth about myself, Laura, that's for sure." He leaned back on one elbow and turned sideways, and with elaborate casualness stretched his legs out behind me. "I should apologize, but I won't. It's the damned Christmas season. In spite of all the best intentions, it can bring out the worst in a person. Besides, this isn't a new side of me. You already know what a cold bastard I can be, it was one of the first things you commented on. Remember?"

I sighed, and rested my head on my tightly-clasped knees. So much for bright promise! Self-pity was one trait I detested, in myself or anyone else. I hated to hear it from Seth. Hated the loss of his warmth, his passion; missed the tender protectiveness he'd shown me so consistently for weeks on end. From the corner of my eye I looked at him again and saw a lounging lord, sardonically smiling at his ease. And then I understood: the coldness and all of that was a pose, behind which he hid his hurt. The distance, the isolation, was for self-protection. Seth had given of himself to me for weeks, and now it was my turn to give to him. How to reach him I had no idea; I could only try.

I let go of my knees and turned toward him. "I know how it feels to want a child," I ventured.

A flicker of pain in the dark eyes. Again, the bitter curve of lip. "I'm not fit to be a father."

I moved closer, imploring. "Seth, I don't like to hear you talk like that. It's just self-pity—heavy, heavy self-pity."

He laughed, but without mirth. "No, Laura. Not self-pity, only the truth. Oh, I've tried to change. Even before I met you, and especially since. But perhaps I can't do it, no matter how much I want to. And I do want to, because *I want you!*"

Suddenly fierce in the firelight, Seth grasped my arms and pulled me down beside him. He kissed me with brutal strength, and yet I responded. His passion had returned, and with it a desperate longing which I recognized even through the roughness of his mouth and his hands which bound my arms in a bruising grasp. I knew that desperation, I felt it, too. I welcomed his rough embrace with an abandon I'd never before known; he could not devour me for I devoured him in return. He loosed his grip, only for my arms to lock around him and pull him closer, my mouth never leaving his. Our lips parted at last for lack of breath, and we lay panting in each other's arms.

Seth pushed himself up into a sitting position, pulled off his already-loosened tie, and unbuttoned his shirt halfway. We had generated heat of our own that was at least equal to that of the fire, and I wished I could find relief so easily. My sweater was damp from the inside out. Seth looked down at me.

"Unbelievable!" he said in a husky voice.

"That's hardly flattering!"

Seth smiled, his most tender smile, and traced my lips with a gentle finger. His eyes glistened; they seemed to be glazed with tears. "Oh, little one, you have hidden depths! You're not as fragile as I thought." He turned his head and wiped his eyes on his sleeve.

I sat up, dazed, unsure what was happening. I had never behaved quite that way before, and if he had gone further I was sure I would have met him equally, every step of the way. Even now, if he were to touch me again . . .

I had no time to wonder why and how he had reached into

me and called forth a response that I had not known was there for any man. Seth was not one who would shed tears easily, and he was wiping his eyes again. He cleared his throat and began to speak, still turned away from me.

"There are dark places in my life, Laura. Things I can't forget, that come back to haunt me. No matter what I do or how much I think I've changed, the darkness is still there."

I crept close behind him on my knees and rested my cheek on his shoulder. "Tell me."

He drew a breath so deep his body shuddered. "I'd hoped I would never have to tell you this. The truth is that I'm responsible for the death of three people, and the injury of over a hundred."

"What?" I moved around him and sat back on my heels where I could see his face. Surely not the face of a murderer! "How, what do you mean?"

"It was seven years ago. One of my buildings collapsed, a six-story office building in Rhode Island. Technically it wasn't my fault, but ethically it was. I'd hired a dishonest contractor. If I'd been in less of a hurry, gotten to know the community better, I'd have heard about his reputation. But I was in a hurry to get on to the next town, the next project, and I didn't know he was substituting substandard materials. And pocketing the money he saved. I was equally greedy, that's why I didn't stay behind to watch him more closely. The only difference between us was that I kept my greed within the bounds of the law. Nevertheless, that contractor put the building up, and it collapsed. And people died!" Seth's face grew lines of guilt, his eyes hollowed, he did look haunted.

"It wasn't your fault!" I cried. "There are building inspectors, it's their job to catch things like that!"

"Yeah. So I told myself at the time. I kept right on, driven to make more money. I couldn't bring myself to do any more office buildings, but so what? I built shopping centers, motels, condos. But you see, I did feel responsible. My life was all out of whack. I'd married the wrong woman for the wrong reasons, fathered a child I could never be a decent father to . . ." His eyes glistened again with tears. "Do you hear what I'm telling you, Laura? I made a lot of money. Period. I gave some of it to my parents because they never had much, and to my sister to help her set up a small business, but otherwise I never did a decent thing in my life until I ended the marriage and came here. I haven't been a good man, much less a good husband or father. It's too late. I'm a fool to think I could change now. Be what I wasn't before."

Boris, who had observed all these emotional goings-on from the warm safety of the hearth, walked in his ponderously dainty way over to Seth and settled against his thigh, and began to purr loudly.

I smiled. "You can't be all that bad. Boris approves of you, and he's very picky!"

Seth scratched Boris behind the ears and looked at me with eyes that were liquid, dark brown pools. The smallest of smiles touched his lips, and was gone. "Unfortunately, I'm not in love with Boris," he said.

My heart missed a beat. And you are with me, I thought. And I may love you, too, or my heart wouldn't do that.

"Seth." I knelt up to him and took his face in my hands. I kissed his eyes, as once he had kissed mine. I kissed his lips lightly and tenderly, as if he were my child. I held his head to my breast and stroked his silver hair, which was thick and wiry under my fingers. I didn't know what to say, I only knew that I must talk and my words must somehow ease his pain. I made my voice soothing, to match my stroking hands.

"Everyone, all of life," I said, "has a dark side. Believe me, I've been seeing a lot of it lately. But the good, the light is there, too. You have to keep looking for the light, and find it, and live in the light—that's all. Sometimes it isn't easy to do. You have to want it so much that you never give up, you keep on trying no matter how often you feel lost in dark twistings and turnings along the way. People do change, if they want to change. Don't give up on yourself, Seth! And don't give up on me, either. Please?"

He raised his head and moved away a couple of feet. I settled back, sitting with my legs tucked in a half-lotus under my long skirt. Boris, whom I had dislodged from his place next to Seth, walked into my lap, turned around once and changed his mind. We were apparently not stable enough company, and since the fire was dying down, Boris went to the bed at the far end of the room.

Seth saw me glance at the fireplace, and got up to put another log on the fire. Still he'd said nothing. He returned to the place he'd been sitting and sat down again, knees and elbows jutting out. Dark hair, as black as his eyebrows, curled in the opening of his half-unbuttoned shirt. When finally he did speak, it was to ask a question that surprised me with its seeming irrelevance.

"How old are you, Laura?"

"I'm thirty-three. How old are you? And what difference does it make?"

"I'm forty-two. Surely you must know why it's taking me so long to know what to say to you, where to go from here."

"Well, no, actually I don't. And I certainly don't know what bearing my age has on anything we've talked about!"

Seth rubbed the back of his neck, something he habitually did to ease tension. "You have such courage. You've been through so much, and you're almost ten years younger than I am. Yet you can say what you did about looking for the good, living in the light. I haven't had one of my black moods like this for a long time. It came on me without warning when I was making the fire, and just swallowed me up. I'd really thought I was over them forever. Now that I know I'm not, well, it changes things. I think perhaps it would be best if I just leave, take myself out of your life. You're young, you should marry again, have children—"

I interrupted him. "Seth Douglass, you're not thinking straight. You're obviously still in your black mood or whatever you call it. You're in no frame of mind to make a major decision."

Now he did smile. "You're right about one thing: leaving you would be a major decision. I think you know I'm in love with you."

I caught my breath, looked away, and then with difficulty

looked back at him. This was a very serious conversation; it might even prove to be our last conversation. Seth deserved both eye contact and honesty. "Yes, I do know that."

"And you don't love me, not yet. Though with what happened a few minutes ago, I might have hopes."

"I don't know for sure how I feel about anyone or anything right now. I could say that I love you tonight, and tomorrow I might regret having said it. My life is in a terrible mess, and I think it may be for months more. At least until I reach some kind of closure about Kathryn." I searched his face, wanting not to hurt him, wanting him to understand. "But in all truth, Seth, something happened to me with you tonight, something I don't entirely understand. I felt something with you that I've never felt with anyone before."

"Yes. I felt it, too. Even though I've known for weeks that you affect me in ways no other woman has done, it was still powerful."

As Seth spoke, I relived that feeling, the strange and wonderful feeling that we belonged together, were right together in a way beyond understanding. Unconsciously I reached for him, and he took my hand across the space which separated us.

"That's why," he said softly, "I'm thinking perhaps I should leave now, before anything else happens. And not see you again."

I gulped. My heart was racing. "Because we may have something very special, you think you should *leave?* That's insane!"

Our hands were locked together, our eyes, too. Seth asked, "You don't want me to leave?"

"No! Of course I don't."

"Then I have to warn you, if I stay, I'm going to want to have it all—oh, don't misunderstand—not tonight, but eventually. I want to marry you, Laura. I want you to have my children—with you, I'd risk fatherhood again."

The fire became impossibly bright. Little points of light, like sparks, like myriad fireflies, filled the air. Spun in a halo around Seth's head. Our joined hands were a lifeline, pulsing and coursing with a golden current of magical energy. I burned in the fire and the light with a terrible joy. I clung to Seth's hand, waiting for the air to clear, waiting for the light to subdue itself to normal, waiting until I could speak.

I never knew how long these episodes lasted, I'd always been alone before when they happened. Seth was looking at me intently when my vision cleared. I found my voice, and it was steady. "If you feel you know me well enough to say what you just said, then you know I can't possibly say anything in return except that you don't know me well enough yet to say such things. No matter how circular that sounds!"

Seth laughed, a full, rich, joyous sound, and he stood up and pulled me to my feet in one motion. "You are so priceless! The best part is that you don't even realize how priceless you are!" He hugged me, a wonderful hug, warm and friendly and loving.

I stood on tiptoe and put my arms around his neck. "Let's settle one thing. Two things. One: I won't say I'll marry you, because it's too soon to even think such things. Two: you aren't leaving me. And I've thought of a third: I don't want to hear any more of this stuff about what an awful person you are. All right?"

"All right, I agree. Seal it with a kiss."

He kissed me and it happened again, the sparks and the light, and the feeling of something strange and wonderful.

"I'm exhausted," I said when he released me.

"So am I. It must be very late. Merry Christmas, Laura."

"Merry Christmas, Seth. Don't forget you're having dinner here with me and Jonathan, two o'clock."

"I won't forget. That sounds like you're kicking me out now." Seth cast a longing glance at the big bed, where Boris lay possessively curled in the middle.

"Um-hm. I'm not ready for that"—I inclined my head in the direction of the bed—"yet."

"Oh, but I could easily make you ready," said Seth seductively. He moved his hands from my back to under my arms, the heels of his palms pressing persuasively where my breasts began to swell out from my rib cage.

I shivered, and acknowledged, "You probably could, but you won't because you're a gentleman and I'm asking you to say good night. *Now.*"

"Good night now," said Seth.

⬛⬛⬛ 10 ⬛⬛⬛

Have you heard the story of the wreck of the *Crissie Wright,* Seth?" asked Jonathan. "I doubt Laura has."

We were walking off our Christmas dinner, a traditional turkey feast I'd arranged through a catering service. Replete and content, I thought for once that the excellence of the food had justified the cost of having it prepared by someone else. Walking between the two men, the one tall and dark, the other rounded and fair, I felt a moment of pure happiness. Then Jonathan, an unlikely Cassandra, began to tell his tale. On his words, a feeling of cold-coming doom slanted into my soul like shafts of winter light.

The *Crissie Wright's* tragedy occurred on January 11, 1886, just over a hundred years ago, Jonathan said. The ship was a three-masted schooner bound for New York when her captain tried to take her into Cape Lookout Bight to shelter from an approaching storm. A sudden shift and quickening of the wind drove the ship onto the reef opposite Shackleford Banks and opened a great hole in her side. There were no life-saving stations on the Outer Banks then; the practice was for the Banker fishermen to go out in their dories. But when the *Crissie Wright* foundered, the high seas and the gales repeatedly threw the small boats of the rescuers back on the shore. There was no choice but to wait for the storm to subside. The Bankers built a bonfire on the beach to let the crew of the *Crissie Wright* know they kept vigil, and to give them hope.

In the meantime the seven men aboard the ship were in danger of being washed overboard, and they couldn't go below because the ship was taking on water faster than her pumps could work. So the captain ordered the men to lash themselves to the foremast, and he did the same.

That night, as the storm continued and the men hung lashed to the mast, the temperature dropped to eight degrees Fahrenheit. The trapped sailors and their captain slowly froze to death. Red dawn came, the gale still blew, and the horrified villagers saw the captain drop frozen from the mast into the raging sea. Two more of his crew followed him. The remaining four freed themselves, and when at last the storm abated and rescuers reached the ship, the four were found covered by sails they had wrapped around themselves. Three were dead, frozen, and the fourth who was on the bottom and protected by the bodies of his companions, was barely alive. This fourth man, the ship's cook, was thawed out and kept his life, but his mind was gone. He died insane a year later. The three sailors were buried together in Beaufort's Old Burying Ground.

Like a horrified watcher of long ago, I saw in my mind those doomed men, lashed to the mast of their ship in a frozen crucifixion, a silhouette of black, silent pain against the red sky. My own blood ran cold as I gazed across the now-peaceful waters of Taylors Creek to the green-wooded Shackleford Banks, where Jonathan said at very low tide the broken-ribbed hull of the *Crissie Wright* could still be seen protruding from the sand. I said nothing, too chilled for words, and the sense of doom that seeped into me became personal, it insinuated itself into sinew and bone and brain.

That night as I lay waiting for sleep, with heavy, bitter irony I thanked God for the gifts I had received on Christmas Eve and Christmas Day: new friends, the knowledge of

Seth's love, and a certainty that the tale of the *Crissie Wright* was a harbinger of evil about to enter my life.

The inn was half-full of guests for the week between Christmas and the New Year. Guests, newspapers, and television were all full of apprehension over the condition of the sea. At midweek we learned a new word, *syzygy*. An unpronounceable astrological term, it meant the conjunction of two heavenly bodies; but in this case, a sort of grand syzygy, sun and moon and earth would all three be in perfect alignment on New Year's Day. Every day now, under the relentlessly increasing pressures of three-fold gravity, the seas rose higher. People who sailed, whether for pleasure or for their livelihood, could talk of nothing else. Our inn guests congratulated one another on having no beachfront property to worry about, and grumbled about treacherous tides that forced them to confine their sailing to short, risky trips. Their complaints had an exhilarated edge—weekend adventurers bravely facing the forces of nature. Syzygy brought the high seas close to home, literally.

I was glad they were enjoying themselves, and wished I could do the same. But I could not. Just as every high tide raised the waters of the harbor higher, so every day my sense of coming doom, of approaching evil increased. I tried to explain it away and very nearly succeeded. I developed an elaborate rationalization about the heightened gravity's action on my body and brain which were, after all, composed mostly of water. I told myself that I merely missed Seth, who had gone to visit his daughter and then his parents, and would return on New Year's Eve. I admitted I felt guilt over excluding Nick from my Christmas party, plus some concern over what his reaction might be if he learned he'd been left out. Surely, I said to myself, the combination of all these things was enough to account for my apprehension! But if naming these minor demons rendered them harmless, there was a greater demon which remained nameless. I sensed this unnamed demon could and would harm me—soon.

When a concrete problem of considerable proportions

occurred at the end of the week, I almost welcomed it. At least it required action; I could *do* something to deal with it. Someone broke into the garage behind the inn, which had been converted into a laundry and storeroom, and went on a destructive rampage. The damage was to Evelyn's domain, and it was she who reported it to me, early on Friday morning.

"You best come see for yourself, Laura," she said. She was as outwardly calm as ever, but her eyes were hard with anger. She didn't even try to describe what had happened, and when I saw I understood why. The violence that had been done was indescribable. Sheets and towels and bedspreads had been slashed and strewn everywhere, like piles of tangled entrails; foam pillows shredded and scattered about like pulpy bits of brain. Boxes of detergent had been gouged open, and their grainy contents spilled from the wounds.

I was shocked, I felt personally violated. My mouth went dry. I looked at Evelyn, realizing that if I felt raped, she must feel even more so. I admired her reserve more than ever.

"This is insane!" I said.

She nodded. "I never seen the likes of such. Now come in the storeroom."

Through a connecting door was the storeroom, filled floor to ceiling with shelves. Under Evelyn's care, the storeroom was always a paragon of neatness, its inventory recorded and kept in perfect order. Now everything had been pulled from the shelves and thrown to the floor in a jumble. As if he, or they, had grown short of time, the supplies which were mostly paper products had not been slashed, as in the laundry. They had been smashed, crushed, as with a huge hammer. Glass bottles of all-purpose cleaner were shattered, and their stringent odor fouled the air. I pictured a half-crazed hulk, pounding and pounding. Someone mentally deficient, surely; no sane person would do such damage.

I let out a long, ragged sigh and ran my hand through my hair, facing the inevitable. "We'll have to call the police. Then I'll help you clean this up."

Evelyn's eyes clouded. "I 'spose you do have to tell them. I feel like this is my fault, but I can't think who'd want to get at me this way!"

"Oh, Evelyn." With dismay I saw her shoulders droop. Evelyn carried her height with dignity, unbent by years of labor some would call menial, and I respected her for it. I couldn't bear to see her slump in defeat. I took her arm and led her firmly from the storeroom, through the vandalized laundry, and didn't stop to speak until we were outside and I had closed the door behind us. "I can understand how you must feel, I know the laundry and storeroom are your responsibility. But I don't hold you to blame, not for a minute. You mustn't blame yourself, either. If anything, it's my fault."

Evelyn's mouth fell open. "I don't see how it could be your fault, Laura! You haven't done anything but good ever since you came here, everybody knows that."

She said it so matter-of-factly, and she was such an honest person. I felt a warm surge of gratitude that was welcome in all this mess. "I could have prevented it, that's why. I realized several days ago that the inn should have an alarm system, but I haven't done anything about it yet. If I'd acted right away, none of this would have happened. Now, why don't you tell Jonathan, and I'll go call the police. I'd like to get them in and out of here before Zelda arrives, if that's possible."

I thought of the prowler on the porch, an episode I'd told to no one and had succeeded in putting out of my mind. The same person? Perhaps. But even before the police arrived in the person of the ubiquitous and slow-witted Sergeant Sanders, I knew I would continue to keep the prowler to myself. I found the local police difficult enough without having to admit my reluctance to call them when I should have.

Sergeant Sanders was perhaps not as slow-witted as I'd thought. He was quick enough to leap to certain conclusions. He asked me, "What connection do you think this destroyed property has with your sister's disappearance, Miss Brannan?"

"Why . . . why . . ." I stammered, taken aback, "none! She's been gone for weeks now."

"You better say what you mean, Sergeant," Jonathan intervened.

"Well, I mean we got two things here that's mighty unusual for these parts. Her sister vanishes, somebody tears her property all to pieces. Looks to me like there ought to be a connection. You sure there ain't something you didn't tell us? Any of you?" His sweeping glance took in Evelyn, and Zelda, who had arrived in the midst of his questioning. We were all crowded uncomfortably into the office.

I swallowed hard and suddenly wished that Seth were here. His had been the significant omission—he had never told the police about the Stone House and his appointment with Kathryn there, nor had I. Nor would I do so now; and to mention the midnight prowler still felt out of the question. Around the room, everyone shook their heads.

Sergeant Sanders said, "Well, now, if anybody thinks of anything . . ." He looked at me with narrowed, unsympathetic eyes. "I'd say, Miss Brannan, that somebody is out to get you, one way or 'nother."

Evelyn and Jonathan tensed, and I spoke up for myself before they could come to my defense. "That's ridiculous. This is just vandalism. Senseless violence for no reason. Surely even Beaufort isn't immune to vandalism!"

The sergeant scratched his closely cropped scalp with the eraser end of the pencil with which he took notes. "Not at this time of the year, we ain't got vandals. Vandals are pesky kids with not enough to do in the summertime. Push over the gravestones in the Old Burying Ground, splatter paint on buildings, stuff like that. No, what you got out yonder weren't done by no pesky kid vandals."

I saw his point, and kept silent. Jonathan, however, did not. He slouched against the windowsill and beamed deceptively at the policeman. Perhaps only I could detect the undercurrent of sarcasm in what he said.

"Let's run that by one more time, Sergeant. I'm a little slow. You say you think whoever's responsible for the violence outside, whatever person slashed up the sheets and all that, that same person, uh, made off with Kathryn Trelawney?"

"Well, now, I didn't 'zacly say that. Alls I said was, maybe there's some connection. What d'you think, Mr. Harcourt?"

Jonathan shoved his hands into his pockets and cocked his head to one side. "I thought you police had closed the book on Mrs. Trelawney. Decided she left here of her own accord."

"That's what the chief thinks, but it's not closed, no, sir. We just run out of places to look is all. If nobody's got anything else to say, I reckon I'll go out and poke around awhile in that storage building. I suggest you go ahead and look into those alarms you said you was going to get, Miss Brannan."

I forced a little laugh. "There's no hurry now, is there? It will be like locking the barn door after the horse has run off!"

The policeman tugged his cap down on his head by its visor. "No, ma'am. I got the feeling you better keep this barn door locked up, horse or no horse. If you take my meaning." He hitched up his belt and moved out the door.

I shuddered and said under my breath, "Maybe the gravity is getting to him, too."

"What?" asked Jonathan.

Evelyn got up hurriedly from her chair. "I'm going after the policeman and make him tell me when I can start cleaning up."

I responded to both of them. "Okay, Evelyn. I didn't say anything, Jonathan. I was just thinking out loud, that's all. You go and get some sleep."

"Right." With a sympathetic pat to my shoulder he left, and I opened the desk drawer and pulled out the phone book. I'd call the chamber of commerce for advice about security systems, I decided. I thumbed through the pages to the Cs when I realized Zelda hadn't moved from her place just inside the door. I looked up at her. "Did you want something, Zelda?"

"I was wondering if you'd listen for the telephone—I'd

like to go out and see what happened, if that's all right with you." Her face was avidly alight.

"Sure. Go ahead." I waved her away, disgusted by the woman's morbid curiosity. Why did I keep forgetting to question Seth more closely about her? Because it's not Zelda's fault that I'm paranoid, I thought, and getting more so by the day.

Facing up to things can quickly become a habit which makes self-deception difficult, if not impossible; including, unfortunately, those petty delusions we use to keep ourselves from seeing the more uncomfortable truths. The uncomfortable truth was that I was not paranoid. If I had still been in Ohio, in my former life, I could have half-jokingly said I was paranoid. But not here. Here, where I was teaching myself to face up to things, to conquer my fears by going into and through them, I had to admit the truth: I was not paranoid. Rather, I was afraid of a very real Unknown. Just because I didn't know the nature of this Unknown didn't mean it was any less real. Until I knew what it was, or who it was, I couldn't safely trust anyone. Maybe not even Jonathan. Certainly not Zelda. I didn't even like the woman—how the heck was I going to trust her?

And Seth? What *was* the relationship between him and Zelda? I remembered, not for the first time, the two of them leaving on Christmas Eve, his arm around her. Surely that persistent remembrance had more than a little to do with why I hadn't asked him about her. I didn't ask him because someplace deep down inside I was afraid I wouldn't believe his answer . . . no matter what it was.

My growing feelings for Seth warred against my need for self-protection. Reluctantly I admitted I had no real reason to trust Seth, either; moreover, I had several reasons *not* to trust him. Hiring Zelda on his word alone had probably been a big mistake.

I shook my head, then took off my glasses and for a moment rested my face wearily in my hands. The awfulness of the truth I had just faced bore down on me with a heavy weight. How terrible to be unable to trust! How awful to want to allow myself to love Seth and be unable to do it, unable even to rely on his word! Slowly I brought myself again under control. This situation wouldn't last forever. In the meantime I had work to do. There was a mess in the converted garage that needed cleaning up; there was an inn to keep, and it needed an alarm system so that no more messes would happen. I turned my attention back to the phone book, glad to have a focus for my attention.

The air was heavy and ominously still. Midnight: the Old Year died, the New was born. I witnessed the transition, intentionally alone.

Shortly before dawn the storm began. Rain came first, and awakened me; it fell relentlessly, the skies dropping their wet burden into the already swollen sea. Day brought gray light and high winds. I got up and dressed quickly in a favorite sweatsuit, superbly soft, its once-bright violet color faded to a pale, shy lavender. With Boris underfoot I climbed to the highest point in the house, the attic over the third-floor dining room. It was cramped, even I could not stand up straight under the exposed rafters, but the one tiny window in the gable-end gave a view as good as the observation deck on the roof of the Mariners' Museum. I'd discovered this aerie a few weeks ago and equipped it with a cushion to kneel or sit on, and a pair of field glasses.

I didn't need the glasses now to show me that what everyone had most feared was now happening: On this New Year's Day 1987, when the sun, moon, and earth in alignment had pulled the ocean to some eight feet higher than normal, a storm now added the final, overpowering blow. Nature, already out of balance, was now completely overbalanced. The ships at anchor in the harbor, and those tied to the docks, rode hard but safe on waters so high that every gust of wind pushed waves from Taylors Creek over Front Street. The rain fell in sheets, and it hit the roof at my head and the window glass in front of my face with the force of thousands of tiny hammers. I raised the field glasses and focused them toward Beaufort Inlet.

My eyes adjusted faster than my brain could make meaning out of the heaving grayness. Slowly I realized how great were the waves, how dark in the trough, yet thin, whitish at the crest; driven by the gale they formed themselves ever higher, monstrously changing shape. Old Fort Macon at the northern end of Bogue Banks was shrouded in rain-veils and assaulted round its base by crashing waves, like some North Sea sentinel.

The storm was awesome. I watched it for a long time, until the sea became anthropomorphic. Great Mother, older than forever, seat of all life, she blesses and curses, gives and takes away. I rejoiced in her power, I feared her wrath, I trembled to know her secrets.

Secrets. Where did the dolphins go, how did they protect themselves when storms such as this shook their watery home?

The rain let go around midday, and the sky lightened perceptibly. The wind backed off gradually throughout the afternoon. Seth, whom I had refused to see the night before, showed up in a borrowed Wagoneer, its high under-carriage and four-wheel drive a protection against flooding. He wanted to take me with him, to see what changes the storm had wrought. I agreed, and we drove out into a gray, wet world. It was low tide. Seth explained that the evening's high tide yet to come would again be many feet above normal. I rode beside him in a sort of daze. It seemed to me that there was not as much damage as everyone had feared, not as much as I would have expected. I said so to Seth, and he agreed that there had been minimal damage to property here. How it might be elsewhere along the coast, no one had yet said. Seth went on about how significant storms such as this one shape the coastline, opening and closing inlets, shaping the sand dunes. Such movement, he said, preserves and rebuilds the beaches.

I was only half-listening, preoccupied with a feeling that had begun as soon as we were in sight of the ocean—I felt hushed, breathless, as if I were waiting for something. For the advent of that Unknown? Perhaps. In the meantime I said my um-hms at the appropriate places, and Seth talked of deep waters building up in the sounds and flooding the mainland. He said this would do more damage than had been done on the beaches, and that roads such as the one we drove on could be overwashed at the next high tide. I noted that already a good deal of debris had washed up near the road—piles of red-brown seaweed, odd bits and pieces of wood, bottles whole and broken, old tires, mounds of shattered shells. I found this tour depressing. I was not sorry when the tide turned and Seth said we must go back to the inn.

"What's wrong with you today, Laura?" Seth asked. "Does it have anything to do with your not wanting to see me last night? I'd hoped to watch the New Year come in with you."

I looked at him then, saw a crease of worry on his brow, and while I tried to frame my answer he spoke again.

"I hope you didn't have second thoughts about me, about *us,* while I was away."

I could respond to that more easily than I could find words to explain my uneasy mood. I managed a smile. "No, I haven't had second thoughts. I'm sorry, I didn't even ask about your trip. Did you enjoy seeing your parents, and your little girl?"

"Yes and no. Seeing Margaret is always difficult, and being with my mother and father isn't much better."

"Well, I expect you'd feel worse if you didn't go."

"Yeah, I do—I've tried staying away, and it is worse. You know, you didn't answer my question. What's wrong?"

"N-nothing. Nothing I can identify. Oh, we did have some trouble at the inn a couple of days ago, but that's not what's bothering me. That's over and done with. There's something about this storm, something . . . something in the atmosphere. Can't you feel it?"

The black brows drew together. "I feel kind of keyed-up, I guess. Sort of excited. It's not an uncomfortable feeling, and not what I sense in you."

"I can't explain it, Seth. I'm preoccupied. I know I'm not very good company right now. Whatever is bothering me will come to a head eventually, and then I'll be fine. We'll be back at the inn in a couple of minutes, and if you don't mind, I won't ask you in. I think I need to be alone."

"I mind, but I do have to return this car. And the tide's coming in. It's probably better for me to go on."

So we parted. I went to my attic aerie and watched until dark. Though no longer stormy, the sea was abnormal, swollen, restless.

The high tide came after nightfall. I saw nothing of it, only heard the wind against the windows. I tried to drown my apprehensions in a novel and told myself I had nothing to fear, the alarm system had been installed on Saturday by a man who grumbled but worked all day to do it. I read for hours, while the sun and moon moved away from their perfect alignment with earth, while the ocean waters rose one last time to an unprecedented high and then retreated, leaving behind on the beaches all manner of matter—lost, abandoned, broken, dead.

The call came at 3:00 P.M. on January second. The caller was a state policeman, I didn't retain his name. He said he had to tell me that a body had washed up on Hammock's Beach, on state park lands, apparently during the New Year's Day storm. It was the body of a female the same height as my missing sister. It was tightly wrapped in sail canvas, secured and weighted with chains. There was no need for me to come to Hammock's Beach, as visual identification was not possible.

I asked where Hammock's Beach was, and he replied just out from Swansboro. I asked why visual identification was not possible, and he said much decomposition had taken place; he said the face was gone.

I registered that, the face gone, and a roaring began in my ears, and through the roar I heard: Full fathom five thy *sister* lies, of her bones are coral made; those are pearls that were her eyes . . . were her eyes . . . were her eyes . . .

I had to ask the man to repeat what he'd said about the state medical examiner, and then I said, "I understand. Thank you."

I hung up the phone and simply sat at the desk in the

office. I felt curiously still, clear of mind, without emotion. I didn't doubt the body was Kathryn's. The Unknown had made itself known, and its name was Murder.

I continued to sit, thinking that the calm I felt was the eye in the center of the storm, in the center of the tempest. At some time I would have to leave this eye and go through the other side, because where there was murder, there was also a murderer.

Eventually I picked up the telephone and called Seth. I wasn't sure he'd be there; I'd never called him at work before. I didn't even know where his office was, only that it was in Morehead City. I was surprised when he answered the ring himself.

"Hi, Seth," I said, "this is Laura."

"A pleasant surprise!"

"Unexpected, yes. I want to ask a favor of you. At such short notice it's probably a big favor. Something has come up, and it's really very important."

"You know I'll always do what I can for you, Laura. What's this big favor?"

"I want you to show me the Stone House, and I want to go now, as soon as possible. Can you do that?"

He hesitated. "I suppose I could leave now. But why? What's happened?"

"I'll tell you when we get there. And Seth, I prefer to drive. If you could come to the inn, we'll go on from here in my car."

Again the hesitation. "Well, all right. Give me twenty minutes."

"Thank you. I'll be waiting." I replaced the telephone receiver. The clock on the desk read three forty-five. I went out of the office and stopped at the reception desk. "Zelda, something has come up and I have to go out. It's kind of an emergency. Please locate Jonathan and tell him he'll have to take the desk if I'm not back by time for you to go home."

Zelda's pointy features sharpened with curiosity. "Oh, I'll stay until you get back! I don't mind, really I don't! An emergency? Is there anything else I can do?"

I didn't welcome Zelda's offer to stay, but I couldn't

readily think of a kind way to tell her that I'd rather see Jonathan's face than hers waiting for me when I returned from what was likely to be an ordeal. So I merely said, "Thank you. No, there's nothing else. This is personal, and I have to handle it myself."

I turned quickly away and walked the long corridor to my room. I still felt that icy calm. Odd, but I was grateful for it. In my room I changed from shoes to high leather boots, put on my winter coat, a classic camel hair, and for warmth and courage wound my bright green cashmere scarf around my neck.

"Wish me luck, big guy," I said to Boris. I picked him up and rubbed my cheek against his soft fur, then put him down again. He eyed me lazily and didn't follow me.

I was waiting by my Subaru, keys in hand, when Seth drove into the parking area. He was casually dressed for the cold, in a suede jacket with sheepskin lining.

"I must say this seems a little mysterious," he said as he left his car and came to mine. "You're sure you want to drive?"

"I'm sure." I opened my own car door before he could do it, and slipped behind the wheel. I called out to him, "It's not locked," and when he got in beside me I said, "I can learn the way much faster if I drive it myself. I need you to give directions." That was not the only reason I wanted my car, but the other I wouldn't tell Seth.

"Okay. Just take seventy toward the coast, and I'll tell you where to turn off."

We drove in silence. I could feel Seth's occasional glances, but I had no desire to talk. I knew what I was going to do, the plan had come to me all in one piece, as if it had been there in my mind all along waiting for this moment. Seth's reaction would be all-important; I hadn't even any hopes, one way or another. And I had my own car in case I needed it, in case I needed to get away.

"Take the next turn on the right," Seth warned. "It's not marked, but it's just this side of a big curve in the road—if you go into the curve you'll know you've gone too far and can turn back."

I made the correct turn, on the lookout for landmarks that might help me remember where it was, but there were none. It was just a narrow, unmarked blacktop road hemmed in on both sides by pine trees and other evergreens whose names I didn't know. Some day I'd have to learn the names of these things, but not now. The growth was thick and let in little light from the clouded late-afternoon sky.

"Now, watch carefully off to your right. You'll see a gravel road—it's little more than a track because it's so seldom used. There's a Private Road sign next to it, but you can't see the sign until you're right up on it."

I strained my eyes through the gloom. "Is that it?"

"Yeah. That's right, go slowly. It's not a smooth ride at the best of times, and who knows what yesterday's storm will have done to it. Fortunately, the Stone House is on high ground. It won't be flooded, except from the rain."

"Um-hm," I said. I had to concentrate on my driving. The gravel track was bumpy and in some places rutted, the ruts filled with water. The trees were not so tall here but grew closer together, their tops flattened and interwoven from resistance to the wind which blew constantly in from the sea. I thought this private road must seem interminable only because it was unfamiliar; must seem threatening only because the trees formed a dark, living wall. I switched on the low beams of my headlights. Once I knew what lay at the end of this road, I'd surely feel less as if I were being swallowed up, never to return.

I broke my silence. "How long is this gravel road?"

"About a mile and a half. We'll be out of these woods soon. You want to tell me yet what this is all about?"

"Not yet. Soon."

It was growing lighter ahead, a damp gray light opening out, and suddenly we emerged from the trees onto a sloping, open area, more field than lawn.

"Stop the car—the chain is up," said Seth, in the same moment that I saw the pillars and the chain stretched between them.

"I guess we'll have to walk from here," I said. The two pillars of roughly piled stone and the chain across them seemed a ridiculous deterrent. There was no wall. Anyone who wanted to pass could simply drive on the grass, around the pillars.

Seth fumbled in his pocket. "No, we don't have to walk. I brought the keys." He caught my sharp look and responded to it. "Kathryn gave me a set of keys to use that day. You remember, I was to meet her out here. She gave me the keys so I could do a thorough inspection, and then she was going to join me."

And you just happened to keep the keys, I thought, while he was saying, "I'll just get out and open the padlock and let down the chain. Be right back."

I hung grimly onto the steering wheel. The gloomy road had opened cracks in my calm.

Seth got back into the car. "You didn't know I had keys? You didn't bring yours with you?"

"No," I said, shaking my head. "I don't have keys. Ah, look! There it is!"

The Stone House was aptly named. From this distance it looked like an ancient Scottish castle, thrown up by some embattled, near-penniless laird. It was crudely but stoutly built of rough stones. The round tower looked to be about thirty feet high; its walls were irregularly pierced with narrow windows. It was flat on top, no battlements or crenelations. As I drove closer, the sun broke through the clouds behind us and touched the Stone House with a sudden warmth of light.

I drew in a quick, surprised breath. "Why, it's almost lovely! Charming!" I glanced at Seth. He had raised an eyebrow and his mouth quirked with amusement.

"I suppose the Stone House has a certain charm. As I think I told you once, no one knows how old the central tower is. It was built of ballast stone. When ships came here from England, or earlier, Spain, they arrived loaded with stones which they then discarded, assuming their ships would be carrying treasure from the New World on their return trip. The builders of this tower seem to have made some attempt to be selective—if you look closely you'll see that most of the stones are light brown in color. Probably rock of that color was common where they came from; it's less common here. At any rate, whoever built the tower chose all light brown stone for it. It's fairly attractive; in sunlight it can take on a golden hue. But when the wings were added years or centuries later the builders weren't so careful. Perhaps the wings aren't even all ballast stones, although from their size they probably are, but there's a lot of our local gray rock mixed in with the brown in the wings."

I had stopped the car where the drive ended abruptly, awkwardly without a turnaround, about twenty feet short of the house. There was no planned parking area that I could see, and no walkway. If there had been once, it was now overgrown with wiry winter-brown grass. There had never been much time in my life for travel, the only castles I'd seen were in books, but even up close the Stone House still looked like a small, eccentric old castle to me. Its stones had not been carved or polished or shaped in any way; they were set in mortar in a manner resembling a fieldstone wall.

I got out of the car, and immediately cold, damp wind bit into me. I shivered, and wrapped my scarf more tightly around my neck. Seth came up behind me, and I shoved my hands into the pockets of my coat and walked ahead, around the outside of the house. The wings spread out horizontally on either side of the tower. They seemed simply built, low, one story only, though the rooms inside would have high ceilings. I noted several squat chimneys but did not count them.

"No architectural integrity," Seth said, coming alongside. "The place is really just a pile of rock. That's why I thought I'd pull it down, just leave the tower. The tower has a certain character, don't you think?"

I thought the tower—in fact, the whole place—had something more than character. To me it had a commanding, almost mythic presence. Though my plan was still clear in my mind, I was tempted to let it go and lose myself in exploration of this place. Its very stones drew me and seemed to hold me. The sound of the sea in the near distance was hypnotic.

I rounded the corner of the wing along which we'd

walked, and stopped to confront Seth. "You aren't going to have the chance to tear anything down," I said.

The wind blew his hair back from his face and carved his cheekbones higher. He had pulled the sheepskin collar of his jacket up to his ears. He frowned, at me or at the battering wind. "Did you get me out here just to tell me that?"

"No. But since you brought it up . . ." The truth was, I hadn't had any thought at all about the Stone House until today; hadn't known I'd say what I did until the words came out of my mouth. Everything I said, everything I did, was coming to me automatically now, as if some spirit guided me. I could only hope the spirit was benevolent.

I held out my hand. "You can give me the keys now, Seth. You won't need them anymore."

He handed them over. There was doubt in the dark brown eyes. "Would you like to go inside? The electricity's cut off, but it won't be dark for a while yet."

"No. I don't want to go inside. I only wanted to see the place today, get an idea what it's like. The outside is enough for now." I turned away and walked toward the sound of the sea.

The Stone House had been built on high ground, no doubt purposely by the tower builders, to provide a commanding view. I saw the ocean as soon as I left the shelter of the house, but not the dunes and sandy beach I had expected. Instead, as I walked across the grass I saw that the rise of land dropped off abruptly. I stood on a bluff; the water crashed in only a few feet below me. The sun had left us again; the waves were gray-green, frothed with white.

"Don't go too near the edge, Laura." Seth had come up behind me again. He put a hand on my shoulder, and I let him pull me back a couple of feet. "The water's high in the sound. It won't come all the way up here, but the waves will undercut the bank. You don't want to fall into Core Sound, I'm sure."

I had forgotten that the Stone House was on the sound and not on open sea. Still, the view was magnificent. The Core Banks were out there, shrouded in gray mist. I turned around and looked at the house, at the tower which had stood for so many years monitoring these waters. Here, now, it was time.

I said, "This is where you were supposed to meet Kathryn that day."

"Yes. That's right."

"Seth, Kathryn is dead." I watched for his reaction. My hair blew into my eyes and impatiently I pushed it back.

Seth's jaw set, a clenching of small muscles that deepened the depression in his chin. His eyes narrowed, his lips thinned. "You know, for a fact, that she's dead?"

"Yes, I do." It was very cold here, cold in a way that passes through clothing, skin, flesh, bones, cold as is known only of and by the winter sea.

"How long have you known this?"

"Not long. I had a call from a state policeman, at three o'clock this afternoon. Some college students went this morning by boat to a place just south of Swansboro called Hammock's Beach. It's some kind of state park, an island with no way in except by boat. The students found a body on the beach, apparently washed up in yesterday's storm. They contacted whoever's in charge of the park, which is how the state police got involved. They, the state police, inquired locally about people missing. The only person missing was my sister, and the body is the right height. And female."

"But"—Seth twisted shoulders and torso in a body movement I couldn't read. He drove his hands deeper into his jacket pockets—"it couldn't be Kathryn. Not after so many weeks! There are predators, natural decomposition, her body couldn't have survived in the water that long!"

"Maybe, if she'd just fallen overboard or jumped in the water and drowned, it wouldn't have. But this body, this female body, didn't die a natural death. She was killed. Murdered. Someone wrapped her body in canvas, the kind of canvas sails are made of, and then secured it with chains. The only part that came unwrapped was the front of the head. The face. Her face is gone. So the policeman said the body would be taken to the medical examiner's office, I think he said in Chapel Hill. They'll make the identification from medical and dental records, and do an autopsy to find out if she drowned or was killed in some other way and then put into the water. I have no doubt. I'm sure it's Kathryn. I can feel it, Seth. My sister was murdered."

"My God!" His voice was hushed. His eyes widened and were darker than ever. There was no light in them, no spark of sympathy; it was as if a curtain had fallen protectively behind those lenses.

He stepped forward, opening his arms to me, but I moved back and he checked his approach. I felt cold, so cold, and excruciatingly rational. His embrace was neither needed nor welcome.

"If she had come here that day," I said, "as she was supposed to do, you might have been the last person to see her alive."

Now Seth folded his arms. A defensive posture, my too-rational mind registered. He asked, "What, exactly, was your purpose in getting me out here today, Laura? It seems you deliberately chose this place to tell me that your sister's body has been found. If it *is* her body. I have to wonder why."

I was acutely aware of the crashing waters of the sound only a few feet behind and below me. I felt dangerously exposed. I shrugged, and began to work my way around him a step at a time as I answered his questions. "With the phone call today, a lot of things came together. Things I haven't consciously thought about, they've just been gathering in the back of my mind, waiting. The body will prove to be Kathryn's, there's no point in debating that. I've known, somehow, that she was killed—you remember, I wanted to hire a detective and you talked me out of it."

"I remember." Seth turned to keep facing me, as I progressed around him.

"And I suppose I've known, too, that this place, the Stone House, has something to do with her death. Perhaps that's why I put it so completely out of my mind until today. It was time, today, for me to come here, and right for you to be here, too. After all, the Stone House connects you with my sister."

"Only in that she owned it and I wanted to buy it. That's

not much of a connection. Why should you think this, this pile of rocks, has something to do with her death?"

I shrugged again and stopped my circling. Now my back was to the house, and Seth's was to the sound. I felt more secure. I answered him. "Well, there's a kind of mystery about it, isn't there? The way she bought it and kept her ownership secret. And apparently she intended to come here on the day she disappeared. Perhaps she did come here, after all. Perhaps the Stone House is the last place on earth where my sister drew living breath."

Seth drew his black brows together and looked down his long nose at me, hawklike. The color of his voice was as dark as his eyes, ominous. "If she came here, she arrived after I'd left. I never saw Kathryn that day."

I said nothing. I wanted to believe him. I wasn't sure that I could. He was wary, defensive, on the verge of anger. The sensitivity he'd cultivated in recent weeks was not in evidence. I'd carried out my plan: I'd confronted Seth here at the Stone House with the knowledge of my sister's murder. Yet I wasn't sure what I'd learned.

I turned away, my mind less clear now that I'd done what I set out to do, my body starting to take over. I was shivering inside my warm clothes. I walked rapidly toward the strange building, on a diagonal that would take me to the foot of the tower, to its heavy wooden door.

"Don't do that!" Seth's voice was brittle on the wind. "Don't walk away from me like that!"

"I'm cold," I called back over my shoulder. "I'm going inside to get out of the wind."

He caught up with me, grabbed and stopped me.

"Let me go," I said.

"No. I want to get this straight. I know you're upset, you have a right to be—"

"I'm not upset!"

"Well, damn it, you believe me, don't you? I didn't see Kathryn, she never came!"

"I don't know whether to believe you or not, Seth. You've never told the police that you were here, that she was supposed to meet you here. I've always thought that was more than a little peculiar."

"I explained that to you. And anyway, even if she had come, I wouldn't have done anything to hurt her. I certainly wouldn't have murdered her. You can't believe I'd do that!" His voice cracked.

I searched his face and saw lines of pain, but the curtain remained shutting off my access to his inner self, through the windows of his eyes. I remembered his anguish on Christmas Eve, when he'd told me of the people who had come to harm in one of his buildings—his eyes had been clear then, liquid, they had poured forth his sorrow. Now there was this curtain. It confused me, I mistrusted it. I wanted to believe, and yet I could not. Something snapped inside me—it was the fragile beginnings of my love for Seth, tearing apart. A violent shudder ripped through my body, my vision blurred, and I swayed.

Seth's hand tightened on my arm. "I knew this was too much for you," he mumbled, deep in his throat. He pulled me firmly against his side and wrapped his arm around my waist. "We're leaving. I'm going to drive you home."

Physical strength had deserted me. I could only walk with him, locked against him, and yet I felt that tower door pulling at me, calling me back. "I did want to go inside!" I protested.

"You can come back another time. The Stone House belongs to you now, or haven't you realized that yet? You can come back whenever you want."

I had to take two steps to every one of his. "Yes," I acknowledged, "I guess I can."

11

I did go back to the Stone House, alone, two weeks later. I went on a sunny day. The graveled private road seemed neither so long nor so threatening with sunlight filtering through the thick growth of trees. The sun warmed the January air slightly, but it did little to warm my heart. I was numb inside. Perhaps the absence of feeling was an unconscious way of protecting myself, I didn't know. I knew that I was functioning well; I seemed stronger than I'd ever been before. If I were grimmer, too, that was to be expected—reality was grim. I had come to the Stone House on this winter-bright day to scatter the ashes of Kathryn Trelawney in the sea.

Her memorial service had been well attended. Everyone I'd ever met in Beaufort was there as well as some I had never met. I expected many had come out of curiosity, because of all the publicity, but still I was grateful for the many expressions of sympathy I received. We had tried unsuccessfully to locate Carroll Trelawney, who was supposed to be somewhere in the Caribbean; he was conspicuously absent from his former wife's services. Absent, too, was Nick Westover, and his absence made me uncomfortable for no reason I could understand. Jonathan and Seth stood by me in the church, and afterward, when we opened the inn to the mourners. Jonathan and Seth acted as family to me, and yet I didn't feel close to them. I felt close to no one. Not then, not now as I held the ashes of my sister in their small brass box in my hands.

I walked slowly to the edge of the land, trying to form a prayer in my mind. No words came. Had my sister loved this place? I wondered. Had she long coveted it and seized the first opportunity to make it her own? Had the idea of selling the property been painful to her? If so, I thought I could understand.

The waters of the sound were not so high now; there was a narrow strip of sand where they washed in below the bluff. I'm not very good at judging distances, but the drop-off seemed at least twice what it had been when I'd stood here before. The sound shimmered blue-green and calm, and the dunes of Core Banks formed an ivory ridge beyond which lay the deeper blue of open sea. I turned and looked back at the tower, its light-brown rocks glowing warm in the sun, its rambling wings reaching out on either side. I could understand how Kathryn might have loved this place. It was unique. It possessed a different kind of beauty—powerful, a little wild.

I removed the top from the brass box, dropped it on the grass beside me, and took the fine powdery ashes in my fingers. I could not drop them into the water as I'd intended, because the wind which always blew in from the sea took the light particles as they streamed from my hand, lifted them and brought them back over the land. So be it, I thought, offering gray ash to the wind until the box was empty. I found I was talking inside my head to Kathryn. I'm sorry, I said. Sorry that you lost more than half the years of your lifespan. Sorry I didn't really know what was going on in your life, didn't know how unhappy you must have been, didn't know you were in serious trouble. Sorry most of all for the way you died, the terror you must have felt.

Soon the ashes were gone. I looked at the empty box, and in a final, furious farewell I threw it as hard as I could out and into the waters of the sound. I went down on one knee, took the brass lid with its little knob on top and hurled it, too, as far as I could. Good-bye, Kathryn. Good-bye, sister.

Where were my tears? Back when I'd first come to Beaufort, I'd cried easily, and more often than I'd wanted to. That seemed eons ago. I couldn't cry now. Kathryn's death was a reality beyond tears. I had driven to Chapel Hill, to the office of the state medical examiner, to hear the full autopsy report. I'd insisted on going alone, though both Seth and Jonathan had wanted to go with me. In all it was over seven hours of driving, and if I'd done any thinking during all that time, I hadn't remembered the thoughts. I only recalled the facts I'd learned: the body was that of Kathryn Trelawney, identified by her teeth and X-rays of a once-broken collarbone. If it had not been for the abnormally high tides and the storm, most likely the body would never have come in on the beach. The forensic pathologist surmised that when she was thrown overboard, a weight of some sort had been attached to the chains which bound her layers of canvas wrappings. But the gases created as her body decomposed slowly brought the body up from the bottom of the sea, where the currents caught it, and at some point the weight became detached. There was no water in her lungs, she had suffocated before she could drown. Death was at the hands of person or persons unknown.

Of course the questions began again, and the police reopened their investigation. This time I told them about the Stone House, and about Seth's part in that. Told them about the money Carroll Trelawney had presumably left, and which was most likely used to buy the Stone House. Told them I'd learned that people hadn't liked my sister, but none seemed to hate her enough to kill her. Told them I'd heard from Nick Westover that she'd had affairs, one of them with him. Why hadn't I told them all these things before, they asked, as I'd known they would. Because, I said rather untruthfully, I believed it wouldn't matter since I expected her to come back, eventually.

Everything was reported in the newspapers. A murder, a body washed up on Hammock's Beach, where people camped and children played year-round, was unusual. Sensational, horrible news. People canceled their reservations at the Trelawney Inn. Why? I asked Jonathan. She hadn't been murdered at the inn. Because of the unpleasant connection with a dead woman, Jonathan said, because the name of the inn was the same as hers. Give it time, people would forget, and they would come again, he said. The regulars, the ones who came one or more weekends a month to stay at night and take their boats out by day, would return soonest.

I sighed heavily, pulled my turtleneck up closer to my ears, and futilely ran my hand through my hair. For now I had done everything I could. The keys to the Stone House were in my pocket; many hours of the day stretched ahead of me. I would explore.

The wooden outer door of the tower was six inches thick, and creaked when I opened it. I blinked, momentarily unable to see because of the contrast from bright sunlight to the shadows within. I stood in the open doorway and smelled dampness, a salty sea-smell trapped and turned musty in its confinement. My eyes adjusted. The tower was, surprisingly, not round inside. It was not at all as I'd thought it would be, rock walls and a winding stair all the way to the top. One of its later inhabitants had turned it into a room with wood-paneled walls and not a single window on this level. No wonder it was so dark! I counted eight corners. This tower room was an octagon, from whose high ceiling hung two medieval-looking chandeliers, iron hoops studded with candle-shaped light fixtures. I looked around and found the light switch and flicked it once, though I knew the electricity would be off. I left the front door open for illumination and walked to the center of the room. My footsteps were loud; they rang off wooden floor, wooden walls, wooden ceiling. I bent down to examine the floor, intrigued by a just-visible pattern in the wood. I saw that it was grimy, but not dusty, my steps had left no footprints. I didn't know what to make of that, but no matter. Under the grime the wood was surely beautiful, hardwood laid in patterns of squares, like fine inlay—the work of a craftsman.

I straightened up again. In addition to the big door I'd left open, there were three other doors spaced around the room. I opened them one by one. Two, on opposite sides of the tower, connected with the wings which I presumed were living quarters. The third revealed a narrow, steep stairway which climbed against the rock wall, winding up and out of sight. There was light here, from the narrow lancet windows. I started to climb the stair but halted on the third step. I mustn't be foolish; I had to stay alive and all in one piece. To climb higher on steps that might be in bad condition was to risk a fall.

I was never sure at what point in my exploration I decided that I wanted to live in the Stone House. Perhaps it was at that early moment when I saw that the floor of the tower room could be a beautiful surface when cleaned, sanded smooth, burnished to a patina, a surface that called out to my dancer's feet. Or perhaps it was later, when I saw that though one of the wings was a shambles, the other had been lived in and not too many years ago. There were four major rooms, all large and high-ceilinged, with fireplaces and wonderful windows now boarded over. The major oddities were that the rooms were all strung together without a hall, so that you had to go through one room to get to the next and the only entrance from the outside was through the tower door; and all the windows in the entire place were on the sound side. No cross-ventilation, I thought. Nevertheless, people had lived here. The kitchen and bathroom were both about 1950s vintage and packed in beside each other, for convenience of the plumbing, I presumed, at the south end of the wing. Of course the inside walls were rock, the same rocks as the outside. The rocks apparently were good insulation since it was much warmer inside than out, but hanging pictures would be impossible. It was then, as I was wondering what I would do with my pictures, that I realized what had happened. I had already decided—I was going to live in the Stone House.

Excited now, I went back through the rooms. I started with the tower room—I would dance here. It would be both entrance hall and dance studio. The first room in from the tower would be the living room, the next would be a combination dining room/study, then a guest bedroom, then my bedroom . . . immediately I could see there would be logistical problems, with the kitchen and the one bath at the far end of the wing. But, never mind, I would solve them. The kitchen would need a lot of improvement. The simplest thing to do would be to gut it and start over. I'd hire a carpenter, get an electrician to check out the wiring, someone to fix the roof in the other wing because I'd want to store what furniture I didn't use in there. It would be useful to have another door to the outside, and I wondered if one could be opened up. Perhaps through the kitchen wall . . . I dug a notepad out of my bag and began to jot down my thoughts.

I was elated, but into my elation came a pang of guilt as I realized how much I was enjoying myself. The Stone House was Kathryn's find, Kathryn's place. Surely I was wrong to enjoy the thought of reclaiming it from its disuse, making it a home for me? I felt I was doing it at her expense, but that was ridiculous. Kathryn was dead, nothing could change that, and she had been planning to sell it anyway. To Seth, who would only tear it down. My guilt and the doubts I had begun to feel were silly, and I dismissed them. I had never intended to live at the inn. I knew well that I was a person who needed my own space, my own nest. I'd always been a nest-maker, even in childhood when the instinct had been confined to my one room. As an adult, having lived for so long in that one impersonal room at the inn had taken its toll on me, as I well knew. To have a place of my own again, to be surrounded by my own things and the family things I had inherited, all the things that had meaning to me and a sense of family history—of course it would be wonderful! For the first time since I'd come to Beaufort, I'd be doing something entirely for myself.

I went back to wandering through the rooms and making notes. I forgot I hadn't had lunch, lost track of time completely. When I began to feel uneasy I attributed it to the failing light. Once my eyes had become accustomed, there had been enough light filtering through the boarded-up windows; but all those windows faced east and as the day wore on and the sun moved westward I lost what little light there had been. I felt suddenly panicked, like a child who has wandered too deep in the woods and with the fall of twilight, knows she cannot find her way out again before dark. My watch told me the hour was not late, but I had to force myself to walk, not run, through the rooms and out the tower door. As I locked that massive door from the outside, I thought that my priorities were falling into place. My first call would be to the electrician, to check the wiring so that I could have the lights turned on!

Jonathan had an old pale-blue sweater he wore every day in winter. It was the V-neck kind, had patches on the elbows, and was practically shapeless. In this sweater he looked more comfortably professorial than ever, and it was hard to disregard his advice.

"I'm not so sure it's a good idea, Laura," he said.

"Of course it's a good idea, Jonathan," I replied. "I need a place of my own, and the Stone House is unique. It looks like a small old Scottish castle."

"I know what it looks like, I've seen it. Of course, I didn't know Kathryn had bought it until you told me. You're sure the title is clear, that it really is yours now?"

"Yes, I'm sure. My lawyer has taken care of all that. You wait until I've fixed it up on the inside. You'll like it then, I know you will. Especially when my furniture comes and I've filled it with my own things. I won't be living in the whole place, just one wing. And the tower room—Jonathan, I'm going to refinish the floor and turn the tower into a place where I can dance!"

Jonathan frowned at me over the tops of his glasses, took them off, and polished them on the bottom of his shapeless sweater. "It's such a long way off, and it's isolated. You'll be all by yourself out there."

My soft spot for Jonathan was wearing thin. "I won't be alone, Jonathan, I'll have Boris with me. I won't feel lonely or isolated. There are telephones. And it's only a fifteen-minute drive from here. Where I come from, that's hardly a commute! I don't understand what's worrying you."

He reached across the table where we'd just had breakfast together and patted my hand in a fatherly way. "I'm concerned about your safety, Laura."

"Oh, Jonathan. You've lived in small towns for too long. I'll be safer at the Stone House than I was in my neighborhood in Columbus! Half my neighbors there had their houses broken into. You learn not to worry about those things." I was nearing exasperation and anticipated his next objection. "I was alone, too, in that house. My husband was a doctor in training, and there were many, many nights he didn't come home. Don't worry, please. Be glad for me. You have no idea how much I'm looking forward to this!"

He pushed his glasses up his nose and smiled, a thin smile. "All right. I do want you to be happy, and I'm sure what you say is true, about the place you lived before. Maybe I'm just selfish and used to having you here. I'll miss you when you're living somewhere else."

"You're sweet, Jonathan. You won't have much chance to miss me, because I'll be here every day, just like I am now, and if you need me at night I'll be just a phone call and a short drive away." I stood up then and did something I'd wanted to do for a long time: I kissed Jonathan on the shining bald crown of his head. "Thank you for caring about my safety."

He blushed, turning a dark pink as only very fair-skinned people can do. "Never mind. Let's just hope I'm worried over nothing."

Seth was less easily pacified. And perhaps I was less willing to pacify. Things had been uneasy between us since that day at the Stone House when I'd told him about Kathryn's murder. He was prickly and so was I, and we both displayed a remarkable talent for saying the wrong things at the wrong times. He was exercising that talent vehemently now.

"You can't do it. You can't move out there all by yourself. The place is a . . . a mausoleum!"

His choice of words pierced into me, as I remembered Kathryn's ashes, blowing on the wind from my hand and falling onto the land, the land on which the Stone House stood, when I had intended them to fall into the sea. But then I flared back at him. "Oh, really? I *can't?* I can see there's no point at all in discussing this with you. You're jealous, that's what. You wanted that property for yourself, and you can't stand to see me doing something with it other than what you had in mind!"

If looks could kill, I thought, as he glared at me for a long moment while he got himself under control. Finally he said, "You're right. There's no point in us trying to talk about it. You've already made up your mind."

"Yes, I have. I sent for my furniture this morning; it should arrive in about two weeks. And this afternoon I had an electrician out there. He has to put in another line for the new kitchen appliances I plan to have, but otherwise the wiring is fine. Day after tomorrow a carpenter is coming out to open up the windows and look at the roof and talk about new cabinets for the kitchen."

"You're too independent!"

"There's no such thing!"

"Yes, there is, when you're so damn set on doing things your own way that you put yourself in danger," he said darkly. He got up from the chair he always sat in when he kept me company at the reception desk, and walked to the door. Hand on the knob, Seth turned and gave me a look that seemed to penetrate into my soul. "What's happening to us, Laura?"

As if afraid to wait for an answer, he opened the door then and was gone.

We were having so few guests at the inn that Jonathan suggested we close down for the entire off-season, change the furniture around in a pretense of redecorating, and open again in the spring under a new name. The break in our operations would give people time to forget, he reasoned, and the name change would further the same end. On the surface it seemed a good idea, but my instincts were against it. So I told him no, we had nothing to be ashamed of, and I didn't want to change the name of the inn. We could sustain the losses for a couple of months. If things didn't pick up in the spring, then we'd see.

Actually, the lack of business activity made it easier for me to spend time at the Stone House. I wanted to get as much done as I could before my furniture came, and even with the professionals I'd hired, there was still a lot to do. I was absorbed in my nest-making to the exclusion of all else. I relied most heavily on a master carpenter who seemed to know his business. He had agreed that another outside door was not only desirable but a necessity; as he pointed out, with only the one exit through the tower the place was a firetrap. He hired a stone mason and they were carefully opening a door from the kitchen to the parking area. His two helpers had first removed the boards from the windows, which proved to be as wonderful as I'd thought they would be. Huge, made up of many diamond-shaped panes of clear glass set in casement-type frames that opened outward. The master carpenter suggested that I install outside shutters which could be closed for protection against storms, and I agreed. While the workmen moved on to dismantle the kitchen, I tackled the years' accumulation of dirt that was everywhere. I resisted the urge to do the tower room floor first. It was more important to get the space I'd be living in ready before the furniture came. And there was the bathroom to think about. Although I was having the kitchen redone, I intended to leave the bathroom as it was. The old fixtures, more thirties than fifties, as I'd first thought, were functional, and I liked their looks. I especially liked the big lion-footed tub, deep as a Jacuzzi. The walls and floor of the bathroom needed work, though, which I could do myself. I would wallpaper the inner wall and cover the floor with do-it-yourself carpeting.

I was staggering out of the car under a load of wallpaper sample books when a masculine voice called, "Yo! Laura!" I looked around and didn't see anyone.

I must be hearing things, I thought, and shoved the car door closed with my knee. I staggered back a couple of steps, bumped into something, and jumped a foot, jostling the top sample book off of my stack.

"Looks like you could use some help here," said Nick Westover. I hadn't seen him standing directly behind me.

"Must you always sneak up on people?" I asked crossly. "What have you been doing, lying in wait for me in the inn parking lot?"

He ignored my questions, retrieved the big book I'd dropped, and took the rest out of my arms. What had been a burden for me was nothing for him—I'd almost forgotten how big he was. How unusually handsome. His abundant red hair and beard waved out from under his navy watch cap, as if he'd let them grow longer for the winter.

"I haven't seen you in a while," I said.

"Oh, I've been around. I heard about your sister and everything. Heard you're doing a lot of work on the Stone House, going to live there. I guess that's what this stuff is for?"

"Yes, that's what it's for. Why don't you bring those things in for me, and stay for a cup of tea?" I went ahead, through the inn's main door. I said hello to Zelda, then stood back and gestured for Nick to precede me into the office. I closed the door behind us, shutting out Zelda's curious eyes and ears.

Nick set the wallpaper sample books down on the desk and leaned up against it, half-sitting, swinging one blue-jeaned leg and seeming very much at home.

I wondered if he'd sat like that, swinging his leg and looking at Kathryn as he now looked at me. I turned my back on him and shrugged out of my coat. I said, "Why don't you take off your hat and coat and stay awhile. I'll call upstairs for some tea."

"No, thanks. I'm not the tea type. Let's go across the street and have a drink instead. You can tell me what you're doing at the Stone House. That's a great place—I envy you!"

"Well . . ." I was sorely tempted. He was offering me something I very much wanted, not the drink, but the chance to talk to a receptive audience. With Seth and Jonathan feeling the way they did about my move, I hadn't wanted to talk about it with them.

"Aw, come on," Nick cajoled, grinning within his beard, sure of his charm. "Like you said, I haven't seen you in a while. I have to make up for lost time, don't I?"

I laughed. He was very nearly irresistible. I put Kathryn out of my mind, as I seemed to have to do so often lately. "All right, one drink and then I have to get back. I take the desk when Zelda leaves."

"Zelda, huh?" Nick took the coat which I hadn't had time to hang up and held it for me. "She looks like a Zelda."

I laughed again. "Yes, I guess she does."

Being with Nick was fun. And he was so good to look at! At the bar he took off his pea jacket to reveal an emerald-green ribbed sweater, exactly the color of his eyes. Without the cap his wealth of hair was beautiful, if a little wild. He made me feel all woman, desirable. If he didn't listen quite attentively as I rambled on about my renovations at the Stone House, if his eyes roved sensually over my body instead, I didn't mind.

When my enthusiasm had finally run down, he said lazily, "I knew you wouldn't be afraid to live there."

I felt a sudden chill stab me in the back, between my shoulder blades. It was a shock, when I'd been enjoying myself so much. "I don't understand. Why should I be afraid?"

"Well, the Stone House is an old, old place. Might be haunted."

I couldn't tell if he was teasing me or not. "Jonathan said he's never heard of it being haunted and Jonathan knows all the old stories. Besides, I don't believe in ghosts."

Nick's eyes glittered. "Everybody believes in ghosts, even if they say they don't. Everybody's got this place inside them that's scared, that remembers what it's like to be a kid and know there's a monster in the closet that only comes out at night."

I shrugged and smiled, but a bit uneasily. "So what? I'm a big girl now. And the Stone House is a wonderful place. I know I'll love being there."

"Maybe you will. I do envy you, it's a place in a million." For a moment his eyes turned hard, and then the look passed. He grinned. "I heard at one time there were pirates there."

"Oh? I heard just the opposite, that the tower was used to watch out for pirates, so the local people could protect themselves."

Nick chuckled. "Maybe the pirates outsmarted them and took away their own tower. I'm pretty sure there were pirates at the Stone House. Back before it was a house, of course. When there wasn't anything but the tower."

I remembered what Seth had told me months ago, about Nick. "You seem to know a lot about pirates," I said.

"Great guys, the pirates. Great sailors, the best. Knowing about pirates is a kind of hobby of mine. They didn't take nothing off nobody—"

I interrupted, amused by his naive romanticism. "I think it's more like they took whatever they could get off of anybody!"

"Well, yeah, they did that, too, but they didn't let anybody screw them over, know what I mean? The pirates were true independent spirits. They were powerful, they'd go up against anybody or anything. Blackbeard, now, he was something else! He got to be a respectable citizen, did you know that?"

I shook my head. "I don't really know much about pirates. But I heard somewhere that Blackbeard had fourteen wives."

Nick leered. "That's right, he did. And I'll bet every one of them worshipped him!"

"I'll bet he didn't give them much choice," I said dryly. "I hate to break this up, but I do have to get back to the inn now, Nick. Thanks for the drink."

"Want me to walk you back?" he asked, but he didn't make a move.

"No, don't be silly. It's just across the street." Then, since he so clearly intended to do it anyway, I added, "You stay and have another drink."

"Okay, I won't argue that. How about an invitation to the Stone House? I'd like to see what you've done."

I paused, touched by his interest. "Of course. I expect my

furniture to come next week, and I'll move in soon after that. You're welcome any time, just call first. The phone's already in, you can get the number from Information."

As I crossed the street I savored the bite of the cold, fresh air, damp from the sea. Nick was certainly a different sort of companion! Maybe he was good for me. Good, at least, for a change. Maybe he wasn't going to win any intellectual prizes, but he was easy on the eyes and his boyish fascination with pirates was entertaining.

So busy was I with the Stone House as the day of furniture delivery drew near that I neglected a similar task close at hand: the clearing out of Kathryn's rooms at the inn. Jonathan brought the matter to my attention one evening when I returned from a productive day of wallpapering. He told me that Sergeant Sanders and another policeman had spent several hours searching through Kathryn's things. They didn't take anything away with them, and if they had made any discovery they didn't say so, but perhaps it was time . . .

His voice trailed off. He didn't need to finish the thought, and I told him so. I'd been remiss and I knew it. After a hot shower and a sandwich, which I ate while I covered the reception desk, I unlocked Kathryn's suite and went in. The police had been neat in their search; nothing looked out of place. What would they have done, I wondered, if I had cleaned up this place right after the memorial service? Then I remembered: the chief of police had told me, "Don't dispose of anything." But he hadn't said not to pack things away, and it was past time for me to do that.

The first room of the suite was a sitting room. Two comfortable chairs on either side of a small fireplace, a loveseat, a handsome antique secretary-desk, low book-shelves under the windows, an oval braided rug on the floor. Near the door where I stood was a small table with one drawer and a shelf below, and on the table a telephone. The police would have looked for . . . what? A diary, a journal, letters, papers, photographs, *clues*. Anything that would reveal things previously unknown about my sister. I stood looking at the room where Kathryn had lived, first with her husband and then alone, and suddenly I felt exhausted. Unequal to the task. And ashamed. For nearly two weeks, since I'd scattered her ashes, I'd been caught in the spell of my nest-making at the Stone House. I'd thought of Kathryn, often, but I'd put out of mind the fact that she had been murdered. That there was a murderer somewhere, going unpunished. It was because of Seth that I'd let myself forget, because I didn't want to suspect him, and yet he was just as much a suspect as anyone else. I owed Kathryn more than forgetting, more than an occasional prick of guilt that in my acquisition of the Stone House I had benefitted from her death.

I squared my shoulders and walked through the sitting room and the connecting bath to the bedroom. A lovely old brass bed took up most of the space, as the room was small, less than half the size of the room I occupied. A handsome quilt in the wedding ring pattern covered the bed. I'll keep that, I thought. It had already begun, the sad, necessary task of sorting through the possessions of the dead. Resigned, I went to the double set of louvered doors across one wall. Such walls were in most of the inn's rooms, concealing the closets which had been added during the renovations. The fact that old houses never had closets never ceased to amaze me. I opened the doors and began mechanically to take down Kathryn's clothes and fold them into neat stacks on the bed. I thought of our childhood, how I'd adored our older brother; loved and hated the little sister who looked so much like me. Where I had loved and hated her, she had been indifferent to me. How odd it was that only now, after she was gone, did I realize that she had been indifferent. Perhaps one has to be an adult to give a name to indifference. She was the youngest, she had somehow claimed all the attention for as far back as I could remember. She'd played with me only when there was nothing better to do. Somehow, even when I was very young, I'd known I was smarter than she. Instead of feeling superior, I'd felt responsible for her. She was always doing stupid things, always getting herself into one scrape or another, and I was always getting her out. If she'd ever said thank you, I didn't remember it.

Oh, God! I collapsed on the bed, upsetting my neat little stacks. She hadn't really ever changed, had she? She'd gotten herself into one scrape too many, and I had come to help, but I'd arrived too late. I couldn't get her out of this one, I could only, only . . . what could I do? All the old emotions of childhood and adolescence rushed over me. I buried my face against one of her dresses, a dress exactly my size, it would easily have fit me—and for the first time since Kathryn's death, I cried.

You're supposed to feel better after you've cried, but I didn't; I hadn't felt better after crying for my mother or my father or my now-divorced husband, either. My glasses were smudged and my eyes and throat felt like sandpaper. I gritted my teeth and finished with the closet, then began on the drawers. By now I had two categories: the things on the bed could be given to charity, and the things on the floor were worn out and would be thrown away. I reminded myself to call Sergeant Sanders first; if he said I still had to keep these things, I'd pack them in boxes and label them "charity" or "trash." I didn't find a diary or a journal, nor had I expected to. Kathryn had never been much of a writer, and if she had turned into one in recent years, I would have been surprised. I didn't find anything hidden in the drawer linings, nor did her shoeboxes hold anything but shoes. So much for clues in the bedroom.

It was around midnight when I progressed into the sitting room. I made piles of magazines to throw out, decided that I would ask Evelyn to pack the books so that I could take them to the Stone House with me. I could never bear to let go of a book. I found an empty wastebasket and filled it with the little personal treasures we all have sitting around on the tops of things—a pretty box of blue glass, a few special seashells, a pottery vase, a teapot covered with tiny rosebuds that seemed unlike Kathryn—I remembered it had been my mother's. These things and her small collection of jewelry I would keep. I opened the front of the secretary-desk. It was disorderly, crammed full of papers. My sister hadn't been an orderly person, her lingerie drawers had been just such a jumble. My scratchy eyes blurred—I was unbelievably tired. I would find nothing in the desk, I thought, nothing but the dead papers of a dead person. If there had been anything significant here, the police would have already found it.

I closed up the secretary and scanned the room a last time. I could come back another day and finish cleaning out the desk and the one drawer in that little telephone table. For now I was simply too exhausted. Suddenly I had an idea which made me feel a little better: I'd give this suite to Jonathan, furniture and all. Give him the furniture to keep, if he wanted it, in case he ever moved on to somewhere else. Unthinkable that Jonathan should ever leave! I relied on him for so much and had given him so little. He deserved a more pleasant place than his cramped third-floor room. Perhaps the suite and the furniture would please him. I hoped so.

═══ 12 ═══

We were having an unusually cold, wet, stormy winter, the local people said. I could count the truly sunny days on the fingers of one hand. When it wasn't actually raining, it was misty or foggy or both. Gale warnings went up and came down, only to go up again. Swash Inlet changed course. Farther up the Outer Banks, at Nags Head, at least two beach houses were about to fall into the sea. Comparatively speaking, I had no problem at all—the Stone House was on high ground and many feet back from the eroding edge of the bluff. But Stone House still had leaks in the roof of the unused wing, where I planned to store my extra furniture, because the roof never dried out enough for the carpenters to work on it. The kitchen was only half finished, but the door to the outside had been carefully framed and set in, and fitted with a good lock. When it rained, the rain came down the chimneys and into the fireplaces, and there was no central heat. I bought two quartz heaters, one for my bedroom and one for the kitchen which could be carried into the bathroom. There were inconveniences, but eventually, if I continued to live here, I would do something about them. For now I was satisfied that I could move in and be reasonably comfortable.

On the day my furniture arrived it was raining hard and the wind blew the rain in near-horizontal sheets. The huge moving van could barely pass through the trees on the narrow gravel private road; in my rearview mirror I saw the high, squared-off metal roof of the van breaking the lower branches of the trees as it lurched along behind me.

The van driver screwed up his face against the wind and rain, said to me, "This is it, huh?" and tramped around the outside of the Stone House making his assessment. He spurned my new kitchen door. "Got to go in through the other side, the big door in the whad'ja call it, the tower. No other way," he pronounced.

Undaunted by anything, he drove his huge, many-wheeled truck across the sodden groundcover of grass and vines, leaving deep, muddy tracks behind him. He maneuvered his great vehicle, looking at one point as if he intended to commit suicide by driving right over the bluff and into the sound. In the end he backed right up to the tower door. My "lawn," such as it was, was ruined; but all my furniture, and the boxes and barrels, passed from the van into the house untouched by the driving rain.

By nightfall the movers had finished and gone. I covered the extra furniture in the dark, leaky wing with plastic sheeting I'd bought and went back to the inn. The next morning I loaded up the Subaru with my things, principally Boris. Untranquilized, he thought he was going to the vet and alternately howled or growled the whole way to his new home. Thus alone and without ceremony, on another cold, rainy, windy day, to the background accompaniment of a howling cat, I moved into the Stone House.

I went in through my new door, which by now I called the back door. Inside, in the half-finished kitchen, all was silent except for an occasional groan of wind down a chimney. I had asked the carpenters to confine their work to the outside for a couple of days, to the roof or the promised shutters, while I put things to rights inside. But it was raining today, and they couldn't work in the rain. I had seldom been here alone over the past weeks, and I found I missed their company. Oh, well, I had Boris. He stopped howling as soon as he'd realized we weren't at the vet, after all.

"Well, here we are, big guy." I put the cat carrier down on the kitchen table and lifted Boris out.

"Grmowr," he said, ears back. His eyes were alert, great tail switched at the tip. He blinked once and looked at me, seeming pleased that the expected shot or whatever had not been forthcoming. He wriggled in my hands and I dropped him gently to the floor.

"This is your new home, *our* new home. That's right, go on and explore. You won't get lost." I watched him sniff at the new-laid vinyl flooring, cross its pristine, shiny surface carefully on velvet-soft paws. The floor was large blue-and-white squares in a pattern reminiscent of delft tiles. The countertops were all in place and were white, of a new material that could be cut and sanded like marble, and was as expensive as I imagined marble would be. The sink was in place, and the stove and refrigerator were hooked up and working; but the cabinets were not all finished. Those that were complete were lovely, solid golden oak, not prefabricated but built on the spot to my specifications. When the cabinets were done, the space between the countertops and the overhead cabinets would be filled in with real blue and white tiles I'd ordered from a pottery in the Piedmont section of the state.

Boris nosed his way around an empty cabinet frame, leaped inside, and after a short prowl jumped out again. He looked up at me, said "Mowr," and padded over to investigate one of the table legs. I liked the way the kitchen was shaping up. The blue and white and the gold glow of oak were pleasant, even on yet another gray day. Another *cold* day. I'd best get busy and make some fires in the fireplaces.

Evelyn had suggested that I pay one of the inn's part-time maids to help me with the unpacking, but I'd declined. I wanted the work, wanted to do it myself. I'd given myself two whole days off, and I'd hired an older woman who was a Historical Association volunteer to do my two hours at the desk each night. She wanted to do it permanently, and I hoped that would work out. I would be glad not to have to take those two hours every night, right at the dinner hour.

I got to work, starting in my bedroom. I had decided after much thought that the room nearest the kitchen should be a library/dining room. The next room was my bedroom. On the other side of my bedroom was a spare room which could be used by guests, if I ever had any. The living room was the one closest to the tower, which one entered by the tower door. I doubted that I'd use the living room unless I had company. My bedroom was so large that I could divide it into living and sleeping areas. I would do my coming and going through the new back door, cook in the kitchen, eat at my mother's tea table, which I'd already placed in front of the windows in the dining room while the big table was in the center of the room, and the rest of the time I would spend in my room.

It took exactly three hours for me to realize how very much alone I was. The rain continued, the carpenters didn't come, and Boris was being a cat, independent and off somewhere doing his own thing. I put a tape in my portable stereo and ignored the eerie feeling which crept up on me no matter how hard I worked. At three-fifteen I called Jonathan and told him how great everything was, how much I was enjoying my unpacking. I was only half lying. At four o'clock I drove to the nearest grocery store, though I'd already stocked the refrigerator, for some things that suddenly seemed very necessary. At five, back from the grocery store, I turned on every light, including the huge chandeliers in the tower room. There was no fireplace in the tower room, and it was as cold and dank as a tomb. I crossed the floor to the massive front door to check it, though I knew I had locked it after the movers the night before. I checked the locks on the other doors, new locks I'd added to secure the other wing and the tower stairs. Then I returned to my own wing and locked myself in. I left the lights on in the tower room. I didn't know why; I just felt safer that way.

I had given no thought to curtains or drapes, and now I was sorry. Very sorry. The sky outside was purple with twilight; soon the huge windows would be black, gaping holes. My head told me that there were no neighbors out here, no one to see in; but my gut, as my psychologist friend would have said, told me that I wouldn't be able to bear those vast dark spaces. Not even for one night. I looked at the windows in dismay—none of the curtains I'd kept from my old house would even begin to cover them, they were just too big. No problem, I told myself, I'll think of something. And I did, but not before I'd begun to shiver almost uncontrollably. I couldn't be afraid, I'd never been afraid to be alone! And I'd conquered my recent fear of the dark. I could cover the windows with sheets—each window was about the size of a double bed. But I hated myself for my irrational fears.

I walked over to the window in my room and looked out. The rain had stopped, and I hadn't even noticed. From the window I saw the lawn, already almost black with approaching night. The sky was a deep blue-purple and so was the sea, broken by a darker ridge that was the Core Banks. No one lived out there on the banks, and no one lived within three miles of me. The Stone House itself was locked up tight as a drum. Still, I *was* afraid. I couldn't stand to think how it would be when the dark was complete, how the dark would come creeping across the lawn, encroaching on the windows, insinuating its blackness through the fragile barrier of my glass. Foolish or not, I would cover the windows. But I swore, as I tacked sheets with hammer and nails to the window frames, that I'd never admit to Seth or Jonathan the fear I felt this night.

My problem with the windows received an unexpected solution when the carpenter and his workmen arrived the next day with the outside shutters. They had built the shutters to measure in their workshop, and had only to hang them. My nighttime fears seemed silly in the light of day, clear and sunny and February-cold. My spirits were considerably improved. I borrowed the workmen to help me put down the rugs, which had been left rolled up by the movers. All were good rugs, Orientals inherited from my parents and a Chinese which was mine. I'd saved up for two whole years to buy that gorgeous rug. I put it in my room, where it defined the living area I'd arranged nearest the windows. The colors and softness of the rugs brought light and warmth into all the rooms. Now the Stone House began to look like home.

When all the shutters were hung, the master carpenter called me outside to show me how the latches worked. He had me open and close them, to be sure I could do it alone. I could, though the latches were barely within my reach when I stood on tiptoe. "You be careful if you do this when there's much of a wind," he cautioned, and I promised that I would. Then he said that since the roof was still too wet to work, he and one of his men would go on. He'd leave the other man behind to check out the tower stairs, see what repairs were needed. Unless, of course, I never planned to climb to the top of the tower.

I hadn't thought about the tower stairs since the day I'd decided not to climb them. It was exciting now to think that the stairs would be made safe and someday soon I could climb to the very top. I could look out from the tower, *my* tower, over the same landscape that others had viewed hundreds of years ago! I thanked the carpenter enthusiastically for thinking of it, and when I went back inside I unlocked the door to the stairs for the workman.

The rest of the day flew by, and I made a lot of happy progress. One by one my possessions emerged from their wrappings, like rediscovered old friends. Boris also enjoyed himself, having a reunion with his favorite chair cushion. The workman came midafternoon and reported that the stairs needed about a week's worth of work to make them safe; did I want to put that much into fixing them? Of course, I said gaily, it will be an investment in history! He looked as if he doubted my sanity, but said he'd go and get the materials and start on it tomorrow.

A happy accident was that my bookcases fit perfectly along the inner walls of the dining room, which I wanted to double as a library. After dinner tonight, I decided, I would start unpacking my books. Then the place would feel even more like home. When the sun moved around to the west and shadows grew in my rooms, I turned on the lights, threw more logs on the fires, and kept right on working. When the blue of the sky began to deepen and the long, low lines of cloud were touched peach and pink with sunset, I stopped my work. Tonight I would *not* fear the coming of darkness. And not just because I had the shutters, either. I put on my coat and went outside.

I did rather miss Beaufort's harbor, I thought as I made a slow circle of the Stone House. The sunsets behind Carrot Island were always beautiful. And, of course, there were always the boats coming in at this time of day. I liked the old boats best, the ones called Sharpies; they'd come flying through the turn into the harbor, their sails catching all the colors of the setting sun. It's beautiful here, too, I thought loyally. I squished over the wet grass to the bluff, then turned and looked back at the tower. Beautiful was not the word for it, I admitted. Evocative? Yes, evocative.

I felt troubled in spite of my best efforts. I didn't want to think what the tower might evoke. Determinedly I paced in the fading light, careful not to go too near the land's edge. I stopped for a moment and stood still, listening. The waters of the sound moved against their narrow strip of sand, not with the lengthy sussurance of ocean breakers, but with their own shorter sibilance. The wind, light, still cold, whispered past my ears. That was all. All else was silence. Not so much as one seagull cry to split the sky. No other living thing in sight, save myself. I did not have to feel lonely, but this was a lonely place.

Time now to close the shutters. I trekked back to the house, avoiding the muddy tracks left by the moving van. By the time I had closed and fastened all the shutters, it was nearly dark. The tower door was closest, but I felt reluctant to go in that way. Outside lights, I thought, that's what I need! And I will have them, I vowed as I hurried around to the kitchen door.

I fed Boris, and then myself. The preparation of a cheese omelet in my new kitchen was a small pleasure. I carried the omelet into my room and watched the news on television while I ate. I was satisfying my hunger, but as soon as I'd been sitting in one place for a few minutes, the rest of my body cried out for attention. I'd worked hard and steadily for two full days, and I had a thousand tiny muscle aches to prove it. I decided that the unpacking of books could wait a while. I finished off my omelet by having a glass of white wine for dessert, and then gave myself a nice, long soak in the lion-footed bathtub.

When the knocking began I barely heard it through the sounds of Crosby, Stills, and Nash singing "Southern Cross" on my portable stereo. I was in the bathroom, naked and fresh from the bath, drying myself in front of a deliciously warm quartz heater. I ignored the sounds. They were probably only my imagination, anyway. I further stopped my hearing by covering my head with a towel and rubbing my damp hair hard, until it was a mass of tangled, half-dry curls.

How strange! The knocking hadn't stopped. It wasn't my imagination, but I shouldn't be hearing it, either. Worried now, I pulled on my blue fleece robe and shoved still-damp feet into slippers. The knocks had become a hard, steady pounding. As soon as I left the bathroom I realized the noise came from the kitchen door. Boris stood a couple of feet back from it, guarding with every sense alert, his tail up straight like a flag.

"It's all right, Boris," I said quietly. But was it? I went to the door, cleared my throat, and called out, "Who's there?"

The pounding stopped. "Laura, it's me, Seth."

My knees went weak with relief. I worked the complex triple lock, glad of its protection even if the person on the other side of the door had turned out to be a friend.

"What in the world are you doing here?" I asked.

"That's some welcome!" he growled. His eyes roved over me, taking in the damp, tousled hair, the squeaky-clean face bare of glasses. "Well, I guess I can understand why it took you so long to come to the door. Did I get you out of the shower?"

"I don't have a shower," I said, closing the door behind him. "I just got out of the tub. Anyway, haven't you heard of the telephone? You could have called. I thought I had the Hound of the Baskervilles or something, pounding on my door!"

"Oh? Well, I didn't want to talk on the telephone, I wanted to see you. I'd have been here yesterday, except that I spent a very long afternoon with our friend Sergeant Sanders, and after that I didn't feel like any more talking. With anyone! God, it's cold in here! Don't you have any heat?"

"Fireplaces. There's one in here, too, but I let the fire die after I finished cooking supper. Come, follow me."

"Wait a minute." From the deep pocket of the trench coat he wore, Seth withdrew a cube-shaped package, a white box tied with a squished silver bow. He grinned lopsidedly as he thrust it toward me. "Housewarming present. Since I couldn't persuade you not to move in here . . . No hard feelings. Okay?"

I smiled back, my dishabille forgotten, starting to relax. "Thanks. Now, do you want to get warm, or do you want the fifty-cent tour first?"

"The tour, I think. I like what you're doing in here." He ran his hand over a smooth expanse of oak. "Nice cabinet work."

"I'm so glad you approve!" Instantly I regretted my sarcasm. He was obviously trying to put our tensions of recent weeks to rest, and so should I. I went on quickly in a more normal tone, "I have a wonderful carpenter. His name is Joyner, which seems like an appropriate name for a carpenter, don't you think?" I babbled on, taking him through each room in turn, stopping short of the bolted door which led from the living room into the tower.

I was dreadfully reluctant to unlock that tower door. I hadn't turned the lights on there tonight, it would be so dark inside. Quivering, telling myself not to be foolish, I put my housewarming present down on a chair and with both hands unfastened the double lock.

"I-I haven't done much in here." I pushed the door open, not looking into the darkness beyond. But I felt its deathly cold. "I'm sure it looks the same as when you were here . . . before."

Seth apparently was not sensitive to whatever it was that bothered me about the tower room at night. He walked past me and was swallowed up. "Where's the light switch?"

"On the wall, to your right about a foot." I ventured in, unconsciously holding my breath.

"Got it." The two huge wheels of light blazed.

I let my breath out, and it formed mist in the cold. I hugged my arms against my chest. "All I've done so far is mop the floor. See how beautiful the wood is?" I traced an inlaid square with the toe of my slipper. "I'm going to have it sanded and refinished, and use it as my studio. Dance studio."

"Um-hm." Seth strolled around, looking down at the floor, touching the wall paneling here and there. He stopped at the door to the stairway, and he opened it. "Did you mean to leave this unlocked?"

My heart gave a huge thump and then missed a beat. "No! One of the men was working on the stairway, and I guess I forgot."

"Well"—Seth poked his head into the stairway enclosure —"no harm done. There's no outside access to these stairs anyway. But just to be on the safe side . . ."

"Right. I'll get the keys." I retrieved them from my bedroom, my glasses, too. I'd been leading this tour half-blind. I was rushing and told myself to slow down. As Seth had said, no harm was done. I *must* stop being so jumpy!

We locked the door to the stairway, Seth double-checked the other doors, and then I settled him in front of the fire in my room. Suddenly I was terribly self-conscious, too aware of him. I wished I'd made more progress on the library/dining room so that we could have sat in there. A comfortable fire burned in that fireplace, too, but most of the floorspace was occupied by still-unpacked cartons of books. Well, I thought, at least I can put some real clothes on.

I went to my chest of drawers and pulled out jeans and a sweater. "I'll just be a minute," I said.

Seth looked up, still holding out his hands to the fire's warmth. "Where are you going?"

"I thought I'd, uh, get dressed." I edged toward the door.

"No, don't. Please don't." From across the room Seth touched me with a gaze soft as deep brown velvet. His voice too was soft. "Stay just as you are. Let me keep on having my fantasy."

"Fantasy?" My skin burned, though I was far from the fire's heat. The soft voice, the velvet eyes, the strong slender fingers held out now to me—all drew me to him. Step by hesitant step.

"I'm pretending that after a long day I've come home, tired and cold, to you. Home to Laura, rosy from her bath, fresh as dew . . ."

"Oh!" Closer, step by step.

"Laura, with her tangle of dark curls, her soft skin . . ." He reached out and plucked the clothes from my arms, dropped them to the floor. ". . . sweet skin . . ." He pulled me to him and buried his face between my breasts, nuzzling aside the blue fleece of my robe.

"Oh, Seth," I sighed. He was sitting, I stood in front of him, feeling heat that was my own or the fire, feeling his lips light as feathers on my skin.

"I'm pretending that you're mine, and I'm yours . . ." The tiny, feathery kisses traveled lower, below the valley of my breasts. His hands left my hips and went to the sash of my robe.

I locked my fingers in his thick hair, silver hair haloed with gold in the firelight. I should raise his head, stop his lips, but there was no strength in me.

Seth's cheek pressed in the hollow beneath my rib cage. He murmured, "I'm pretending there is no one, nothing in the whole world but you and me . . ." He loosened the sash without opening the robe. His hands moved to cup my buttocks, pressing me closer in to his burrowing head.

Seth's fantasy became my fantasy. The world fell away. Weeks of tension, days and days of stifled sorrow, simply disappeared. There was only me and Seth in our circle of firelight, only Seth warming me with the magic glow of his love. Only his hands compelling me to him. And his mouth, more insistent now, moist and hot, moving at the indentation of my waist, down to the slight swell of my abdomen. Then his tongue stabbed my navel, a sharp, sweet sword.

I gasped, my whole body turned liquid. I hadn't known how much and for how long I'd wanted him, I hadn't let myself know. Even as I bent to him and my own lips sought his temple, his cheek, the hollow behind his ear, my saner mind called to me: to love Seth Douglass is dangerous, it's unwise. But the call came from too far away, and it came too late, for his hands imprisoned my head and his lips closed over mine in a kiss that became my whole life. His tongue probed deeper, swelled, and filled my mouth, and yet I wanted more.

The fire was hot but our bodies flamed with a heat that was hotter still. Mouths joined, we tore away the clothing that separated us, needing the feel of skin on skin. The proof of my desire for him flowed wetly between my legs. When his lips and tongue left mine, I placed his hand on my wetness and whispered, "Here. Now." I sank to the floor and pulled him with me, guided him into me. When he would have held back I urged him on. He caught my need, and my hunger, and rode me hard—thrusting, thrusting, until we both exploded with a force greater than anything I had ever felt before.

I held him on top of me, his head in the hollow of my shoulder; I welcomed his weight and rejoiced in the feel of him in my arms. Gradually our muscles relaxed and he slipped from within me, then eased his body over to lie at my side. I thought, at least I still have his spent seed inside of me. Then, reluctantly, I opened my eyes.

The first thing I saw was Boris. He sat on the chair where Seth had sat, paws tucked under his chest, looking down at us where we lay naked, legs entwined, on the rug. Boris blinked his round blue eyes, and I could almost hear him thinking, What fools these humans are!

I laughed. The sound came out in a happy gurgle.

Seth opened his eyes. Such long, black eyelashes he had! He said, "I didn't think we were funny!" But he was smiling.

I leaned up on one elbow and traced a finger down his very straight nose. With that finger I touched his lips, lips that had given me such pleasure; I opened his lips and kissed him. A long, lazy kiss of perfect fulfillment. Then I said, "I wasn't laughing at us. At him." I nodded up in Boris's direction.

"I didn't realize we had an audience. I don't think I've ever done it with an audience before," said Seth. He tousled my already-tousled hair. "Did anybody ever tell you what wonderful hair you have?"

"No." I sat up and felt around the floor for my glasses. "I think what I've heard most often is that it looks like a mop. A curly mop." I put on my glasses and the real world sharpened into focus.

Seth sat up, too, and took my glasses off again. "And your eyes . . . such an unusual color, like green smoke. Why don't you wear contacts instead of hiding them behind glasses?"

I snatched my glasses back, pretending to be offended. "Oh. We make love *once,* and you start to criticize! Well, for your information, my eyeballs are allergic or hypersensitive or something. I just couldn't learn to tolerate contact lenses. As long as we're being critical, has that long body of yours ever seen the sun? You're as white as . . . as a ghost!"

"I can't say I like your analogy, my dear." Seth drew his heavy brows together in mock concern. His body, white or not, had pleased me and he knew it.

I hugged my bare knees to my bare breasts and watched him dress himself. Everything about Seth was long and lean and hard, and that fair skin was furred on chest and abdomen, arms and legs, and of course between the legs, with hair black as night.

I asked the question I was thinking. "How did you get so completely gray on your head when all your other hair is so black?"

"Heredity. Unfortunate family trait."

"I don't think it's unfortunate. I like your hair—all of it." I grinned.

Seth, standing and buckling his belt, smiled down on me. Then he reached for me and gathered me up into his arms. "I'm glad you like it, because I love you. Every inch of you. And as soon as the sun is warm enough, I'll get a tan. I'll get as dark as Othello if it will please you, my love!"

"Oh, I think a light shade of toast will be good enough." I shivered in spite of Seth's embrace. The fire was dying. Our magic time was drawing to a close.

Seth felt my shiver and retrieved my robe from the back of the chair, where he'd put it. "As much as I like to look at you, little one, I think you'd better put this on. And I'll fix that fire."

I belted the robe around me and went in search of a hairbrush.

"I hope you have a good supply of wood," Seth muttered. "I must admit, I still have reservations about your living here."

"Don't. Just don't," I cautioned. I didn't want him to ruin the peace, say or do anything that might weaken the bond between us. But already I felt how fragile, how tenuous was our linkage. We had come together out of need. Perhaps out of love. I wasn't quite willing, yet, to use that loaded word. The real world was so complex, so full of different motivations, of deceptions . . . As completely as the world had drained away, so now it returned and claimed me once again. The brush in my tangled hair hurt my head. My tangled thoughts hurt my heart.

Under Seth's care the fire blazed up again. He turned his back to it and addressed me across the room. "I don't understand, Laura. I don't understand why you're so insistent on turning this unsuitable place into a home. And I've never understood what you had in mind that day you had me come out here with you. That day, you know, when you told me Kathryn's body had been found."

Wearily I sat on the loveseat in front of the shuttered windows. I looked at Seth, loving his lankiness and the way his collarbone showed in the open neck of his shirt. I wanted to go away with him, far, far away, where we would both get tan and he'd never wear a tie again. I said, "I have to stay here. I don't expect you to understand. There's no one reason. It's complicated. This place seems to . . . to call out to me. The Stone House wants me here, I can feel it. I don't always like it"—especially at night, I thought, and shrugged the thought away—"there are inconveniences, but nothing that can't be fixed, in time. I need a home, Seth. I'm a natural nest-builder, and I never intended to stay so long in one room at the inn. You know how seldom a house comes up for sale in Beaufort—this was a good solution for me."

Seth came and sat beside me. "You're not telling me everything. You've seemed so driven. Almost obsessed."

I sighed and ran a hand through my hair. "Okay. I know, I just *know* that somehow this place is connected to Kathryn's death. Her . . . murder. It's important for me to stay here. It's the only thing I know to do"—I raised my eyes to his in a challenge—"and I'm doing it."

"The police will find your sister's murderer. If he, or she, can be found."

"Do you really think so? I'm not so sure." I felt old doubts of Seth, unwanted but definitely there, pricking at my mind. "Maybe you should know. You said you spent a long time with them yesterday."

"I certainly did. Oh, I'm sure they're satisfied that I had nothing to do with it, or I'd have gotten a lawyer before answering all their questions. What it comes down to is, when I realized Kathryn probably wasn't coming back, I should have gone to them and told them that I was supposed to meet her here."

"Why didn't you?"

Seth rubbed the back of his neck. "The truth is, I don't know. I guess it's like I told you when you talked about getting a private detective. I thought, why not leave well enough alone?"

"Um-hm. Well, we can't do that anymore, can we?"

"No, we can't."

"If they don't suspect you, what *are* they doing? The sergeant and one of his cronies came to the inn and went through Kathryn's rooms, but I don't think they found anything. They certainly haven't had any news for me."

"I'm not sure. From the kind of questions they asked me, I think they've decided there was something shady going on in Kathryn's life. Forgive me for asking, but was she hooked on drugs, anything like that?"

"If she was, I didn't know. I think Jonathan would have known, and he didn't say anything like that. She certainly didn't die of a drug overdose. The autopsy would have shown it."

"I suggested to Sergeant Sanders that they track down Carroll Trelawney and find out more about his activities, current and past. It was a logical suggestion, but you should have seen their reaction! You'd think I'd attacked a local patron saint!"

"Carroll? Why Carroll? According to Jonathan, he practically *was* a saint!"

Seth got up and started to pace, rubbing his neck all the while. "She must have been killed by someone we don't know. Must have! All the local, uh, suspects are accounted for, or they would have hauled somebody in by now. To me, that points to her husband, associates he, and maybe she, may have had from the past. Something like that."

I mulled over this. I was so in the habit of trusting Jonathan's judgment that I found it difficult to suspect Carroll of anything. Except, of course, wanderlust and excessive love of the sea.

Seth had stopped pacing. He sat down again next to me. "Here. You never opened this."

"My housewarming present . . . I can't believe I forgot. I guess we got involved in other things!" Our eyes met, we shared a smile, and for a moment we were united in memory. Then I untied the crushed silver bow, and opened the box. Inside was a dazzle of color and captured light. "It's beautiful! But what is it?"

Seth was amused. "Take it out and you'll see."

Among the colors I discerned a fine silver chain. I grasped the chain and lifted it up. The gift was a mobile of jewel-like abstract shapes of stained glass, set in and balanced on silver wires, hung from a silver chain. I held the mobile at arm's length, where it quivered and turned delicately in response to the slight motions of my hand. "This is magnificent, Seth. It's a work of art! Thank you."

"You're welcome. I thought the glass, the colors, would be nice in the light from one of these big windows."

"Oh, yes, it will be beautiful. Help me hang it? I can hardly wait to see it in the morning sun."

Seth hung the mobile from the ceiling near my bedroom window. I didn't ask him to stay and see it in the morning sun, nor did he seem to expect me to. When he had left, the Stone House felt empty. Cold. Cold and empty as a tomb.

"Tell me again what happened," I said, and Zelda repeated what she'd said on the telephone. She had left the desk to go to the bathroom, and she'd turned on the answering machine as usual. She couldn't have been gone more than ten minutes. When she'd returned, this mess was what she'd found: the long metal file box in which we kept cards on this month's and next month's reservations had been overturned, its dividers scattered, and the cards themselves were gone. The filing cabinet was pulled open, much of its contents ripped and strewn over the desk, the chairs, the floor. Zelda stood to the side nervously, her hands fluttering and her eyes darting back and forth, from me to the mess. She looked like an ungainly, frightened bird.

"Do you want me to wake Jonathan and tell him?" she asked.

"No! Of course not. There's nothing he can do." I felt revulsion so strong that it was physical, I was close to tossing my recent breakfast. And I felt, too, the icy grip of something very much like fear closing around my spine. This was too much like the destruction of the laundry and storage room. This was a clear threat.

Zelda kept glancing at me, and then away. Trying to judge my reaction? I looked steadily at her until I captured her darting eyes. Why couldn't I feel sympathy for this woman? I couldn't. Her excessive nervousness only annoyed me. I said in an even voice, to calm her, "It's not your fault, Zelda. Stop grieving and start cleaning up. I'm going in the office to think about this."

"Will you call the police?" Her voice came out of a throat so constricted that she squeaked.

I paused, hand on the office door. "As I said, I'm going to think. Police or no police, we can't do business like this. If anyone came in and saw this mess, they'd turn right around and leave."

"But . . . but the police should see it, like it is!" Her bird-eyes glittered.

My annoyance passed the breaking point. "Look, Zelda, either you start putting the reception area back in order, or you can leave and I'll do it myself. But if you leave, you won't be coming back. Do you understand?"

"Yes, but—"

"But nothing! Someone is trying to drive me out of business, and I won't stand for that! If someone, *anyone*, came in here and saw this, this destruction, the news would be all over town in a minute. The only guests we'd get after that would have to be blind, deaf, and dumb! Now, are you going to clean it up or not?"

"I'll clean it up."

"Good!" I shut the office door on her and leaned against it. My knees were weak. I closed my eyes, fighting down nausea. When it passed I went to my desk, sat down, opened the bottom drawer and pulled out a hard-bound record book. Thank goodness I'd been keeping this book ever since my concerns about Polly. I had a handwritten duplicate here of all the reservation records. I also had my own copies of the typed lists of names and addresses of former guests, in the same bottom drawer. The vandal, or whatever he/she was, hadn't done as much damage as he'd hoped. The file contents, though, were another matter.

I went and told Zelda not to throw anything away, we might have to piece the torn papers together. She nodded obediently. I must have put the fear of God—or more likely of losing her job—into her, I thought with some satisfaction. I sat down again to do what I'd said I'd do. Think.

Talk about the fear of God, or just plain fear—someone was trying to put it into *me*. Trying, and succeeding?

No, damn it! I slapped the palm of my hand flat against the desk, hard. It stung, and the iciness that had gripped my spine dissolved in the heat of my growing anger. My anger gave everything clarity and my mind ticked along, hyper-rational.

I did have to tell the police, there was no way to avoid that. But I wouldn't have them come here, I'd go to them. I wouldn't have good old Sergeant Sanders here again with his police car outside, advertising: There's been more trouble at the Trelawney Inn! No way. I'd go to the police only when things were physically in order, and my thoughts in order as well.

I thought all the way back to the intruder on the porch, and I admitted a pattern was emerging. That had been no Peeping Tom, I knew that now. Had it been a man or a woman? Could have been either. The height of the shadow had suggested a man, but shadows can be deceptive. Male or female, that person must have been trying to find an alternative way into the inn. Probably wanted to do damage, way back then. Subsequently he or she, prowling around, found the converted garage and did the damage there. It hadn't amounted to all that much in dollars and we did have insurance, but the shock value had been terrific. Now this—if I hadn't kept duplicate reservation records, we'd have been crippled by this attack. And it was shocking, too. The criminal, what from lawyer days I recalled the police call the perpetrator, had destroyed a lot of records in a short time.

Suddenly, horribly, I realized we'd been watched. Some-one knew Zelda left the desk unattended for a brief time each morning, and presumably knew how long that brief time usually lasted. Someone also had waited until a morning when I hadn't come in, which was a rare occur-rence. I thought with some satisfaction of the shadowy Someone waiting morning after morning, freezing his balls off, waiting in vain for Zelda to be alone. Since the two days I'd taken off at the time of my move, some ten days ago, I'd kept exactly the same daytime hours as when I'd lived at the inn. Why had the Someone not struck during those two days? Impossible to know. There were too many potential answers to that question.

I didn't like where my thoughts were going, but I pushed the hair back out of my eyes and doggedly went on. So. Either this Someone had watched the inn every day until this morning, or had just decided that today was the day and lucked out, *or* had been watching . . . *me.* Whom had I told that I would be staying at the Stone House this morning to hang drapes? Jonathan, Zelda, Seth, the carpenter and his two helpers. It couldn't have been the latter three because they'd all three been working, at last, on the roof when I got Zelda's call.

Oh, Lord. I didn't like this. Not one little bit. I got up and went to the window because my thoughts made me too uncomfortable to sit still. I paced back and forth in front of the window, then stopped to look out. It gave onto a small landscaped courtyard and across that, the parking lot. To the left, out of sight, was the converted garage. In the parking lot were five cars: mine, Zelda's, and those of our two single guests and one guest couple. Not much cover for someone who wanted to hide and watch.

I chewed at my lower lip. My throat was tight. Tears pricked in my eyes. I blinked and swallowed. My thoughts had led me to a place I didn't want to go. I backed up, mentally, and tried another route. Not who, but why? Why threaten me, why try to get at me through stupid attacks on the inn? Maybe not so stupid, but there was an adolescent quality about this maliciousness. Why? Well, to make me give up. Close down the inn. The inn was my only reason for being in Beaufort. Maybe someone just wanted me to leave Beaufort. Maybe this Someone had killed Kathryn, and my very presence, especially with my physical resemblance to her, was a reminder of a crime he wanted to forget. If I left town the police might feel under less pressure to keep on looking for her murderer. And I, myself, wouldn't be looking for the murderer if I were gone—not that my looking had produced any results.

A worse idea: What if this Someone was a complete crazy.

Totally insane, though he walked around appearing normal. Had hated Kathryn, killed her off, and then found there was yet another Kathryn. Me, her almost-twin. He would have transferred his psychotic hatred to me. First he would do threatening things to me until I was terrified, and then he would kill me, too. The idea fit, in a way; it was consistent with my first reaction to the violence in the laundry and storage room, that it was the work of a sick mind. But . . .

I put that idea away. It was too bizarre. Nobody that unbalanced could seem normal on the surface day after day. On the other hand, a very smart person could do things and make them look crazy. And there I was, back in the place I didn't want to be. I'd trapped myself.

I went back to the desk, walking on feet that felt like lead. I took off my glasses and covered my face with my hands. Pressed the heels of my hands hard against my cheekbones, told myself, Hang on! I felt myself out on the edge again, this time teetering, about to fall off the edge and into the abyss beyond. Deep inside me, so deep I had to spiral down into the depths of my consciousness to get there, a dialogue was going on. A dialogue more personally threatening than anything that had happened at the inn, for the dialogue threatened *my* sanity. I knew if I were to keep from falling off the edge I had to bring that dialogue up, acknowledge the two parts of me that were at war. Slowly, painfully, I brought it up.

One side was screaming, Don't take him away from me, too! Don't make me lose Seth, not now! Not now that I've allowed myself to want him, and to begin cautiously to love him! The other side, serious, unscreaming, said: I told you it was dangerous and unwise to love Seth Douglass. I warned you, and you didn't listen to me!

I fell back in my chair, tears streaming down my face. Never mind the tears, the worst was over. I had gone into that place I didn't want to go, and now I was facing what I found there. My on-the-edge status was preserved; I wasn't going to fall off. Yet. Who might want me to give up and leave Beaufort? Seth Douglass. Why? Because he wanted the Stone House. Wanted it more badly than I could ever have imagined. Seth knew well the workings of the inn. He had known about my plans to hang drapes this morning. And—sickening thought!—even if he hadn't known schedules, routines, or anything, he had his confederate. Zelda. Right here, on the spot. What if Seth had planted Zelda here, to spy? God, the scenario got worse and worse. Worse, because it was so possible. Quite possible that Seth had put the snake, Zelda, in my bosom so to speak. Zelda could have destroyed the records herself!

I decided that I had better listen to the other part of me, which was practically jumping up and down for attention. Yelling, Seth loves you! Seth loves you!

Oh, but does he? How should I know? I'd been mistaken, painfully mistaken, about love once before. Seth was an incredibly complex man; it would take years for me to know him well. And he had intelligence along with complexity. Such a person could be capable of anything. Anything except insanity. For certain, Seth was not insane.

I argued with myself a little longer: the Stone House, no mere piece of property, was worth killing for. Even committing acts of threat and violence for. Certainly not the Stone House, a somewhat isolated rock pile. Seth wanted it, but not *that* much. He does want it, said that persistent doubter inside me. Look what he's doing, he's covering all his bases. If he can't frighten you away, he thinks he'll make you love him, and then he'll marry you. Either way, the Stone House will be his!

My tears were spent. I had torn myself apart, split my own heart in two. I ached, I yearned for simplicity, just a plain, simple life. What was that song, that old Quaker or Shaker early-American song? "'Tis a gift to be simple, 'tis a gift to be free . . ." Oh, yes, what a gift that would be! To simply love Seth, to be free of all doubts, free of all the threatening, terrible things that were happening.

Keep it simple, I told myself. No one can do more than one thing at a time. Don't hide from the truth, don't twist the facts, but don't overreact, either. Most of all, hang in there and survive. I felt a little better. My tortured mind grew calm. I mustn't dash out and accuse Zelda of destroying my records and being in conspiracy with Seth. Nor should I fire her, no matter how great the temptation. It was better to have her here where I could keep an eye on her.

I took up my record book. Zelda could set up a new reservation file, which might or might not make her happy. Then I would go to the police station and tell them exactly what had happened. Just the facts, ma'am, like in that old TV show *Dragnet*. No doubts, no fear, no wild guesses, just the facts. And what to do about Seth? I could only move ahead one step at a time. I didn't have to decide the Seth-step yet. I was glad, though, that I'd already told him I wanted a firmer foundation of friendship between us before we were intimate again. He'd caught me in a weak moment that night, I'd said. I didn't say that since we'd made love I grew weak at the first velvet softening of his brown eyes. I would have to deal with my weakness, however difficult that might be.

I rose from my desk, pulled my body to its fullest height, drew a deep breath, and took the first of my one steps at a time. I went to see Zelda, carrying my record book before me like a shield.

▰▰▰ 13 ▰▰▰

Noon, February fourteenth, St. Valentine's Day. I climbed to the top of the tower. The climb was not physically hard—if the tower had been a modern office building, it would have been only about four stories high. Psychologically, though, it was difficult indeed. The tower seemed to twist both time and space. The stairs clung to its perimeter, and for the first twelve or fourteen feet the effect was claustrophobic. Steep, narrow wood steps squeezing round and round a huge, many-angled box that was the tower room. I felt I couldn't breathe, and knew it was an illusion, for the narrow slits of windows let in both light and air. I felt that those angled wooden walls might start at any time to move and crush me. I couldn't look at them, so I looked instead at each step as my feet gained and left it. The steps were new, pristine, walked upon only by the workman who'd replaced almost all the treads with these new boards. My breath came hard, but not from physical effort. This climb was, I thought, a microcosm of my present life: one step at a time. I pulled a grim smile, realizing that here as I climbed the tower I was literally between a rock and a hard place—the rock being the rocks of the tower wall, and the hard place being the wooden walls of the inner tower room.

At last I ascended free of that octagonal wood box. I clung to the handrail, which was not a rail at all but a heavy, ancient chain bolted into the rocks, and looked out over the roof-ceiling of the tower room. It was perfectly flat. I could have walked right across it if I'd wanted to—I didn't. My relief at being rid of that encroaching inner wall was swiftly replaced by stomach-sinking insecurity. Too much open space where so shortly before there had been none, it was profoundly unsettling. Though I knew the tower was about twenty feet in diameter, I'd paced off the tower room, it seemed now vast. Vast and gloomy. Far across I could see the stone steps growing out of the stone wall, winding up and up and up.

The workman had warned me, the wooden steps stopped at the level of the tower room ceiling. He thought they'd been built because in the construction of the tower room the original stone steps had been damaged. I stood now on the last of those wooden steps. If I put my foot on the next step, I would tread upon stone. Old, old stone, part of the tower, built into its walls from the very beginning. The workman said the stone steps were perfectly safe, he'd climbed to the top himself and looked out from the tower. How was the view? I'd asked. Pretty good, he'd replied, he guessed it was worth the climb. I looked up into space that seemed darker than it should have been at midday, and I felt paralyzed. Unable to go up, or down. Time stopped.

I looked down at my feet, small feet, human feet. Move! I commanded them, Climb! And they did. I clung to the chain railing and I went up and up, one step at a time. At the top was an old door, smaller than the front door but just as heavy. Before the door was a landing only a little longer and wider than one of the steps. I stood on the landing and slowly, carefully, turned around. Looked down. When my heart stopped swooping around in my chest I thought, I did it! I made it all the way up out of that dark, gloomy place! Then I turned easily, effortlessly, pushed open the door, and stepped out into the sun.

I looked up at the sky. Beautiful, beautiful blue, a shade the local people called "Carolina Blue." High, wispy clouds like angels' gossamer sleeves. I lifted my arms up and out, a gesture of elation.

I had emerged on the land side of the tower. Its stone formed a circular wall at my waist's height, and I walked along, trailing my hand over the rough rock, following its curve until I beheld the sea. The Core Sound, the uninhabited Core Banks, the great Atlantic Ocean. These were treacherous waters; many ships had met their end out there. Yet today all was so innocently blue and white. I stood in my high place with the steady, cool wind lifting my hair and the salty sea-tang staining my lips, and I sealed a love affair begun months before, my love for the sea. So many have fallen for this Indifferent Lover. I, too. Never again, if I were given a choice, would I live out of sight of the sea.

I do not know how long I stayed on top of the tower. I do know that was when I truly understood what Seth had told me about the beaches in general and the Outer Banks in particular. I felt their wildness, the rule of nature here; felt it in a way beyond words. Felt a power I did not need to understand in order to know that if I did not abuse it, I might share it. Into my mind came an image of the dolphins—this was their element and they gloried in it, they knew and shared this power.

Finally, reluctantly, I left. Going down through the tower was no easier than coming up had been. I clung to that chain on the wall as if it were a lifeline. I found myself thinking that the octagonal tower room should never have been built, it was an instrusion into this ancient place. Perhaps Seth was right, perhaps none of this place was meant for human habitation, and all should be torn down except the ancient tower.

When I reached the bottom step at last, I went and stood in the center of the tower room. I looked up at the lighted rounds of the chandeliers, looked out at the paneled walls which I had rubbed and polished until they gleamed, and down at the floor which I still had not refinished. Then I closed my eyes. My eyes would not tell me what I wanted to know. It was a feeling-thing I sought to identify. The feeling was very different here and on the stairs, than on the top of the tower. Here, I felt something . . . wrong. As if the tower housed a . . . a bad spirit.

My eyes flew open. I'd shocked myself, coming out with such nonsense! There are no bad spirits, only bad people. What this tower room needed was exactly what I intended to give it, music and dancing. My dancing. Perhaps that was why the Stone House wanted me, so that I would dance in the tower room and drive the bad feeling away. I shook my head, as disgusted and yet baffled by this thought as I had been by the bit about bad spirits. Only one thing was certain: the sooner I got the floor refinished and my stereo hooked up and a practice barre installed, the better!

Mother Nature was teasing us this Valentine's Day. With dreadful swiftness the weather turned. The wind rose up and grew teeth of cold—straight off the water it blew, a Nor'easter. The great storm-wind. It forced its way in through the lancet windows and howled in the tower. Boris, who is afraid of almost nothing, hid. I ran outside and struggled with the shutters. I would get one side halfway closed and the wind would slam it open again. If I hung on, my feet would leave the ground and take me with it. I soon learned why my carpenter had said to be careful. The strength of my hands and arms was not enough; I had to lean all my body weight into swinging each shutter closed. I was determined to get it done before the rain began.

When I had conquered the last shutter, I looked out to sea and watched the gathering storm. It had taken me so completely by surprise. I thought how awful it would be to be out in a boat when this happened! Awful, and yet the power in the gale and the rolling, thundering waters was thrilling. Now that my shutters were closed and I knew I could return to the safety of my rock walls, I felt excited. I let the power flow through me and fancied that I could participate unscathed in this storm.

The temperature was dropping rapidly. I knew that it seldom snowed here on the coast, but there was an icy bite in the wind that meant snow to me. Too, the wall of clouds advancing from the horizon were the heavy dull gray of snow clouds. Instead of getting drunk on nature's power, I'd best do the things one does to dig in for a winter storm.

First I called Jonathan. It was a Saturday and we had no guest reservations at the inn for the whole weekend, so I'd given myself the weekend off. I told Jonathan he could close down if he wanted to, we certainly wouldn't be getting any drop-ins with this sudden storm. Then I carried in several loads of wood for my fireplaces. I debated whether or not to make a dash to the grocery store and decided I wouldn't. My Subaru had taken me through lots of Midwestern ice and snow, and if I had to, I could go out in just about any kind of weather.

I made a pot of tea and settled down with a book in front of the fire in my room. Boris, having gotten used to the howling in the tower, jumped up on the chair with me. He kneaded himself a place alongside my thigh and settled there, purring. I felt warm and cozy. A little smug, to be so comfortable in the face of a coming storm.

Sleet hit the shutters like thousands of tiny knives. I drank my tea and read on. The wind slammed in gusts against the walls of my stone fortress.

Boom! Boom! Boom! That was not the wind! Boom! Boom! The blows fell hard, their boom echoed, reverberating a bass continuo under the staccato pricking of the sleet. Boom! I couldn't place the sound, it wasn't thunder, it was not anything I'd heard before. Boris had jumped down and run from my room, run in the direction of the tower—which was odd because Boris hated the tower for some reason; he wouldn't even go in there with me. Boom! Boom! I put my book aside and followed Boris. I was into the living room before I realized the booms were not a sound of nature. The booms were someone or something at the tower door.

If Seth had frightened me briefly by banging on the door of the kitchen, this was much worse. I took a deep breath and unlocked the door from the living room into the tower. Boris hissed and arched his back and held his ground in the living room. Boom! Boom! Boom! The thought that propelled me forward into the dark was that someone could have been stranded in the storm. The sound of the wind in the tower above me was horrific. I found the light switch and flipped it. The booming stopped. I crossed the floor swiftly, unlocked and opened the big door.

"Oh, for God's sake!" I nearly collapsed with relief. It was Nick Westover, crusted with ice crystals from head to foot. "Come in! You do turn up at the oddest times. What are you doing here?"

"Like they say, any port in a storm!" He winked at me and pushed the heavy door shut behind him. "I was beginning to think you couldn't hear me, though, over all the wind. Mind if I stay awhile?"

"Of course I don't mind. Come on, the first thing we need to do is get you warm." I led the way, talking over my shoulder. "What happened? Were you out in your boat, or what? How did you get here?"

"Yeah, I had the *Hellfire* up around Portsmouth Island, checking out Swash Inlet. You know it moved, closed over for a while? Anyway, this storm came up real fast. I thought I could make it back through the sound, but it was too tricky. . . . Say, this is nice! This is great!" Nick stopped in the middle of my room and turned a full circle, looking.

"Thank you. Uh, let's go in the kitchen. There's a fire there, too, and I'll make you something hot to drink. You really are frozen, aren't you?"

"Sure am. Say, you have any brandy?"

I plunged on toward the kitchen, sure he'd follow. "No, I'm sorry. I don't drink much, and I just haven't thought to stock up on those things. Here we are—I'll just put another log on the fire, and you get that wet jacket off."

I worked at the fire, then brought a chair to hang Nick's jacket on so the fire could dry it. The jacket was heavy wool and soaked clear through. So was the knitted cap he pulled from his head.

"Oh, dear," I said. "You're wet to the skin!"

"Yeah, I guess I am," Nick agreed. He didn't seem the least bit distressed.

"I can't think what to—I mean, you're so much bigger than I—but you can't stay in those wet clothes!"

Nick was amused by my confusion. He stood with his back to the fire and watched me flounder around. I couldn't have him sitting naked in front of the fire in my kitchen! If he had any other ideas, he didn't offer them. Instead he started to pull his damp turtleneck sweater off over his head.

"Wait! You'll . . . get chilled," I improvised. "Let me get you something to wear before you take those things off."

What I got for him was a blanket, rather old and rather pink, but it would cover him. I turned on the quartz heater in the bathroom and put him in there with it, and hoped for the best. When he came out with the blanket wrapped around himself I had coffee on and was making grilled cheese sandwiches to go with the vegetable soup I'd planned for my own supper. From the corner of my eye I watched Nick spread his wet clothes in front of the fire. He sat on the floor facing the fireplace, legs folded under him Indian-fashion, blanket around him also Indian-fashion.

He didn't talk. I took him a mug of coffee. He asked for sugar, then went back to looking at the flames. His hair, drying now, repeated their coppery-red. I thought he must be colder and more tired than he wanted to admit. This quiet contemplation of the fire was quite unlike the Nick I'd known so far.

The sandwiches were ready for grilling, but I hesitated. Nick seemed to need more time and I wasn't really hungry yet. I'd busied myself with the food mainly to have something to do. I poured my own mug of coffee and stood at the counter, listening to the storm. It must have been terrible for him, out there all alone. He still stared into the flames, motionless. I took my coffee and joined him on the floor.

"Nick, you haven't touched your coffee," I said gently.

He didn't answer. He seemed hypnotized.

I picked up his mug and put it in his hands. "Drink that," I said more forcefully, "you need it."

"Huh?" He jerked his head around, a strange look in his eyes. "Oh, yeah. Thanks."

He really has been off somewhere, not in this room, I thought. I sipped at my coffee and allowed myself to relax enough to enjoy it. At least he wasn't coming on to me. I certainly wasn't afraid of him—in fact, his repeated attentions had been flattering. Nor could I be too critical of him since I had in the past found his sexuality compelling, though merely in a physical way. I had responded to it whether I wanted to or not, as he well knew. I stole a sideways look at him. Yes, he was still sexually attractive, even with his whole body hidden under a faded pink blanket.

The silence lengthened and still Nick did not even move. He sat as still as one of the stones from which my house was built. I found this disturbing, especially as it was so unlike him to be both still and quiet. Perhaps he was simply exhausted. Yes, that must be it. But then, he'd had such an odd look in his eyes. . . .

Boris distracted me. He crept up beside me, on the side away from Nick. I rubbed his fur idly, then had a sudden, shocking recollection of that long gash he'd clawed into Nick's cheek. Dark blood welling, the white scar that remained. I looked down at my cat, realized that he wasn't purring. His body was tense, ears back, and he glared at Nick. Boris, too, remembered.

Nick came abruptly and completely out of his reverie. Whatever had so absorbed him, it had not brought him peace. He was frowning. He asked without preamble, "What's going on with you and Seth Douglass?"

"We're friends," I replied warily, "good friends."

"He's a wimp."

I almost laughed. Seth was often too serious, sometimes cold, and he could be maddeningly reserved at times, but I of all people knew there was nothing "wimpy" about Seth. I faked a cough and when I had myself together I said, "Oh, really?"

Nick nodded. "Believe it. You gotta stop spending so much time with him."

I was more curious than annoyed. "How would you know what kind of time I spend with Seth, or anyone else?"

"I know. I get around. I talk to people, they talk to me. I come around to see you, his car's always there." He narrowed his eyes, glowering. His hair and beard had dried into a furious, burning bush out of which those green-slitted eyes glowed. "He's no man for you!"

"And you are, I suppose?"

My sarcasm was wasted on Nick, he didn't even hear it. Instead, he was pleased. He went from Old Testament fury to overgrown kid in about two seconds. "You got it! I am!"

Chuckling, I shook my head and my own hair fell into my eyes. "You're impossible, Nick Westover!" Unwilling to continue along this line, I coaxed him to the kitchen table and gave him a bowl of soup to work on while I grilled the cheese sandwiches.

It took three sandwiches to satisfy his hunger, and still he hadn't talked of what I most wanted to hear. How he'd been caught in the storm, where he'd left the *Hellfire,* how he'd managed to get from his boat to my tower door.

Finally, as I put a plate of cookies on the table for dessert, I simply asked him.

It was never hard to get Nick to talk about himself. He said, "Oh, it's a bad storm, all right, but I know these waters pretty well. If I'd tried to keep on going down to Cape Lookout, that would be the danger. You know, when you're out in a boat you can see the tower here from anywhere in the sound. And there's lots of places along the coastline to shelter a boat. So that's what I did."

"I see. You think the *Hellfire* will be safe?"

"Sure." Nick tipped his chair onto its back legs, a movement that caused his blanket to slip from one shoulder, leaving most of his broad chest exposed. "This isn't near as bad as that New Year's storm with all the high tides. The sleet is bad; it'll turn to ice. The deck will get slick as glass, but I took the sails down and buttoned her up tight. She'll do."

I was momentarily distracted by his smooth skin, hairless and still tanned, stretched over splendid musculature. It seemed unnatural for his chest to be without hair when there was so much of it on his face and head. In spite of all his gorgeousness, I managed to ask my next question. "How did you get from there to here?"

Nick laughed.

"I walked, of course!"

"It must have been a long walk, no wonder you got so wet. And how did you make it up the bluff, to the Stone House?"

"I climbed up the old path. You didn't know you got an old path?"

I shook my head.

"I guess you don't know your own property too well, then. You got a real prize of a place here, Laura. If it was mine you can be damn sure I'd know every inch of it!"

I felt defensive. Even as I wondered how he had come to know about this old path, my defensiveness took over and I heard myself making excuses. "I've been concentrating on making the house livable. There's been so much to do inside, I haven't been around the grounds much. And then, too, the weather has been bad most days, and I've had to be at the inn most of the time. . . ."

Nick brought his chair legs back down with a little thump and leaned across the table. The other side of the blanket fell away. I trusted it still covered him from the waist down. His emerald eyes flashed. "Maybe tomorrow I'll show you where the path is. You'd like that I'll bet, wouldn't you? We could, uh, explore together."

"Explore. Tomorrow. Yes." Mention of tomorrow brought home to me the fact that Nick would have to stay the night. I couldn't very well put him back out in the storm, nor would he want me to drive him to town when he'd only have to come back to get his boat.

We got through the evening with a minimum of tensions, sexual and other. Nick, more or less wrapped in his blanket, watched television and drank a bottle of white wine I opened for him. I spent a good deal of time fixing up the guest room for him, then joined him in the library, where I resumed reading my book and he continued watching TV. We were surprisingly companionable.

Nick apparently felt the same, for at one point he said, "I like this."

I looked up from my book and asked, "Good TV program?"

He smiled. "The program's okay. I mean I like being in a

199

real house with a nice fire and all, while it's storming outside. Feels real cozy. What I like best is, you made it this way. And you're here, too."

Boris was not disarmed, he kept his distance from Nick, but I was. As the hours wore on and the wind still howled in the tower, I went from being reconciled to Nick's presence to being positively glad for the company. When bedtime came it was comforting to know that Nick would be sleeping in the next room. Provided, of course, that he *stayed* in the next room.

The storm, or something, had made Nick docile. He seemed content with one small good-night kiss, and we went to our separate beds.

I swam upward through layers of sleep and left my bed like a sleepwalker. I didn't remember turning on a light, yet I could see. I didn't feel my feet on the floor, I glided like a wraith in my white nightgown from room to room to room. I searched, and did not know why I searched. I searched, and did not find. I came at last to a doorway filled with darkness. There, I would not go. Puzzled, I glided back through the rooms, back to the waiting softness of my bed. I swam down and down, where deep sleep waited and claimed me once more.

In the morning I awoke suddenly, instantly alert. Most unusual for me! I hurried, shivering with bitter damp cold, to build up the embers of my fire. As I knelt with hands spread to the kindling flames, I shivered again—not with cold, but with memory. How strange, how very, very strange!

Boris left his place at the foot of the bed and joined me on the hearth.

"Mowr?"

I scratched his head and sat back on my heels. "I had the strangest dream, big guy. At least, I think it was a dream."

"Mowr. Mowr-ur-urr." He rubbed against me and I stroked him.

"Yes, you're a beautiful cat. Beautiful, soft cat," I said out of habit. I wasn't thinking of Boris, I was wondering: what if it wasn't a dream? What if I'd really gotten out of bed, half asleep, and gone from room to room? Why would I have done such a thing?

My heart began to thump. I remembered Nick, sleeping in the next room. I whipped my head around. The door was closed. Both doors were closed, to the library on one side and the guest room on the other. But they'd been open, both of them! And Nick . . . where had *he* been?

Oh, geez, Laura! Get hold of yourself! I shook my head, as if that might separate out the crazy thoughts from the reasonable ones. It didn't. By the time I'd dressed in the bathroom, in several layers of clothes because it was the coldest morning yet, I had decided the crazy idea was correct. I might have been half asleep when I'd prowled through the house, but I had done it. It was no dream. So then where was Nick? He hadn't been in his bed when I'd passed through that room in the night.

His clothes were still in front of the fireplace, and all but the jacket were dry. I got a new fire roaring and turned the jacket inside out to dry it the rest of the way. I folded his other things, then made coffee and drank a glass of orange juice. Nick still hadn't showed, so I went to wake him. I knocked on the door to the guest room. "Nick? Good morning, Nick!"

Not a sound. Not even the rustle of him turning over in bed.

I knocked again, harder. "Nick! Wake up, sleepyhead. I'll be making breakfast. I'm leaving your clothes right outside the door here."

He must have heard me. I put the clothes down and went back to the kitchen. Nick was sure to be the bacon-and-eggs type. I could do the bacon first, and by then he'd be up and could say how he wanted his eggs. I put strips of bacon in a pan over low heat, then opened the back door to see what the storm had done.

Light dazzled my eyes. Everything was covered in a thin layer of snow and ice, and where the sun touched it sparkled like diamonds. The air was cold enough to take breath away. I put a tentative toe outside. Slick as glass! Until the sun was warm enough to melt this, we were stranded. I closed the door and went back to my cooking.

The bacon was done, the table was set, bread waited in the toaster, and still no Nick. What if . . . ? Oh, nuts! I ran my hand through my hair and slumped over the sink. My nerves weren't what I wanted them to be, that was for sure. Nick wasn't gone, he couldn't be. He was in that bed, and he was just a heavy sleeper.

Well, then, argued the opposing counsel inside me, where was he when you were walking around in the middle of the night? Good question. He had to have been in the one place I didn't go, in the tower room. But in the pitch-black dark? Now I was confused again. Maybe it *had* been a dream. There had been light in the other rooms, no one in the bed in the guest room, the feeling that I was searching, and door after door already open for me to pass through—until that last, dark door. Nick wouldn't have been in the tower, in the dark. It made no sense.

Oh, this was maddening! And it was stupid, when all I had to do was go in the guest room and wake Nick up and ask him what the heck he'd been doing in the middle of the night. I stomped through the library/dining room and across my room to the guest room door. The neat pile I'd made of his clothes was still there. I picked it up and knocked on the door again.

"Nick?" This time I didn't wait for an answer.

He was there all right, a big, bulky shape under the covers, red hairy head half-on, half-off the pillow and his face turned to one side. I let out a little sigh of relief. Some part of me had been afraid he might have disappeared, I didn't want to even wonder how.

"Come on, Nick." I clutched his clothes to my chest with one hand and gave his shoulder a shove with the other. "Wake up, will you *please?*"

The next thing I knew I was on the bed with him, and the covers were off of him and tangled around me. Trapping me.

"You—you turkey!" I yelled, flailing at the covers. "You tricked me! You weren't asleep at all."

He just laughed. He was stark naked and for once I didn't appreciate his body. Not even his stunning erection. I struggled more, then realized I'd never get out of this by physical effort. He was far too strong for me. Words were my best defense.

I glared at him and opened my mouth to speak—and as soon as my lips parted, his mouth came down on mine. His tongue pushed past my teeth, and I bit it.

Nick's head jerked up. "You little hell-cat!"

I hadn't really hurt him. He must like a fight—his green eyes danced. Before he could come back for more, I let fly a volley of words. "What do you think you're doing, Nick Westover? Don't you know it's not nice to attack a person who gives you food, clothing, and shelter? Let me up, let me go, right now!"

"Aw, come on, Laura. I need you, you see how much I need you." He bent closer, and closer. His lips fastened on my neck, plying, seeking to arouse. His breath fell hot upon my ear. "You'll like it. Just relax—"

I'd worked my left hand free and I grabbed a handful of beard and pulled, hard.

"Owww!" His right hand went up to rub his bearded chin. "You fight dirty!"

With only one of his hands on me and his attention diverted, I managed to wriggle free of the entangling covers. But he still had me by one shoulder, and I was very angry with him. I spat, "What did you expect, you . . . you barbarian! If this is the way you go about making love to a woman, you have a lot to learn!"

Nick had remarkably expressive eyes, and I was learning to read his facial expressions, too, in spite of the covering beard. His eyes flinched and appeared briefly puzzled, then wounded. He pulled away completely. A leering grin faded, his jaw went slack. He looked down at his now-limp penis, and then back at me; and though he said nothing I could almost hear him thinking, Now see what you've done!

A bit late, Boris appeared on the scene. Oh, no, I thought, go back, big guy! But Nick had seen the cat. He fingered the white scar on his cheek. Boris had heard the alarm in my voice and he stared at Nick, ears back, growling deep in his throat.

Quickly I scrambled up and put myself between the cat and the man. "No harm done. I forgive you. Just don't . . . don't come on so strong, okay? I brought your clothes, they're around here, somewhere. Get dressed and come to the kitchen, I'm cooking breakfast." I scooped Boris up into my arms. In the doorway I stopped and asked brightly, "By the way, how do you like your eggs?"

"Eggs? Huh!" Nick snorted. "You gotta be kidding."

I scrambled the eggs because that's how I like them. Nick came to the kitchen table fully dressed. He had even made an attempt to discipline his hair. He said nothing as he ate, which I could understand. No doubt I'd wounded his ego. From time to time I caught him looking at me in a strange, considering way as if I were some newly discovered life form.

"It's all ice outside," I said at last. "I don't think you can get back to the *Hellfire* for a few hours."

"I'll see about that," he mumbled.

"Perhaps, after a while, we could go out and see just how slick it is. I'd really like to get the shutters open, if you'd help me."

He pushed back from the table, measuring me. "Can't do it alone, huh?"

I wanted to ease things between us, since he was likely to be here a while longer. It wouldn't hurt to flatter him a little bit. "I can, but it's hard for me to reach the latches. I'm afraid I might slip. But you're so tall, you could do it easily!"

His lips curved up, a little. "Yeah, I guess I could do that. The shutters are new, aren't they?"

"Yes, they are. How did you know?" Instantly, I tensed.

He shrugged, and took a long pull at his coffee mug. "I've explored around the coastline a lot. I like to look for places where the pirates might have been. It's like a hobby of mine, you know?"

"Yes, I remember you said pirates had been in the Stone House, or at least in the tower. And I said you were wrong."

"Maybe I was, maybe I wasn't. Anyway, this was a while back and the Stone House was deserted, nobody lived here, so I looked around. I didn't know it belonged to you."

"It didn't until my sister died. The Stone House belonged to Kathryn."

"Oh, yeah?" One bushy eyebrow went up. "How about that? She sure didn't let it be known much, did she?"

My tension dissolved. Of course Nick hadn't known the secret, only Seth had known. It was natural enough that a man like Nick, a sort of adventurer, would poke around an uninhabited old landmark. Especially one which had a tower, an obvious relationship to the sea.

Now that Nick seemed thoroughly placated, I could ask him what I longed to know. "Nick, last night something woke me up. I don't know what it was. And you weren't in your room. Where were you?"

His eyes narrowed. "You woke up?"

"Yes, I did. And got up, too, though I was half asleep."

"Well, I heard a noise. Like somebody messing around where they shouldn't have been. So I got up and looked around. I looked in your room, and I thought you were asleep. I looked in all the rooms and I never did find anything, so I figured I must have been dreaming. After a while I went back to bed."

I felt enormously relieved, and touched. He'd actually been trying to protect me! I wished all mysteries were as easily and happily solved. I said, "Thank you, I shouldn't have worried."

"Not with me here!" He smiled, showing his even, white teeth. "Old Nick takes care of his women!"

Here we go again, I thought. I couldn't stop myself, I had to say it. "Nick, I'm *not* one of your women!"

Now he was impervious. "You will be, Laura, you will be."

Nick opened the shutters for me while I cleaned up the kitchen. When he came back in he said the crust of snow and ice was beginning to melt. He offered to take my car and go to the store for me. It was the least he could do, he said, to repay me for feeding him.

He saw my surprise, and laughed. Of course he could drive, he said. He couldn't get everywhere he needed to go by boat, could he? He had a car which he kept in a rented garage in Beaufort.

Well, why not let him take my car. Shopping wasn't my favorite thing to do anyway. I made him a shopping list and gave him my keys. I stood at the kitchen door and watched my dear old Subaru disappear into the trees in the distance. I was sorry now that I'd let him have it. What if he had a wreck? My inner voice chided me: You know you have to start trusting somebody sometime!

How true, I thought. I'd just have to make more of an effort.

Seth called. I said, Yes, I'm fine, and No, don't come out because I'm busy and don't want to be interrupted right now. He didn't ask what I was busy with, fortunately, since I hadn't thought of an answer for that question. The last thing I needed was Seth and Nick both on the premises at the same time; it would be a thousand times worse than Nick and Boris!

I was being super-careful with Seth these days, making an effort which painted me. It was hard not to fall into the relationship he offered. Harder still to realize that only when Kathryn's murderer was found could I let go of this miserable control over my feelings for Seth. The murderer might never be found, and what then? Sometimes I thought I would even prefer to have Seth proved the murderer than to go on living with my doubts. Every phone call, every span of hours spent with him was a kind of tortured pleasure. I really didn't know how long I could stand it.

When I hung up the telephone my hands were shaking. I sought out Boris and found him curled up on my loveseat. I picked him up and held him close, comforting myself as I stroked his softness. His purring restored my spirits. "What would I do without you, Boris, old friend?" I murmured.

Nick was gone a long time, longer than I would have

thought necessary for a short list of groceries. I told myself that the roads were bad, not to worry; I worried anyway, not for Nick but for the Subaru. I had no doubt that in a wreck Nick would walk away whole—he had that indestructible aura about him.

I was never good at waiting. I felt restless. I looked out of the windows and saw that the lawn was now a patchwork of brown and white, muddy grass and melting snow. I pulled on my boots and my blue poncho. I'd go outside—perhaps I could find that old path on my own. Though I held the door open, Boris declined to come with me. The ground was too cold and messy for his fastidious cat-feet.

There was a high, thin overcast to the sky, straining the sunlight. My feet alternately squished and crunched as I made my way to the bluff. Midway I stopped, considering. Should I angle right or left? I knew what lay straight ahead, so it couldn't be that way. I chose left and set off. As I scrunched along I thought about Nick, struggling up here in the sleet and the stiff wind and the near-darkness. Along the way a pile of rocks farther left caught my eye. I hadn't seen that before, and I went over to investigate.

I didn't realize what it was at first, city-bred woman that I am. A circle of stones about a yard in diameter, broken down now in places, it was covered over by weathered boards roughly hammered together. Its significance nagged at me until I captured it: a well! An old well, no longer of any use. I went closer and with some effort pushed the covering of boards partially aside. There was still water in there, not too far down, either. Five or six feet, I guessed. I wondered if the water was still good, and decided it didn't matter. I tugged the cover back in place and went on.

There wasn't any old path, not really. What there was was a gouge in the bluff that signaled the top of a series of steps gouged into the land and loosely fitted with chunks of rock. A primitive stairway clearly belonging to the Stone House— I'd have recognized those buff-colored stones anywhere. They led down to a small cove that was scarcely more than a dent in the shoreline. In the cove the *Hellfire* rode at anchor, looking none the worse for her night in the storm.

I was pleased to have found a way down to the water and the strip of sand. It was like having my own narrow beach; on warmer days I could lie in the sun and dabble in the water. I lifted my chin and held my face to the ever-present wind—too cold today, with that bone-piercing cold I never seemed to get used to. Yet I wanted to go down there. In fact, I almost felt I *had* to go down there.

I set my foot on the top step, such as it was. My ears started to ring. Must be the wind. I put my hands over my ears and brought my other foot onto the top step. My ears rang louder. I reached down with my foot for the next step. My body swayed, I was dizzy. I gasped for breath, my vision blurred, the milky sky and the gray-green sea slid past each other and formed a whirlpool. In the center of the vortex was the *Hellfire*, in full sail . . .

I sat down, hard, on the top step. Let go of my ears and clutched at the solid rock on either side of me. The ringing in my ears faded and gradually my vision cleared. I was panting for breath, grateful beyond measure that I hadn't fallen to the bottom of those rough steps. I'd have been battered to pieces!

I'm tired of living on the edge, I thought, sick and tired of these experiences. This had been the worst one yet, and the most dangerous. What did it mean? Why had it happened? I ran my hand through my hair, trembling, still afraid to move.

A pair of hands gripped my shoulders and I jumped a mile.

"I see you found the path," said Nick.

"Y-yes," I answered through chattering teeth.

He moved around me and stood on the step below, offering me a hand. "Want to go down, help me check out the *Hellfire?* I tied up my lifeboat, it's down there someplace. You won't get too wet."

"No, . . . no, thanks." I ignored his outstretched hand. "I'm cold. I should have worn something warmer than this poncho. I think I've caught a chill." I looked at Nick and then down at his boat, and I felt an inexplicable revulsion so strong that it terrified me.

"What's the matter, Laura?" asked Nick. "You don't look so much cold as—sick, or something."

I seized the excuse and rose unsteadily to my feet. "I'm sorry, I think maybe I *am* getting sick. I'd better go back to the house."

"Okay, I'll come with you. Say, I put the things you wanted in the kitchen."

I nodded, unable to say anything. Nick insisted on putting his arm around me, and since I was far from surefooted, I couldn't object. But the closer we drew to the house, the more determined I became that he should leave. I was baffled and frightened, and I needed to be alone so that I could try to understand what had happened. But Nick was enjoying playing Comforter of the Sick, and it wouldn't be easy to make him go.

I made the first try when we rounded my wing of the house on our way to the kitchen door. "Thank you for going to the store for me. I hope I haven't kept you too long. You must want to take advantage of this better weather and get back to the harbor at Beaufort!"

He didn't answer, just tightened his arm around me.

I stopped at the door and removed his arm, giving it a hearty pat. "You've been a big help today. You needn't come in with me, really. You can go straight back to the *Hellfire.*"

Now he was getting the message. He scowled, and I could see his anger rising as he looked down at me. "Just like that, you're kicking me out?"

"Not kicking you out," I insisted. I licked my dry lips. A few moments before I'd been afraid of I knew not what; now I was afraid of Nick's anger. I felt very small and very vulnerable, but I knew I must never let Nick know that I feared him. "Just letting you go so that you can get to your dock while you have good weather. Oh, yes, you have my keys. I'll take them, please." I held my hand out, palm up.

He looked at my open hand, then into my eyes. He was angry, his rising color attested that, but his eyes were sly. Those eyes told me he was determined to have his own way. Nevertheless, he dug into his pocket and dropped the heavy ring of keys into my hand.

"I don't want to be let go," he said. "I did your shopping. I want you to cook for me, but if you don't feel up to it, I'll cook. I know how. I want to stay again. I'll go back to Beaufort tomorrow. Maybe."

A sudden gust of wind caught my poncho and lifted it, a swirl of blue. His possessiveness, his self-assurance disgusted me. I felt invaded by this man, and not for the first time. Damn it, the Stone House was mine, *my* space! The solid weight of the keys in my palm confirmed it. Anger of my own swept into me and pushed all other emotions away. "Oh, no," I said, my voice low and hard. "I took you in last night because of the storm, but the storm is over now and it's time you were on your way. You're not invited for another meal, Nick, and certainly not for another night. Good-bye!" I turned on my heel and reached for the doorknob.

Nick grabbed my arm and jerked me back, roughly. "Don't do that, Laura Brannan. You're making me mad," he growled.

"Well, then, that's two of us! You're rude, Nick Westover, and you have an exaggerated sense of your attractiveness to women. If you don't leave *right now,* I won't want to see you again, ever!"

He dropped my arm. I had to be impressed with the visible effort it took for him to choke off his anger as he backed away. "All right, all right," he said, holding his hands up, palms toward me. "You're sick, that's what. You're sick, that's why you talk that way to me. I'm going. I don't want to catch whatever you're sick with anyway. I'm outta here!"

14

I threw down the pencil in frustration. There was no point in trying to make revenue projections for the inn, not in our situation. I was spending my own money now in order to pay salaries, and I had to set a limit. One more source of tension, I thought grimly. I clenched my teeth and took up the pencil again. I'd always been a great little problem-solver, hadn't I? No need to be sarcastic with myself, it was true. I knew that if I made a workable plan and stuck to it, even if it was a disaster plan, at least I wouldn't be worrying about the what-ifs. I'd put off making decisions about the inn for long enough. The inn's problems were concrete at least, and I could get a handle on them. Which was a heck of a lot better than some other problems I had!

I started over. I would assume *no* guests. Some sort of advertising campaign just before Easter. Maybe Jonathan was right about changing the name. Maybe we needed a new image. I took up my calendar, to see how many weeks there were until Easter.

A polite tap came on my office door—I knew Jonathan knocked like that. I called out, "Come in!"

It was indeed Jonathan who opened the door. "Morning, Laura. May I talk to you for a few minutes?"

"Yes. Sit down, please. A talk with you is exactly what I need right now, but I thought you'd be asleep. It's not even noon yet."

He slouched into the chair. "I'm a little off my schedule, since we closed the inn over the weekend."

"Oh, sure. I didn't think of that. Well, you first. What's on your mind?"

Jonathan put his fingertips together and regarded me over the top of the steeple they made. "You know I've moved into Kathryn's suite, as you said I could. I'm not sure I've thanked you properly for that."

"You don't need to thank me, Jonathan." Smiling, I shook my head at him. "You deserve a place to live; you give so much more than you get around here."

"Well, thank you anyway. What I wanted to see you about is the papers in the desk."

"Oh," I said in a rush, "I forgot all about them! The night I sorted out her things, it got late and I was too tired to deal with the papers. I meant to go back and do it, but Evelyn offered to box up the other things for me and so I just never got back to it. I'll do it right away, today, whenever it's convenient for you."

"There's no need. I'd like to do it myself, if you don't mind. Only I don't want to simply box them up. I want to go through and look at those papers. Read through them carefully. I realize it's an invasion of privacy, so I'd like your permission, Laura."

I looked at him curiously. He sat relaxed as ever, fingertips together, glasses halfway down his nose not helping his soft blue eyes a bit. "You don't look much like a detective, Jonathan," I said, not sure whether to be amused or concerned. "What are you up to?"

He chuckled. "Probably nothing. But then, you never can tell what a detective looks like, can you? They're like criminals—the best ones always look like something else. I just thought, since the police don't seem to be getting anywhere and I knew both Kathryn and Carroll pretty well, maybe I might find something in that desk that they missed. If it's all right with you."

"Sure. It's all right with me, although your idea about stuff in the desk is probably no better than mine about the Stone House . . ." I let my voice trail off. I was really only thinking out loud.

Jonathan moved onto the edge of his chair, hunched forward, alert. He pushed his glasses up on his nose. "You have an idea about the Stone House?"

I waved a dismissing hand, sorry now that I'd said anything. "It's not an idea. It's silly, really, just a feeling I have about the place. That I have something to learn from it. Or, if you want to get spooky about it, that the house has something to say to me. I know how ridiculous that sounds—"

Jonathan broke in, "Actually, I don't think it's ridiculous at all. It may make a lot of sense."

That was a rather mysterious thing for Jonathan to say, but it went over my head at the moment because I was thinking of something else. "Jonathan, is that table still in your suite, the one with the telephone on it, just inside the door?"

"Yes. Why?"

"Because I forgot to look in there. It has a drawer, and I didn't even open it. You might find something in that drawer."

He shook his fuzzy-haloed head. "There's nothing at all in that drawer—at least there wasn't. I opened it looking for a phone book, and it was empty. So I brought my old phone book from upstairs and put it in the drawer."

"Well," I said, "so much for that idea." But I thought that in a way it was even more peculiar for Kathryn to have a completely empty drawer than if it had been filled with exotic junk. Kathryn didn't clean out, didn't throw things away, she stuffed things in drawers. I was sure it hadn't always been empty. Could my benevolent-looking Jonathan be lying about that drawer?

"What?" I realized he'd asked a question and I'd missed it. "I'm sorry, I got distracted. What did you say?"

"I said, it's your turn now. What can I do for you today?"

I shifted the subject to the running of the inn and outlined my plan, as far as I'd gotten. I said we might as well stay open because I didn't want to stop paying anyone's salary, but I'd have to figure out how many weeks I could do that assuming we had no guests. I told him I wanted to keep Mrs. Trowbridge, the woman I'd found at the Historical Association. I'd found out that she could type, and I wanted Jonathan to train her so that she might substitute for Zelda and perhaps someday take her place.

Jonathan nodded his approval of these things, though I knew he didn't share my negative view of Zelda. Finally I said that the inn needed a new image and an advertising campaign. I was beginning to think he was right about changing the inn's name. Would he help me with ideas for the advertising, and to think of a new name?

He beamed. "I'm glad to see you taking control again, Laura. I was afraid we were losing you to your new interest."

"My new interest?"

"The Stone House. You've been so wrapped up in that place, I was afraid it was becoming an obsession."

Seth had used the same word, obsession. "I just had a lot to do there, and maybe I had to get some distance from Kathryn's death before I could deal with the inn again," I said decisively. "Now, let's brainstorm on names for the inn. Okay?"

We brainstormed for an hour and I wrote everything down. Our names ran the gamut from exotic to trite. Never ask a writer to help you find a name for something, I thought after Jonathan left me alone with a list as long as my arm. His mind was a fertile field; he'd obviously never forgotten any name he'd ever heard! I did quite a lot of marking-out with my pencil and then made another list from what was left. I would carry this shorter list around with me, live with it awhile, and maybe eventually I'd develop a clear preference.

I broke for lunch and tackled the less-fun job of finances. I could make it until Easter with Jonathan, Evelyn, Zelda, and Mrs. T. And the expense of the ad campaign I'd keep low-key. Low-key, but effective, I hoped. After Easter we'd have to have at least a third of the rooms occupied, or I'd have to either borrow operating capital or close down.

I'd done more than a good day's work when I locked my office and went home to the Stone House. I felt healthily tired, and that was good. Perhaps I'd sleep well. I hadn't slept well since . . . since when?

I was driving on my narrow private road, hemmed in by trees that consumed the light so that it was dark before time, when I admitted the truth: I hadn't slept well any night since I'd moved into the Stone House.

I paid a man to refinish the floor in the tower room. He sanded it with a machine one day, polished it the next, and sealed it with some kind of high-tech finish on the third day. He insisted on roping off the doors to prevent anyone from going into the room, though I told him it wasn't necessary, there was only me and Boris. He didn't care, he said, he always roped off his rooms and that was that. Since I couldn't be entirely sure I wasn't sleepwalking these nights, maybe the ropes were just as well.

I invited Seth for dinner, and also to help me hook up my stereo, the first night the ropes came down. The sealer had taken forty-eight hours to dry, and I was anxious to see the results—I hadn't been allowed past those ropes myself. Seth followed me in his car when I left the inn, so we arrived together.

I didn't even stop to build up the fires, I was so excited. I ran through the rooms, turning on lights as I went. I unlocked the door from living room to tower and threw it open, ignoring the dark and the cold that rushed to meet me. With Seth right behind I plunged in, feeling along the wall for the light switch.

The great chandeliers blazed and the floor, gleaming, reflected their light. I kicked off my shoes and pirouetted into the center of the room.

Seth stood aside with his hands in the pockets of his trench coat, his often-serious face now smiling. I spun to a stop and he called out, "Beautiful!" The word echoed off of eight walls.

"Yes, it is," I agreed, looking down. "It's even more beautiful than I thought it would be."

He crossed the floor to me, his hard-soled shoes ringing hollowly with every step. "I didn't mean the floor, little one, I meant *you.*"

He reached for me but I went down on hands and knees, tracing the inlaid woods with my fingers. I ignored his compliment. "There must be at least three different kinds of wood here," I said. "Walnut, pine, do you think this is maple?" I looked up at Seth through the mop of my hair.

He knelt on one knee for a closer look. "Could be. If you really want to identify the wood, it would help to know when this room was built. Myself, I wonder *why* it was built."

My skin tingled with the closeness of him. I pushed my hair out of my eyes. "I've often wondered that myself, but I don't suppose we'll ever know. It doesn't matter anyway. All that matters is that I'm going to dance again, right here!" I jumped up, did a few more turns and a leap for sheer joy. "Oh, Seth, would you mind very much if we hooked up the stereo now and had dinner after? I'm too excited to cook!"

Seth chuckled, warm and low. "Will you dance for me, if I say yes?"

Suddenly I felt self-conscious. I'd been whirling and leaping around like an idiot! And I hadn't danced for anyone but myself in a very long time. Hesitantly, I said, "I don't know. I only dance for myself now. It's a . . . a very private thing."

Seth came to me, put his arms lightly around me, and kissed my forehead. I quivered inside. "You're adorable," he said softly. "Just now you looked like an appealing little girl. We'll give you music now, if you want. Music is more important than food, any day."

"I didn't know you liked music," I said as we took off our coats and dropped them in the living room, where I'd piled all the stereo components, and the extra wiring for the speakers.

"There are quite a few things you don't know about me," he said with a wink. "Yet."

"I can imagine," I commented dryly.

Seth raised a very black eyebrow and shouldered a speaker. He was a strong, willing helper, and in about half an hour the tower room was filled to the brim with the heartrending strains of Tchaikovsky's music. My feet could not be still, and I forgot myself. I danced, for both of us; I was the Swan Queen in a sweater and skirt and pantyhosed feet.

"It's been too long," I panted when I came to a stop sooner than I wanted to. "I'm in terrible shape."

"You look in wonderful shape to me," said Seth. He sat on the floor with his hands clasped around his knees, and the softness was in his eyes. "You really are a dancer, Laura! You're so graceful, so exquisite, you have wings on your feet!"

"Your Scottish ancestors, as they must be with a name like Douglass, would cringe to hear you—you sound like you didn't just kiss the Blarney Stone, you swallowed it!" I pulled him to his feet. I'd worked up quite a sweat, and it was too cold in the tower. I'd have to do something about that, I thought, but right now there were other rooms, other rooms with fireplaces. "Come on, I'm starting to freeze!"

Seth worked at the fireplaces while I changed into a warm sweatsuit in the bathroom with its welcome quartz heater. Then we went into the kitchen, where he had the fire blazing, and I started dinner.

I had everything cooking when suddenly I missed Boris. "Seth, have you seen Boris since we came in?"

"No, I haven't. But we were so busy, I wasn't particularly paying attention."

"Maybe he's just annoyed with me for being in the tower for so long," I said, and I sat down at the kitchen table with Seth.

"You mean because what we were doing in there delayed his dinner?"

"That, too, but for some reason Boris just doesn't like the tower room. He explored it once, and now he won't go in there again. Maybe it's only that it's too cold for him . . ." I ran my hand through my hair. "Keep an eye on the chicken for me, would you? I think I'd better go look for him."

He wasn't in the bathroom, where I feared I might have accidentally shut him in. As I went through the other rooms, searching and calling, I had an uncomfortable recollection of our first few days at the inn. Boris, hiding so frequently under the king-size bed—I'd ignored his behavior at the time, thinking it some kind of moving trauma. Now I wondered what had frightened my brave cat so much that it had forced him into hiding. And where was he now? Not under my bed this time, nor under the bed in the guest room. Not in the pine wardrobe that served as my closet, or behind the larger pieces of furniture. Not roosting on top of the bookcases, one of his favorite places.

I had an ominous feeling as I gave up the search and returned to the kitchen. "Can't find him," I admitted. I checked the chicken Marengo on the burner and the broccoli casserole in the oven. Then I opened the back door.

"Boris! Here, big guy! Come on, Boris!" I called out into the darkness. Damn, I thought, why hadn't I had those outside lights installed? "Boris! Here, kitty, kitty, kitty!" I hadn't called the big guy "kitty" since he was a kitten. Nor had he run off since he was a kitten. I closed the door behind me, hoping I'd be able to see better if I shut out the contrasting light, but I couldn't. There was no moon. The darkness was absolute. This complete absence of light on moonless nights was something I had never experienced before coming to the Stone House. Always before there had been street lights, lights from nearby houses, but not here. I found it unnerving, and I wasn't sure I'd ever get used to such smothering blackness.

I called again. Since my eyes were of no use, I listened. Oh, I would have given the world to hear that "Mowr." Even if he sounded sick, or injured. But there was only the sound of a moderate wind wrapping itself around the stones, and when I listened very hard, the farther-off rhythmic motion of the sound's waters.

Wordlessly I reentered the kitchen and opened the cabinets one by one even though I knew Boris would not be in them. He'd have heard our voices and been loudly demanding to be let out, long ago.

"Hey," said Seth, "he's probably out prowling around. He'll come back, he'll probably be right outside the door tomorrow morning."

"I wish I could believe that." I said no more, but set places for us at one end of the big dining table in the library/dining room. Candelabra, good silver, the works. But my heart wasn't in it. In my mind I kept seeing Boris, normally so fearless, cowering under that bed at the inn. His eyes, glinting silver in that cramped dark space, haunted me.

If the chicken or the broccoli or the chocolate angel pie were any good, I couldn't taste them. I drank an extra glass of wine to help me choke down food that had the texture of cardboard. Seth's conversation seemed to come from miles away.

His hand closed over mine as I reached once again for my wineglass. "I'm glad we've had this time together tonight, Laura, because tomorrow I'm going away for a few days."

"Going away?" I felt a pang at the words. Now he had my attention.

"Not far, only to Raleigh. I've been appointed to the Coastal Management Commission."

I swallowed my own concerns, the feeling that I was being left alone when I needed him. "Oh, Seth, that's wonderful! Congratulations!" I squeezed his hand. "How long will you be gone?"

"Three or four days. There's a hearing I'll be sitting in on, and I want to get there a couple of days early. As the one new member of the commission, I have a lot of catching up to do, documents to study, that sort of thing. And I'm not sure exactly how many days it will take for the hearing."

"You're going to love every minute of it, I know." He already loved it; his face was all eager anticipation like a boy about to receive a coveted prize. My heart went out to him. "Tell me more about what you'll be doing."

On this subject it was never necessary to ask Seth twice. Sometimes it wasn't even necessary to ask him once! I appreciated what he said, but more than that I enjoyed the way he said it. He was more than knowledgeable, he was passionate; and his passion transformed him. His severe good looks became charisma. He compelled belief in the things he said.

"You know," I observed when he finally ran out of words, "this really is an important beginning for you. If you keep on going like this, I can easily believe you'll end up in the legislature!"

"Would you vote for me?" he asked, eyes twinkling.

"Sure"—I grinned—"twice!"

I kept having the irrational feeling that I was not alone in the Stone House. Of course I couldn't sleep; I missed Boris's familiar weight at the foot of my bed. I thought I must be feeling his presence, that somehow he had gotten himself stuck in a place where he couldn't get out and I just hadn't looked for him hard enough.

You know how it is when you desperately want to recall something that matters very much to you—the more you replay it in your mind, the less and less certain you are about what really did happen. I had been very sure Boris had been in the house, not outside, when I'd left for the inn that morning. Prompted by the eerie feeling that I was not alone, I got up twice in the night and went through the rooms. I felt afraid and told myself for no reason, there was nothing to fear. The Stone House was like a fortress, my fortress. These stones had stood for years; in the case of the tower, for hundreds of years. The doors were all thick, all locked. Windows locked, too, and though I no longer closed the outside shutters unless the winds or rains were heavy, every window now had thick drapes which I drew at night. No one could get in. So how had Boris gotten out; if I hadn't let him out myself? I was no longer sure of anything.

In the small, dead hours of early morning, hovering on the border of sleep, I thought I heard a sound. Only once, a dull thud. My body shook so hard it shook the bed. There is nothing to fear, I repeated, but my body continued to shake. My jaws clenched so tight I felt as if I had lockjaw. The thud did not come again, and gradually my fear subsided. Eventually I convinced myself it had been a night-prowling animal, or an off-course bird, bumping into one of the doors. Pale gray predawn light filtered around the edges of my drapes when at last I slept.

Less than two hours later I was up, pulling a coat on over my blue fleece robe, jamming bare feet into boots. Outside, my breath turned to ice as I called and called for Boris. I grew frantic; I ran and stumbled and fell to my hands and knees on the frozen ground, got up and ran again, calling, calling. I lost all reason, I stood at the edge of the bluff and screamed out to the sea, "Oh, my God, Boris, where are you?"

It was not until near nightfall that I found him. I'd gone to work and made it through the day, I didn't know how. When I returned home I began my search again. I unlocked the door to the tower stairs and climbed halfway up the claustrophobic steps, calling. With a powerful flashlight I went over every deserted inch of the disused wing, startling at the unfamiliar lumps that were my shrouded furniture, cringing at rotting things I preferred not to try to identify. By the time I went outside, a dreadful certainty had settled in me. Boris was dead. If I found my cat at all, I would not find him alive.

I walked the grounds in ever-widening circles, driven by grim determination. If an animal had killed Boris, I might find his body anywhere on this huge field of a lawn. I kept my head down, scanning, scanning the tangled brown grasses. Eventually I came to a place I recognized, the circle of stones that was the abandoned well. Something was wrong here, it didn't look right, but I couldn't quite say why. My heart was in my throat as I stepped up to the well-wall, bent over, and looked in. The dark water was not far down, and on its surface floated my Boris. Drowned. Dead.

My legs wouldn't hold me. I collapsed. A voice shrieked Why? Why? It took some time to realize that the voice was mine. I clamped my mouth shut to stop the awful sound. Ding dong bell, pussy's in the well, ding dong bell, pussy's in the well—the mocking rhyme stuck in my head, bouncing off the walls of my mind. "Stop it, just stop it!" I yelled. The words stopped, but as they did I could have sworn I heard laughter. Hoarse, cruel, cosmic laughter which was definitely not my own.

Finally I got to my feet. I had to get Boris out of the well—I couldn't leave him there. I forced myself to look in again, to judge the distance. I couldn't get to my poor cat without a net, or some sort of scoop at the end of a long pole. I didn't know where to find such a thing.

I turned to go back to the Stone House. The tower rose up against a darkening sky. No rosy-golden sunset this day. The stones of the tower seemed to feed upon the dying light. It swelled and grew as the day waned. This was not the quaint, eccentric little castle of my foolish fancy. I knew now what the tower evoked: Death. Death and darkness and evil. Even as I watched, the tower grew larger, blacker, until it loomed over me and blotted out the sky.

Gasping, I shut my eyes to escape the sight. Only the thinnest thread linked my sanity to me. I waited, said the familiar words to myself: This will pass. This is an illusion and it will pass. I pressed my fingertips hard against my temples; I felt the blood, my mortality, thundering through my veins, pulsing to the beat of my living heart. I am alive, I affirmed, I am alive! My life and my mind belong only to me! Leave, death and darkness, *go away!*

Control returned slowly. I realized night was near and I would not be able to get Boris's body from the well until tomorrow. Now I needed light, and warmth. I had to take care of myself.

It was late, near midnight, when I thought to call Jonathan.

"Are you all right, Laura?" he asked immediately. "It's not like you to call this late."

"Yes, I'm all right," I said, and then, "Well, no. I'm not, not exactly. I, uh, I don't think I'll be coming to the inn for a couple of days, Jonathan. You and Zelda and Mrs. T. can manage, don't you think?"

"Of course we can, but how about you? Are you sick? Do you need anything?"

Did I need anything? I was so far beyond need of any one thing, I almost laughed hysterically. But instead I answered his other question. "I'm not sick. Something has happened to my cat. Boris." My voice broke on his name. "He's dead, and I—" I stopped abruptly, unable to go on.

Jonathan, too, was stunned to silence. When he spoke again into the line, his voice was soft, kind. "I'm sorry. I know how important a part of your life Boris was. He was a very special cat. How did it happen?"

"There's an old well here. I guess he was exploring, and he fell in and drowned. Only, only—" Again, I couldn't go on. I had struggled with this for hours.

"Only . . .?" Jonathan made the one word a gentle encouragement. I took heart and put my doubts into words for the first time.

"Only I could have sworn that I covered the well again after I explored it. And yesterday, when I first missed him, I was so sure that Boris was in the house when I left for work. Jonathan, Boris was a clever cat, and surefooted for all his size. I can't imagine him falling into that well!"

"You think, ah, you think he had help?"

"I don't know," I wailed, "I just don't know anymore what to think! Maybe my memory is playing tricks on me. Maybe I did forget to let him back into the house before I left yesterday. Maybe I did forget to put the cover back on the well. But if I did, then my memory is really shot to pieces, because I don't even remember taking the cover all the way off in the first place. I think I only slid it to the side, because it was pretty heavy."

"I see," said Jonathan, and then he fell silent again. I could almost hear him thinking. "I don't like this, Laura."

"I know," I agreed, "neither do I."

"Maybe you should come back here to the inn. At least for a few nights."

I'd thought of that. The Stone House seemed so empty without Boris. But I knew that if I went to the inn, there would be people and work, many distractions, and I needed above all else to think, to feel. Something was brewing here at the Stone House, and more than ever I felt I had to be here. So I said, "No. No, thank you, Jonathan. Losing Boris is a blow, I admit. It's like . . . like *overkill*. Do you know what I mean?"

"Yes, I do. That's why I think you should be here with people who care about you and not off miles away, all by yourself."

"Not this time. He was important to me, but if I can keep my perspective, Boris was after all, a cat. This is not as bad as when Kathryn's body was found, though right now I feel it is. You were a wonderful help to me then, Jonathan, but this time I need to be alone. I can't explain it. Just trust me, please, and give me a few days."

He agreed reluctantly. I thanked him for his understanding and said good-bye.

Something primitive stirred in me, grew, and took hold. A vengeful, atavistic anger, huge in its proportions. I had obtained a net on a long pole from a fishing tackle place on Harkers Island, and a sharp pointed spade from the hardware section of the K Mart. First I dug the grave, defiantly, in the very shadow of the tower. Then I netted that sad, sodden body, unbelievably heavy in death. It weighed as much as a child. All the while the primitive element grew and grew in me, directed me to bury Boris with a ritual that came to me as if in a race-memory.

I tore apart the cushion that had been his favorite and I wrapped his body in its velvet cloth. Into the grave I put his bowl and a ball with a bell inside, a special toy saved from kitten days. I laid his body among his things and wondered if cats have souls, wondered if I performed this ritual for Boris or for myself.

I took off the silver ring I wore and placed it in a fold of Boris's velvet shroud. Then I filled in the grave. Huge anger carried me now. On top of the grave I built a pyre, a pyramid shape of dry kindling wood which completely covered the disturbed earth. I went into the house then, and cleansed my hands and face. Dressed in my blue poncho and removed my shoes.

The pyre blazed. I could not have said why I trod around it, my bare feet beating the cold earth. My dirge-dance came from my heart, from the deepest, oldest places in my soul. As I wove around and around the grave, almost in a trance, the blazing pyramid threw its challenging light against the tower.

15

I slept for a very long time. Heavy, exhausted sleep from which I awoke with leaden limbs and aching head. It was raining again. Good, the rain would wash away yesterday's funeral ashes. Ashes to ashes, dust to dust, for all living things.

I knew what to do for my heavy muscles. I dressed in layers that I could peel off as I warmed up—leotard, tights, loose knitted vest, leg warmers, an oversize sweatshirt that hung to my knees. I stuffed toe shoes into the sweatshirt's kangaroo pocket and carried the quartz heaters, one in each hand, into the tower room.

My music filled the air; my feet claimed the floor; I made the room mine. I danced for release, and renewal, and found both. It would be a long, long time before I could dance for joy. If I ever could, in this place. Dripping sweat, I shivered in spite of the heater nearby. I sat on the floor with legs and toes turned out, and through the mop of my damp hair I contemplated the walls around me. What must I do to learn their secrets?

"I won't be defeated," I said to the eight walls, "and I won't be driven away. I *will* learn the truth!" The atavism was still with me, under a layer of firm resolve.

Later in the day I called the police station and told them I wanted Kathryn's car released from impoundment; I would send Jonathan to pick it up. Then I asked what progress they had made. Continuing the investigation, they said; going to do some polygraph, lie detector, tests. I asked on whom, and of course they wouldn't tell me. Interesting idea, I thought when I hung up—at least they were doing something. I called the inn next and asked Zelda to have Jonathan walk over to the police station later in the day to get the car. I explained we'd keep it for inn business, and Jonathan was to feel free to use it whenever he liked.

Strange woman, Zelda. She had been so formal, so distant over the phone. Hadn't asked how I was, hadn't asked when I was coming back to work. Maybe she wasn't so strange, at that. The clear truth was she just didn't like me. She'd be happy as a clam if I never came back to the inn. I didn't know why that should bother me as much as it did, since I didn't like her very much, either. Was Zelda a piece in this malevolent puzzle I couldn't put together, or only an outside irritation?

As the day wore on, I thought it was remarkable how much stronger I felt. The ritual or whatever it was I'd done for Boris seemed to have cleansed me, and I found that what I wanted most was simply to get on with my life. Let the police take care of the mystery surrounding Kathryn, let Jonathan work at it if he wanted to. As for me, I would let it go. I realized I'd been motivated by a guilt I no longer felt—it seemed to have been burned away by the light of Boris's funeral pyre. That guilt had been unreasonable, largely left over from childhood, and I was glad to be free of it. This whole puzzle was one *I* didn't have to solve! I swept the pieces away, clean and clear.

What I didn't count on was that some events once they are set in motion will continue of their own momentum until they either run down or something stops them. Nor did I know that though I might decide to let go, I was so firmly enmeshed in the pieces of this puzzle that it would not let go of me.

* * *

The next day I was making chocolate chip cookies and listening to Neil Diamond tapes when I thought I heard a car outside. It's Seth, I thought with a little leap of gladness, come back early from Raleigh. I put down the big spoon and went to the door.

Not Seth, but Jonathan, getting out of the old Olds that had been Kathryn's. "Come on in," I called out, "though I feel a bit like you've caught me playing hooky. I'm not exactly in deep mourning. I'm making cookies."

"Sounds good. You don't owe me any explanations, Laura. I'm certainly not checking up on you." Jonathan came into the kitchen and removed his old tweed hat. "What kind of cookies?"

I closed the door. "Chocolate chip, everybody's favorite. We can have some soon. In the meantime, would you like some tea? Or perhaps you'd like to look around. You haven't been here before. You can even climb to the top of the tower if you'd like."

He was turning slowly around as he scanned the kitchen, nodding appreciatively. "You've got it looking very civilized in here."

"I should hope so! There are quite a few dollars' worth of civilization in this kitchen!" I went back to my bowl of cookie dough. "Ah, Jonathan, what brought you out here? And how is the car, by the way?"

Jonathan seemed unusually somber. "The car's none the worse for having sat behind the police station for a couple of months, though why they had to keep it for so long I don't know."

"That's my fault. I didn't push to get it back, and I imagine they just forgot about it."

"Well, it does seem to be fine, and I appreciate you letting me drive it. I usually have to borrow a car from friends when I need one, and I'm glad not to have to do that. Anyway, more to the point: I came out on impulse. Wanted to see you, have a couple of things I want to talk to you about. Tell you what, you keep on with your cookies, and I'll just look around on my own. How do I get up into the tower?"

"I keep the door locked; you'll need the keys. There's an

extra set in that drawer under the counter, nearest the door. You get them, my hands are all sticky."

Jonathan deposited his hat on the end of the counter and found the keys in the drawer. "Got 'em."

"Okay. You just keep going from room to room, and on the other side of the living room is the first locked door. That one's the square-topped key, the others are round. When you get in the tower room you'll see two more doors. Three, counting the outside door, the big old one on the sea side. The stairs are more or less opposite the big door, and the other door is to the wing I don't use. There's nothing in there but stored furniture and assorted vermin. Just be careful on the stairs."

"Right. Thanks, Laura. I'll be back in a few minutes."

I waved him on with my sticky spoon. I didn't expect him back for a while if he intended to climb the tower, and he wasn't. When he did return my blue and white kitchen was sweetly filled with baking smells, and I had tea and a plate of still-warm chocolate chip cookies on the table. I could barely contain my curiosity while Jonathan shrugged out of his jacket and plumped down into the other chair. He took off his misted glasses and began to polish them on the hem of his sweater.

I couldn't stand the suspense. "Well?"

There was a faraway look in his eyes. He hooked the glasses over his ears and slowly brought his gaze to meet mine. "That's quite an experience, that tower."

"What did you think? How did you feel?"

He looked away and made an unnecessarily big deal out of pouring a cup of tea and adding sugar. Finally he said, "The view from the top is terrific. I don't think there's any doubt the tower was built to give people a lookout over the sound. Of course, there's a lot of mist today, but—"

"But nothing! Jonathan, I really want to know what you thought and how you felt *inside* the tower." He reached for the cookies and I pulled the plate back out of his reach. "No cookies until you tell me the truth!"

"All right. I felt strange. Damn strange. And too old and too fat to be comfortable with nothing but an old chain on the walls for a railing!" The old twinkle came back into his eyes. "Now can I have a cookie?"

I smiled, but part of me was anxious as I pushed the cookies back in his direction. "There *is* something about the tower, isn't there? I just wish I knew what . . . why . . . I guess I was hoping you wouldn't feel anything at all. Then it would have to be all in my imagination."

"Not your imagination, no, sirree." He munched thoughtfully. "Now, the rest of the place is nice, with your furniture and your rugs and all."

"Thank you."

"Listen, Laura, I'm sorry about Boris."

I shrugged, but I felt the prick of tears behind my eyes. "That's over, in the past now. I've buried him, and made my peace with it."

"Um-hm. Life goes on, etcetera."

We had our tea and cookies in silence for a while. It was Jonathan who finally spoke. "Laura, I did have a reason for coming out here today."

"Oh?"

"I mean besides wanting to see what you've done with the place. I want you to go somewhere with me, there's someone I want you to meet."

"Today?"

He nodded his large, half-bald, half-frizzy head.

I looked down at my faded old jeans and baggy pale pink sweatshirt. "Oh, not today! I hadn't planned on going out, I'm not dressed to meet anybody."

"Believe me, the person I want you to meet won't care." Jonathan chuckled. "There's no telling what she'll be wearing! Come with me, Laura, it could be important. And I have a feeling today is the perfect time."

I sighed, resigned. "All right, Jonathan. It's hard to refuse you anything. I'm ready whenever you are. Are you going to tell me who this person is, and what this is all about?"

"Her name is Belle Helen. No last name, far as I know. She's a Wise Woman, with capital Ws. Some people would call her a witch."

* * *

Belle Helen was impressive, and she didn't look in the least like I'd have expected a "witch" to look. In the car I'd pressed Jonathan for more information, and all he'd say was "You'll see."

We drove south and inland and were soon in deep green woods, pine and cedar and yaupon, their trunks straight, close together, tops lost in the mist. These woods felt old, pure, peaceful. The house we came to was white frame, spectacularly clean. It rambled through its little clearing every which way with porches and added rooms. Flowers bloomed around the front steps, yellow and blue-purple crocuses, the first flowers of spring and the first I'd seen in a very long time. The woman who stood at the top of the steps wore the colors of the trees and the flowers. I knew without asking that this was she of the unusual name, Belle Helen.

She was a stately woman, large but not fat, tall, strong-featured. Her skirt was full, forest green, and came nearly to her ankles. On her feet she wore soft, moccasin-like boots of brown leather which disappeared beneath the longish skirt. A loose, long-sleeved tunic of periwinkle blue flowed over the skirt well past her hips, and over the tunic she wore yet another flowing garment, this one sleeveless, open in front like a long vest, in a clear yellow. Her hair flowed too, long, full, unbound, dark auburn mingled with strands of silvery gray. She held out both hands in welcome, and I saw that she wore no rings, no jewelry of any sort, which was somehow not what I expected. Her colors were her adornment.

"Jonathan," she said in a voice which matched her strong features, "you've brought your friend! Welcome, both of you."

Jonathan introduced me and we went into the house, cozy with low ceilings and bright rag rugs. Plants, some of them blooming, hung in every window. The air had a clean herbal smell. It was impossible to be uncomfortable in this place, so full of the fragrance and color of nature.

"Now," said Belle Helen when we were seated, "what has our friend Mr. Harcourt told you about me, my dear— Laura? You won't mind if I call you Laura?"

"Please do," I replied. "He told me very little. Only that some people might call you a witch, but he considers you a Wise Woman. I admit I'm terribly curious! You couldn't be a witch and live in a place like this!"

She laughed, a rich, vibrant sound. "Wise Woman sounds a lot more flattering. I am called wise by some. The term *witch* is so often misunderstood. I am simply a practitioner of the Craft, the pre-Christian religion of the Celtic people. It's called Wicca, or Wicca Craft, which has been corrupted to "witchcraft." But we of the Craft are a long way from the popular concept of witches. Our first rule is Do No Harm."

I glanced at Jonathan, who had his hands folded comfortably over his round middle. This was interesting, but what had it to do with me? "Ah, have you known Jonathan long?"

"No." She smiled, a lovely, serene smile. "He found me only a few days ago. But once we'd met I felt I'd known him forever."

I answered her smile. "I know exactly what you mean."

Jonathan shifted in his chair. "I found Belle Helen because I've been looking for anyone who could tell me something about the Stone House. She has some interesting things to say, and besides she has exceptional . . . I guess you could say credentials . . . for what she will tell you."

I wasn't smiling anymore. I shot Jonathan a look which said, Who asked you to do this? But I held back the words.

Belle Helen leaned forward. Her large hazel eyes were sincere, and compelling. "Look at me, Laura, and give me your hand." For long moments she said nothing, but her grasp was full of strength and her eyes reached deep, deep inside me. "I feel your losses," she said, "and I feel that you have made peace with them. There are traces of guilt, but faint. That's good—we deplore guilt, it drains energy and blocks spiritual growth. Oh, but you didn't come to hear those things. I'll tell you now what I know about the Stone House. I must ask you to open your mind, because what I have to say will be out of the realm of your usual experience. Will you do that?"

I nodded. I was impressed with her and willing to listen without prejudice.

She began. "All people have access to a power or energy that exists both in us and outside of us. In the Craft we consciously use and develop this power. It's commonly called psychic, though actually it's more than that. Mine is well developed—and still growing, I trust. I work alone, I've chosen the solitary path, although when I'm asked I may join with a group, a coven, for a particular purpose. Several years ago I was asked to join with a coven at the Stone House."

I drew in a sharp, involuntary breath. "The Stone House?"

"Yes. The place which Jonathan tells me was bought by your sister who has been murdered, which now belongs to you. In previous years it was a rental property, and the coven had leased it with an option to buy. The coven did want to buy it. It had, seemingly, all the attributes they needed: isolation, for privacy; a large, open, outdoor space and the large indoor space in the octagonal room; sturdy, unpretentious shelter for those of the coven who wished to live there. And as if these things, ordinarily so hard to find all in one place, were not enough, there was also the proximity to water. But there was a significant problem, and that is why they called on me."

"What sort of problem?" I asked.

Belle Helen stood up, went to a window, and stroked the leaves of the plants hanging there, as if she might draw strength from them. She turned back to me. "That is difficult to explain to someone unfamiliar with our way of life, but since you have been living in the Stone House, perhaps you will understand. Places and inanimate objects can store energy from the thoughts and emotions of people who have been there. Sometimes the stored energy is powerful. Always it reflects the nature of what has happened there, positive or negative. When the coven gathered at the Stone House to perform their rituals, they sought as always to raise positive power. In particular when they called me in, they wished to use the power to heal a seriously ill child. But it proved difficult. The place itself seemed to block them."

"Oh!" My stomach had turned cold and wrapped itself around my spine.

Belle Helen sat again, regarding me closely as she continued. "They called me then, because there are ways to clear the negative energy from places and things. I have done it successfully a few times. So I went to the Stone House. The negative energy is very, very strong there. It is centered in the old tower."

"I . . . thought so," I said hesitantly. "I've felt something myself. It's like there's a . . . a kind of presence there. Sometimes I've felt it was trying to, ah, communicate with me."

She grasped my hands tightly. "If that is so, you must never listen, never respond, never! Let me tell you the rest, everything I know. In the Craft we don't talk of "good" and "evil," because those are loaded words; we say instead positive and negative. Nevertheless, there *are* people now, and have been in all ages, people who intentionally do evil things. The negative force in the tower of the Stone House is so strong that even I am inclined to call it evil. I could not clear it. Not alone, and not with the combined powers of the entire coven. And we were afraid to call down help, because like attracts like. There's no telling what horrors we might have brought down if we'd tried. So the coven broke their lease. It was the most promising place they had ever come across, and yet they did not stay, they simply left."

"You lost me there, I don't understand." I shook my head. "What do you mean, call down, and like attracts like?"

"The principle of like attracts like is so common in our earthly plane of existence, in the world, that we're usually unaware of it. The country folk have a saying: What goes around, comes around. That's a perfect example of like attracts like—what you put out is what you get back. For a simple instance, if you walk down the street smiling, people will smile at you in return. Are you with me so far?"

I nodded.

"All right, good. Remember that I told you we Wiccans consciously develop and use our power, that which is often called psychic. When one uses the power alone, it's called a spell; when we use it together, it's called a ritual. In our spells and rituals, when we seek to influence another person or event, as in curing an illness or to insure a good crop, we trust that the positive power we put out will eventually come back to us, because like attracts like.

"Now, Laura, here is the part I know will be hardest for you to accept. Up until now I've been talking about using, we say 'raising,' the power that all of us living here on earth have. There is another location of the same power, not on this earth-plane but beyond, or above—the plane where the spirit goes when it is not in the body. We can contact those spirits and obtain their help. When we do this it's 'calling down' power. Raised or called down, it's all the same power and the same principle applies, like attracts like. Believe me, we have the very strongest of reasons *not* to do black magic, *never* to call down the power of a very negative spirit such as the one the Christians have named Satan or the Devil. In fact, I use called down power myself very seldom because no matter how carefully I prepare, I know how risky it is."

Jonathan whistled softly and said, "Far out!"

I scowled at him, though I was thinking something similar.

Belle Helen nodded, her face serene. "That expression dates you, Jonathan, but it's the usual reaction."

"Let me be sure I understand you, Belle Helen," I said. My lawyer training was asserting itself in spite of the cold dread that gripped my spine. "Essentially what you're saying is that just as there are people who do bad things, there are also these, uh, people without bodies hanging around out there somewhere who also do bad things?"

She nodded again, and I went on. "And you're saying, too, that if a lot of bad things have happened in a particular place, the place itself becomes a bad place?"

"Not exactly," she said. "The place itself is neutral. The stones of your tower are just stones. But negative thoughts and emotions are stored in the place, in the stones if you will, in the form of energy. Therefore, the entire Stone House property and the tower especially have what you might call a "bad feeling" to them. I would call it a negative charge."

"Okay," I conceded, running my hand through my hair, "let me go on. Finally, you're saying that these negative bodiless beings, evil spirits or whatever you want to call them, are attracted to the Stone House? Because of this like attracts like principle? So if you or the . . . the coven, or I—" I struggled with the strange words, with unfamiliar, frightening concepts. "Oh, nuts. Give me a minute to figure out what I want to say."

I walked to the window as Belle Helen had done and stood among her plants. I had just enough of the lawyer left in me to keep me rational, and I needed every bit of rationality I could find. Far out or not, what Belle Helen said made more sense than I wanted it to. The trouble was, I felt crazy just thinking about it. As if I were losing my grip on the only world I'd ever known.

There was not a sound from the two people behind me, and I could feel them watching, waiting. I took a deep breath and turned to face them. I began where I'd left off. "If anyone in the Stone House did anything to more or less open the door to the spirit world, what you'd get would be the negative spirits because the place itself already has all this negative energy stored there?"

"Yes," said Belle Helen.

I glared at Jonathan. "If you say 'far out' again, I'll throttle you. After all, you brought me here. You must have known what she was going to say!"

He looked sheepishly over the tops of his glasses. "I won't say a word, Laura. You're doing fine, just fine."

I wasn't so sure about that. Now I was cold all over and my head was trying to spin, but I kept mentally jerking it back, holding it still. Now I pressed my fingers to my temples, as if I could physically still the spinning thoughts. "I don't know," I murmured, "I thought it was just me, just this living on the edge . . ."

Belle Helen came to me where I stood in the window, put her arm around me, and led me back to my chair. She sat me down, sat herself opposite, held both my hands, and looked into my eyes. "Please tell me what you mean. Please tell me about living on the edge."

I laughed a little. The laugh sounded fake. It *was* fake. "It started about a year ago. I have these episodes that are strange, to say the least. Sometimes they're mild, just a brief period when my senses are all too sharp—light is too bright, normal sounds hurt my ears, music is so beautiful it's like, like—well, like sex. Pleasure so strong it almost hurts, you know?" Embarrassed by my analogy, I glanced at Jonathan.

"Go on," Belle Helen urged. "I do understand. What you're telling me is important."

Her strong face, a brow so smooth it might never have known a frown, her steady, fathomless eyes, invited trust. In spite of her odd beliefs I wanted to confide in her. But I said, "I can't."

Somehow she understood. She gently let go of my hands and turned to Jonathan. "I think Laura and I need to be alone, Jonathan. Perhaps you might go for a walk in the garden, or make yourself comfortable in the kitchen?"

He didn't seem to mind, and said equably, "Sure, I'd like to see your garden," and shambled out.

I opened up then. I told Belle Helen about all the episodes I could remember, both the pleasant and the unpleasant ones. Told her how time seemed to stop, how my perceptions altered so much I couldn't be sure what was really happening, how secretly afraid I was that one day I might say "this will pass" and it wouldn't, and I'd be trapped. I'd have lost my mind.

"You see," I concluded, "why I didn't want Jonathan to hear. Not just that these things are so personal, but I don't want him to think I'm crazy. I certainly don't want him to think I'm incapable of running the inn!"

Belle Helen was deep in thought, her face averted so that I saw her profile. The fact that she said nothing alarmed me, and further loosed my tongue.

"So often," I said, "I seem to be in touch with the dark side of things. What you'd call the negative, I guess it is. And that was happening before I got to the Stone House. So I thought, I assumed what I've felt about the tower, that was where it came from. If the tower is as you say it is, could it . . . could it have somehow killed my cat?"

Her head snapped around, sharply. "Please explain."

I did, and I told her how I'd buried him and made the pyramidal pyre and danced around it, not knowing why I did these things.

A trace of a smile touched her lips, but not her eyes. Belle Helen's eyes were very serious indeed. "Afterward," she asked, "how did you feel?"

"Emptied out, clean inside. And I haven't grieved for Boris. It was as if somehow I, or the fire, somehow we released Boris and he went on to a better place. I know that sounds childish, Boris was only a cat, but that's how I've felt."

"It's the farthest thing from childish that I can conceive of. I believe you did exactly that, and more. I believe that your depth of feeling for your animal companion combined with the light of the fire you built and drove back the darkness of the tower for a space and time. Your ceremony was powerful, filled with symbolism you don't consciously understand—it came from deep inside of you, from a memory you didn't know you had. What you've called 'living on the edge' is like a crack opening between the everyday world you've lived in and another dimension of reality, one most people experience only in dreams. You certainly won't go crazy! If you wanted to you might encourage this ability and learn to control it. I could teach you; it's a part of that power I told you we all have."

I shook my head vigorously. "No! All I want is for it to stop, go away!"

Belle Helen sighed. "I'm sorry you feel that way. However, if you want it to stop, I'm sure it will. There is great strength in you, Laura. But still I am concerned. You should not stay at the Stone House. It's a negative place, and I'm afraid only negative things can happen there. Truly, you should leave."

I jumped up, pushing the hair out of my eyes. "That's really why Jonathan brought me here, so you, too, would tell me to leave the Stone House!" I rushed out of the room in the direction Jonathan had gone, calling him. I soon found him in the kitchen and dragged him back with me. I knew I was overreacting, but I didn't care. "I want you both to hear this: No, I will *not* leave the Stone House! Belle Helen, I'm sure you are wise in the ways of your Craft, but your ways are not my way. Maybe I can put some positive stuff into those stones—I already thought of that, without any powers or second sight. Oh, I'll be careful—I'm not about to raise anything, or call anything down—but I am most certainly going to stay there."

Jonathan and Belle Helen looked at each other, then back at me. She said, "I still believe it's dangerous. I don't know the history of the place, only what I've told you. But I would be willing to bet that in the last two hundred years or more, *no one* has been able to live there for very long at a time. That in itself should tell you something, Laura."

I didn't reply. I folded my arms and stood my ground.

"Well, that's that, I guess," Jonathan said. "At least you've told her what you found there. Thank you, Belle Helen. We'll go now."

Belle Helen touched my arm. "Wait, please. There's one more thing I must do. Just a moment." She left the room with swift long strides, seeming to leave ripples of green and blue and yellow hanging in the air, an after-image. She was back almost instantly and came to me.

I looked up at her. She dwarfed me in every way, and yet I felt none of the discomfort I usually feel around very tall women. Rather, I felt protected. Even loved.

"I give you a gift, Laura," she said, "and yet not a gift, for this is already yours. It was meant for you, as surely as if it had come to me with your name on it. I have only been the keeper."

She pressed an object into the palm of my right hand. Tiny, it was, and cool, and my skin tingled where it touched. I felt instant, leaping joy so keen that for a moment I dared not see what she had given me, and I closed my eyes.

"Oh!" I breathed.

"Yes," murmured Belle Helen, her voice like music, "the dolphins do belong to you."

Nestled in my hand, two small silver dolphins entwined in a double leap. They were exquisitely detailed, with smiling mouths and tiny sapphire eyes. The dolphins were a pendant, on a slender silver chain. "Oh, I couldn't!" I protested. "This is far too valuable a gift."

Belle Helen smiled and picked the dolphins from my palm. She slipped the chain over my head and the dolphins settled in the hollow between my breasts. "Valuable for you, yes. Valueless for me. The dolphins came to me some time ago—never mind how—and I kept them although I never wear metal of any kind. Why do you protest? This talisman is yours, Laura, and you know it. Don't you?"

"Yes," I whispered. But how could *she* know, how could this happen?

"You have an affinity for the dolphins," she said, answering the question I hadn't asked aloud, "and they for you. Not these silver creatures, they are only the symbol. It is the real dolphins who are your friends. As soon as you told me the story of your encounter with them, one of your 'living on the edge' experiences, I knew for whom I have kept the talisman. From your bond with the dolphins the talisman will draw its power."

I was speechless.

"Listen to me, Laura Brannan. Dolphins are special creatures. Intelligent, emotionally sensitive, highly social. Many people believe that dolphins, like humans, have souls; and further, that the dolphins' souls may be more highly evolved than ours. To know this you need only to look into their eyes, for eyes are truly the windows of the soul. Wear the talisman, Laura," said Belle Helen. "The eyes of the dolphins will protect you."

16

"There's an important message on your desk, Laura," said Zelda.

"Good morning to you, too," I said. "You're looking well, Zelda. New outfit?"

She bobbed her head up and down, too rapidly. "The blouse is new. Really, Laura, I promised——"

"Whatever it is, surely it can wait two minutes. What about guests? Reservations?"

"We have a couple and two singles, all four from out of state. No reservations in the time you were out."

"I'm sorry to hear that. But I'm working on it. I'll take care of that message now," I added over my shoulder as I went into my office, "It's good to be back!"

I thought, as I closed the door, that Zelda did look better than usual. She must thrive on my absence. I pulled the blue poncho off over my head and hung it on the old-fashioned coat rack, tossed my head to readjust my unruly hair.

There were several messages on my desk. The most recent, on top, said: Please call Sergeant Sanders, ASAP.

"That explains everything," I muttered, and reached for the phone. In mid-motion, I withdrew my hand. I preferred not to talk to the sergeant within proximity of Zelda's avid ears. The skies were clear today, and there was a hint of spring in the air—a good day for a walk to the police station. I could get some exercise and keep Zelda Crabtree out of my business at the same time. A winning combination!

I was wearing a smock-dress in brushed cotton flannel, with a round white collar, a comfortable dress which I liked in spite of the fact that its innocent style made me look like a child. I stuffed a twenty-dollar bill into one of the deep pockets in the skirt and left my purse under my desk. Perhaps it wasn't such a bad idea to look like a child on a visit to the police station. I wondered what the sergeant could want as I put the poncho on again.

"I'm going to see Sergeant Sanders," I announced, breezing past the reception desk. "I'll be back when I can."

The walk was pleasant. I noted crocuses beginning to bloom in the yards I passed, though none were as far along as Belle Helen's; and slender green spears that would soon produce daffodils pushed up through the earth. With a welcome lightness of heart I realized that spring would come earlier to Beaufort than I was accustomed to, and it promised to be beautiful. With half a chance, I might even enjoy it!

Maybe the sergeant would tell me they'd caught the murderer. But no, that was wishing for too much. My mind supplied me with a more realistic thought: Seth could return today. I felt my heart beat faster and my breath catch in my throat. Telltale signs I hadn't felt for years, but impossible to forget. For better or for worse, I was in love with that complicated man. I smiled and quickened my step.

Beaufort's police station, like the town itself, was small and quiet. Not the kind of place you'd think of a murder investigation going on, even if you were capable of imagining that the victim had been your own blood kin.

"Nice to see you, Miz Brannan," said Sergeant Sanders, "but you could've called. You didn't have to come down here."

In spite of myself I was growing to like him, his easy manner, his unpretentiousness. "I was glad to have an excuse to get out and walk, Sergeant. It's such nice weather for a change."

"It is," he nodded, rocking back on his heels. "It most surely is. Well, seeing as you're here, let's get us a private place to talk."

He took me into a small room with a table and several straight, hard chairs around it. I tugged off my poncho and sat. I said, "Go ahead."

The sergeant seated himself at the end of the table. He puckered his forehead in a puzzled frown. "Go ahead?"

"Yes. *You* called *me,* remember?"

A slow grin spread across his face. "Yes, ma'am, I did that. Thought I'd tell you we won't be wanting you for the lie detector test. The motel manager where you stayed verified the time you said you left on the day your sister disappeared. As you said, you weren't even here, so you're in the clear."

I eyed the sergeant. What a devious mind he had behind that bland exterior! "You didn't seriously think me capable of doing away with my own sister?"

The grin stayed in place. He drawled, "Could be. Such things been known to happen. People are a whole lot more likely to be killed by somebody in their own family than anyone else, did you know that?"

"I seem to have heard it someplace," I said dryly. "Are you looking for Carroll Trelawney?"

Instantly his eyes were alert. "Maybe. Ain't found him yet. You didn't know him, did you?"

"No, only what little I heard from Kathryn when she came to Columbus when our parents died. And what I've heard here, of course."

"What'd she say to you?"

I paused, remembering. "Not much. She said he changed in the months before he left. When he was alone with her he was too quiet, moody. She assumed, and it made sense, that the change in him was because he wanted to get back to the sea again. And of course she also thought he was no longer in love with her."

"She think that before or after she started fooling around with other men?"

I felt as if he'd zapped me between the eyes. I started to snap at him, and thought better of it. "I don't know anything about that," I said evenly.

"Don't know? Or won't say?"

"I don't know. If she did have a relationship, or relationships, outside of her marriage, do you think it's relevant? I suppose you got the idea from Nick Westover, you must have talked to him."

Sergeant Sanders scratched at the back of his head. "Yeah. Odd bird, that Westover. The killer could have been a lover. Trouble is, we don't know who her lovers were. Nobody will admit to it."

"Maybe you should give your lie detector test to Nick Westover, then. He was one. He told me so himself."

"No need to put Westover on the polygraph." He waved his fingers in dismissal. "He's weird, but he's been real cooperative. And he's like you, he wasn't anywheres near Beaufort that day. He was out off Shackleford for them Dolphin Guards. Got a log to prove it, plus the word of that woman who's the coordinator."

"Oh. Well, I'm glad to hear that. Do you have any other leads, that you can tell me about?"

"Nope. More's the pity. And we've had near 'bout half the adult male population of Beaufort in here for questioning. Right many of the females, too."

No wonder I can't get any customers at the inn, I thought. But I was glad to know the police were working so hard.

"Who do *you* think killed your sister, Miz Brannan?"

I blinked, startled by the direct question. "I, uh, I don't know. Seth Douglass thinks——"

The Sergeant broke in. "I already know what he thinks, in great detail. You're a sharp lady. You really got no ideas?"

"No," I said nervously, not wanting old doubts about Seth to surface. "But I'm beginning to think Seth may be right. The murderer may be someone who's not from around here. Maybe the Trelawneys, Carroll and Kathryn, were involved in something besides the inn."

"Maybe. We're looking into that." Sergeant Sanders

leaned on the elbow he had cocked on the table. "Your boyfriend tell you he refused to take the polygraph?"

I pushed the hair back out of my eyes. "My boyfriend?"

"Yeah," he said with a sly smile, "Douglass. Don't look so surprised. This is a small town and you been seen together a lot. For a while there I thought the both of you were in on it. Maybe for the money. Then I found out you got more money than your sister ever had anyways, and Douglass is rich as Croesus. He could buy the Trelawney Inn and the Stone House five times over and never miss the money. No motive there."

"And there is the small fact that I never set eyes on Seth Douglass until *after* Kathryn was murdered!" I felt indignant to have been doubly a suspect. More strongly than that, though, I was worried about Seth again. "Did Seth say why he refused the lie detector, the polygraph test?"

"Yep. Said it's against his principles. Invasion of privacy."

I forced a smile. "Seth Douglass does have strong principles, Sergeant."

He rocked back on his chair legs. "I reckon."

"If there's nothing else," I said, "I think I'll be on my way."

"Lemme ask you one more thing. You ever hear tell of buried treasure on that Stone House property of yours?"

"Buried treasure!" The idea was so preposterous that I laughed. "Really, Sergeant. Are you so hard up for real clues that you're going in for fairy tales?"

He frowned at me. "Blackbeard's treasure ain't no fairy tale. The pirate himself said he'd buried his treasure in a place where only the Devil could find it. I reckon folks'll be looking from now to Doomsday. Half the land from here to New Bern's been dug up at one time or another. That's a strange enough place you got out there; I just thought I'd ask, that's all."

I gathered up my poncho. More insinuations about the Stone House, and from someone as unimaginative as Sergeant Sanders, were too much to take. "Maybe I should have a contest: Submit your spooky fantasies about the Stone House! The winner with the spookiest fantasy will receive a one-day all-expense-paid round trip to the top of the tower! Honestly, Sergeant! I'm living there now, doing my best to make a home for myself. How do you suppose that makes me feel?"

A surprisingly gentle look came over his plain face. "I'm sorry, Miz Brannan. I truly am. I'm just looking for a motive, is all. We seem to have us a motiveless murder here, though of course there's no such thing. The chief is about give up, and if I don't get a lead that pans out pretty soon . . ." He shrugged.

"I understand. Now, I think I will go." I dropped the poncho over my head and stood up to find Sergeant Sanders also standing, smiling at me.

"You be careful out at the Stone House, you hear?" he said. "It's not in our jurisdiction, but if you have any trouble, you go straight to the county sheriff."

"I'll be all right," I said. I had said those words so often, they sounded like a litany.

On my way back from the police station, I stopped at the public library and checked out several books about dolphins. I strolled the rest of the way to the inn, enjoying the sunshine and the salt-tangy breeze off the harbor. Suddenly I had a creepy feeling on the back of my neck and between my shoulder blades. I stopped short and whipped around, poncho flying. There were a few people scattered behind me, none of whom I recognized and all of whom continued on about their business.

It was the first time I felt that I was being followed.

Seth didn't come back that day, but he did call. He said he was learning so much and making such good contacts in Raleigh that he'd decided to stay a full week. He said he missed me, and I felt that now-familiar hitch in my heart. I told him about Boris, making the cat's death sound like an accident. He said he wondered if it really had been an accident. Since I was no longer so sure about that myself, I lied. I said, "Of course it was." Just before Seth hung up, he said "Get a dog, Laura. A big dog."

I got a dog. A big, bouncy sunbeam of a dog, a half-grown female golden retriever. I named her Aurora and called her Rory. Rory was semi-obedience trained, emphasis on the semi. She was so big she took up most of the backseat of the Subaru, though she would have preferred the front, with me. After dignified Boris, who had been fond enough of me but in general skeptical of the merits of human beings, Rory was quite a change. Rory did not know how to walk. She ran or trotted or jumped in the air, but her usual mode of perambulation was bouncing.

I knew when Seth said "Get a big dog" that he had meant a Doberman or a German shepard or a Great Dane, something fierce and formidable. But when Rory and I saw each other, it was love at first sight. She not only bounced, she also smiled—all the time. At the kennel she smiled and bounced up to me, and I was a goner.

"At least you're past the chewing-on-everything stage," I said to her one night, after her wagging tail had made a clean sweep of the top of a chairside table in my room. She smiled and panted and looked at me with adoring golden eyes, and I smiled, too.

"Sit, Rory!" I commanded, and she sat. "Now lie down." She stretched out reluctantly and put her head on her paws. "Good dog." I patted her vigorously on the back and picked up the magazines and paperbacks she'd knocked off the table. The offending tail thumped rhythmically on the carpet.

I sighed and refocused my attention on the letter I was trying to write to my friend the psychologist in Columbus. It was rough going, I kept having to leave things out. I couldn't very well write, "Dear Elizabeth, Since my sister's body washed up and we found out that she had been murdered, I've moved into this place called the Stone House which looks like an old Scottish castle, and somebody or some thing killed my cat. And I met a witch who says there are evil spirits in the Stone House tower. And, I'm in love with a man but he might be the one who killed my sister; and there's this other very good-looking and sexy man who seems really attracted to me—he has a great boat, but he's a little weird—he's obsessed with pirates. And oh, yes, I got a dog." No, I couldn't write that. By the time I'd edited out all the outrageous stuff, I ended up with something that sounded a lot like a letter home from camp: How are you, I am fine. Love, Laura.

Oh, well, I thought as I licked the envelope flap, it's better than nothing. And so are you—I looked down at Rory. You can't turn a cat person into a dog person overnight, but I was getting there. Dog's can't talk; Boris's "mowr" had had a hundred inflections. Dogs don't purr, a major disadvantage. Boris had been discriminating and mysterious; Rory was about as discriminating as a garbage collector and as mysterious as a comic book. But Rory had other advantages. She was unfailingly good-natured with her always-smile. And she was funny, still as clumsy as a puppy, and she could do a puzzled facial expression that was a riot. And she was *big*. When I walked her on the leash after dark with my new super-flashlight, I did feel more secure. I was sure that in time I could turn her into a real watchdog, if I could ever teach her how to wipe that smile off her face!

Rory's one great advantage over the late Boris was that she would come with me into the tower, whether she liked it or not. And she didn't like it. The tower was the only place where Rory didn't bounce; in fact, the first time I took her there, she growled. When I said "Come!" she hung back, and I had to repeat the command. She came then, cautiously, head down and sniffing. I never had the problem I'd anticipated, that when I danced Rory would want to jump and play and get in the way. Instead she would sit wherever I told her to sit, and her eyes would go from me to the walls, from me to the walls.

She slept at night on the floor beside my bed. Even on her first night Rory made a large, comforting presence. On her second night I discovered that my smiling golden dog was worth more to me than gold.

"Good dog," I murmured, more than half in sleep, and reached down to pat her where she lay beside the bed. My hand groped in air.

"Grr-oof!" Half growl, half bark, low in her throat—an ominous sound I'd never heard Rory make before. It brought me fully awake. I lay absolutely still, eyes searching in the darkness, ears straining for the smallest sound. I heard only the faint hiss of wind at the windows. But Rory's ears were keener than mine. She growled, low and threatening. I shivered in spite of the warm bedcovers; all the tiny hairs on my arms stood on end.

I sat up and called softly to the dog. "Rory! Come here, girl!"

She came, not bouncing but suddenly mature in her alertness. In the darkened room she found me with no trouble and pushed her nose into my outstretched hand.

"Good girl," I said again. I got a grip on her collar. Rory stood still, but I could feel her flesh quiver, like my own. I tried to think straight. Reason told me whatever Rory had heard must be outside, and yet I had it again—the feeling that I—we—were not alone in the Stone House. I knew I wouldn't sleep again unless I checked this out.

I talked it through to the dog, hoping that the sound of my voice might calm both of us. "Okay, Rory, this is what we're going to do. We're not going to turn on any lights, because if anybody did get in we want to surprise him. Right? So we have to get to the kitchen because that's where the flashlight is." For a moment I was stuck. I'd never make it quietly in the almost complete darkness as far as the kitchen without bumping into the furniture or something, particularly holding a big dog by the collar. And if I let her go, there was no telling what she'd do. I began to talk again, thinking out loud. "What we'll do is . . . is use the big fireplace matches to light our way to the kitchen, and we'll get the flashlight, and then we'll work our way back through the house to the tower. If we don't find anything,"—I silently hoped we wouldn't—"and if I feel very brave, we'll check outside."

I worked my feet into the slippers I'd left beside the bed,

but I didn't want to let go of the dog to get my robe. I had on a flannel granny gown, so I wouldn't freeze. "All right, here we go!" As soon as I stood, Rory pulled hard in the direction of the tower. I pulled equally hard the other way, whispering, "Not that way! Not yet."

I inched my feet along and felt in the black air with my free hand for pieces of furniture, until I reached the fireplace and located the box of long matches. I struck one against a stone, and we proceeded in that small circle of light. Rory padded carefully beside me, not bouncing for once. She was so big I had to stoop only a little to keep hold of her collar, and our feet on the rugs made no sound.

"This is silly, we're not going to find anything," I muttered when we reached the kitchen. But I went on with the plan. Still holding the dog by her collar, I felt in the drawer for the flashlight, and when I had it I switched it on. It was a big one, the kind that takes four batteries, and after the darkness its white light was intense, stark. I swept the light through the kitchen, into all the corners, and as I'd expected, nothing unusual appeared. I grinned at Rory, but the dog wasn't smiling.

"Yeah, I know. We're not out of the woods yet." I grabbed my keys from the drawer and got a new grip on the dog's collar. She began to tug me back the way we'd come. Not too fast, a slow steady pulling, but clearly she went after the sound she'd heard. Though she'd only been in my house for two days, she seemed to have no need of the flashlight I kept trained down at the floor.

Rory led me to the tower. She stopped dead still in front of that locked door.

"Uh-huh!" I said. I let go of her collar. If anyone, anything waited in the tower room, I wanted Rory free to attack or to do whatever she wanted to do. I unlocked the door and stepped back, letting it swing open onto cavernous dark.

Rory did not attack. She took two paces into the doorway and stood there still as a stone. I sucked in a deep breath. The flashlight beam wavered in my trembling hand. Suddenly I wished I had my dolphins with me—the pendant was on my bedside table because I'd never liked to wear anything about my neck when I slept. I vowed I would put it on as soon as I got back to my room and never take it off again until . . . until all this, whatever it was, was over.

Courage! I told myself. I moved beside Rory, my knee against her warm side, and I raised my beam of light.

For a heart-stopping moment I thought I heard laughter, insane laughter. I wanted to turn, to run, to slam the door behind me—but my dog advanced into the tower room and I went with her. My slippered feet whispered on the bare floor; Rory's nails clicked. The powerful flashlight which had seemed so bright before was lost in this room, a mere pencil-beam. Rory paced purposefully, and I stood in the center of the room and tracked her with my light.

My imagination worked hugely, frightfully, and I wished that Jonathan had never taken me to Belle Helen. It was one thing to fight heavy feelings of dread when I thought they were only in my mind, quite another to have them confirmed by one who was called a Wise Woman. The sense of another presence worked on me. An evil presence. Yet it seemed not to want to do me harm; rather it pulled at me, called to me. It wanted me. These stones, this tower wanted me.

"No!" I screamed aloud.

Rory whimpered, and skittered backward away from the door to the tower stairs. I ran to her and went down on one knee and hugged her to me with my free hand. "Not you, good dog, not you! Oh, Rory, there can't be anyone in the tower, there just can't! But God help me, I feel *something!*"

I hugged the dog tighter and buried my face against her neck. When I lifted my head I trained the flashlight on that stairway door. Mercifully, it was closed. I rose, went to it, and found it locked. Rory whimpered again, pushed past me, and pawed at the doorframe.

"It's locked, old girl. I think you've caught my susceptibility to spooks. Whatever it is we're feeling, it was here long ago, not now. The only way it can hurt us is if we give in to it and let it make us crazy." I raised my voice and swept my light, my circle of light, around the octagonal room. "I don't believe in you! Do you hear me? I don't believe in you, so *leave us alone!*"

Rory caught my energy and barked three times.

"That's the spirit," I said. "Good dog! Come on, I've had enough of this place, and I'm sure you have, too. And I'll be darned if I'll go outside."

My dog and I went back to the kitchen, and along the way I turned on all the lights. I knew I wouldn't sleep any more this night, and so I built a fire and started a pot of coffee. Rory looked at me expectantly, smiling again now, and I gave her a couple of dog biscuits. While the coffee dripped I returned to my room and took the pendant from my bedside table. It was foolish, of course, superstition. Or at best wishful thinking. These silver dolphins with their sapphire eyes could not protect me. Nevertheless I held the talisman in my hand while the night hours crept by, and when the sky began to lighten toward dawn, I slipped the chain over my neck before I went back to bed. I fell asleep with my hand clutched against my breast, holding fast to the dolphins.

"Hello, Nick. I didn't think you knew how to use the telephone," I quipped.

"Huh? What you mean?" he asked.

I'd forgotten Nick lacked a subtle sense of humor. "I was only kidding. I meant you never call. Whenever I see you, you just kind of turn up out of nowhere. I'm glad you called."

"Yeah, sure. You're not still sick, are you, Laura?"

"Sick? No, I'm not—" Just in time I remembered. "I'm much better now, thank you. What's on your mind?"

"Actually, I thought you were all right, I've seen you around. Saw you did what I wanted you to do." His voice turned seductive, smooth as silk. "That's good, Laura. I like that."

"Well, it's nice to have your approval, but the truth is I have no idea what you're talking about."

"You stopped seeing the Douglass guy, like I told you. Like I wanted. You understand now, I know you do."

There was a note in that silky voice that made me wary. "What is it I understand, Nick? Maybe you better tell me just in case I've made a mistake."

He chuckled deep in his throat, still seductive, very pleased with himself and with me. "That you're my woman, that's what. You love me. You don't need Seth Douglass, so you told him to get lost."

I ran my hand through my hair in the nervous gesture, glad we were having this conversation over the telephone. I chose my words carefully. "Uh, how do you know I haven't seen Seth?"

"Simple. He has a black BMW, right? And his car hasn't been around, not at the inn, not at the Stone House."

"You've been watching me." I liked this less and less.

"Oh, I walk over to the inn, drive out to the Stone House now and then. I like to know you're there, that's all. But since you didn't come by the boat I thought maybe you still didn't get your strength back. Now I know you did, I'll come over."

"Wait! Nick, it's ten o'clock at night, too late for you to come here."

"Ten o'clock isn't late, not when we've got all night." His voice slid along the telephone wires. "I have great plans for us, Laura. I've been working it all out."

My mouth was dry. I spoke in my firmest, most no-nonsense tones. "No, Nick. Listen to me. I want us to be friends, you and me, just friends. You can be a lot of fun and I like to go out on the *Hellfire* with you, but that's all. You've got it wrong about Seth Douglass, I haven't stopped seeing him. He went to Raleigh on business, but he'll be back and when he is, I'm sure I'll see him again."

In a brief silence I heard the sound of Nick's hard breathing. He said, "I can't have that, Laura. You can't be seeing another man. That's not in my plans for us."

I sighed, not at all liking what I had to do. Leaving aside that strange episode on the steps down the bluff—which strangeness had surely come out of the atmosphere of this place and not from Nick himself—I *did* want us to be friends. Apparently, it was not going to be possible. "I won't stop seeing Seth, Nick. I'll be your friend, if you can accept that. But I will not be your woman. Please don't come out here anymore unless you're invited. Don't even drive by. If simple friendship isn't enough for you, then I won't see you again."

His long silence was as loud as thunder. Finally he said, "You'll change your mind."

"No, I won't," I said. But it was too late. Nick had hung up.

Mother Nature had changed the rules of the game again. In celebration of the month of March she conjured up her winds and hurled them in our faces. They came galloping out of the sky in great, heaving gusts that whipped the tops of the waves to froth and sent the seagulls wheeling. They scoured the heavens and left them a deceptively beautiful blue while day after day gale warnings were posted on the banks and in the channels. The waters were so turbulent you could get seasick just watching the boats ride at anchor in Beaufort's harbor. Walking along the boardwalk was a challenge; walking atop the Stone House bluffs was an elemental adventure even Rory couldn't enjoy for long.

I indulged my fascination with the sea from behind glass windows. At the inn I took my work upstairs to a table in the dining room, with its splendid view of the harbor. I savored the clear skies, the visibility, and forgave the wind its fierceness, for it had driven away winter's gray storms. From time to time I climbed to my attic aerie where I could look farther out to sea. I was supposed to be working on a new ad campaign, planning strategy, choosing a new name for the inn, but my progress was slow. Like my mind. I hadn't slept straight through the night for a very long time, and the lack of real rest was wearing on me. It was no longer dreams which disturbed my nights—it was whatever awoke me from the dreams.

A major advantage to working in the dining room was that it put me in proximity to Evelyn rather than Zelda. When she finished her cleaning at mid-morning, Evelyn, too, would sit in the dining room with her work. Sometimes she planned the breakfast and supper menus, sometimes she had bedspreads or sheets and pillowcases to mend by hand, sometimes she came out of the kitchen with something she'd baked from scratch. Soon we were sharing the same table, talking as we worked.

At the Stone House, too, I chose to stay out of the wind. I let Rory exercise on her own and sat at the library/dining room window with my books about dolphins spread out over mother's tea table. Reading about dolphins was like Evelyn's presence—it calmed me. The books I'd chosen were not myths and legends, they were scientific accounts by marine biologists and psychologists. What I read was factual, reported in a straightforward style, yet often it touched such deep chords in me that I read with tears in my eyes. Even the most objective marine biologist's comments would reveal a growing emotional attachment to the dolphins he or she observed; over time this attachment evolved into admiration. I did feel an affinity for them, as Belle Helen had said, a kinship; but the more I read, the more I learned, the more I realized there was nothing mystical about my feeling that way. Any reasonably thoughtful person given the same information I now had would have felt the kinship, too.

It was easy to dismiss the mystical aspects of dolphins and the spooky stuff about the Stone House during the bright, windy days, but not so easy at night. Increasingly I dreaded twilight, which was distressing because it had always before been my favorite time of day. I sat at my window and felt threads of apprehension stitch along my arms as the first sunset colors tinged the clouds. If I wanted a walk before dark, it would have to be now. I decided against it, and let Rory out to race and play tag alone with the wind. A few minutes later I was glad of my decision, for otherwise I'd have missed Seth's call. He was back!

He declined my offer of a casual supper but said he would be over soon after. I wrapped myself in the sound of his voice, let knowledge of his nearness seep gladly into me. I had missed him. Gone only a week, and oh, how I'd missed him!

I ate quickly, called Rory in and fed her, then ran from

room to room closing drapes and straightening up. How one woman and a dog could make as much mess as we did, I'd never know. When those things were done, I turned my attention on myself.

Vanity and self-indulgence—not my usual style, but everyone's entitled once in a while. Especially when she's in love, and I was. Unwise or not, my love for Seth was a truth to be acknowledged. Maybe enjoyed. I prepared to enjoy. I filled the huge tub with lily-of-the-valley scented bubbles and got out the new dress I'd bought for this occasion. Luxuriating in the warm, silky water, with eyes closed, I moved the washcloth over my body. I remembered Seth's fingers, his lips, here and here and here . . . I sighed and let my mind go where it would. For a long time I'd known that my husband had been too self-centered to be a good lover. Seth was not. Our first coming together had been hurried by the sudden, swift passion that had swept us both along, and yet Seth had touched depths in me I hadn't known existed. I wanted to savor this wonder with him, to taste the delight again, and again.

I grinned and splashed my way out of the tub. The truth was, I wanted to seduce Seth! I was getting on with my life, putting the past and the dark things behind, claiming some of the happiness I'd had precious little of. Seth loved me, I loved him, we should be together—it was that simple.

Oh, but it's not that simple, argued that bothersome opposing counsel in my head. I refused to pay attention to its argument. I buffed myself with the towel until my skin tingled. I'll make it simple, I will! I promised, and used the towel on my damp hair. I reached for my robe but stopped in mid-motion, drawn to the full-length mirror on the bathroom door. Curiously I examined my reflection. For years, ever since I'd known I would never dance professionally, I'd avoided looking at this body. Dancers spend a lot of time in front of mirrors, perfecting gestures, ever seeking the graceful arch, the length of line. And when there was no longer a purpose to look for these things in myself, any looking became painful. Now it was different. Now this body was again my instrument, an instrument of pleasure for myself and my lover. I touched the cool glass, wiped away its haze with the flat of my hand. I saw again in my body the proportions one dance teacher had called perfect —more rounded now and more mature, but the breasts were still full yet high, the rib cage narrow, and waist more narrow still; a feminine curve to the stomach, legs slender and long for my height. Take off ten pounds and it was still a dancer's body, except for the too-pretty, highly arched feet.

I looked down at my feet, and then my gaze, startled, flew back to the mirror. I strangled on an in-drawn breath. What *was* that? For a moment I thought I'd seen a face there, not my own, a dark and hideous face. I backed away, groping for my robe. I'd turned cold, the fragrant warmth of the room had fled. My teeth chattered as I belted the robe around me.

Ridiculous, I chided, stupid, stupid imagination! I forced myself to look again into the mirror as I opened the door. Of course there was nothing in the glass, nothing but a pale, heart-shaped face with baffled gray-green eyes lost under a tangle of black curls. Laura's frightened face.

I jerked the door open and nearly tripped over Rory. She smiled and thumped her tail. "You're a sight for sore eyes, Rory girl," I said, not minding the cliché in my relief. "Come on, you can help me dress."

My new dress was the sort of thing your well-bred yachtswoman might wear after a hard day on deck. I'd bought it in a typical Beaufort shop, a deceptively plain storefront, and the inside full of elegant, expensive goodies. I loved the clothes people wore here, comfortable, classic, good stuff. Like this dress, which I'd gotten for a bargain because it was a winter item now on sale. Even on sale it was a delicious extravagance, a full-length wrap-dress of cashmere, so soft it was like wearing a cloud, its color a muted gray-green that matched my eyes. I wrapped its softness over my bare skin, slipped only bikini panties underneath, and felt elegantly wanton. The dolphins on their silver chain were my only jewelry. I brushed and brushed my hair, to no avail, of course, but it felt good. My scalp tingled pleasurably, and I tingled all over. The brief horror in the mirror was forgotten. Last I put on my glasses and rummaged through my shoe collection until I came up with a pair of silver-gray velvet slippers I'd forgotten I had.

Rory heard Seth's car before I did. Incipient watchdog that she was, she bounced in the direction of the back door, barking.

"Hush, Rory!" I dashed after the dog and grabbed her collar. My heart pounded, I was out of breath, and neither was due to chasing Rory. I tugged her backward to the vicinity of the kitchen table, cautioning, "It's Seth, and he's a friend. Now, *sit*."

I pushed my hair up and back at the temples, told myself to be calm. I heard his car door slam, waited for his knock. It came.

I was going to count to ten and stroll languidly to the door, but at the knock Rory went "Woof!" and bounded forward, so I bounded right behind her.

"Woof, woof!"

"Hush, Rory!" I got Rory behind me, but I forgot to tell her to sit and stay. With my heart in my throat I opened the door, said "Hi, Seth," got one glimpse of the marvelous silver hair and the black eyebrows before I became no more than an obstruction in the way of Man Meets Dog. Or vice versa.

Rory bounced about as high as my shoulder, smiling gleefully. Seth might have said, "Hi, Laura," or he might not have; he might have reached for me or he might have reached for the bouncing golden retriever—I didn't know because I did the sensible thing, I stumbled out of the way. So much for my intended glamorous greeting!

"You said to get a dog," I said wryly.

"Hey, boy, look at you! Nice dog, good fella!" Seth babbled to the dog, rough-housing amid much bouncing and sniffing and licking.

I got around the two of them and shut the door. Fists on hips, I said, "She's not a boy, she's a girl. Like me. Female, you know?"

"What? Oh, yes." Now Seth straightened up. He looked lanky and sexy and wonderful in his worn old suede jacket with a brick red sweater underneath. His eyes went over me and into me. The eyes, his whole face, softened.

"Female. Yes." His voice came from deep in his throat. "I seem to recall something important about females."

I forgot Rory. The hounds of hell themselves couldn't have kept me from Seth when he looked at me like that. My fisted hands uncurled, left my hips, went out to him. And that was enough. He took one long step to me and I was lost in his arms, lifted up against his hard body. First on tiptoe, then my feet left the floor as my lips, my heart, my soul melted into him.

"I missed you," I said, unnecessarily.

"I'm so glad you did," he murmured against my cheek, then he claimed my lips again. Slowly, gently, he set me on my feet. He cupped my face in his hands, and the look on his own face was so open, so vulnerable, and so puzzled it pierced my heart. "I never expected such a welcome from you, Laura," he said. Then he grinned, tousled my hair, and the seriousness was over. "But I won't say I'm sorry to get it!"

I laughed. "It's been an interesting week, and I've made some changes. I'll tell you all about it, but first, let me properly introduce you to this bundle of joy in dog form. This is Aurora, Rory for short. She's a golden retriever, seven months old." Recognizing her name, Rory bounced over to me, grinning so widely her pink tongue escaped one side of her mouth. "Rory, this is Seth Douglass."

"Sit, Rory," said Seth. He winked at me and bent to the dog. "Shake hands?"

To my surprise Rory lifted her paw and put it in Seth's outstretched hand. "She's never done that before!" I exclaimed.

"Either someone taught her, or else she's a fast learner," said Seth, rubbing her silky ears.

"She deserves a treat for that trick." I turned away and went for the dog biscuits.

Behind my back Seth asked, too casually, "How is Rory as a watchdog?"

"She's learning. I know you probably wanted me to get a Doberman or something that at least looks vicious, but . . . well, you see how it is with Rory. The darn dog is irresistible. The way the two of you have taken to each other, I just hope she won't want to leave with you!"

Seth wrapped an arm around me. "Maybe I won't want to leave, myself."

We settled on the loveseat in my room, with Rory in front of the fire gnawing away on one of her giant-sized dog biscuits.

Seth told me about his week in Raleigh, and I told him about my decision to put the past behind me, to let the police do what they could and get on with my own life.

"Do you really think you can do that?" A dark eyebrow arched. He looked skeptical.

"Of course I can. Didn't anybody ever tell you you can do anything you really want to do?"

"Um-hm. When I was maybe fourteen. The world has gotten a little more complicated since then."

"Not for you, surely. You've done very well for yourself. Sergeant Sanders said—" I stopped short, but not in time. My mention of the sergeant had taken our conversation in a direction I hadn't meant to go. "Uh-oh. I think I just put my foot in my mouth."

Now both of Seth's eyebrows went up. "Then perhaps you'd better take your foot out of your mouth and tell me what the sergeant said, *and* what you were doing talking to him in the first place."

I hedged, made a futile attempt to move the conversation away from this. "You know, Seth, if you shaved those eyebrows off, you'd lose half your repertoire of facial expressions."

He tweaked my earlobe. "And if you, my dear, shaved your head, nobody would recognize you without the mop-top! Now, answer the questions, both of them. Please."

"The sergeant said you were, quote, 'rich as Croesus.' I guess he investigated you."

"I expected to be investigated, but Croesus? Who would

have thought Sanders capable of coming up with an analogy like that! And what were you doing with him?"

"Just . . . talking. I think I misjudged him. Maybe you did, too. He's smarter than I thought, and he's really working very hard. I'm willing now to believe the sergeant will find Kathryn's murderer, if he can be found."

Seth frowned. "Not unless he's got something better up his sleeve than his damn polygraph."

"Uh . . . I heard you refused it." I felt increasingly uncomfortable, a tinge alarmed.

"That was some conversation you had with Sergeant Sanders! Yes, I refused it. He had no legal right to ask, he was just floundering around, grasping at straws. If they want to charge me, then I'll take their test. Otherwise, I'm entitled to my privacy and so is everyone else in Beaufort!" He rubbed the back of his neck and turned his face away.

There was now a palpable strain between us.

I tried to placate. "They did take your suggestion about Carroll Trelawney seriously; they're looking for him."

No reaction.

"Let's drop this, Seth. More brandy?"

"Hm? Oh, yes. Thanks."

We were quiet together, our silence slowly smoothing away the strain. All couples have tensions, I told myself. Rory snuffled in her sleep before the fire. Seth put his arm around me and drew me close. I snuggled against him, content with the silence. He hadn't isolated himself from me, and that was important. That was progress.

He nuzzled my ear. With a sensitive fingertip he traced the V neckline of my dress. Delicate shivers of pleasure followed where he touched.

"I like your dress," he murmured, "it's so soft. And it matches your eyes."

"Thank you." I was almost afraid to breathe.

His stroking finger moved to my chin, my nose, and lightly brushed one cheek and the other, a butterfly fluttering beneath the lower rim of my glasses.

"But I think," he said gently, "for all your brave intentions, all is not well with you, little Laura. There are shadows under your eyes. You aren't sleeping well."

A note of alarm, unwelcome, rippled down my spine. "I sleep all right. It's just that I . . . I wake up sometimes."

The muscles of the arm around me tensed. "Bad dreams? Anxiety? What wakes you?"

My alarm increased, became an icy weight which settled on me. How had we gotten into this? This wasn't what I wanted. What had happened to seduction? One glance at that severely handsome face, now drawn in lines of concern, and I knew I had to tell him the truth; he would be satisfied with no less.

"Not dreams," I said. "Maybe it's a kind of anxiety, I don't know. I wake up with the feeling I'm not alone in the house, but I am. I've searched the place, and I know no one has broken in. There's no way anyone could get through all the locked doors, anyway."

"You're sure about that?"

"I'm sure. You know how massive the main door is, and in addition to the old lock it has that beam you can put across from the inside. Anyone who wanted to come in that way would have to hack their way through, and it's six inches thick. The other three doors into the tower didn't have locks, so I had them installed. They're brand-new and absolutely cannot be opened without a key, which only I have. Besides, they're all inner doors. You have to be in the house first before you can even get to the tower room. Unless, I guess, you're a bird or a vampire or Superman, in which case you might fly to the top of the tower and come down from there!"

"Very funny." Seth ruffled my hair. "I don't like this, Laura. I don't think you're the type to imagine things, in spite of all the strain you've been under."

I wasn't going to tell him about the visit to Belle Helen and her conviction that some sort of dark force was at work in the tower. Privately I thought that had something to do with why I woke up, but Seth of all people would scoff at such an idea. I took another tack. "Well, it's probably only some sort of residual paranoia, left over from when I was so concerned about Kathryn. Once or twice in Beaufort I've felt someone was following me, but that was silly, too. No one was.

"Listen, Seth, I'm going to say something once and for all, and then I don't want to talk about it again. Sergeant Sanders and the police seem to think now that Kathryn must have been killed by someone from outside of Beaufort. I think so, too; and you yourself had a hunch along those lines. There is no reason whatever for anyone to want to harm me or frighten me. I know that, so I'm just not going to pay attention to whatever is waking me up or making me feel followed. Eventually, it will stop. And that's that!"

"Easy, Laura, easy. I hear you, there's no need to shout."

I hadn't realized I was shouting, but I said defiantly, "It's my house. I'll shout if I want to."

"So little, and yet so fierce!"

I retreated into my corner of the loveseat. Put my feet up, gulped brandy, and glared. "Don't be fooled by my size, Seth. I may buy my jeans in the boys' department, but I'm a full-grown woman. I hate it, I've always hated it when someone pats me on the head and talks down to me. And while I'm on this subject, I'd appreciate it if you would stop calling me 'little one.'"

Seth's face clouded. I was making him angry, I knew, but I couldn't seem to stop myself. I was determined to make the problems go away, by sheer force of will if there was no alternative, and I wouldn't have him shaking my resolve.

"Be fair, Laura," he appealed. "When I call you 'little one' I mean it as an endearment. You *are* small. Your size is one of the things I like most about you. It makes me feel protective. Is there anything wrong in that?"

"Only that I hate the traditional male-protector thing. We had this conversation once before, remember? I don't want or need to be protected. I just want to be—" my voice broke—"l-loved."

Something was going terribly wrong inside of me. I huddled to myself in the wake of my huge admission, my head down on the knees I clasped tightly to my chest. I felt Seth's hand stroke the nape of my neck, but I couldn't look at him.

"Sweet," he whispered. "Sweet Laura. I do love you. I'll love you just as much as you'll let me. That's all I've wanted for a very long time." He kissed my neck where he'd stroked it. I didn't move.

"Not all you wanted. You wanted the Stone House." I heard the words come out of my mouth and couldn't believe I'd said them.

The stroking hand moved to my hair, tracing circles in the curls around my ear. "Not the house, sweet, only the land, but it belongs to you now."

"Exactly." I raised my head; his hand fell away. I dared to look into eyes I knew would be like brown velvet, eyes whose softness had the power to rob me of reason. Words I'd buried under layers of my longing for him continued to pour out, without my volition. It was like running downhill, once I'd started I couldn't stop. "Love me, love my land, that's how you think. If you have me, then you'll have both."

The hand which had lately touched me so gently flexed, fisted, pounded once against a lean thigh. The brown velvet eyes wavered. On an indrawn breath, Seth turned away. "Damn, if you aren't a hard woman to get close to, Laura. I feel like . . . like you keep inviting me in, and when I'm in the doorway you slam the damn door on me!"

"I know," I whispered. I clung to my knees and watched helplessly as Seth got up and paced once around my room with long, angry strides. It was my mistake, a heart-breaking, awful mistake to let myself fall in love with a man I couldn't trust. Now I had to endure his anger; I'd earned it.

He strode back to me. His voice cut like steel. "I thought tonight, the way you were when you said you'd missed me, I thought we'd turned a corner. I could have sworn you wanted . . ." He bent down, grabbed my clasped hands, and wrenched them apart, tore them from my knees, and pushed my knees down so that my feet hit the floor. "Just look at you! I'm no kid, Laura, I've been around the block a few times. If you have anything on under that soft, sexy dress, it sure as hell isn't much. There's a word for women who do what you've done to me tonight, and it's not a nice word. How do you like being a tease, Laura Brannan?"

"I'm not!" I cried. "I didn't mean to, I did want—! Oh, Seth, I'm sorry. *Please* sit down, I can't talk to you way up there."

He sat, stiffly, warily. Rory, awakened by our tones of voice, was alert by the fireplace.

A cold calm took me over. The words still seemed to pour out on their own, but I sounded completely rational. "I made a mistake. You and me, Seth, it just won't work. Because I can't trust you. I've tried and I just can't do it. I don't think I ever will. It's over, that's all. Over. We both have to accept that."

"I see." He peered down his long, straight nose, disdainful, aristocratic. "Do you mind telling me *why* you don't trust me?"

I shook my head. "I just don't. There's no point in going into all the reasons; that would only make everything worse than it is already."

"All the reasons? My God, woman, that's enough! If you think I'm going to hang around and pry these so-called reasons out of you so that I can answer them one by one, you're wrong. You might try realizing that you have problems with trusting *anyone.* Sure, you have good reason to be that way, but I have my limits." He got up then, and strode to the door of my room. I stood, too, but he turned in the doorway. His voice was still hard. "I made you promises, and I meant every one. But if you say it's over, it's over."

"Well, it's not working out for us, is it, Seth? It's better for us both to accept that it's over. I have to get on with my life. And so do you." I ignored the pain that raced throughout my body.

Seth drew his great brows together, his face dark as a thundercloud. "So be it," he said. "Stay where you are. I'll get out on my own." He turned and walked away.

I went hesitantly after, somehow needing to watch him go.

I heard him say to himself, under his breath, "It's this damned Stone House. I swear, just about every time I come out here, something bad happens!"

When the kitchen door closed behind him, I locked it, leaned against it heavily. Rory, who had padded along beside me, cocked her head. She'd caught the mood, and she wasn't smiling.

Hours later I awoke to the now-familiar feeling that I was not alone. I grasped the silver dolphins at my breast and mumbled out of my exhaustion, "Oh, whatever you are, just go away and leave me alone!" Either it was the right thing to say, or I was just too worn out to care, for I turned over and went right back to sleep.

The next morning as I forced my weary body to dance in the tower room, I realized that I had done it after all. Done what Nick Westover wanted: I'd sent Seth away.

17

I sat in the inn's dining room with my list of names. Most of them were crossed out. I had two left to choose between, Creekside Inn and Harbor House. Both were acceptable, and neither was very exciting. It was time to make up my mind. The name change was a big undertaking, a project that got bigger every time I thought about it, and I couldn't delay any longer. But these two names were dull; and the more exciting ones, culled from the recesses of Jonathan's fertile mind, were all too imaginative. What I needed was something in between, a compromise. Suddenly inspiration struck, and I had it! I took a Jonathan-word, *Voyager.* Put it together with a Laura-word, *Haven.* Voyagers' Haven. Perfect! Voyagers' Haven—I had to try it out on somebody, right away.

Evelyn was in the kitchen; I'd try it out on her. I threaded my way through tables and chairs. In my excitement I called to her when I was only halfway across the room. My calling her out of the kitchen at that precise moment saved her life.

The sound of the explosion was a *Whump!* Huge, heavy, horrifying. It blew out the walls of the small kitchen, blew Evelyn out with the walls. I saw her hurled through the air as I was flung to the floor by the force of the concussion.

"Evelyn!" I screamed, fighting my way up through a torrent of chair legs. Black smoke roiled through the air. I coughed and screamed and somehow got to her. Her back was all flames. I beat at them with my hands. I got her rolled over, which put the flames out. She was unconscious.

The corner where the kitchen had been was burning. My eyes streamed, my nose and throat burned from the heavy smoke. If I didn't get us out of here the heavy smoke would kill us both. I grabbed Evelyn's arms and dragged the dead weight of her unconscious body through a forest of tables and chairs. I couldn't breathe. My hands hurt, my arms ached, I was pulling them from their sockets. There was so much smoke, I couldn't see . . . I wasn't going to make it.

I collapsed on the floor next to Evelyn. There was air here, precious little, but air. I gulped at it, and everything went black.

I came to fighting. Somebody was trying to smother me! There was something covering my nose and mouth! I tried to rip it away, and somebody held my arms.

"You're all right now, just breathe normally. This is oxygen. Breathe normally, deep breaths. That's right."

The voice was soothing. I opened my eyes. Gradually the panic left me. I wasn't being smothered, it was an oxygen mask. I stopped gulping and tried to breathe normally, as the man said. He was young, very blond with blue eyes, and he wore some sort of uniform . . .

I remembered: *Whump!* Smoke, fire—Evelyn. I started to shake uncontrollably. Began to cough, deep, wracking coughs.

The man removed the oxygen mask. He said, "Don't worry, coughing's normal. You've still got some smoke in your lungs, and your hands will be tender for a while, but you'll be fine."

I nodded, still coughing.

"Want to sit up?"

I nodded again. With the man's help, I got in an upright position. The blanket he'd put over me fell away. I sat on the grass in the courtyard behind the inn. I looked around, saw

Jonathan and Zelda nearby, and what looked like the entire adult population of Beaufort in the driveway.

The young fireman put the oxygen mask in my hand. "Just put it up to your face when you want more, okay? I'm going to see how they're doing inside."

"Okay. Where's"—I coughed again—"Evelyn?"

"The black woman? Rescue Squad took her to the hospital."

"She's . . . alive?"

"Yes, ma'am. Unconscious. We didn't try to revive her because her back is burned pretty bad; she'd be in a lot of pain if she was conscious. Don't worry, they'll take care of her at the hospital."

I moved, preliminary to standing up, and a gray wave washed over me.

"Take some more oxygen. Don't try to get up yet. You rest here until the chief comes. He'll want to ask you some questions. Okay?"

"Yes. Okay." I breathed more oxygen.

As soon as the fireman left Jonathan came and plopped down on the ground next to me. He was only half dressed, in pajama bottoms and an ancient plaid bathrobe. His corona of fair hair was frizzier than ever. He said nothing, just sat. He seemed to be more in shock than I was.

I reached out with my free hand and took Jonathan's hand in mine. I needed the warmth of a human touch. We held hands in silence for perhaps five minutes, and then the fire chief came. His boots and his yellow overalls were wet, his helmet under his arm. He was middle-aged, rugged, with a salt-and-pepper beard and hair, and kind eyes.

"You're Miss Laura Brannan, you're the owner?"

"That's right."

"There's not too much damage inside. That back corner room, I guess it was a kitchen, it's gone. But the rest of the inn wasn't touched. It wasn't actually a very serious fire, mostly a lot of smoke. We wet the walls down good in that kitchen area, it'll take a couple of days to dry out, but mostly what you've got is smoke damage in the dining room and some in the hall on that floor."

"You're sure? It was so *awful!* And poor Evelyn!"

"Yes, ma'am. Can you tell me what happened?"

"There was an explosion, a big whumping sound. I was crossing the dining room, calling to Evelyn, and she was coming out of the kitchen door, and then there was this . . . this blast. It knocked me down, but I saw it blow the walls out and blow Evelyn out, too. After that I don't remember anything except smoke. So much smoke!" I began to shake again. I took the blanket that had been over me when I was lying down and pulled it around my shoulders.

"Evelyn's the black woman, she was the inn's housekeeper, right?"

"Right," Jonathan answered for me.

"Well, it's a good thing you called her out of the kitchen when you did. If she'd been right on top of that explosion, she probably wouldn't have survived. You almost got the both of you out of the dining room before we arrived. You passed out within five feet of the door. That's a long way for a woman your size to have dragged an unconscious woman her size."

I looked at Jonathan. "You called them?"

"Yes, I did. The noise woke me up. Zelda's no good in a crisis, she was halfway up the stairs, wringing her hands and screaming her head off. Soon as I saw the smoke I called the emergency number. There was so much smoke in the dining room it took me a while to find you, and then the firemen were there. I have no idea how long all this took, how long you were lying there on the floor, but it probably wasn't more than a couple of minutes. God, what a terrible thing to happen!"

I didn't realize we'd been joined by another person until I heard an all-too-familiar voice. "More trouble, huh, Miz Brannan?"

I shaded my face with my hand and looked up at Sergeant Sanders. "I should have known you'd show up."

"Yep." He grinned at me, then turned and spoke to the fireman. "Got any idea how the fire started, Chief?"

"Explosion in the kitchen, not a very big one, fortunately.

The housekeeper woman's back was burned, and there's some property damage."

"Think it was an accident?"

The chief glanced at me and Jonathan, then back at the sergeant. "Why don't you come on up there with me and we'll see. We wet it down so much, I expect what's left of that kitchen will be cool enough to poke around some. "'Scuse us, Miss Brannan. Mr. Harcourt."

I watched them walk away. That was no accident, and I knew it. "Jonathan, I want you to do something for me. Something I'm not strong enough to do right now."

"Anything, Laura, just name it."

"Go over there and tell Zelda I'm closing the inn, and when I reopen I won't be needing her services. I'll send her two weeks' pay in the mail, but she's no longer employed here as of this minute. I don't ever want to lay eyes on that woman again."

He looked doubtful, but he must have seen on my face the resolve I felt. He pushed his glasses up his nose and went and did as I'd asked. I watched with narrowed eyes. Was I being unfair, jumping to conclusions? I didn't know, and I didn't care.

Jonathan wanted to come back to the Stone House with me, but I declined, just as I declined to be checked out at the hospital's emergency room. I was bruised, and my hands were red and sore, but that was all. I wished the same could be true for poor Evelyn. Before I left the inn I called the hospital and learned they were making arrangements to send her to a Burn Center in Chapel Hill. Her husband was with her, there was nothing I could do. So I drove myself home and soaked my aching body in the tub.

My arms were really sore, I found as I put first one and then the other into the sleeves of my soft fleece robe. The rest of me wasn't much better. My whole left side was turning blue—I must have landed on that side when I was thrown to the floor.

271

"You're going to have to take it easy on me for a few days, old girl," I said to Rory as I came out of the bathroom. She bounced a couple of times and pushed her nose into my hand.

The telephone rang; I answered it and recognized Seth's "Hello, Laura."

"News travels fast," I said by way of greeting.

"You're all right?"

"If I weren't, I wouldn't be at home, I'd be in the hospital like Evelyn. I don't want to talk to you now, Seth. Goodbye." I didn't give him a chance to say anything, I just hung up.

Damn! I swore under my breath. Seth's call had started me shaking again. Gingerly I made my way into the library, where I kept my paltry liquor supply in a sideboard. I choked down some brandy which burned and then numbed my smoke-parched throat. When I'd stopped shaking, I went into my room and called Sergeant Sanders from the bedside phone.

"Looks like somebody connected up some kind of a bomb to your microwave," he said. "We'll have more specifics tomorrow."

"I'm not surprised," I said grimly.

"Miz Brannan, that's just about the most interesting thing you ever said to me. You want to elaborate on that?"

"I can't. But the housekeeper was badly hurt, she could have been killed, and nobody was after *her*. Whoever it is who's doing these things, he or she is getting at me. I hate to admit it, but you've been right about that. I have no idea why, but I have some suspicions about who. Sergeant, I want you to question Zelda Crabtree."

"Say more."

"All right." I took a deep breath, which hurt a little. "I can't really accuse her of anything, I just think she's involved in these things that have happened at the inn. And I think if she is, she's not in it alone. She's nervous and high-strung and if you work on her, shake her up, get tough with her—however you do these things—maybe she'll tell you something."

"We'll get right on it. You happen to have her address handy?"

"Not here, I'm at home. I think she lives in Morehead City. You can call the inn and Jonathan will give it to you."

"No need to bother him. I'll find her."

"Sergeant, one more thing." I faltered.

"I'm listening."

"Zelda used to work for Seth Douglass. I'm sure there's still something between them." My heart was going like a jackhammer. Every beat was pain.

"Well, well. The boyfriend."

"Not anymore, he isn't. Good-bye, Sergeant."

"Yeah, good-bye. And thanks."

It was several hours later when the full import of what had happened hit me. I was deeply involved and had been all along; there was no way to put Kathryn's murder and all the things that had happened since behind me, no way to simply let go. Everything was related, had to be, even the killing of my cat which I had long since admitted to myself wasn't an accident.

I thought back to the time, not so long ago, when I'd felt irrationally afraid. I hadn't had a name for what I feared, I'd labeled it the Unknown. Then Kathryn's body was found, and I'd thought the Unknown was Murder, the act itself. Now I knew more. Not the Unknown, not Murder, but the Murderer—Kathryn's murderer was after me. No longer vague, no longer irrational, and somehow the fear was the worse for being focused, and rational.

Maybe now the murderer only wanted to frighten me, harrass me. Pretty serious harrassment; Evelyn had become its victim and she was seriously burned. I could have been the one to go into the kitchen and turn on the microwave, and then I would have been the one burned, possibly . . . killed. But *why?* I couldn't imagine, unless my first instincts had been right and all this was centered somehow on the Stone House. Yet, my opposing counsel argued, most of the "accidents," all of them, in fact, except the one to Boris, had happened at the inn. No matter how I turned the thoughts in my mind, it made no sense to me.

I sighed. I was very tired, I felt battered both in body and in spirit, yet my mind twisted and whirled. I couldn't shut it off. Perhaps if I walked outside with Rory, the fresh air and exercise would clear my head and help me sleep. I slipped my poncho over my robe, took her leash and the flashlight and my keys from the drawer. The dog raced back and forth gleefully from counter to kitchen door. I envied her that simple happiness as with a tremor in my hand I fastened the leash to her collar. The night held no terrors for Rory, as it did for me. I went out into it anyway.

A shadow within a shadow. The light of a three-quarter moon gave the bare grounds an eerie glow, like a snow-field scarred by black tracks of winter's old ruts. Against this background the tower's shadow fell in high relief, starkly black, a dead zone. And in that absolute black, I thought I had seen the movement of something blacker still.

Rory romped ahead. My arms and hands hurt too much to hold her back. "Heel!" I said in a loud whisper, which she ignored. She was young, barely trained, and I'd used the wrong tone of voice. The truth was, the dog was walking me—I must either drop the leash or follow her. I followed, twisting half-backward and straining my eyes to see within the tower's shadow. There was no time to think, with every second Rory pulled me toward the bluff, away from the tower. So I raised my voice, called clearly, "Heel, Rory, heel!" and she did. I switched on the flashlight in spite of the bright moon, and with the dog at my side I stalked back to the tower.

I kept the flashlight beam trained straight ahead of me. It cut cleanly through the night and soon pierced the tower's shadow. There was no foliage to conceal a person or a large animal. Foot by foot I turned the dark to light. It was an empty blackness which I illuminated; there was nothing there after all.

I went down on my knees and hugged Rory, rubbing my cheek against her smooth coat. "You would have protected me, wouldn't you, girl?" I murmured. She turned her head and swiped at my hairline with a friendly tongue.

I scrambled up heedless of my sore body, not wanting to

stay in that shadow a moment longer. "Come on, Rory," I cried, "let's run!"

Voyagers' Haven was out—I would always associate that name with the horrible sight of Evelyn being blown across the room with her back in flames. I settled for the more mundane Harbor House and proceeded with organizing my ad campaign. Since the inn was closed, Jonathan was sleeping nights like the rest of the world and by day supervising the clean-up and repairs on the third floor. I'd called Chapel Hill each of the three days since the fire for news of Evelyn, and she was holding on, stable, but she would need skin grafts. I'd told her husband they weren't to worry about money, and I had my lawyer working on all the insurance details. In other words, I was once again getting on with life as best I could, but I felt as if I were playing a grown-up version of the children's game "Heavy, Heavy, Hangs Over Your Head."

Jonathan came into the office. I looked up and said, "Hi. What have you got there?"

His cheeks were flushed—he was clearly excited about something. "I think I've found a clue or something, Laura. Look here—this is the drawer out of that telephone table in my sitting room." He turned the drawer upside down and set it in front of me on the desk, right on top of my papers. "Now do you see?"

I shook my head. "Maybe I need new glasses. It's just . . . an upside-down wooden drawer."

"Here, right here. Look close."

I bent over and looked more closely. There were numbers written in pencil on the unstained wood. "You mean these numbers?"

Jonathan nodded. "What do you make of them?"

"Not much." There were two sets of numbers. The top one had eight numbers and the bottom one ten. "Some kind of manufacturer's code? No, obviously nothing so dull, to judge by that gleam in your eye. Why don't you sit down and tell me what you think these numbers are."

He dragged a chair over and sat on the edge of it. "Well,

you see, after the explosion I kept thinking there must be something I could *do,* so I went through all the stuff in the desk again. Didn't find anything. I don't know why, I just decided to take all the drawers out of the desk and look on the bottoms of them. They were clean. Then just for the heck of it, I took this one out of that table and turned it over, and there were these numbers. At first I thought, like you said, they were some kind of ID, serial numbers, like that. But the bottom numbers nagged at me, reminded me of something. It was maddening, like having something on the tip of your tongue and it won't come out, you know?"

I said, "Yes, I know," and looked at the number again. Now I saw what he meant.

"Read them aloud, Laura, the bottom numbers."

I did. Read aloud, the ten numbers fell into a familiar rhythm. "A phone number! Is it a phone number, Jonathan?"

He beamed and rocked back in his chair. "I think so. The first three are a Florida area code. So I called the number, just now."

"And . . .?"

"Well, it was a legitimate number, but it's out of service."

"Oh. Well, now what?"

"I'm going to take this drawer to the police."

"You think Carroll Trelawney wrote the numbers on that drawer? I do know it's not Kathryn's writing."

"Yep, that's what I think. Maybe the police will have some idea about the top row of numbers, and maybe they can find out who had the bottom number when it was in service. That top row, that's a puzzle. I can't think of anything that comes in a sequence of eight numbers, can you?"

I thought for a minute. "Social security? No, that's nine. Maybe the ID number of a bank account, something like that. The bottom number *might* be something other than a phone number, that could be just a coincidence. But I agree, you should tell the police. *Anything,* any clue at all, would be a big help right now."

Jonathan bobbed his head and picked up the drawer.

"That's what I thought, too. So I'm going on over there, if that's okay with you."

"Sure, you go ahead."

He went out the door. I jumped up and ran after him, caught him just outside. "Wait, Jonathan! I thought of something you should tell them."

Jonathan waited, and I went on.

"You said when you moved into the room that drawer was completely empty. To have an empty drawer *anywhere* was extremely unlike Kathryn, wasn't it?"

"Yes," he nodded, "yes, it was."

"So, whatever was in that drawer, Kathryn took it out, and we've never found it. Maybe it's not important, but tell the sergeant. Or whoever you see."

My friend Jonathan positively twinkled, and I understood why. We were desperate for anything, no matter how small, that might make us feel we were getting somewhere.

"You're right," he said, "I'll tell him. Hey, maybe we've got something here!"

"I hope so, Jonathan. I really do hope so."

No sooner had he left and I settled down to work again than there was a series of sharp raps on the outside door. What now? I thought impatiently. There was a "Closed" sign as big as your face on that door, and it was locked besides. Another round of rapping convinced me that the knocker wouldn't go away, so I left my papers once more and went to open the door.

"Hey, lady, I came to see how you're doing." Nick leaned one arm against the door frame and flashed his white teeth.

As always, the first sight of him took my breath away. No male human outside of the movies had a right to such flaming good looks. The warmer weather had brought his physique out into the open again, in a thin, once-yellow V-neck sweater over bare skin and tight old jeans. I pushed my hair out of my eyes and, in spite of myself, smiled. "I'm fine, Nick, but I'm pretty busy."

"Busy? How can you be busy?" His green eyes roamed over me, as if he could see beneath my overlarge pink shirt and gray trousers. "Your sign says Closed."

"It doesn't seem to be very effective, does it?"

"Huh?"

I looked down at my feet, trying not to laugh, and thought, Oh, Nick, you're really not too swift! And I said, "Effective against you, you big idiot. My Closed sign didn't do much to keep you out, did it?"

"Nope." He grinned. "So can I come in, or what?"

"All right, you can come in," I stepped backward out of the doorway, "but really not for too long. I do have a lot of work to do."

He strolled into the reception area. "I'd like to see where you had the fire. How about you show me, Laura?"

"Well . . . okay. I guess it wouldn't hurt for me to see how they're doing up there.

Nick made an exaggerated, sweeping bow. "Ladies first, and all that."

I went ahead. As I climbed the stairs I reminded myself of Nick's last phone call to me. Reminded myself what I'd said about us being just friends. After my ex-husband Roger, I didn't want any more possessive, overbearing men. Easier said than done—it had always been the overbearing ones who were able to break through all the walls I'd recently begun to understand I threw around myself. I had a history of fatal attraction to the domineering type, and Nick was more domineering and more attractive than most. I was too conscious of him on the stairs close behind me.

"You can see the smoke damage on the walls, starting here," I pointed out. The clunking sounds of work in progress grew clearer as we reached the third floor, and the walls grew blacker. I made a mental note to choose new wallpaper soon—no use trying to wash this mess.

"Say, you had a lot of smoke up here!" said Nick.

"Wait till you see the dining room." I went on to speak to the work crew and left Nick to ogle on his own. The work was still in the tearing-out stage, and the destruction was horrible. Every time I came up here, I had to fight off a case of the shakes and tell myself how much worse it could have been.

Nick ambled up, the tips of his fingers stuck in the back pockets of his jeans. He made a low whistle. "Big mess you got here, Laura. Got any idea what really happened?"

I stuck to the cover story Sergeant Sanders had insisted on, in case this incident were in some way connected with Kathryn's murder. Nick could have read it in the paper. If he ever read a newspaper. "The microwave oven blew up, for reasons we'll never know, and the explosion started a fire." I squared my shoulders. "If it weren't for Evelyn's injuries, I might consider this a blessing in disguise, because I get to put in a new kitchen and the insurance money will pay for it!"

Nick appraised the ruined corner with glittering emerald eyes and a half-grin, half-leer. I thought what an unfortunate human trait it is, this fascination with disaster. He turned to me with that leer and his voice rose over the hammering and ripping. "Lucky it was her instead of you in there."

My cheeks flushed hot. He'd put into words something I tried never, never to think. I said, "Let's get out of their way, Nick. I'm sure you've seen what you wanted to see."

On the way down the stairs he said, "I guess you have to fix up the damage before you can sell the inn. I guess you wouldn't get your money out if you let whoever buys it do the fixing."

I stopped on my step and turned around, wavering a little as I looked up at him two steps above. With his abundant red hair and muscular, tall body, Nick filled the stairway and towered over me. "Why would you think I'm selling the inn?"

"You are, aren't you? You're closed and everything."

"I'm closed until we get the damage taken care of. And I'm using this time to get ready for our reopening. In fact, I've got some pretty good plans, including a name change. That's why I'm so busy, I'm working out my plans. Which reminds me, I do have to get back to it." I turned around and stomped down the remaining stairs and into my office, where I sat down determinedly behind my desk.

Nick dawdled along, looking around, taking his time.

Eventually he parked himself on a corner of my desk. "You don't look much like a businesswoman, Laura. Are you sure you want to keep on with all this stuff?"

I leaned back in my chair and leveled my gaze at him. "I've never been more sure of anything in my life, Nick. When I came here last fall I intended only to help Kathryn out for a while. Now it's different. I have something to prove. I have a . . . a deep personal investment here, and I'm determined to make it pay off."

Nick smoothed his beard and stared at me.

I stared back, and the phone on my desk rang. All calls were now forwarded from the big electronic unit on the reception desk to my office. I picked it up and said hello, and heard the voice of Zelda Crabtree. A very distressed Zelda Crabtree.

She said, "Laura, I have to see you. I really, really do."

I glanced at Nick, who watched and listened with undisguised interest. I could think of no reason why he shouldn't hear my end of a conversation with Zelda, so I went ahead. "Zelda, anything you have to say to me I'd much rather you said it to the police instead."

"I did. I was there"—a brittle catch in her voice—"a long time, I told them over and over and I don't know if they believed me. I have to tell *you,* Laura. Really, because of what happened to Evelyn!"

"Evelyn?"

"Yes, f-for poor Evelyn. Please, Laura."

She had invoked the one name I could not refuse. What the heck, my day was more than half shot anyway. "All right. How soon can you get here?"

"Right away. Fifteen minutes. Thank you, oh, thank you!" she half-shrieked, half-sobbed.

"I hope she's not too upset to drive," I muttered as I replaced the receiver.

"Old Zelda? What's she got to be upset about?"

"I'm afraid that's none of your business, Nick. She wants to see me, so it's time for you to go." I stood up. "Thanks for stopping by."

Nick didn't budge. He sat on the desk, swinging one leg,

grinning like a huge orange Cheshire cat. "I knew you'd be glad to see me again."

"It's always good to see a friend," I said carefully.

"Weather's getting better. Warmer, not so windy. I bet you'd like to come out on the *Hellfire* with me, wouldn't you?"

I studied him, felt a smile coming and allowed it. He had been, for him, polite; he'd kept his hands to himself; and that boat of his was an irresistible enticement. The dark side of my previous day on the *Hellfire* was forgotten; I recalled only the fresh feel of the wind on my face, the thrill of flying over the water. "As a friend—just a *friend,* Nick—I'd love it. You do understand what I'm saying?"

"Oh, yeah. Loud and clear." Nick put both feet on the floor and stepped away from the desk, his back to me for a moment. His shapely buttocks and strong thighs moved inside the tight jeans. He turned around. "So let's go, then. How about tomorrow?"

I shook my head, and my hair fell into my eyes. "Not this week. I'm working on a tight schedule and I have to get a bunch of stuff to the printer by Saturday noon. How about next Monday or Tuesday?"

Now he really smiled, a genuine smile that crinkled the corners of his eyes. "Monday, then, unless it rains or there's too much wind. *Hellfire* 'n me will be waiting for you, Laura!"

I came around the desk then and urged him toward the outside door. I paused before opening it. "Nick, you remember when you told me that sometimes you checked to see if Seth's car was here or at the Stone House, and I asked you not to do that anymore?"

"Yeah. I remember."

"Well, did you stop, ah, checking on me?"

Nick shrugged. "I didn't want you to be mad at me, Laura. And you sounded pretty mad."

"Okay, Nick." I sighed. "I'm not mad anymore. I was just asking." Just asking because I still had the feeling that I was being watched, and followed—not that I particularly cared anymore. There is something that happens when you finally admit to yourself that someone wants to do you harm. I imagine it's like knowing you have a chronic illness that is not always, but is occasionally, fatal. You come to terms. You stop being angry, because anger takes a lot of energy and doesn't change anything. You stop being quite so afraid, your heart doesn't try to beat its way out of your chest every time you feel there's someone behind you, stalking you. You live normally enough from day to day, you get the fear down to a level where you know it's there, but you can cope with it. You don't want to provoke a crisis, but you aren't going to avoid one when it comes, because most of all what you want is for it to be over, you want resolution. Even if the resolution means your own death.

So I said again to Nick, "Just asking. Never mind."

"I want to tell you what I did do, and what I didn't do," said Zelda. She sat on the edge of her chair, bony knees protruding from under the edge of her skirt. Her blouse was as wrinkled as if she'd slept in it; her eyes looked more as if she hadn't slept at all. She wrung her hands this way and that.

I inclined my head in assent, without speaking. My voice might well have betrayed the skepticism I felt.

She rushed on with her explanation. "I did take the reservation records that day. I . . . I put them out in the trunk of my car and later I dumped them into the dumpster behind some condos. And then when I came back in from putting them in my car, I just pulled papers out of the file cabinets and tore them up and scattered them all over. I wanted to make it look like somebody had broken in. I got the idea from the way the laundry room and the storage room had been messed up. But I didn't do it that first time, Laura, and I didn't cause that fire in the dining room, either. I only took the reservations and tore up the files a little, that's all."

I laced my fingers together, as if holding my own hands could help me hold my temper. "Why on earth would you do that, Zelda? Keeping the reservations was *your* job. Taking them was like stealing them from yourself!"

She wrung her hands more. I wondered she didn't crush her own knuckles. She said, "I know, I know! I thought nobody could possibly suspect me if it was my own work I destroyed, I thought I was being smart. And I never dreamed you had duplicates." Her throat was so tense, she squeaked. "S-so it didn't even do any good, I mean it didn't work. I worried so much, I really agonized over doing it, that I might get caught. And then, because you had the duplicates, all that worry was for nothing. It just made a lot of mess and no results at all!"

"You can't expect me to feel sorry that your destructive plans didn't pay off!" I snapped. "And you still haven't said why you'd do such a thing."

With a pointy tongue she licked her dry, thin lips. "I wanted you to get discouraged and quit. Go away, go back where you came from."

"I gave you a job when you wanted one, Zelda. I thought you wanted to work here."

"I did, but that was before, before—"

"Spit it out!"

"Before I found out how Seth feels about you." She hung her head, and her lank, stringy hair fell around her face.

Well, well, I thought. I stared at her, my narrowed eyes challenging her to go on. I let an uncomfortable silence fall.

Her eyes when she looked up at me had a glazed, faraway quality. "Seth is such a wonderful man. He's always been so nice to me, I mean, he went out of his way to do little things, and I knew he was lonely. He watched out for me, even when I wasn't working for him anymore. Like getting me the job with you. So I thought, I mean I hoped, that one of these days he'd, you know . . . But then he got interested in you and I thought it wasn't right. I mean Seth and I, we're so good together. When I was his assistant I always knew what he was thinking and how he was feeling and what he needed and . . . and everything. I just wanted you to go away, that's all. That's why I did it."

And now, as a result of this performance, I'm supposed to believe it was all one-sided, that the closeness I'd sensed between those two was all on Zelda's part. For just a moment I felt sorry for her, for her ravaged appearance. But if ever there had been a faithful retainer, a woman who would do anything for the man she adored, Zelda was it. She would lie for him, steal for him, possibly even take the fall and go to jail for him if it came to that. Pathetic. My heart ached and not entirely for her, because in a deep part of myself I understood. I still loved Seth myself.

"All right," I acknowledged, "you've confessed. But I gather because you made this confession I'm supposed to believe you had nothing to do with the other two incidents?"

"Oh, I didn't! Poor Evelyn! I would never, never do anything that could hurt someone. It's so awful that she got burned, and I'm so sorry. That's why I had to come here and tell you in person. I can't bear for you to think I'd do something like that. Really, I just can't bear it." Now she was whining.

I asked, "Is that what the police think, that you did all three things?"

She wrung her hands, leaned forward, and thrust them between her bony knees. "I don't know. I told them the truth. Not about how I feel about Seth, they don't have to know that, but about what I did. That sergeant just kept on and on at me. He kept asking was I doing it for someone else, or did I let anyone in, anything like that."

"Well, did you?"

"No. You believe me, don't you, Laura? You've got to believe me."

I ran both hands through my hair, expelled a breath I seemed to have been holding forever, and turned my face away. Without looking at her I said, "If you're really sorry about Evelyn, write to her. Send her some flowers. Offer to help her when she comes home. Do I believe you?" I faced her again. "I don't know. Time will tell. You can be sure we'll get to the bottom of this, one of these days."

18

I worked longer than I'd meant to on the Harbor House brochure. I would have to push if I were to be back at the Stone House before dark, and I had to stop at the supermarket on my way home. I checked the position of the sun behind Carrot Island as I drove away from the inn and judged that I had half an hour of light left, at most.

I was stopped at a traffic light halfway to the shopping center when the back of my head began to feel peculiar. Not now, I thought, I don't have time for one of those on-the-edge episodes now! I hadn't had one in a long time, since before meeting Belle Helen, and I'd thought they were over for good. But my head felt strange, creepy, as if a spider with a hundred legs had tangled in my hair and every one of its legs pricked into my scalp. "No, damn it, stop!" I said aloud. "I don't have time for this now!"

The light changed and I drove on. By the time I pulled into the supermarket's parking lot I recognized the pricking for what it was, a heightening of the being-followed feeling. My senses were all alert, but not abnormally so. I didn't lose track of time, didn't have the unreal sensations of former episodes. This was something new, then, as if my mind and body had refined the intensity of all those earlier experi-

285

ences, kept the parts which were most useful, and threw the rest away. If I were really being followed, it would certainly be useful to know.

When I got out of the car I dropped my purse, on purpose. Nothing spilled out, but I pretended otherwise, I fussed around on the pavement picking up imaginary objects and dropping them into the purse, while actually I looked around from under the mop of my hair. Three cars parked while I played my charade. People got out of two of them; whoever was in the third car stayed put. My stalker? Perhaps. I noted where that car was parked, all I had time to do without being obvious, and went on to do my shopping.

Twenty minutes later when I returned, the same car was still there. It was a black car, I thought, though we were at that time of day when there is not enough light to see well and not enough dark for the automatic sensors that control these things to switch on the parking lights. So it could have been dark green or dark blue, as well. I couldn't tell if the person inside was a man or a woman, much less what he or she looked like, because I couldn't see through the glass. Again, that had to be a trick of the light. The car could be innocently waiting to pick up a shopping spouse, but I didn't think so.

I put my two bags of groceries on the other side of the front seat, pushed the button which automatically locks all four doors, started the engine, fastened my seatbelt, and drove away. I wouldn't look in the rearview mirror, not yet. That creature with the hundred legs sticking into my scalp had left me while I was in the supermarket, but now it was back again. Pricking, pricking.

Twilight gloom engulfed the car. I turned the headlights on low beam and allowed myself a glance in the rearview mirror. I'd been foolish to think I could tell if that dark car in the parking lot followed me. I could tell only that there were other cars behind.

I shuddered, thinking of the dark, close confines of the private road to the Stone House—not a place I would like to be trapped, forced off into the deserted woods. When my turnoff came I passed it and continued on, driving north on

Route 70. I'd been this way only once before, with Seth. The memory was distant, hazy, as if from another lifetime. I'd been upset that day, but now I couldn't recall what had upset me. Nothing could be more upsetting at this moment than the glaring reality of a pair of headlights behind me.

I reached up and flipped the mirror to night vision. It was not yet completely dark; rather I moved through that muted dying of the light which distorts distances and inflames the imagination. At this time of day it is easy to see things that are not there, and not to see things that are. The practical side of me, which until this strange past year had always been the dominant side, asserted itself. A glance at the speedometer verified that I was driving faster than was safe for the time of day. I fought the increasing panic which pressed my foot too hard against the accelerator, and the Subaru slowed.

A horn blared, lights flashed, and the car behind me roared past, crossing the center line of the two-lane road. "Idiot!" I muttered, my attention still focused on safe driving. Next I felt briefly disoriented, as if I had missed something important and had no idea what it might be; then I laughed. It was nervous laughter, but laughter all the same. That was the car I'd thought was following me, but when I'd slowed down, it passed! My pursuer was gone, he wasn't after me at all!

Why then did the pricking of my scalp continue? No matter, as soon as I could find a place to turn around I'd be on my way home. Before long I'd be safe in the Stone House, in my blue and white kitchen, with a fire for comfort and Rory for companionship. Unfortunately there was no place to turn on this narrow road. I tried to remember from that one drive with Seth what this stretch of road was like, what would come up next. I strained my eyes against the increasing darkness, and suddenly with no warning the car left trees behind and I was in another world.

This I remembered. This, I hadn't liked then and I didn't like it now. Ahead of me the road stretched for miles, straight and narrow; on either side extended the marshes—barren, sodden, abysmally lonely. In this open and isolated place there was, for now, more light than had been earlier when the road ran through the trees. But even as I looked the light was dwindling, dying. The sky was a dark blue with here and there an early star, diamonds on blue velvet. Below, black night oozed from the marshes. The night would soon claim all this world, including me, for I was on the causeway now and there was nowhere to turn around. I had no choice but to drive on, all the miles to Cedar Island.

The pricking on my scalp converged into a cold, stabbing jolt that struck at the base of my skull and traveled down my spine. Involuntarily my eyes went to the rearview mirror. Like baleful, glowing eyes two headlights hung there. It's my nerves, I thought, they're not real. I'll close my eyes and when I open them again, the lights will be gone. But I didn't dare close my eyes on a narrow, unfamiliar road at nightfall. I looked over my shoulder instead. The lights were real, all right; there was a car behind me after all.

I counted to ten, trying to regulate my breathing and get my heartbeat back somewhere near to normal. Then I twisted around and deliberately looked at the following car for as long as I dared take my eyes from the road. There was just enough daylight left for me to see that the car was very much like the one from the supermarket parking lot. Of course, it could just be someone who lived on Cedar Island and happened to own a black car, driving home. No need to jump to conclusions, especially since there was nothing I could do except drive on.

And what would I do when I got to land's end, the point where I could drive no farther? I tried to think it through, and I couldn't. I was simply too scared. It was all I could do to keep my hands on the steering wheel and my attention on the road. The intensity of my fear made my vision blurry and I kept blinking to clear it. Night closed relentlessly around the car, and soon I drove through the darkness with only the white line in the middle of the road to guide me. The glaring round eyes of the following headlights still hung in my mirror.

It was a nightmare of a ride. Finally my high beams picked a roadside sign out of the black: Cedar Island ferry,

1.5 miles. Soon there were lights, blessed bright lights on poles, shedding their illumination in a wide circle over an asphalt parking area. And buildings, cars parked—people! Where there were lights and buildings and cars, there must be people.

Relief flooded through me. I pulled my Subaru up next to an already parked car and expelled a long, heavy breath. What now? In front of me was a café and gift shop and its lights were on, people inside. I felt safe for the moment, and I wanted desperately to know if that car had really been following me and who was in it. So I turned off my engine and headlights and scrunched down in the seat. By turning my head I could barely see out of my side window.

I didn't have to wait long. In the brightly lit parking lot the black car that had followed me revealed itself. It was indeed black, jet black. And fairly new, American-made, large and heavy. A Ford Taurus, something like that. I couldn't see the license plates, nor could I see inside. It rolled along spookily, as black within as without, looking like a driverless car. I realized it must have tinted glass, the kind you can see out of but not into. I scrunched further down, hoping the driver would think I'd gone into the gift shop and would leave his car and go in, too, then I could see him. Or her—learn the identity of the person who stalked me. I waited, and waited more. Finally I peered over the edge and out the car window. The black car had stopped near where the road entered and exited the parking lot. Its light were off, it looked dead. So, he was waiting, too.

People came out of the gift shop. Inside, someone turned off lights. Everyone was leaving. Well, I would leave at the same time, there is safety in numbers. As the other people got into their cars I sat up and started mine. When the first car pulled out, I swung the Subaru right behind, and almost shouted for joy when another car came right behind me. Please, oh, please, I prayed, let me have the company of these anonymous, normal people for at least part of my way home!

My prayers were answered. I was sandwiched safely in a procession of several cars, all going south on 70, back the way I'd come. One by one I lost my escort to driveways or side roads, but by then the causeway was far behind. I drove faster on the dark, deserted two-lane highway, no longer caring about safety or anything else except getting home. I took my turn-off at a speed that made my tires screech; hurtled down the bumpy private road heedless of the jarring punishment to the car's joints and my own. More than once my eyes cut to the rearview mirror, but if the black car had joined our procession I'd left it far behind. I had, at least, made it safely home.

The next morning I was once again up and functioning on too little sleep. Not, this time, because I'd awakened in the night, but because I'd never been to bed at all. All night I had sat in the chair in front of my fireplace. When I cried, as I did from time to time, Rory would rouse herself and put her head in my lap. She was such a comfort, almost as much as Boris would have been. Finally, toward dawn, when the light began to come, I had fallen asleep. Still in the chair.

I hadn't slept long in that uncomfortable position. Just as well—there was much I had to do today. I must go over the brochure one last time and take it to the printer. See if on a Saturday I could reach an electrician about outside lights—something I should have done weeks ago. And I intended to pay a visit to the county sheriff's office and ask them to put a watch on the Stone House. Even here in my fortress, in my quaint castle, I didn't feel safe anymore.

My body ached. My soul ached. I sat slumped at the kitchen table and drank enough coffee to give the jitters to a small army. "I don't know how much longer I can stand this, Rory," I said, "I really don't."

Sunday morning I dressed in my best leotard, which happened to be lavender and long-sleeved, over my new pink spandex tights. I wrapped the satin ribbons of pink toe shoes carefully around my ankles, did a few stretches in front of the big, sunny windows in my room, and then went to the tower to dance. Rory trotted along beside me.

I snapped on the lights and the wood paneled walls glowed, the parquet floor shone. A beautiful room and yet for me it was increasingly oppressive. I decided to open the big door and let in some fresh air and sunlight. My arms were still sore and protested the effort of lifting the heavy beam, but I did it and was rewarded by a tantalizing hint of spring on the in-rushing air. Rory bounded through the open door, and when I didn't follow she turned, smiling and panting with her tongue hanging out. "Go and play!" I called to her, and off she went.

Dancing didn't work for me anymore, I couldn't lose myself in it. Music and motion—these had always been a balm for me, a healing force. But no longer. Still, I danced on. Stubborn and willful, my mother had called me when I was a child, and it was just as true of the grown-up Laura. I put a tape of Stravinsky's *Firebird* into the deck and leapt into one of the most difficult pieces ever choreographed.

Later, after all that, I still felt restless. I did the only remaining thing I could think of: I called Jonathan and invited him to the Stone House for brunch.

He said, "I'd like to, but I'd planned to go to church this morning. Why don't you come to church with me, and afterward we'll go out to eat?"

I hadn't been to church in years; maybe it was time. "I'd like that. I'll be there soon." I had already bathed, and now I dressed again, this time rather conservatively in a gray spring suit and white blouse with a lace panel, and gray high-heeled shoes.

We went to the Episcopal church in Beaufort, and then Jonathan drove us to a place that was new to me, a restaurant in Swansboro where we had a table that seemed to hang over the water. Only glass separated us from boats and gulls and waves broken by an occasional jumping fish. I watched the boats go back and forth under the bridge and wondered why nothing, not this lovely scene nor the reassuring ritual of the church service, could ease the terrible restlessness in me.

Jonathan quaffed a strawberry croissant and chased it down with something he'd ordered for both of us called a Sunrise Cooler. It was a mixture of white wine and various fruit juices, but I wasn't enjoying mine nearly as much as he enjoyed his. I smiled affectionately across the table. He looked quite distinguished today in a dark blue suit and a yellow tie. What would I do without him?

"Eat, drink," said Jonathan with a wink, brandishing his fork, "be merry!"

"I think the rest of that quote is 'for tomorrow we die.' Seriously, Jonathan, I'm trying. But I don't think I can manage the merry part."

He studied me over the rims of his glasses. "Anything new wrong, or just the same old things?"

"I just feel so restless today." Impatiently, I pushed the hair out of my eyes. "I know this sounds crazy because I've never had any children, but I feel preg-pregnant. Not in a happy way. I just feel as if something big is about to happen, and I'm so heavy with it I can hardly sit still!"

Jonathan put his knife and fork on his empty plate and looked pointedly at my full one. "Pregnant women have to eat, Laura."

"I know." I picked at my shrimp salad. "It's really very good."

"You're probably right. I expect something big will happen very soon. Maybe as soon as tomorrow."

"What do you mean?" I looked across the table, alarmed, but Jonathan was smiling.

"Well, I shouldn't tell you, Sergeant Sanders wouldn't like it, because all the results aren't in yet, but seeing as how you feel the way you do . . . Remember that drawer with the numbers on the bottom?"

I nodded.

"The bottom one *was* a phone number. It had been the unlisted telephone of a man on Captiva Island. That's in Florida."

"I know. Lots of people from Columbus go there in the winter. Sanibel-Captiva. So?"

"So this man was known to be a middleman for drug deals. And the sergeant thinks the numbers on the top— remember there were eight of them?"

I nodded again.

"He thinks they're coordinates. Degrees and minutes of

latitude and longitude. Those particular eight numbers mark a place out in the ocean off Diamond Shoals. So, in spite of what we all thought of him, it could be that Carroll Trelawney was involved in some sort of drug dealing."

It made sense, but somehow didn't ring true for me. "How do you know all this?"

"From Seth Douglass." He saw me stiffen, and put his hand over mine on the table. "Laura, I know you and Seth have had some sort of misunderstanding, he told me so himself. He came to see me and asked if I knew any reason why you shouldn't trust him. I told him I didn't. He was plenty upset."

I looked down at my plate. I had nothing to say, because there was a huge lump in my throat.

"Look, Laura, everything will be out in the open very soon. Right now I can't say any more because I promised Seth I wouldn't, but he went to Florida with Sergeant Sanders. They'll be back tomorrow, and then I expect we'll know a lot more than we know now."

Slowly I raised my head. I almost didn't dare hope, but at least part of Jonathan's information must be true. "I knew the sergeant was out of town," I said.

"How's that?"

"Oh, I called him yesterday and the man who answered at the station told me he was out of town. That's all." I resumed eating my salad, pretending more interest in the food than I felt. Jonathan was quiet and I knew he was looking at me.

He asked the question I'd hoped he would omit. "Has anything more happened to you? Something I don't know about?"

"Someone has been following me, Jonathan. It's nothing new, it's been going on for a while. But night before last was the first time I could be sure it wasn't all in my imagination. I saw the car, it followed me all the way to Cedar Island, but I managed to lose it on my way home."

"Cedar Island? I realize it may be none of my business, but what were you doing all the way out there at night?"

"Trying to get away from the car that was following me. I

didn't want it to force me off the road in that isolated stretch just before the Stone House."

"What kind of car was it?"

"A black car, with the kind of glass you can't see into. Creepy looking, but new. I think it was a Taurus."

To my surprise, Jonathan looked relieved. He leaned back in his chair and said, "I'm sure that's nothing to worry about, just one more thing that will be straightened out when Seth and the sergeant get back. Now, what do you say we have another one of these Sunrise things. They're pretty good, don't you think?"

"Your reaction is very interesting, Jonathan. If you know something you aren't willing to tell me, perhaps you'll be willing to tell it to the Carteret County sheriff's office. They think I'm a neurotic woman—they didn't seem to believe there could be anyone following me, thought it was all in my head. I asked them to watch the Stone House, and they were pretty noncommittal about doing it. Seems they haven't enough manpower." I was disgusted. Not even Jonathan seemed to take me seriously on this.

"Sheriff?"

"Yes, the Stone House is in their jurisdiction. That's why I called Sergeant Sanders, out of courtesy, to tell him I was going to the sheriff."

"Well, no matter." Jonathan smiled and bobbed his head. "Everything will be fine, everything will work out. You'll see. Let's have that drink now."

I was dubious, but I kept my doubts to myself.

19

Rory and I ran along the bluff in the clear, cool morning air. The sun just risen out of the Atlantic made a golden sea-path and scattered sparkles over the waves. It was a beautiful day for a sail, a perfect day for me to go out on the *Hellfire* with Nick Westover.

Maybe I should give up dancing and take up running instead, I thought when I returned to the Stone House and got busy in the kitchen. The brief run had loosened my muscles and cleared the night's cobwebs from my head. And besides, if I ran I didn't have to go into the tower.

I fed Rory and sat down to my own breakfast. As I ate, I made an admission to myself: living here was not working out, it was a mistake. My tower might be old, it might have historic value, but it was a blight on my life if not on the landscape. I should have listened to Belle Helen. Her ideas were strange, but deep inside I knew she was somehow right. All that business about evil forces was a bit hard for me to swallow, but facts are facts. It was a fact that I had done everything I could think of to make the whole Stone House, including the tower, a pleasant place to be. And it was a fact that tower was still anything but pleasant, even dogs and cats didn't like to be in it. Not to mention that I myself would seize on almost any excuse not to dance in there. It was a fact that no matter how picturesque the whole place was, at odd moments it could turn on you and give you the creeps—like that horrible face I'd thought I saw in the bathroom mirror. Now every time I took a bath I had to cover the mirror with a towel. Maybe that was a small thing, but it was symbolic of the larger problem. And it was no way to live.

My opposing counsel argued with me. Said Oh, but you've put so much energy, not to mention money, into the place! Which was also a fact.

The heck with it. I didn't feel like arguing with myself right now. But it was something to think about, moving out, tearing down the tower or maybe even the whole place. I got up from the table and got busy making a picnic lunch to take on the *Hellfire*. I figured if I came with lunch already prepared I could say I wanted to eat on deck, and thus avoid being alone in the close confines of the cabin with Nick. Why I thought I could fend him off better in the open air I didn't know, but I did. I intended to enjoy this day out on the sea, away from all my troubles. I wasn't about to let Nick create any new ones for me! Far in the back of my mind, where I'd thrust it, was a tiny hope that Jonathan was right. That today Seth and Sergeant Sanders would return with answers for everything. Maybe, just maybe.

I packed the lunch in a canvas beach bag and topped it off with a couple of my blue and white checked napkins. Over the jeans and plain white sweatshirt I wore, I put my old yellow windbreaker, stuck a scarf in the pocket, and I was off. I left my car at the inn with a note on the windshield addressed to Jonathan in case he wondered why the car was there and I was not. As I walked briskly along the boardwalk, I touched my hand to my breastbone where the silver dolphins rested under my sweatshirt. I'll see them, I thought. Today I will see the dolphins!

Some ten feet away from the *Hellfire* I stopped, my breath caught in my throat. On deck with his back to me, Nick raised his arms above his head and tugged at a line on the mast. His gorgeous copper hair glinted in the sunlight, his splendid muscles rippled smoothly beneath a tight-fitting silky jersey. Almost a perfect replay of the first time I'd seen him, right down to my appreciation of a beautiful male body. I watched, expecting him to move that quarter turn around the mast, and he did, revealing his bearded profile.

This time there were some differences. He wore more clothes than he had that day, but they fit so well he might as well not have had them on. The most important difference was in my physical response—muted, much less than it had been on first sight of him. That was good. I didn't expect to be immune to the man, but I did want to be in control of myself.

"Hi!" I called out, waving. "Ahoy there, or whatever it is you say!"

He stopped in his work and smiled. "Ahoy, lady! Come aboard."

I jumped from dock to deck, taking the hand he offered to steady me. Nick kept the hand and pulled me into a crushing hug.

"Hey, that's a little too much welcome," I protested, pushing against his chest. "People will talk, you know."

"I don't give a damn what other people say," he growled. But he released me.

"Yes, I guess you don't. Anyway, it's a beautiful day and I'm glad we're doing this." I held up the beach bag. "You go on with what you're doing, I'll just put my things down in the cabin. All right?"

"Sure, Laura. This is great, having you here. You take your time. I have a few more things to do before we get under way."

"Right." I smiled, then went below and stashed my sandwiches in the back of his refrigerator. The other things, fruit and cheese and homemade brownies, would be fine left in the bag. I wished he hadn't made that remark about not caring what people said, because people were saying things about Nick Westover. Long before coming to Beaufort I'd made it a practice never to give credence to gossip, a practice which had only been strengthened by the harm such gossip had done to the inn. Therefore I refused to believe what was said about Nick, but still I'd heard it: that he had been high in public more than once in recent weeks, on drink or drugs or both; that on at least one occasion his behavior had been offensive, verbally abusive. Even if the rumors were true, I didn't for a minute think that he would be that way with me, but I would have preferred not to be reminded by his remark about not caring what people say.

When I came back up on deck Nick paused in the middle of pulling a sweater over his silk jersey undershirt. He flashed me a brilliant smile. I smiled back, and went and stood in the stern, out of the way. I knew the routine by now. I found with pleasure that knowing what to expect only heightened the anticipation. I lifted my face to the breeze, which would be stronger when we were out of the harbor. There was spring in the air; it smelled and tasted different from fall's air. It teased rather than bit with its salt-edged tang.

Nick started the motor, and my heartbeat quickened. Did this happen every time for people who sailed often, this excitement on leaving land behind? We rounded Carrot Island and made for the inlet. Being lighter and faster, the *Hellfire* passed a shrimp boat with its heavy burden of dark, furled nets. Nick waved to the fishermen who waved back, and I waved, too. I felt no disorientation today. I felt I belonged on the water, that the water was my home, my true element. It had just taken me thirty-three years to find it.

Slowly, holding to the brass railing with one hand, I walked around the deck, visually drinking in all there was to see. Hearing, too, smelling, feeling, feasting all my senses. This was wonderful, the most wonderful experience I could possibly have! I knew that I must learn to sail, must have a boat of my own. And being of a practical turn of mind, it occurred to me that if I sold all or some of the Stone House's acreage, I could afford to buy my own boat. I looked up at Fort Macon as we sailed by. Another, much larger fortress with none of the Stone House's malevolence. I shivered, shocked that my mind would produce such a word. Perhaps I really should get the whole place out of my life.

Nick, at the wheel, motioned for me to join him. I knew I

was all smiles as I looked up and said, "You wanted me, Captain?"

"Yeah, I thought I'd point out the sights. We've got an almost perfect day. You're gonna love where we're going. Now look off to port side, that's Shackleford Banks."

"I know," I nodded.

"Okay. Now look on out that way." He pointed, ahead and less sharply to the left. "That's Cape Lookout. Soon you'll be able to see the lighthouse. We're going right on around Cape Lookout Point and north along Core Banks and Portsmouth Island to Ocracoke Inlet. Everything's favorable, we ought to make good time."

"Sounds wonderful," I said sincerely. "Is there anything I can do, anything at all? You could teach me—"

"No!" Nick scowled. "A woman shouldn't be a sailor, a woman should be a passenger. You just watch. Relax and enjoy yourself."

My hands itched to try the wheel, to feel it under my fingers, but I shoved them into the pockets of my windbreaker. I knew better than to argue with Nick and his eccentric ideas. "Aye, aye, Captain," I said. He grinned, liking to be called captain, and I backed away.

When we were well away from the inlet, Nick left the wheel, cut the motor, and raised the sails. The *Hellfire*, long and sleek and sharp-prowed, was graceful enough under power, but the act of unfurling her sails was an apotheosis. She became a magnificent, winged goddess upon the sea.

"Aaah!" I sighed, entranced.

It was mid-morning before I realized that Nick had been below several times. The *Hellfire* didn't require all his attention, and yet he was leaving me alone. I was glad of that. It must be that he was taking seriously what I'd said about being friends. I had plenty to occupy me. I was absorbing the beauty of this voyage through every pore. And watching and waiting for the dolphins.

Thus it was that I didn't notice any peculiarity in Nick's behavior until my stomach growled with hunger and I made my way to him. He was near the wheel studying charts or maps or something in the shelter of the windscreen. I hadn't worn a watch, I never wore a watch anymore, but the sun was past its zenith so it should be later than midday. Definitely time to eat.

"You must be hungry, I know I am," I said when I stood beside him.

"Hungry?" He jumped as if I'd startled him. His eyes were blazing but for a moment unfocused, as if I weren't there at all.

"Yes, hungry." The intensity of his eyes startled me, but even more disturbing was the wild, avid look on his face. What could be in those charts he studied, or was it something else that produced such an expression? I forced a smile, and touched his arm in a gesture meant to be reassuring. "It must be well past lunchtime, and I brought a picnic lunch for us. A gift, a surprise, for you and me, Nick. I brought everything but the beer, I knew you'd have that. I'll bring the lunch up on deck now, shall I?"

His green gaze when it focused practically burned a hole through me. But all he said was, "I'm not hungry. I don't want anything to eat. You go ahead." And he went back to his charts.

I backed away from him a step at a time, both puzzled and disturbed. Something was wrong, I could feel it. Nervously I looked out across the water. On my right lay the vast open sea, blue on blue on blue; on my left at some distance, was land. The Core Banks, or Portsmouth Island, I didn't know which. I only knew that it was deserted, sandy, windswept, and too distant to be of any comfort. I was quite isolated with Nick on this boat, and there was something wrong with him.

I told myself not to be silly. Nick might have his strange moments, but he was an excellent sailor and, if anything, too fond of me. I would come to no harm. I took a deep breath and affirmed silently: I will come to no harm.

Probably everything would seem better once I had some food in my stomach. I went quickly below and put the lunch together. I added Nick's beer to the things I'd brought, hurrying. In spite of what he'd said I took all the food back up on deck—he might change his mind. He was preoccupied with his charts, that was all; he would come out of his intense, faraway mood, and when he did he'd want his food.

I sat down on the polished deck with a coil of thick rope at my back, planted my sneakered feet wide apart, legs bent at the knee, and spread my lunch in the space between. Nick's portion I left in the canvas bag with the top folded over to keep it cool. One bite of sandwich and my appetite took over. I glanced at Nick from time to time, but mostly I just ate while the *Hellfire* sailed on. We sailed smoothly, Nick handling his craft as well as ever. Lulled by a full stomach, by the sound of the wind flapping in the sail and the shushing of the hull through the water, I fell asleep.

"Hey, come on. Wake up! There's things I want you to see. Wake up!" Nick's voice was gruff and he poked me, not gently, with his foot.

"Sorry!" I scrambled to my feet before my eyes were really open, responding automatically to that demanding tone of voice. "I'm up, I'm up!"

"Come on." Nick pulled me by the hand, hard, and pain shot through my still-tender shoulder socket.

"Ouch! I'm coming, Nick. Not so rough, okay?" I stumbled after him, shaking my head to clear the muzziness. I'd been deeply asleep, but the pain in my shoulder brought me sharply, rudely awake.

"You stand right here. Right here!" Nick shoved me against the bow railing. I snatched my hand away from him and grabbed the brass rail with both hands. He moved behind me and gripped my shoulders. "Look, Laura. Out there, that's the start of the most dangerous waters on the East Coast, from here to Hatteras. It's called the Graveyard of the Atlantic."

I looked, but there was nothing to see on this calm day. The salt water was the same unrelenting blue, the waves were no bigger or smaller than elsewhere. But Nick's tension traveled from his hands into my shoulder muscles and radiated down my arms. What in the world did he expect me to say? My voice came out too high, almost a squeak. "I see."

Still crushing my shoulders, he brought his head close to

mine. His voice was heavy, loud in my ear. "There are shipwrecks out there, lots of them. Spanish, English, American, pirate ships, treasure—all under the water. I've got them on my maps. And there are ghost ships, they come in the fog and the storms, come right up out of the waves!"

"Have you ever, uh, have you ever seen one of these ghost ships?"

"Nah, I don't go out in bad weather and that's when they come. Sometimes, lots of times, I sail at night, though. I think I'll see one at night sometime. That would be great, to see a ghost ship. I think they must be the ghosts of the pirates, don't you think so?"

"Yes, that would make sense," I said. He sounded a little more normal, and pirates were something I expected him to be excited about. I relaxed and looked around farther afield than he had pointed. We were drawing closer to land, and I saw a lighthouse. I looked up at him and named the most famous lighthouse on the Outer Banks. "Is that the Hatteras Light, Nick?"

He snorted at my ignorance. "'Course not. That's Ocracoke. Hatteras is farther north." He let go of me, at last. "You stay there, Laura. I'm taking the *Hellfire* through Ocracoke Inlet."

Nick Westover was a man much more in command of his boat than he was of himself. The mast creaked, the great sails swung, the deck tilted slightly as he changed course. He yelled over the wind, "Blackbeard did this hundreds of times, he came right through here. This was one of his favorite places!"

Blackbeard. Of course. The pirate was Nick's hero. I didn't know anything about Blackbeard, but from both Jonathan and Seth I'd learned about Ocracoke Inlet. Nick's mind was on the pirate, but I thought of those eighteenth-century merchants of the sea who had to negotiate this inlet as their entryway to the wide waters of the Neuse River. They would sail up the Neuse to New Bern, where the colonial governor had his seat at the Tryon Palace. An unlikely port, New Bern, and yet it was only from there that roads spread out to the rest of the state. No wonder North

Carolina had had to struggle for only moderate prosperity in the days when all luxuries and many necessities came by sea. Even a novice seafarer like me could have no difficulty understanding how much easier it would have been to take a ship from Virginia on down to Charleston in South Carolina and skip North Carolina altogether.

To me, Ocracoke Inlet seemed narrower than Beaufort Inlet, and it certainly seemed wilder, for once through the small arms of land there was no welcoming harbor full of boats and civilized bustle. There was only more water, as far as the eye could see. Where was Nick taking me?

I looked nervously back at him. He wore no cap, his unbound copper hair streamed in the wind which parted his beard and sent it too streaming back from his face. His frowning concentration suggested that even in good weather it was no easy task to sail through Ocracoke Inlet. As I watched him he brought the *Hellfire* about by ninety degrees. In dismay I saw the sails automatically lowered. What was he doing? And why was I so nervous?

Nick cut on the motor and I breathed easier. Its mechanical throb was reassuring. I looked around and felt better still. The ninety-degree turn took us closer to Ocracoke Island. On the ocean side Ocracoke was all empty dunes, but here on the sound were little houses, and trees, and we were coming up on a crescent-shaped harbor.

Throbbing along under power, we bypassed the harbor. Anxiety threatened. I wanted to know where Nick was taking me, and yet I was afraid to ask. I worried, too, about the time. Unless we turned around and started back now, I doubted we could make Beaufort before sundown. I had no intention of staying on the *Hellfire* overnight with Nick! Unconsciously I pressed my right hand to the hollow between my breasts and felt the silver dolphins there. My talisman, the dolphins.

I may need you, my friends, I thought. But for now I knew I had to find out what Nick had in mind, though I was more than half afraid of the answer. I walked carefully down the deck to where he stood at the wheel.

"Where are you taking us?" I asked.

His white teeth split the red beard in a grin. The avid look was in his eyes. "There's a place up here I'm sure was Teach's Hole. You know, Edward Teach was Blackbeard's real name. Nobody ever marked it on a map, except me. I call this place Teach's Hole and I'm going to show you."

"Oh." I shoved my hands in the pockets of my open windbreaker and gathered courage. "Uh, Nick, don't you think we should start back for Beaufort? I mean, I do have to get back before nightfall."

He simply ignored what I'd said. "Got any of that lunch left?"

"Yes, but—"

"How about you get it together, and a cold beer, while I take us in the Ole Hole, huh? I'll throw out the anchor and show you where Blackbeard careened his ship." He ruffled my hair, and I took a step away. He winked at me. "If you be real good, maybe I'll let you see my maps, and the charts. All the shipwrecks and all the secret places, I got 'em all marked on my charts and maps!"

"I . . . oh, okay." I couldn't see any alternative for the moment, but my mind raced as I grabbed up my canvas beach bag and took it below with me. I knew I would have to make fresh sandwiches, the ones I'd brought for him wouldn't have held up for so many hours in the sun, even inside the bag.

I found ham and Swiss cheese in the refrigerator. If I hadn't been working in the galley, I might not have noticed the door ajar, opposite the door to the head. And if I weren't a compulsive door-closer and drawer-shutter, I might have left the door ajar. But I did see it, and I did stop in my sandwich-making long enough to close that door, and when I touched it curiosity prompted me to look inside. What I saw appalled me.

It was a closet of sorts, beautifully fitted with shelves and all kinds of custom-made nooks and crannies. But *in* the nooks and crannies were objects which immediately I labeled instruments of torture. Handcuffs and leg irons. Explosives that looked like big firecrackers. A coiled black whip. A deadly, gleaming collection of knives nestled lovingly among black velvet-lined dividers. Some drawers were closed. My hand crept out to open one—I snatched it back. But curiosity once again won out, and I opened the drawer to find knotted lengths of rope, and something old and strange. In a moment I had its name: a scourge. I closed the drawer with a hand that trembled now. This was all pirate stuff, I guessed, but somehow it was too much. This was going too far. It gave me the creeps.

I was about to close the door when something else caught my attention, above my eye level so I'd almost missed it—a bottle of rum, open, and more than half gone. Well, of course, Yo Ho Ho and a bottle of rum! I was not amused. On that same shelf next to the rum was a plastic bag containing some white stuff. I stood on tiptoe and craned my neck. I'd never "done" drugs, never so much as seen a quantity of cocaine. But I knew the paraphernalia and he had them here: a tiny spoon, gold, like a demitasse spoon; a square of mirror with a few white flecks clinging to its surface; a slim gold tube, like a straw. Gold, yet—only the best for the rich bum.

I carefully left the door just exactly as it had been, ajar. I wasn't sure whether to be glad or sorry for my compulsive door-closing tendencies. Now I understood the wild look in the eyes, the tension, all that. Nick had been drinking rum and snorting coke all morning. The rumors I'd heard in Beaufort were true. Nick was getting high these days, if he hadn't always. I would have to be careful—if he were verbally abusive in bars, perhaps after all he could be the same on the *Hellfire* with me. And worse, if I angered him and the abuse turned physical, he had all those . . . those pirate things to be physically abusive with!

I ran my hand through my hair and went weak-kneed back to the galley. I was probably better off knowing about this, I could be doubly on my guard. But oh, it was bitter, bitter to have more of my illusions shattered. Nick Westover wasn't the handsome, harmless, not-too-bright nonconformist I'd thought. He was a man living and playing on the edge, an edge far more dangerous than mine had ever been. His pirate obsession wasn't amusing anymore.

I wrapped the sandwiches with extra care. I took a can of beer for Nick and a bottle of Perrier for me from the refrigerator, hurrying now. I'd been down here too long. I could only pray he wouldn't notice.

He didn't, he was too busy taking his boat into a scooped-out little bay with a sandy beach. A pretty place—on another day I might have liked to take the inflatable dinghy over to that little beach. I'd been a good paddler in my canoeing days. But today all I wanted, desperately, passionately, was to get safely back to Beaufort.

I watched Nick drop the anchor over the side. Anchor and chain were mechanized like everything else on the *Hellfire,* and even if it hadn't been, I knew Nick wouldn't let me help. I stood with his food in my hands and little pieces of observations snapped into place, like a significant chunk of a jigsaw puzzle: Nick's attitude toward me was antique. I wasn't to do any work, I was to be decorative. Cooking, preparing and serving food was okay, woman's work; making a home of the Stone House was even better. But sailing a boat, merely handling the wheel—that was not, and neither was owning and running the inn. Sailing and business, those were the man's job. If Nick was the Pirate, I was supposed to be the Pirate's Lady. I was part of his dangerous fantasy.

Nick wolfed his food while he stood at the railing and told me how the pirates careened their ships to make repairs and scrape the hull. He had the peculiar, overly detailed knowledge which accompanies obsession. I said "Oh," and "Ah!" but all the while, I was thinking God, Somebody, get me out of here! I knew instinctively that returning to Beaufort would have to be Nick's idea. If I insisted, he would get angry. But how I could manipulate him into wanting to go back, I had no idea.

I prayed for another boat to come. Instead, came the dolphins.

I felt their coming before my sight confirmed it, felt them as a steady, vivid pulse coursing through my soul-blood. Heard their brilliant whistles and clicks. I heard Belle Helen, too, saying, The eyes of the dolphins will protect you! I dared not move from Nick's side, but I knew the dolphins neared. I felt them calling me and silently I answered: Yes, come, come to me!

Nick wiped the back of his hand across his mouth. "Time to go below," he declared. "Be back in a minute."

No sooner had he disappeared than I saw the dolphins. Swiftly, sleekly, they swam two by two in a double line. Joyfully I ran to the stern, held out my hands, not speaking yet pouring out my hope, my fear, my need.

The dolphins formed a circle around the *Hellfire*. They circled in their ancient, stately pattern, weaving their spell of protection. I felt the silver chain at my neck and drew out my talisman, raised it to my lips. "My friends!" I whispered, and my whisper tumbled and rustled across the water. Two dolphins broke from the circle and leapt, twining their shiny-wet dark gray bodies. They dipped and arched to me. Very close, they stood up in the water, turned their heads with their smiling mouths, and looked at me with dark, liquid eyes.

"Thank you," I breathed. "Oh, you are so beautiful and so very, very welcome!"

The pair ducked their heads, tucked themselves into a dive so neat they left scarcely a ripple in the water. The other dolphins continued in their circle, making a space for my two special friends to rejoin them.

"Where the hell did *they* come from?" Nick growled. He shifted his weight from one leg to the other, back and forth in agitation, strong thighs working.

I called to them and they came, I thought, but I said, "They just swam up. I think they came to see us. Oh, Nick, aren't they beautiful?"

"I can't see it myself," he muttered. He began to pace the deck and I followed him.

I chattered deliberately, bombarding him with a subject I knew made him uncomfortable. "I've read a lot about dolphins since that time you took me out in the fall. Did you know dolphins are almost perfectly social creatures? They have a kind of society many people long for but think humans are too imperfect to achieve—they live together in perfect peace. They are always cooperative, they will never compete with each other even in captivity. Researchers have tried to teach dolphins to play competitive games, but in the end the dolphins taught the researchers a new game instead, a game of sharing and taking turns. Mothers watch each other's babies. If one dolphin is sick, the others will support it in the water . . ." I went on and on, spilling fact after fact.

Marvelous to me, this information, but an abomination to Nick Westover. Five times he circled the *Hellfire*'s decks. I chattered; he grunted and growled and with every circuit he made, the looks he threw the dolphins grew increasingly haunted. I clutched my talisman in my right hand, rubbed the tiny sapphire eyes with my thumb.

The fifth time around I saw that I need talk no more. Nick couldn't stand the circling dolphins—their progress was as relentless as it was dignified. I sensed what he felt: the dolphins had labeled him a rogue, an outsider, and by their circle they isolated him. Somehow the gentle creatures of the sea controlled this man. He stood in the bow, towering, huge, the angry flame-haired god, and screamed.

"Leave me alone! Go away! I should get my gun and shoot you all. I'm the captain of the *Hellfire*—fear me-e-e-e!"

Nothing phased my dolphins. They swam on. They only tightened their circle, imperceptibly, but I saw. And Nick's will was broken.

"I'm getting out of here," he muttered. "Damn dolphins. Can't shoot the damn things. Fucking stupid Protection Act. Not worth the trouble it would cause to shoot them."

"We're leaving?" I asked in a carefully neutral voice.

"Yeah. Stay out of the way."

Nick did not go through Ocracoke Inlet again; he took the *Hellfire* down Core Sound instead. The dolphins followed us and I stayed in the stern, alternating between keeping a watch on Nick and casting grateful glances to my waterworld friends. Nick muttered and cursed under his breath. As we passed Portsmouth Island on our left, he raised the sails. They caught in the wind and the *Hellfire* took flight, flying before a strong tailwind.

Nick raised his arms and shook his fists at the sky. "Eee-yah!" he cried. He spun around. His eyes were a green blaze, his voice a harsh scream. "I fly before the wind like a bat out of hell. You hear that, you damn dolphins? Hellfire and damnation. Eee-yah!"

I grabbed the railing and hung on, assaulted by the rushing wind and Nick's guttural, demented laughter. It was indeed a hellish ride, frightening yet thrilling, exhilarating. In what seemed like no time at all the Stone House tower rose up, its stone glowing golden in the afternoon sun. It seemed small and very old after the Ocracoke and Cape Lookout lights, seemed the relic it was of an earlier age. Nick turned and grinned over his shoulder, motioned to me to join him.

I went, treading carefully and clinging to the rail. I wished I had a life jacket, but Nick never wore one and had never offered one to me. When I drew up level with him I turned and kept the railing at my back. I tried a smile, which trembled but held.

"There it is, your Stone House," said Nick. "You should make it a—what d'you call it?—a shrine. A monument to Blackbeard."

"Why, Nick? Pirates are your thing, not mine. There's not the least bit of evidence that Blackbeard or any other pirate was ever at the Stone House."

He smote the wheel with his palm and the *Hellfire* lurched. Through clenched jaws he insisted, "He *was* there! I know he was. Someday I'll prove it to you."

I raised a hand to hold the wind-whipped hair out of my face. I felt strangely calm. "That's not necessary. In fact, it would be a waste of time. You see, I'm most likely going to tear down the Stone House. Including the tower."

His expression was horrified. "Why?" The question came as a gasp.

"Because I'm very uncomfortable there. I can't live in it, Nick. Not much longer."

He shrank from my words as if I'd hit him. "No! You can't do that!" He seemed desperate, not angry. He whipped his head from side to side, red hair and beard flying. *"They* made you say it. You don't mean it!"

"They?" I didn't understand, not his words, not his

reaction. I only knew that, all unplanned, I had spoken truth.

"Them. Those big fish." He pointed a sweeping finger at the escort of dolphins beside and behind the *Hellfire*.

"Dolphins aren't fish, Nick. You must know that, you're a Dolphin Guard. They're mammals, warm-blooded, just like you and me. They have brains like ours, they communicate with each other, and care for each other just as we do. The dolphins are more 'us' than 'them'!"

"I don't care, I hate 'em." His eyes were wild. "They get inside you and do things to your head. Get me a drink, Laura, bring the bottle. I can't sail the *Hellfire* on automatic, the wind is too stiff. Help me, please, I've got to have a drink!"

He whined, he cringed. The wide swing in his behavior was a sign of how sick he was. "All right, take it easy. I'll get it. You just . . . just take good care of the *Hellfire*. Okay, Nick?"

I brought him the rum and a plastic glass. He ignored the glass and drank from the bottle. The drink seemed to quiet him, but even so I wondered what in the world I would do if he got too drunk to get us back to Beaufort Harbor. I thought about a radio—that would be no help, I doubted I could control the boat until someone might come even if I could figure out how to call them. I wandered around the deck until I came to the inflatable dinghy. It had directions printed on the pack, which I read carefully. I looked over the rail and saw the dolphins—if I had no other alternative, I could jump overboard. Perhaps it was only fantasy, but I thought they might help me, care for me in the water as if I were one of their own.

The sun set as we passed between Harkers Island and the Shackleford Banks. The dolphins were still with us, they herded Nick and the *Hellfire* as a Highland collie herds his sheep. The sky was deep navy blue and dotted with stars when we rounded Carrot Island and Nick lowered the sails. Two by two then, the dolphins retreated, leaping, whistling, clicking into the night.

"Good-bye," I whispered after them. "And thank you."

By the lights along the boardwalk I saw two figures near the empty berth where Nick would dock his boat. One was tall and slim with silver hair that shone in the muted light; the other was shorter and rounder and had a fuzzy halo of a head. Seth and Jonathan waited for me.

"You can't do it, you can't go to them. That's not how it's supposed to be!" Nick insisted.

But I knew he couldn't stop me, he would be too much occupied with fitting the *Hellfire* between the boats on either side of his space. I was ready, I had gathered my things and tied the silk scarf over my tangled, matted hair, cleaned the salt spray from my glasses. There would be no polite good-byes this time, no chance for Nick with his strength to overwhelm me with unwanted kisses. Not tonight and never again. A part of me felt sorry for him. He was addicted and mentally unbalanced and he needed help. But a much larger part of me knew that the dolphins had been my salvation from some crazy scheme of his. And as soon as I could leap from the *Hellfire*, before Nick was free to come after me, I would do so.

"I have business tonight with Seth and Jonathan," I said, raising my voice to be heard over the throbbing engine, and keeping my place at deck's edge. "Remember, I told you I had to be back by sundown."

I felt the *Hellfire*'s soft thud against the dock, and I jumped.

"Laura-a-a-a!" Nick called my name in a coarse wail. I felt his eyes, their emerald fire burning a hole through the night, searing me to the skin.

I didn't even say goodbye, just got my feet under me and walked swiftly, decisively away. Seth and Jonathan were soon with me, one on either side.

Seth began my name, "La—" and I cut him off. His hand closed around my arm and I shook him off. "Not a word," I cautioned. "Just keep walking. He may be very angry, so just keep walking."

When we reached the inn's darkened parking lot, I stopped and looked up at each of them in turn. "I've got to

311

get home to the Stone House. I never thought Nick would keep me out so long, and I have to get back to Rory. I think I know why you were waiting for me, and I do want to know what happened in Florida. I'd be glad for you to follow me home, and then we can talk."

"Fine," said Seth.

"Sure," said Jonathan.

I unlocked my car door and Seth took hold of its frame while I slid behind the wheel. "I'll ride with you," he said.

"No." I started the motor. I didn't dare look into those brown eyes. My emotions were nearly in shreds from the ordeal on the *Hellfire*. My heart leapt within me like one of the dolphins. I was much too glad to see Seth, I wanted nothing more than to bury my head in his chest and dissolve in his arms. "Nothing has changed between us, Seth. It's better for you to ride with Jonathan."

I gained a measure of control over myself as I drove toward the Stone House. I sensed that after months of confusion and uncertainty and just plain waiting, events were converging. It was like running downhill with a stitch in your side, not wanting your feet to carry you overfast and trip you up before you reach the goal at the bottom of the hill. Surely I could keep my feet under me a little while longer!

Rory was overjoyed to have me home. I hugged her in mid-bounce and didn't mind a face full of wet licks. When she heard the second car she ran outside, barking. I left the door open and went into the library, turning on lights as I went.

"We'll talk in here," I called out when I heard the men in the kitchen. "Leave Rory out, she needs to be outside for a while." I pulled off my scarf and shrugged out of my windbreaker, then set out my stock of liquor and mixers on top of the sideboard. I was glad I'd recently refurbished and enlarged the supply—if ever in my life I had really wanted a drink, I wanted one now. I opened the next cabinet so that each could choose his own glass, then I brushed past Seth and Jonathan on my way back to the kitchen for ice. I took a moment to clean myself up in the bathroom, then joined the men in the library.

"Drink before talk," I said in the process of fixing myself a stiff Scotch. "I had quite a day. And if you, Seth Douglass, even think of saying I deserved it, I'll throw you out on your ear."

Jonathan chuckled. Seth said to him, "Feistier than ever, isn't she?"

I plopped down in the chair at the head of the table. They sat on either side, across from each other. Slowly I relaxed, taking long sips of Scotch that stung and renewed. I loosened the laces of my sneakers and worked my feet out of them, socks, too. I wriggled my toes, and sighed.

Jonathan and Seth smiled at each other, and at me.

"Well?" I asked.

"When the sun went down and you weren't back, we worried," said Jonathan. "We decided to make sure Westover's boat was still out, and when it was, we waited there for you."

"You're all right?" asked Seth with a frown that drew his black brows together. "He didn't hurt you, or anything?"

I could feel his caring in spite of his boardroom-like posture. I steeled myself against that caring, even as I hoped that soon he would tell me something to take away the barrier between us. "No, he didn't hurt me. He doesn't want to hurt me, but Nick is . . . sick. He's not quite right in the head. I didn't realize it until today. He needs help, but unfortunately I'm sure he doesn't think so. Look, you two, you weren't waiting for me because you wanted to talk about Nick Westover. So—out with it."

They looked at each other. Seth gestured toward Jonathan. "You tell. After all, it was your clues that cracked this thing open."

Jonathan beamed and pushed his glasses up the bridge of his nose. "It was the numbers on the bottom of that drawer, Laura. Of course, it's not a happy story, it's nothing to be pleased about exactly . . ."

I helped him out, saying gently, "I'm sure it's all right to be pleased if the mystery is solved, Jonathan. My sister was *murdered;* a nice, pretty solution to murder is an impossibility. Go on."

He looked relieved, cleared his throat, and continued. "Right. Well, that bottom number led the police to a man who was a Florida drug dealer, a middleman with connections to Colombia. The Florida police were already holding him on another charge. When Sergeant Sanders went down there, the man spilled out the whole thing that happened here two years ago."

"Probably because it was much less serious than some other charges, it didn't hurt him that much to come clean on the North Carolina deal," Seth inserted.

"Right," Jonathan took up the narrative again. "Two years ago the heat was on the Florida guy, so he came up here to the Outer Banks to find someone he could delegate a couple of shipments to. After Florida, North Carolina is the next most popular place for drugs to enter the country."

"The coastline, I suppose," I said bitterly, "attractive now just as it was for the famous pirates, and for the same reasons."

"Exactly!" In his excitement Jonathan missed my bitterness. "Well, this guy got to Beaufort and he delegated a kind of trial deal to—I'm sorry to say—Carroll Trelawney."

"Carroll!" I was shocked.

"Yeah, it surprised me, too, but not Seth. Anyway, it's some consolation that Carroll had never done that kind of thing before, so they didn't trust him with much. Now, those other numbers were the coordinates of a drop-off point. Carroll must have written all that under the drawer in case he forgot them. He took his boat, the *Mary Stella Maris,* out to that place in the ocean, Diamond Shoals, and picked up some marijuana. Not much, because it was a trial thing to see if he could become the North Carolina middleman. And it didn't work out. Carroll was supposed to get $250,000 for that marijuana, then he'd keep a percentage and turn over the rest to the Florida guy. He picked up the marijuana on schedule, but he never turned over the two-fifty. I think he only took the deal in the first place to give himself some money to get out of here with, and to leave some for his wife—but then, I liked the man, I'm just guessing. Your turn, Seth."

Seth leaned forward, speaking earnestly. "I talked Sergeant Sanders into letting me go down to Florida with him because I have friends in Sanibel, and I thought maybe not being a policeman I could ask around and learn something. We made a mistake—we thought the man with the phone numbers was a friend of Carroll's, and I was looking for Carroll. As it turned out, I needn't have gone down at all because once the drug dealer started talking he told everything."

"Well," I urged, "what else did he say?"

"That Carroll took the money and left the country. The Colombians caught him in the Bahamas and killed him, and then they came back on our Florida man. It seems Carroll didn't have all their money, he swore he'd spent it, but they checked around and he had nothing to show for it, so they didn't believe him. Our Florida fellow didn't have it, either, and he just barely got himself off the hook with the Colombians because he swore he'd never seen it, and he'd never cheated them before."

"Kathryn!" I breathed.

"Afraid so," Seth said, and Jonathan nodded. "We think the money Carroll gave Kathryn came from the drug payoff. She may or may not have known where it came from. My guess is that she did. She did a pretty smart thing, she immediately bought the Stone House in secret. I think the reason she was so desperate to sell was that either the Colombia people or the Florida people had caught up with her. She was going to get her money out and run, but she didn't make it in time. One or the other group killed her. Most likely neither Carroll's body nor his boat will ever be found; Kathryn wouldn't have been found, either, if not for that storm."

I looked from one man to the other. Both were intelligent, and they seemed well satisfied. I wanted to be, but I wasn't.

The lawyer in me felt loose ends and was bothered by them. I didn't say anything. I reached for the Scotch bottle in the middle of the table and freshened my drink. Maybe I should drown the loose ends in too much Scotch. I sipped my drink, tempted to do just that; but then I put down the glass. "I'm going to let Rory in," I said, and left the table.

I lingered in the kitchen to feed the dog and took a can of honey-roasted cashews back to the library with me. I was too tired to bother with a bowl, I put the can unceremoniously on the table and slumped down in my chair.

"That was good work, both of you," I said honestly. "Sergeant Sanders, too. So what happens to the Stone House now? Will the government confiscate it for being bought with illegal money?"

"Well, no," said Seth. "You see, our Florida man didn't say a word about Kathryn having the missing part of the money, though he was perfectly open about the Colombians killing Carroll. Sergeant Sanders expects he probably killed Kathryn himself, and, of course, he wouldn't want to admit to murder. Nobody knows whether he'll ever confess or not, and there isn't a shred of evidence against him for her murder. This is all just us guessing, me and Jonathan. I'm not sure what the sergeant will tell you, he won't tell anybody until after he's filed his report. At any rate the money Kathryn used to purchase this place is long gone and untraceable, so no one could ever prove where it came from. No one is going to take the Stone House from you, Laura."

"I see," I said. "Thank you for telling me so promptly. Now, if you don't mind, I'm awfully tired, and my clothes are stuck to me with salt-spray. Forgive me, but I'd like you both to leave now."

Jonathan shot me a measuring look over the tops of his glasses, but he immediately pushed his chair away from the table. Seth seemed stunned, eyes wide and blank of expression. His finely shaped mouth formed itself around several words before any came out.

Finally he managed to say, "You don't seem satisfied. All that, and you're still not satisfied. My God, Laura! What do you want, what will it take to satisfy your doubts, woman?"

My voice sounded chilly and superior, even to me. I didn't care. I said, "The truth, Seth. The whole truth."

A little over an hour later I'd bathed and eaten a cheese omelet and a salad. It wasn't quite cold enough for a fire, so I had the quartz heater on low in my room. Supposedly I was reading a paperback novel, a piece of high-class trash that had seemed delectable in the K Mart but was just so many words to me now. It wasn't the book's fault. It was all those years at law school plus quite a few in practice, subconsciously working away at loose ends. I knew when I was licked; it had been like this when I'd tried to put away a case everybody said I should be comfortable with, and I wasn't. I put the book aside and got pen and paper. I started to make notes to myself:

1. *$250,000 is not a lot of money in the drug business.*
2. *When someone crosses a drug dealer, the drug people will kill for (a) vengeance, (b) to teach a lesson.*
3. *Killing Kathryn did not fit their usual pattern. She hadn't been involved in the original deal and might not even have known about it. She wasn't killed until two years later. Considering all this, I don't believe the drug people killed her.*
4. *The murderer is still out there somewhere.*

As I contemplated my last sentence, the telephone rang. I walked to the bedside table, dragging my feet, and picked up the receiver.

"Laura, Jonathan. I'm sorry to bother you, but I'm concerned. I know it's not really my business, but I think you know I have more, er, feelings for you than the employer-employee thing."

I thought I knew what was coming, and suppressed a sigh. "Of course, Jonathan. I feel the same. So what's so much on your mind that it couldn't wait until the morning? I'll be at the inn at the usual time."

"It's Seth. He counted so much on what we had to tell you making things right, and when it didn't seem to he . . . well,

317

he's all broken up about it. I thought you should know, even if he kills me for telling you. I don't really know what's wrong between you, but he knocked himself out these last few weeks working on this murder stuff on his own. He's even been paying a security guard to follow you, watch over you any time you're not at the inn, to keep you safe."

I exploded. "Oh, my God! So *that's* who's been following me! I've been scared half out of my wits! I could kill him for doing that to me!"

"Hey, whoa. This was for your protection. The guard didn't invade your privacy, he never came all the way up to the Stone House, he watched the private road because it's the only access."

"Oh, no," I said sarcastically, "he didn't invade my privacy. He just terrified me. I suppose this guard has a black car?"

"Yes, he does."

"And you knew and Seth knew. Why didn't you *tell* me? Can you imagine what it's like to feel someone following you and then finally see the car and know you were right? It's horrible. You should have told me."

"The guard wasn't supposed to let you see him. Really, Laura, I'm sorry you were frightened, but try to understand Seth's side. If he'd told you about the guard, you'd have refused it, wouldn't you?"

"Yes," I admitted, more calm now, "I guess I would."

"Seth meant well. I think he'd rather have had you a little frightened and safe, than all alone and in danger. He would have protected you himself, but he said you wouldn't let him near you anymore."

"That's right. I have my reasons, Jonathan. Since you and Seth have apparently become friendly while working on the things you told me tonight, I doubt you'd appreciate my reasons. They're best kept to myself."

"Um-mm. Well, I'm afraid I've done more harm than good with this call. I thought maybe you were unaware how much the man has missed you, and, uh, cares about you. Heck, Laura, since I'm in over my head anyway, I may as well call a spade a spade. Seth is nuts about you, he loves you. And I thought you were in love with him, too. I'm just a sentimental old busy-body—I'm sorry. For what it's worth, Seth called off the guard today. You won't be bothered anymore."

"Jonathan, wait! Don't hang up. I do appreciate what you've tried to do." Tears were running down my face. I tried to keep them out of my voice. "I can't tell you how much I wish things were different, but they aren't. Not yet. There are just . . . just too many loose ends. Thank you for telling me who was following me. It's a big relief to know, even if I did blow up about it. Thank you, Jonathan, thank you for caring."

I barely responded to his goodbye, for I'd shoved my knuckles against my lips to keep from sobbing out loud. I'd wanted to tell him that I loved Seth, too. Wanted to tell him that I, too, was broken up and somehow it was worse for knowing that I had to do it to myself. I collapsed back on the bed and cried until I was empty. I kept wanting to scream, What about *me?* Don't you realize somebody is terrorizing me? And it surely isn't drug dealers!

Rory licked my face. I opened one eye and saw her goofy grin. "Woof!" she barked, and bounced from my bed to the door and back. I squinted at my bedside clock—6:20 A.M. She didn't usually have to go out this early. She repeated the routine: lick, woof, bounce.

"Okay," I said groggily, "if you gotta go, you gotta go." I put on my glasses and my robe and followed her in bare feet.

"Woof! Woof-woof!" She bounced to the kitchen door and looked expectantly at it. I was getting almost as good at decoding woofs as I'd been with mowrs, and I could have sworn that Rory thought there was someone she liked on the other side of the door. But I must be wrong—I never could think straight when I first got up. She must just want to go out and greet the dawn. After all, I'd named her Aurora.

"Okay girl, here you go. For whatever reason." I opened the door and gaped in astonishment. "Belle Helen!"

"I'm sorry to be so unconventional and impolite, but I must see you. To call would have meant delay. May I come in?"

"Y-yes. Of course."

She took time to pat Rory, who was wagging her tail a mile a minute and smiling her widest smile. "Good, beautiful dog. Go now, Aurora, Rory, run and play. Go and greet your namesake!"

I couldn't believe my ears. "How did you know her name?"

"You were thinking of it when you came to the door just now. I picked it up from you."

I stepped back for Belle Helen to go past me into the kitchen, and tried to get my mind in gear as I followed after her.

Belle Helen harmonized with the colors of my kitchen decor. She wore an aquamarine cloak, the color of the sea on a spring day. The cloak was full-length and hooded. She pushed back the hood to reveal her gray-streaked auburn hair.

"P-please," I stammered, "sit down. I'll make coffee. I'm not worth a thing until I've had my coffee. Shall I make breakfast, too? It's so early, you can't have eaten."

"I suppose there is time. Coffee, yes. Not breakfast."

I still struggled to bring myself fully awake. "Excuse me, I have to —"

"I know," she interrupted gently. "I got you out of bed. You go ahead, but please, be as swift as you can. I'm not sure how much time we have."

Mind-reading, hooded cloaks, no time—nuts. I stumbled into the bathroom and closed the door, being careful not to look into the mirror. When I left the bathroom I brought its quartz heater for the kitchen. If we didn't have much time, whatever she meant by that, she surely wasn't going to want me to make a fire, and the house was chilly.

When I had finished the first cup of coffee, I could think straight. My first thought was that with all I had to do today, Belle Helen was one thing too many. My next thought I put into words. "I know, I've got it! Jonathan told you."

"Told me what?"

"The dog's name, of course. I can't believe you read my mind. Especially through a closed door!"

Belle Helen smiled. How extraordinarily handsome a woman she was. Not conventionally beautiful, but she radiated inner strength and grace. She had removed her cloak to reveal a loose, flowing peach-colored dress whose long, full sleeves fell back when she lifted her coffee mug. "I'm not a mind-reader, Laura, or a charlatan. Our survival in what we must do this morning may depend on these abilities of mine which you're so reluctant to believe in."

I suddenly felt very cold, cold as death. I gulped hot coffee which warmed me only a little.

"You must learn to trust again. It is not necessary for you to be quite so alone as you feel yourself to be. I believe I can help you, that's why I'm here. Remember that I gave you the dolphins you wear. You can trust me."

My hand went automatically to the talisman beneath my robe, beneath my nightgown. "That's right, you did. And you knew, without my telling you, how I feel about the dolphins. All right, then, tell me—everything."

Belle Helen put down her coffee mug. She closed her eyes. She seemed to gather stillness to surround her. Her facial muscles relaxed and smoothed, she looked ageless. She opened her eyes and spoke.

"The Dark Force, in the personification the Christians call Satan, has been summoned repeatedly to this place. Not to this lovely room, but to a chamber in the tower."

"Oh," I said impatiently, "you've already told me that. I even think you may be right. That's why—"

Belle Helen held up her hand, palm out, a sign for me to be quiet. "I don't mean in the past, I mean in recent weeks. The one who summons Satan is growing stronger. Very early this morning as you lay deep asleep, he almost succeeded. I saw this in a dream, a dream which persisted after I woke and became a vision. There is danger to the summoner, of course, but he has chosen his path and I would not interfere with his free will. I sense also grave danger to you, Laura, and that is why I came when I did. The one who calls to

Satan calls you also. I don't know why. My vision was unclear. I must find the chamber in the tower. In the chamber the vibrations will be strong, and I will learn more. But I need your permission, your help, and your support."

"But there's only the one room. Just that and the stairs up inside the tower. I've been all the way to the top, and there's nothing else. You have my permission, sure, and if I can help you I will, but—" I broke off, tugging my hand through my hair. What she said made awful sense. Truly awful. I *had* felt called, or something, but I'd thought it was the Stone House itself that called to me. Even so, I just couldn't accept anything so . . . so outrageous without questioning. "It's impossible. There *is* no other room in the tower. And no one can get into the house or the tower, I've checked again and again. And if all that's not enough, I just learned last night that a security guard has watched the Stone House, watched the private road, and that's the only way in. As you must know yourself!"

Belle Helen said calmly, "I have seen what I have seen. The answers will be in the chamber in the tower."

It's funny how, when something is too big to comprehend, your mind will seize on a very small piece and you think, if I can understand this one piece, then the rest must follow. I did that now. I told Belle Helen about the dark, ugly face which came and went in the mirror on the bathroom door.

"I want to see this mirror," she said. "It is a beginning. Are you ready, Laura?"

I looked down at myself, my bathrobe and my nightgown, my bare feet. I said, "No, I'm not dressed. I mean, dressed right. Tell me what I should wear."

She nodded, smiling her serene smile. "You have wisdom you barely recall, but it is there. Remember the ritual for your cat? You should wear anything which fits loosely, with no metal buttons or hooks or zippers, in white or a clear color. Shoes or slippers to protect your feet. I think I had better come with you while you dress. It's better that we not be apart from now until all is finished."

I understood. She left her cloak in the kitchen. In my

room I took from the wardrobe a hostess gown I seldom wore, which had attracted me because of its sumptuous fabric. I chose it because it was the only garment I owned which resembled in style the gown Belle Helen wore. Mine was cut velvet, its color aquamarine, almost the exact shade of Belle Helen's cloak, though I'd thought of it as simply green. I slipped the gown over my head, and it fell free from a high square yoke, and the long, full sleeves covered half my hands. Now I remembered why I'd worn it so seldom in the years I had owned it—it felt like a costume. In this gown I felt like a medieval princess.

"Perfect!" said Belle Helen.

I smiled. "May I wear the dolphins? They're metal."

"Yes—they are your special talisman. Wear them."

As I searched for a pair of slippers that felt right, I asked her why not wear metal.

Belle Helen gave an answer I didn't understand but I accepted. She said, "Because even small amounts of metal can disrupt the energy field."

"Oh." I'd found the slippers I wanted, old soft kid with flat heels. "I'm ready now."

Belle Helen hugged me to her and held me still. I felt her strength, her power, flow into me. "We are surrounded by the light," she said in a clear voice.

I knew what to do next. I led her to the mirror. Unhesitating, she stepped directly in front of it while I stood beside and slightly behind her.

For long moments she seemed to do nothing, and yet I felt something I had no words for, no previous experience of. It was a change in the atmosphere, like the perceptible change of summer air before a thunderstorm. I knew without asking that I felt Belle Helen calling up her own power.

"Show yourself!" she suddenly commanded, in a voice that seemed to echo.

As I watched in growing horror, the dark face grew in the corner of the mirror, exactly where I'd seen it. In response to Belle Helen's command, the face grew sharper, clearer than it had ever been for me. It was hideously ugly, like a closeup of some gargoyle lurking under the portal of an abandoned monastery. She studied this horrible visage without fear. She did not move a muscle. Her serenity clothed her like a blessing. I felt some of that serenity, enough to keep me from dissolving in fear.

"Go away, demon of the mirror," she said simply. And it vanished.

I was flooded with relief to see how easily she made it leave, and yet when she turned to me her expression was grave. "There was your small demon, Laura, all too real. We must find that room. The one who called this visage can call others, bigger, stronger. We must go now, to the tower."

I got my keys from the kitchen, and we walked through the house hand in hand. When we neared the door from the living room to the tower, Belle Helen stopped. She said, "Remember that we are surrounded by the light. It is the light which protects us. You may feel fear. If you do, say to yourself: I am in the light and of the light. Say it once for me."

"I am in the light and of the light."

"Good. I may go into a trance. I may speak, or I may communicate with you directly by my thoughts, but even those thoughts you will hear in my voice. If you hear another voice, not mine, you may listen, but *do not respond.* If anything threatens you, tell it to go away, just as I did the apparition in the mirror. Do you understand?"

"Yes."

"All right. Unlock this door, and leave your keys in this room. We will not need them."

"But—"

"We will not need the keys."

I did as she said, trusting her.

Belle Helen moved slowly, stately, into the center of the tower room. I didn't know if she needed the lights, but I did. I touched the switch and light flooded down from the great wheels near the ceiling. I watched Belle Helen. She stood in the exact center of the room. She raised her arms straight out from the shoulders, with her palms open and out. Her sleeves flowed down, her gown flowed over her tall body to the floor, she glowed like a creature of the sun. She revolved, full circle, seeming to feel the room through her open hands. I saw that her eyes were closed.

I caught my breath. I felt the aura of her psychic search proceed outward from her center in concentric circles, felt her power probe through me and pass on. How? I wondered, how can she do it? But I believed. I had seen her call the demon in the mirror and send it away. Now I felt the strength of her mind, her spirit, and knew that I could believe without understanding.

She dropped one hand and let the other lead her forward. I followed. She stopped three feet from the panel next to the door which led to the tower stairs, and turned to me. Her smile was there, she looked perfectly normal. "Have you wondered, Laura, why this room is an octagonal shape?"

"I certainly have. I've tried to imagine, and I can't. Unless it was just built that way for convenience, to fit straight sections of wood into a round space."

"I've just learned the answer. This room was made about a hundred years ago by a man named Martin or Martine, I'm not sure which, but that matters little. The man was a spiritualist. A fake, most of the time. Every one of these eight panels is a door and will open if touched in the right way. This was useful, for he could bring his special effects in and out of anywhere in the room; and of course he had complete control over the lighting, when he wished it would be absolutely dark, impossible for his clients to see his fakery. Once, however, he called up something genuine, something he hadn't arranged himself. It was a horrible thing and frightened him half to death. That is what I saw. I would imagine he left not long after that. A pity, to leave when he'd spent so much money to make this special room—but he was dishonest, it was no more than he deserved. Now. The panel I must open is this one. The locked door beside it leads to the stairway, doesn't it?"

"Yes, it does." I was fascinated.

Belle Helen called up her power again. I felt it increase,

like the turning up of a rheostat. I also felt something growing inside me, small and thrilling, a kind of humming deep, deep within, from my soul.

She said without looking at me, "It's all right, Laura. You have the power, too, everyone does, but yours is closer to the surface than in most untrained people. Feel it, let it come."

So I did. I went and stood beside Belle Helen at the panel. Her eyes were open, her right hand she held gracefully moving over but not touching the wood panel. My own hand twitched, my fingers tingled. I let my fingers follow their tingling and I forgot Belle Helen. I forgot everything except the mellow, golden hum within me and my fingers which felt as if stars danced on their tips. My fingers moved over the panel, my mind said, There! And I pushed. Pushed again, harder, leaning on the heel of my hand the second time. The panel creaked open, with much protest.

My humming stopped. "I found it!" I cried, amazed.

"Yes, so you did. But I'm confused. This panel has obviously not been opened in a very long time. Well, no matter. I'm sure the room we seek is beyond this panel. I'd best go first." She pushed the panel wider, no easy task. It was very dark inside.

"I'll go get a flashlight," I said.

"We'll go together. Not a flashlight, but candles." Together we strode back across the tower room.

"Why? A flashlight won't go out."

"Because its batteries have magnetic poles. The energy we read or feel, and interpret, is stronger without the magnetic interference. You do have candles?"

"Oh, yes. Lots."

Belle Helen chose white candles about eight inches long, one for each of us. My gown had no pockets, so she put two more candles and matches in a big pocket concealed in her skirt. She winked at me like a conspirator. There was a comradely enjoyment in what we did, in spite of the dangers. She said as we returned, "If you should decide to dress habitually in the way I do, which we call 'unbound,' you'll soon learn to look for things with pockets. Or have them made for you—these clothes aren't easy to find!"

"I'll remember that," I assured her.

We lit our candles and went through the panel, into the dark beyond. I shivered, suddenly afraid. "I am in the light and of the light," I said. My fear retreated to a governable level, but it was still present. This was a fearsome place.

Our candles were pitifully small illumination. I felt Belle Helen's power grow and fight against the darkness. She went ahead of me. Turned left. We were now under the stairway. She stopped, holding her candle high. "You will not like this, Laura. He comes through that locked doorway. Come, look—there is just enough room for a person to pass between that corner and the bottom stairs."

She was right. He came through my locked doors. Nothing was impossible anymore—this fact slammed into me as if I'd walked into a wall.

"Here is the door we seek," she said, pointing downward. It was not a true door, but a trap door under the stairs, its outline barely visible at our feet. I doubted I could have been strong enough to raise it by its ancient iron ring, but Belle Helen could, and did. She handed me her candle and pulled on the ring with both hands. The trap door was old and thick, like the main door of the tower. It opened onto a square of blackness. Going down there would be like descending into hell, and yet that was where we must go. Belle Helen took her candle and stepped into the black. I followed her.

I had to touch the wall as we descended, to keep my balance. I shrank from it, expecting it to be slimy, but it was not. It was hard and rough and cold—more stone. I counted thirteen steps down. The floor when I reached it was hard-packed dirt. This hidden room was a large pit, the walls lined with stone blackened by age and smoke. There was ventilation from somewhere, the air was not as stale as it might have been. My candle flickered.

My inner humming began, but it was faint, dulled perhaps by my curiosity. Belle Helen walked slowly around the periphery of the room. She seemed to be in trance, oblivious to me. I gave rein to my curiosity and simply explored.

In dismay I saw that someone had been here, recently.

There were many candle ends and a discarded flashlight against the wall—whoever came here either didn't know or didn't care about the magnetism. There was a circle inscribed in chalk on the floor, roughly made, imperfectly round, with symbols around its edge which I both recognized and could not name. I walked through the circle, holding up my candle. Against the far wall was a rickety old table and an equally old chair. On the table were two things which told me all I needed to know.

My humming stopped. I went closer to the table, not wanting to believe what I saw there: a bottle with an inch of rum remaining in it, the label familiar, Nick's brand of rum; a square of mirror. I bent over to look more closely at the mirror and saw the telltale traces of white powder. There was also a candle stuck in a bottle, the latest of many which had crusted its sides with spilled wax. I felt physically ill. How many nights had Nick Westover sat here in a drugged state, doing whatever he did, while I awakened upstairs to the eerie sense of someone in the house with me? Well, at least I had been right—someone had indeed been in the house with me.

My knees threatened to give way. I couldn't breathe. The black walls closed in on me. From far, far away I heard a harsh laugh. I'd heard that laugh before, in the tower. Was it Nick, or some evil thing he brought into that circle on the floor? My head spun, the room tilted.

I was at the bottom of a dark, dark pool. I was Boris, clawing and terrified, drowning in the well. I was lost, lost . . . "Go away," I gasped, "I am in the light and of the light. Go away, be gone, leave!"

With every word I grew stronger. I swam up through the whirling dark. "I am in the light and of the light," I said again, firmly, and I was in the room again. My candle had tipped and spilled hot wax over my hand.

Belle Helen was speaking now in that echoing voice. "It is a face surrounded by flames. He is a young soul, and ignorant, but his belief is great. Obsession. So great it gives him power he would not have otherwise and does not know how to use. He allies himself with an ancient, evil soul, dark through many, many lifetimes. That old soul's name is Edward Teach. Blackbeard!" The name exploded out of her. She turned around three times for a reason only she knew, and then she spoke again.

"In the name of Edward Teach he calls the Devil to this room. The Blackbeard also called the Devil in this room, and when the Blackbeard called, Satan came. Belial, Asmodeus—" Her voice wavered and lost its echo. She gasped harshly. "No! Be gone! I stand in the light, I banish you from the light!"

For one endless, terrifying moment a darkness heaved and gathered, hovering in the air, swirling black on black, forming a center. It hovered in front of Belle Helen. My whole being began to thrum and I flung the power out of me in the words which came. "Be gone, Satan!" I screamed. "We are of the light!"

Panting, I watched the darkness fold in upon itself, over and over, smaller and smaller, until it vanished. But it left behind a stench which fouled the air and devoured its oxygen. Both our candles went out. There was no light at all, and I was terrified. I dropped my candle.

"We are in the light and of the light," said Belle Helen. My voice joined hers, we chanted. She struck a match. It went out. She struck a second match and lit her candle. Then she took another from her pocket, touched it to hers, and handed it to me. "We must leave now," she said, "hurry!"

I didn't need to be told twice. I couldn't get out of there fast enough.

20

utside." With her long legs she strode across the tower room, and I ran to keep up with her. "Help me to open the door, Laura. My strength is gone."

I felt weak myself. The bar I had often removed by myself from the door now required both of us to lift it. "I need the keys. You have to unlock as well as remove the bar." I knew on looking at her that Belle Helen could not go with me for the keys. She leaned against the door, gasping for breath. She looked haggard, years older. "I'll hurry!" I said, and she nodded.

I gathered up my long, heavy skirts and ran. Just as a dancer focuses on one unchanging point to ward off dizziness as she pirouettes, I focused on my one goal, the keys in the living room. All around me, unseen but real, was that force which wanted to capture me and keep me in the tower. I shut it out, I intentionally called up my humming, and my feet grew wings. I reached the keys and returned safely, but that last spurt of effort had used nearly all my strength. I couldn't fit the key in the lock.

Again and again the key aimed for the lock and glanced off to the side. "You must help me, Belle Helen," I said, my voice now as rasping as hers had been. She placed her hand on mine. Together we inserted the key. Together we turned it, and together we pulled open the door. We ran out into the sunlight.

Exhausted as I was, I could not leave that door open. Irrational or not, I feared that the Thing inside might come out after us. I left Belle Helen and went back. "I *will* close this door!" I said stubbornly with what remained of my voice. I clung and pulled with my whole body, and finally the door slammed shut. At the last it felt as if someone inside had given a tremendous push. Anyway, it was closed, and I felt relief.

With our arms around each other Belle Helen and I walked to the edge of the bluff and sat on the fresh, dewy grass. We gazed at the waters of the sound, aquamarine like my dress, like Belle Helen's cloak. Rory, my golden sunbeam of a dog, bounced up. Sensing that we were too tired to play, she lay down between us.

I lifted my face to the sun, breathed in the clean, tangy air, felt my strength return. I tried my voice and found it normal. "Did what I think happened really happen in there?"

Belle Helen nodded. She looked much better, but her voice was still weak. "If you had not been there, Laura, I would not have survived."

"The dark cloud I saw forming, was that—"

"Don't speak the name. It was the Dark Force. It tried to draw on my strength in order to materialize, and very nearly succeeded. It distracted and tricked me into speaking two of its names . . ." Her eyes deepened with sadness. She looked away, out across the water. "This Stone House is a terrible place, Laura."

I glanced over my shoulder at the tower. It looked so normal. I remembered how enchanted I'd been—my quaint old Scottish castle. So charming!

Belle Helen said quietly, "There is dark enchantment, and evil charms."

I was no longer surprised that she should know my thoughts. And I understood what she meant. "Yes. What can I do to put a stop to all this horror?"

"To begin with, you are still in danger. Both from the presence in that hidden room which wants you for your inherent power as it wanted me for mine, and from the misguided person who has awakened that presence again. You must never set foot in the tower again, nor is it worth the risk for you to continue to live in the Stone House."

"After this morning, believe me, I have no desire to live there. I can stay at the inn until I find another place. I'll hire people to come back and pack everything up for me. But beyond moving out, what shall I do? I can't just leave that . . . that *thing* in there. How can we get rid of it, send it back where it came from or whatever you do with such things? You talked about Blackbeard in there, do you remember? Is the pirate really the one who started all this?"

"I think so. The pirates were a strange, sad lot of men. They were outcasts, often through no fault of their own. They played on the fears of the sailors whose ships they wanted—thus the flag with the skull and crossbones. They purposely made themselves as fearsome as possible, and boasted they were in league with the Devil. Some of them came to believe it, and in written and verbal history Blackbeard claimed to worship the Devil and called himself a devil in human form. The vision I had in the hidden room confirmed the presence of Edward Teach, and more. I can tell you what to do, if you're willing to destroy your own property."

I swallowed hard. Though I had expected this, it was still difficult. "I'm willing."

Belle Helen placed her fingers to her temples and closed her eyes. When she opened them, she said, "Tear down the whole place, stone by stone. Remove the stones which line the walls of that hidden room, the pit in the ground. Fill in the pit, with soil brought from elsewhere. Scatter its stones. There may be more you can do—I'll have to do some reading."

I stroked Rory and had a very mundane thought. How much money would all that cost me, and would I be able to sell the property after? It was so ludicrous, I laughed. "You're trying to turn me into some kind of mystic, but it won't work, Belle Helen. I'm just too practical and I overanalyze everything. I hate like heck to admit it, but I'll probably be a practicing lawyer again one of these days. My days of living on the edge seem to be over, and I find that I don't hate the law as much as I once thought I did."

Belle Helen only smiled and looked very wise, as if she knew all my secrets. Probably, she did.

I sighed, wanting to move on and away from all this. "The man who was in that room, his name is Nick Westover."

"So. You do know him, then."

"Yes. What shall I do about him?"

She gazed out over the sound. "In my dream I saw you threatened by darkness. That was the force in the tower. And I saw a man's face in flames, which must have been this Nick. Appropriate name—perhaps you've heard the devil referred to as 'Old Nick.' I confess I am not sure what to do about him."

"He has a lot of red hair and a red beard; that's probably why you saw him as if his face were in flames."

Belle Helen mused, "Odd, how we so often choose our own symbolism. I can only tell you about this Nick that in doing what he has done, because he is a young soul and ignorant, he has probably destroyed his mind and set his soul's progress back many lifetimes. Stay away from him, and protect yourself from him. He will soon destroy himself."

I shivered. I should tell Belle Helen of my near-escape yesterday and how the dolphins had come, but I would do so another time. Now I had to move on. I stood up, and Rory bounced up with me. "Oh, dear. What will I do with Rory? I can't take her to the inn; she's just too big and she needs a place to run."

Belle Helen rose and held her hand out to the dog, who came and eagerly pushed her nose into the inviting palm. "I will take your Aurora home with me until you have a place for her."

I changed hastily into more normal clothes and threw a few things into a suitcase. Belle Helen refused to leave me alone until I was out of the house. Then she drove away in her own car with Rory, and I left right behind her. With all that had happened, I would still arrive at the inn no later than my usual nine-thirty. Amazing, how things happen which alter the very fabric of life, and yet the day goes on.

I was preoccupied as I pulled into my parking space at the inn, thinking of all I had to do and wondering where to start. I would take my suitcase and choose a room first, I thought. I got out of the car and opened its rear door.

An arm came around my throat from behind, choking me. I saw flashes of light dance before my eyes.

"Make one sound, lady, and I'll bury this knife—" a long, sharp blade flashed in front of my face—"right up under your sweet rib cage and into your heart!"

I felt the point of the knife in my ribs. The voice was Nick's. I was silent. I knew now how dangerous he was.

"All right. We're going on a little trip, and if you don't cooperate with me, I'll kill you, just like I did her. Only I won't be as neat with you as I was with her—I'll carve your guts out all over this damn fucking parking lot. I don't care anymore if I get caught. You understand?"

"Yes," I croaked. The arm around my neck loosened. He handcuffed me to him but I scarcely knew what he did, my thoughts tumbled so.

"Now, we're holding hands, nice and normal. You just walk along with me and I won't hurt you."

My vision became very sharp, my hearing, too. It was like being on the edge, but I wasn't, not anymore. I was very much in the real world. My mind, too, became remarkably clear. I thought concisely, logically. I walked across Front Street and onto the boardwalk with a madman, a murderer, and I was not afraid.

We boarded the *Hellfire* and went below into the cabin. I knew, now, why he had chosen the name for his boat. Blackbeard, the devil, hell, *Hellfire*—all made sense. Nick removed his half of the handcuffs and cuffed both my hands behind me. Then he sat me down on a bunk, surprisingly gentle.

I tossed the hair out of my eyes. "You did it," I said, "you killed Kathryn."

"Yeah, I sure did," he drawled. He laughed. "It was pretty funny, too, what happened. You scared me half to death the first time I saw you. I thought you were a ghost! She was dead right here in this cabin, lying right there on the bunk, where you're sitting, I smothered her with a pillow. It would have been pretty funny if you'd come on board when I asked you to that day; it would have been like having the same person two ways, alive and dead."

Not to me, it wasn't funny. Bile rose in my throat; I was revolted. "Why did you do it, Nick? Why kill my sister?"

"Oh, she deserved it." He shrugged, uninterested. Got up and went into the galley. I shuddered, thinking of the closet and its torture things, but he only asked, "Do you want a drink? Rum or brandy? I forgot, I put the cuffs on you. Well, if you want a drink I'll take 'em off. I just want you to stay with me; I won't hurt you unless you try to leave. You look like her, but you're not like her."

If he'd said that once, he'd said it a hundred times, but I was no longer tired of hearing it. My difference might keep me alive. I said, "Yes, I'd like brandy."

Nick brought the brandy in one of his cut-crystal glasses. It seemed wrong for someone so ugly and twisted inside to have possessions of such clear beauty. He removed the handcuffs, which was what I wanted—not the alcohol. He wasn't rough with me. I looked at him sadly. This man was insane. What a waste! I wanted to keep him talking, and I wanted to know more. "Why did she deserve to die, Nick?"

He sprawled on the bunk opposite. "She was a bitch. She crossed me twice. We had a thing going, you know. Not like I said, I didn't screw her just once or twice, we had a real thing going. Then I found out she was doing it with other guys. I beat her up a couple of times. She took it real good—I think she kind of liked it. Anyway, the next time I beat her, she said she'd make a deal with me. She was going to sell the Stone House, and she said if I'd leave her alone she'd sell it to me. I wanted the Stone House real bad, see, I'd found a way to get in through that crummy wing, the one where you keep the rest of your furniture now. And I'd messed around in there and learned my way around the old tower and found a place where Blackbeard used to go—so I wanted it real, real bad, and I told her we had a deal.

"And then I found out Kathryn was a liar. She was going to sell the Stone House to that bastard Douglass. I knew I'd never get it from him, he hates me. Wouldn't sell me this place I wanted on Ocracoke a while back. I couldn't let her go back on our deal, you know? I was just going to remind her, like. I got her to meet me that night out by where I keep my car, and when it was real late I brought her back here . . ." He paused and looked puzzled, oddly boylike. "I was gonna beat her, but I ended up screwing her first—I don't know why, I usually do that after—but anyway she started to make a lot of noise, just a real lot of noise, and I put the pillow over her face and kept it there and after a while she stopped thrashing around, and she was dead. I didn't mean to kill her, but I looked at her dead there, and I thought, Oh, well, that's no great loss. At least it meant she couldn't sell the Stone House to Douglass, I'd still have a chance at it."

"I see," I said noncommittally. I sipped at the brandy, glad now that I had it. Strange, how I felt. Horribly as he'd told his story, I was enormously relieved. The truth, at last. And how simple it was after all. I felt a residue of grief for Kathryn, and some traces of the childhood guilt. And I was glad, so glad, that it hadn't been Seth. Seth was not a murderer! When I got out of this, I would go to him.

Nick chugged rum and lay on his side, devouring me with his eyes. What would he do? Rape me?

"You weren't very nice to me, Laura. Yesterday you ran away from me, that's why I had to get you and make you come. I wanted you to come to me on your own, but you didn't. I didn't want to hurt you or force you or anything." The puzzled look came back. "I think I love you. I never loved anybody before."

"I'm sorry." Playing for time. "I didn't know how you felt."

Nick had one of his lightning-fast mood swings. He bristled, fierce, and jumped from his bunk. "Oh, yes, you did. But at least you're not a whore. You're just too damn independent, that's what's wrong with you. You need to learn how to be a real woman, a man's woman. I tried to show you with little lessons, nothing big, that you needed a real man, and not an inn and all like that, but you wouldn't learn."

He loomed over me and I lay back slowly, forcing myself to be casual, relaxed. "Those little lessons, you did them at the inn?"

"Yeah." He sat down on the bunk and began to unbutton my blouse. My skin crawled, but I didn't try to stop him.

"One of those lessons wasn't so little, Nick. You hurt Evelyn badly. If I'd been the one to turn on the microwave, I might have been killed."

He looked up from what he was doing, pulling my blouse out from my skirt, and the regret in his eyes seemed genuine. "It wasn't supposed to happen that way, was supposed to be just a little fire. But I don't know much about explosives. I got a book, but I must have done it wrong. Made a great mess of your dining room, didn't it? A real explosion, huh?" Regret changed to glittering madness, all in an instant.

I flinched involuntarily, and he saw it. Quickly I said, "I feel so bad about Evelyn. I guess it's my fault. Nick, don't you want another drink?"

"No, can't. You know, I was at the Stone House. That guy who's been watching you, he really fouled me up. I had to go to my secret place by taking the *Hellfire*, 'cause I couldn't use your road. But he wasn't there last night. I was going to bring you with me when I left this morning, I left my car in the woods, but this woman came. Who was that woman? She screwed up my plans. I guess this is okay, though." His fingers traced the outline of my bra.

"She's just a friend. She, uh, she had a problem and we took care of it. You're very clever, aren't you? You sail the *Hellfire* up the sound and leave her down there where you showed me once, and then you climb up the old steps cut into the bluff, and you come in through a place you found a long time ago in the other wing, the one I don't live in. But how do you get into the tower room?"

He grinned and dug in the pocket of his jeans. "Keys, see? I have to keep going to my secret place, I feel kind of funny, bad, when I can't get to it. I felt bad a lot when you had the locks put on, but then you let me stay that night. You were so nice to me, until you got sick. You gave me your keys, and I had some made for me when I went to the store for you."

He kissed me then. The kiss was disturbing. In spite of everything this man's sexuality was powerful, he could arouse me, and I fought against it as I always had. Only this time, fighting was a mistake.

Nick pulled away and said gruffly, "You'll act different soon. Right now I got to go up on deck, and I'm gonna fix it so you don't try to run away again." He dragged a canvas chair from the galley area and put it in the space between the bunks. From the other bunk where he'd left it, he picked up the long-bladed knife. "This is your punishment for not kissing me back, Laura. That's how people learn, they get punished when they don't do things right."

My mouth went dry, my eyes felt as if they bugged out of my head. Whatever he did I wouldn't resist, I resolved. He was much too strong for me to fight him physically. And I'd never, never let him see my fear.

"Stand up!"

I stood up. With the tip of his long knife, Nick cut through the threads that held the two buttons at the waist of my skirt. It slid down my hips and fell slowly into a puddle of cloth around my feet.

Next he went behind me. Being unable to see what he did was terrible. The knife was razor-sharp, it sliced through my sweater and my silk blouse right down the middle of my back in one long, nerve-rending stroke. Nick laughed and peeled the halves of the blouse and cardigan from both my arms. While he did this he held the knife in his teeth, pirate-style.

"You're ruining my clothes," I said. It was the kind of humor he had never been able to understand.

"I'll buy you more, lots more, when you learn to be good."

He came very close to me then, and sank his teeth into the curve of my neck. He sucked hard, bruising my skin, and as he worked away with lips and teeth and tongue at my neck, he slid his knife point down between my breasts.

I bit my tongue to keep from crying out. I was gripped by an incredible range of feelings, aroused and disgusted and afraid. He had sliced through the elastic alongside the clasp at the front of my bra.

"I've marked you, you're mine now." He lifted his head, pleased with himself. He held the knife in his teeth again and pushed the bra from my shoulders. I was afraid that he would tear the dolphin pendant from around my neck but he didn't. He paid no attention to it at all. I dared not look down at myself, I knew my nipples were taut, aroused.

Nick brushed his hands across my breasts. He took my nipples one by one between fingers and thumb, rolled and pinched. I bit my tongue again. Then he jerked my half-slip down, not bothering to cut it. He chuckled, his emerald eyes gleamed wickedly. There was no way, I thought, no way at all that he could cut through skin-tight pantyhose without cutting me. I readied myself to feel the pain.

He did it from behind. He split the pantyhose down the backseam very, very slowly. It was agonizing for me—I expected at any moment to feel blood trickle down my legs. But he didn't cut me. He urged the split hose down my legs with the flat of the knife.

"You can keep that on, I guess." He referred to my panties, which were the minimal, string-type bikini I wore under pantyhose for comfort.

I was angry now, so I didn't let myself respond with the sarcastic *thank you* I felt. I wanted to throw myself at Nick Westover and scratch his eyes out, make much bigger scars on his cheeks than Boris had made, pull out his beard hair by individual hair!

"Sit," he said, and I sat in the chair. He tied my ankles to each chair leg, and my arms to the chair arms. The rope was relatively soft, but he made the knots tight and the position was uncomfortable. He stepped back, admiring his tie job or me, or both.

"Where are we going?" I asked.

"I guess I can tell you. You sure aren't going to get away this time. I was gonna take you yesterday, but the dolphins messed me up. I fixed up a whole house just for you, Laura. It's on Portsmouth Island. There's a whole village there nobody lives in anymore and I bought up a whole block of it. The whole island's deserted, nobody lives there anymore." Nick knelt in front of me and slowly, sensually, stroked the triangle of cloth between my legs. "It's a nice house, I've been working on it for months. You're going to live there all by yourself, Laura. The only person you'll ever see will be me. I'll bring you food and stuff. And after a while you'll have learned not to be so independent, because you'll depend on me. Nobody but me, see? You'll love me then, you'll beg me to make love to you. But I won't do it until you beg me. I'll tease you,"—his stroking hand moved in light circles up and across my belly, inside my thighs, and returned to its rhythmic stroking—"but I won't make love to you until you beg me. You resisted me too many times, you see, and that's your punishment."

I glared at him while I silently screamed *Never!* And he went on deck and left me tied to the chair.

When the time came, it was relatively easy to escape from Nick. He had brought me up on deck as soon as we were well underway, still all but naked and with my hands tied in front of me. He drank steadily and inhaled coke, and he was increasingly out of his mind. I could walk, though haltingly, and I inched away from him a little at a time. Since I couldn't take off my glasses to clean them, they were misted with seaspray and I saw everything through a blur. I got used to the blur, just as I got used to the chill air on my bare skin. The sun was warm, and that helped.

I knew the dolphins were coming. All the time I was alone in the cabin I'd sent mental messages to the dolphins, and to Jonathan and Seth as well. They will hear me, I insisted fiercely. Doubt and rage crept in, but I pushed both away and kept sending out my messages. It was all I could do. I dared not try anything until I had a reasonable chance of success. Nick had to think everything was going his way. He mustn't know that I intended to escape.

The dolphins were coming, and the sight of them would torment him. He'd be distracted, and I'd jump overboard with the inflatable dinghy. Maybe the dolphins really would help me in the water, maybe that wasn't just a fantasy, but I preferred the boat. The problem was, I had to get my hands untied.

I'd done as they do in the movies, looked for a sharp piece of metal to saw the ropes against. But this was not the movies, and though there was a lot of metal about the deck, Nick kept his boat so well that there wasn't a jagged edge in sight.

My friend the psychologist always said when you want something, ask for it. She said it was amazing how often people would be devious and manipulative and make elaborate deals, when they hadn't tried asking first. So I took her advice. I edged my way back to Nick, and when I was near I deliberately stumbled and fell against him.

"Hey, steady there. Don't want to fall and hurt yourself." He turned from the maps he pored over obsessively and set me on my feet. He looked me up and down, grinning. I knew by now that he liked my body and I was glad; at least he hadn't tortured it.

I held my bound wrists out to him. "Please, Nick, won't you untie me? I have to go to the bathroom and there's no need for you to come with me. Untie me, please? We're in the middle of the ocean; I'm not about to run away. Please?"

My friend the psychologist was right. I asked, and he did it. He untied me, just like that. I did have to go to the bathroom and so I went. On my way back to where he wanted me, near him, I lingered to be sure I understood the directions on the inflatable boat. That was when Nick began to scream.

"Aa-a-agh! Go away! Go away!"

The dolphins had come.

Nick left the wheel and forgot to engage the automatic pilot. He raced into the bow, shaking his fists and screaming, "Yah! Yah! Yah!"

The *Hellfire* without a hand at the wheel lurched and tilted and began to turn. I looked uneasily up at the sails. I didn't know what to do. If the boat ran loose in the water, she might run over me when I got into the dinghy. I decided to make one effort to calm Nick down.

He was pathetic. He shook all over as he stood in the bow. He tore at his hair and his beard. He had the staring, tiny-pupiled eyes of a reptile. He saw me and he babbled, "Make them go away, Laura, please. I can't stand it any-more. They hate me. But they like you. Make them go away."

"I can't, Nick," I said calmly. "They're wild animals. Why should they hate you?"

The skin stretched taut across his forehead and his cheekbones. The old Boris-scar was livid. Nick pulled and pulled at his beard. He looked at me, then out at the dolphins, who were now forming their circle around the boat. He whispered hoarsely, as if he didn't want the dolphins to hear. "They saw me. They're smart, you know? I used to watch them and I kind of liked them till that day. I didn't know they were there or I would've waited, or gone somewhere else. They saw me throw Kathryn Trelawney's body overboard. They stood up on their tails and looked at me with their eyes. Their terrible eyes! I dream about those eyes. Accusing me. They know, they know how bad I am . . . !"

Nick had cracked. He fell to the deck, sobbing, helpless as a child.

"Hush," I said, "it's all right." But I didn't linger. He was volatile, he might be helpless now, but in a minute he could snap to in a murderous rage.

I wished I'd thought to grab one of his shirts when I'd gone to the bathroom, but I hadn't, and there wasn't time now. I went over the side of the *Hellfire* wearing only the smallest of panties and a pair of silver dolphins with sapphire eyes.

I'd tossed the dinghy, tab pulled according to direction, ahead of me when I jumped, and I took one oar with me, in my right hand. The dinghy inflated as it was supposed to. I had cold salt water in my eyes and my nose and my mouth, and I lost my glasses when I went under at first, but I didn't care. I flopped into the dinghy and looked back at the *Hellfire*. She was making a wide circle, away from me, and the dolphins kept their watch.

All except two. My two dolphins came to me; they smiled and clicked and dipped their heads. I laughed. I was in their world now, on their level, and they knew it. They kept me company as I paddled toward the sandy Core Banks. They were with me when a power boat roared up and nearly swamped my rubber dinghy. I didn't know the man who drove that boat, but I knew its two passengers, Seth and Jonathan.

⬛⬛⬛ AFTERWARD ⬛⬛⬛

"It's a shame," said Seth, "but I suppose you were right. The land is more valuable this way, believe it or not." He stood behind me, his body molded to mine, his hands on my shoulders, his faintly cleft chin resting on top of my head.

I raised my hand, the left hand with the engagement ring which was not a diamond but the aquamarine I'd asked for. I stroked his cheek. The Stone House was no more. Tonight Belle Helen and her friends would come to perform a ritual I would be no part of. The mystical life was not for me; I was studying for the North Carolina Bar.

I turned in Seth's arms and put my face up for his kiss. I knew there were tears in my eyes. I would not hide my tears from Seth, nor anything else. We were together now and would never be apart. I trusted him.

When his lips left mine I looked deep into his eyes. Eyes, the windows of the soul. I answered what I saw there with my own eyes, and with my voice. I said, "I love you."